MW00834652

THE CORNISH PRINCESS

TANYA ANNE CROSBY

OLIVER
HEBER
BOOKS

SERIES BIBLIOGRAPHY
THE GOLDENCHILD PROPHECY

This one is dedicated to the real Gwendolyn of Cornwall... because we should all be a little more Gwendolyn.

Acknowledgments

Mad love to Kerrigan Byrne for propping me up when I worried about straying so far from the genre I cut my teeth on.

And also to my agent, Christine Witthohn, whose patience is boundless, and whose belief in me goes the distance, even when I tell her I'll give her a new proposal soon, then veer WAY off course to pen a book of the heart. *Thank you, Christine.*

To my longtime reader Barb Batlan-Massabrook, a warrior in her own right, whose been my cheerleader throughout most of my thirty-year career.

To my daughter, Alaina Christine Crosby, for all her wonderful feedback and loving suggestions. And, to her husband, Thomas... just because. (Finally, I'm writing a book you'll read!)

Also, to my husband, the original dún Scoti, who never said, "That's bloody crazy!"

And finally, to Kathryn Le Veque, for reasons I won't go into here. You're a true friend, Kat, and I love you dearly.

I am blessed.

READER'S GUIDE

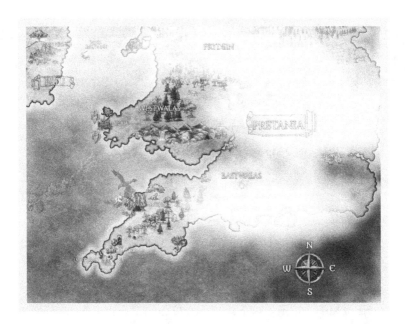

Main Characters

Albanactus - Brother of Locrinus; "founder" of Alba

Brutus - King Brutus; Trojan by birth, "founder" of Britain

Bryn Durotriges - Shadow Guard to Gwendolyn

King Corineus- *[cor-en-ee-us]* vassal of Brutus

Gwendolyn - Daughter of King Corineus and Queen Eseld

Queen Eseld - Queen consort and princess of Prydein

Kamber - Brother of Locrinus; "founder" of Cumbria

Locrinus - *[lock-ren-us]* Son of King Brutus of Troy

Málik Danann - *[mah-lick dah-nuhn]*

Elowyn Durotriges - *[El-oh-win]* Bryn's sister, and Gwendolyn's dearest friend

Caledonia (n) - Scotland/Scottish

Cymru - "Land of friends"

Dryad/Drus - Faerie oak spirit

Dumnonia - Ancient Cornwall

Ériu *[eh-ru]* - Ancient Ireland

Hyperborea - Fabled land whence the Tuatha Dé Danann may have hailed

Loegria - Essentially Wales. Old English, meaning "land of foreigners"

Pretania - Ancient Britain

Prydein - Welsh term for the isle of Britain; for The Cornish Princess, specifically Caledonia/Scotland

Sons of Míl - Hiberians who conquered the Tuatha Dé Danann and settled Ireland

Tuatha Dé Danann [*too-uh-huh dey -dah-nuhn*] - "Tribe of the gods," ancient race in Irish mythology. Also, *Sidhe [*shē*], Elf, Fae*

Wheals - Mines

ysbryd y byd - Spirit of the world.

The Four Talismans of the Tuatha Dé Danann

Claímh Solais *[Klau-Solas] - The sword of light*

Lúin of Celtchar - Lugh's spear

Dagda's Cauldron - *[DAW-dYAW's Cauldron]*

Lia Fáil [*lee-ah-foyl*] - *The stone of destiny, upon which even Britain's current kings are crowned.*

Awenydds - Philosophers, seeking inspiration through bardic arts

Gwyddons/Gwiddons - Priest-scientist, believe in divinity of and for all: *gwyddon, male; gwiddon, female*

Druids - Priests, teachers, judges

Llanrhos Druids - The most ancient order of Druids occupying the area now known as Anglesey

dewinefolk - *Witches, faekind*

The seven Prydein tribes

Caledonii - Scotland during the Iron Age and Roman eras

Novantae - Far northeast of Scotland, including the offshore isles

Selgovae - Kirkcudbright and Dumfriesshire, on the southern coast of Scotland

Votadini - Southeast Scotland and northeast England

Venicones - Fife (now in Scotland) and on both banks of the Tay

Vacomagi - Region of Strathspey

Taexali - Grampian, small undefended farms and hamlets

Four Tribes of Ancient Wales

Deceangli - Far northern Wales

Silures - Southeast of Wales; "people of the rocks"

Ordovices - Central Wales; area now known as Gwynedd and south Clwyd

Demetae - Southeast coast of Wales

Three Tribes of Ancient Cornwall

Dumnonii - British Celtic tribe who inhabited Dumnonia, the area now known as Devon and Cornwall

Durotriges - Devon and parts of Dorset and Somerset

Dobunni - West of England

Remaining tribes of Ancient Britain

Atrebates - Far south of England, along what is now the Hampshire and Sussex coastline.

Brigantes - Northwest of England; Manchester, Lancashire and part of Yorkshire

Iceni - East coast of England; Norfolk

Catuvellauni- London, Hertfordshire, Bedfordshire, Buckinghamshire, Cambridgeshire, Oxfordshire, parts of Essex, Northamptonshire

Cantium - Far Southeast England, Kent and a small part of Sussex

Parisi - North and east Yorkshire

Trinovantes - Essex and part of Suffolk

THE GOLDENCHILD PROPHECY

It was Brutus of Troy, a king slayer, who first came upon these lands at the edge of the sea... One day, out hunting, young Brutus sent an arrow through his father's heart, and for this, he was banished, cast away on an endless sea to seek his fortunes amidst more savage lands.

But little did they know Brutus was favored by gods.

He set sail upon his galley with the serpent prow and arrived at Land's End with such splendor that he turned the heads of all who knew so little of his kind—those red-cloaked warriors with their golden helms, golden hair and eyes.

Indeed, he came, he saw, and he conquered, yet not so boldly as stories might later claim.

To be sure, there's much to be told that transpired hereafter, but this will be fodder for another tale. Enough to say that by the time the sun set on Brutus' first year on the Tin Isles, he was already High King, while my father, a true son of Dumnonia, was essentially his vassal, bending the knee to a foreigner, whose weapon of consequence was not cold, hard steel, but a sharp mind and tongue.

But also, because of a prophecy... the first of two fated to change our destiny evermore.

"As I have come, one day, my people will, too," warned Brutus. "They shall rush upon your shores as a red tide to wash your sands with blood. Embrace me, I shall defend you."

And who in all of Cornwall should have called him a liar?

After watching his sturdy ships conquer our storm-ridden bays, my father could do little but welcome a new High King. Thus, Brutus of Troy became Brutus of Pretania, and within one swift blink of an immortal's eye, the Old Ways were swept away, like sand before a storm.

And still, this land remains an Old Land, steeped in Old Ways.

Our ancestors are no less children of gods.

I am Gwendolyn of Cornwall, princess of the Dumnonii, and this is my tale...

It begins on the seventh eve following my birth, in the room where my cradle lay... beneath the light of a pale moon. Here, in the wee hours, I was visited by two ancient creatures, and the only witnesses therein were my mother and her dutiful maid.

"She is beauteous," said the younger of the two, whose eyes were as icebourne as a Winter sea. She clapped her delicate hands as she peered into my crib, nails long and curved like claws.

"She'll turn heads," said the elder with satisfaction, but then she cautioned, "Perhaps she'll never know her true worth, lest she know the soul of each man who pursues her."

"Oh! I know what to do," exclaimed the younger, with a sparkle of cunning in her brilliant eyes. "I will bestow upon Gwendolyn of Cornwall the gift of reflection."

Excitedly, she touched a finger to my brow, and whispered sweetly—or as sweet as a ravening voice may be. "Now, all who gaze upon her face will spy their own true selves in her countenance, and depending upon their virtue, she will be the loveliest maid in all the

2

land... or the most hideous." She laughed delightedly, tickled by her tricksy gift.

"Esme!" said the elder. "You did not consider this well enough. Unless a man's heart be true, this poor child will be coveted for her worth, yet despised for her face."

The younger fae's shoulders fell. "Oh, dear," she said. "Oh, dear. Yes, I see." Dismayed, she blinked at the moonlit crib, and the silence as she contemplated her folly grew deep.

From the doorway in the same room, neither my mother nor her maid dared reveal themselves, and now my mother worried her soft hands whilst the maid held her by the shoulders, desperate to keep her mestres from the room.

"Fret not," said the elder fae as they watched. "I know how to fix it. I will bestow upon this child the gift of a golden mane, wherein every lock of her hair will turn to gold, provided 'tis cut by her one true love. This is how she will know."

"Indeed, this is how she'll know," echoed the younger, whereupon the elder bent to touch a finger to a wisp of yellow hair, and for an instant, the golden locks blazed like the sun's rays.

Only it was then, in that instant, the elder creature caught my mother's mortal scent, and now she turned to address her timid audience.

"I see you, mestres of Dumnonia!" she said, standing tall—and this was not very at all, because, although she was really quite tall for a fae, she was actually quite small.

The beauty of her was astounding, her skin translucent with stardust, and eyes that radiated with the light of two suns.

"We come in peace, though with foreboding," said the elder. "The doom of our kind was foretold but fell upon deaf ears. Still it came to pass, and now you, too, will face the Twilight, and your daughter is the hope of all kind. Heed my words, mestres! You must unite the draig banners to stem the Red Tide!"

"Romans!" hissed the younger, with a tremble in her lips, and this single word filled the room with a bone-deep chill that caused both mortal women to clasp their breasts with wary arms.

"Is that my child in the crib?" asked my mother, not comprehending a word of the faerie's crosstalk, only fearing to the depths of her soul that they'd left her with a changeling.

Both creatures smiled then, revealing sharp, savage grins.

"Child of your womb," crooned the elder.

"Child of the Aether," said the younger, before both vanished like frost from moist lips.

So, there I lay... in my cradle, in a room silvered by moonlight, with a nursemaid and mother now uncertain of my humanity. And yet, no matter their disquiet, both crept to my bedside to peer inside the cradle...

One saw a child disfigured, the other, my face as it is.

CHAPTER ONE

Gwendolyn heard the wail of a sentry's horn but thought little more of it. Rolling onto her back, she yawned, then stretched, basking like a cat beneath a warm swathe of morning light that spilled in through her high window.

Trevena was a bustling city, luring merchants from as far away as Phoenicia and Carthage. She was thoroughly accustomed to the hurry-scurry, and yet no one but Ely or Demelza ever dared disturb her here in her private quarters. Therefore, when the rap sounded on her chamber door, she started. Rolling quickly to find her feet, she misjudged the distance to the edge of the bed, and with a yelp of surprise, landed in the rushes.

Unfortunately, at this hour, her antechamber would be empty with no one available to greet her mystery guest.

Another knock came, rude and insistent.

Stifling a groan, Gwendolyn scrambled to her feet, hurrying to locate her gown. No doubt, Demelza was still preoccupied with her mother, and, not for the first time, she wondered why Queen Eseld steadfastly refused to assign her a lady's maid, when there were plenty of worthy applicants who coveted this position, her best friend Ely being one.

The answer was obvious, of course, and it vexed Gwendolyn to no end, because it gave her mother another means to spy. Meanwhile, this wasn't the first time Gwendolyn had gone clambering from her bed only to don yesterday's attire.

Worse yet, her tunic had a large blueberry stain—irrefutable evidence she'd been flouting her mother's wishes again, sneaking about the cook's house in search of pastries. Infuriating as it was, her mother was right: At this rate, her wedding gown probably wouldn't fit by the time she must wear it, and despite this, Gwendolyn couldn't help herself. She was nervous.

One more sharp rap on the door, and she cursed the day she was born—not for the obvious reasons, but for the one curse those damnable *faeries* never confessed to. She wasn't clumsy precisely, but neither was she so gracious as her Queen mother.

And regardless, while Gwendolyn admired her mother's indefatigable determination to be what she was not, she wanted more from her life—*so much more.*

She wanted to travel, not merely to see Pretania, but to look upon Cnoc Fírinne in Ériu and see with her own two eyes the last bastion of the Tuatha Dé Danann.

Someday, she also wished to meet her grandparents.

Also she meant to visit the new Temple of the Dead in Eastwalas.

Most of all, she yearned to be accepted and loved for who she was, regardless of how one perceived her face.

Sighing gloomily over the thought, Gwendolyn rubbed at the stain on her bosom, then went stumbling toward the door, and drew it open.

"Yestin!"

"*Myttin da,* Highness," said her father's steward. "I've come to tell you that your attendance is required in your father's Konsel—forthwith."

Gwendolyn blinked. "Mine?"

She tapped a finger to her breast, one brow lifting in surprise. Really, it wasn't so much that her father had need of her. These days, he needed help in performing many of his duties. It was more the early hour. Though perhaps it meant he was feeling better?

The steward's eyes narrowed on Gwendolyn's stain; and then, perhaps recalling where it lay and whose breast it occupied, he lifted his gaze to glower at her, as though it were her fault his eyes had wandered. Lifting a grizzled brow, he said again, "Forthwith." As though Gwendolyn hadn't heard him the first time. And then, he refused to say aught more, except to reveal that a messenger had arrived from Loegria. It wasn't until she slid into her chair at the far end of her father's war table she learned the dreadful news...

King Brutus' son, Urien the Elder, her betrothed, was dead.

Deader than a doornail, so they claimed, and equally stiff, considering he'd been gone now for more than a fortnight, and his father was only now imparting this news.

Groaning inwardly, Gwendolyn slid down into her chair, some part of her fearing the worst—that *she* had somehow been the cause of this, that one look at her countenance had driven the poor prince to his grave. And now they would foist her upon the younger...

Prince Locrinus.

Clearly, negotiations were over, and despite that no woman should know her true worth, Gwendolyn did: seventy heads of cattle, two hundred goats, fifty hens, two peregrines, and two thousand ingots of Loegrian steel. Additionally, because Prince Urien's death was not perceived to be her fault, thank the gods, her dowry should remain the same, and her bride price was expected to rise by another twelve aurochs, thirty goats, and one more cartload of ingots. Overall, not such a terrible sum, but none of it was worth more than the Loegrian steel—that strange, precious metal that arrived on their shores along with Brutus and his warriors.

As usual, there appeared to be some complication, and judging by the pinched look on her mother's face, Queen Eseld had already grown impatient with this discourse. Her displeasure intensified with Gwendolyn's arrival, and seeing her mother's soured expression, Gwendolyn wished she were anywhere but here.

Anywhere, truly.

Anywhere.

In the freezing rain.

Midwinter.

Stuck in a fen.

With no way out.

Alone.

With spriggans creeping her way.

Nor would Gwendolyn's voice be welcomed—not in this matter. Her only chance to speak against the new betrothal would come *after* she and Prince Locrinus had met. However, given what she knew of Prince Locrinus, the thought of marrying him did not displease her. In fact, some part of her rejoiced over the news—not particularly Urien's death, but the good fortune that she would now be wedding someone closer to her age.

Poor Urien had been a full score years older than Gwendolyn, a man fully grown when he and his father arrived in Pretania. When she was still only a babe in her crib, he was already wielding a sword by his father's side. Consequently, by

8

the time Gwendolyn grew to be his age, if he had lived, she might be commanding nursemaids to feed him and wipe his drool. *Or worse.*

It was not a very appealing thought.

Moreover, not that it should matter, considering her own malediction, but at twenty, Prince Locrinus was also said to be the fairest of Brutus' four sons. Even as far as Land's End, bards sang songs to his visage. They claimed he was golden like the sun—skin bronzed, hair yellow and shining, his intellect surpassed only by the beauty of his face. Yet, though she worried he might think her unworthy in comparison, it was his mind Gwendolyn admired most, and she hoped he would value the same in her.

But perhaps he would?

He was said to be a dedicated scholar, and Gwendolyn understood that as a young boy, his father had spared him to study with the Llanrhos Druids, so he could better know Pretania's ancient tribes.

She also heard he'd taken a pilgrimage to Ériu, and more than Gwendolyn dared to confess, it titillated her to learn more about this experience.

Indeed, whatever his faith, solely by his actions, Gwendolyn already adored him. How could she not, when they seemed to be like minds?

She, too, ached for more and varied knowledge, and, far more than fear and might, Gwendolyn believed true peace could only be achieved through mutual understanding and respect.

She only hoped that Prince Locrinus might be persuaded to make another pilgrimage to Ériu. *Why not?* They should have many, many more years to travel before they would be called upon to serve.

Mulling over the possibilities, Gwendolyn sat listening to

the present discourse, feeling something like bees hum through her belly. As best she could determine, neither of her parents had any true objection to the younger Prince. Nor did most of her father's aldermen—most, because there were, indeed, a few who seemed unsettled by this news, Aldermans Ailwin and Crwys being the most vocal of the lot. Yet in terms of protests, neither had much to say about the Prince himself, instead returning time and again to matters of state that hadn't so much to do with Gwendolyn's betrothal as it did with the possibility of renewed conflict with the northern tribes.

And this seemed to be the true quandary: Her mother's people were so firmly entrenched in the Old Ways that, until recently, they had steadfastly refused to trade with the "foreigner." Now, at long last, after twenty-one years wed to a daughter of the most powerful Caledonii tribe, the Caledonian Confederacy had officially elected her father as their ambassador. This news came swiftly on the heels of the Loegrian messenger this morning, and it didn't sit well with some elders, who believed it was one thing to negotiate with Loegria for the sake of the southern tribes, yet another to barter with anyone on behalf of Prydein.

"Wildlings," her father had once called them to his Prydein wife's face. And yet, regardless of the reason, Prydein had been quiet now for years, sending delegates instead of raiders to deal with Cornwall.

"It does not behoove us to jeopardize this alliance," said the Mester Alderman. "Entirely for Cornwall's sake, not for Prydein."

Curious to see his response, Gwendolyn's gaze slid across the table to First Alderman Bryok, who sat with eyes closed, perhaps contemplating a rebuttal. And nevertheless, the Mester Alderman spoke true. The alliance with Loegria had proven mutually beneficial, not the least for which their Cornish armies now had access to the finest of weapons and armor, thanks to Brutus' new alloy.

Made with inferior materials, their old weapons oft broke merely by striking one's foe, even against soft flesh and bone. Loegria's new alloy was like magik—strong, lightweight, more flexible. It formed a deadly blade.

However, it wasn't merely the new alloy to be considered. Ending the alliance would also weaken their position against the rest of the tribes. After all, as symbolic as it was, it wasn't her parents' marriage that finally settled the querulous northern tribes. It was the strength and solidarity of the Cornish-Loegrian union.

Alone, King Brutus would be difficult to defeat. Together, Cornwall and Loegria made a formidable pair, and so her father claimed, fear was the greatest of arbiters.

"I agree with the Mester Alderman," said Bryok, after a moment.

His avowal was met with silence and pursed lips.

Two, against ten... or nine?

Judging by body language alone, Gwendolyn couldn't tell. But it wouldn't matter. Of the twelve, the Mester Alderman's voice spoke loudest, and today, he was supported by his successor. Together with the king's voice, this sacred trinity was the law of the land. The remaining aldermen hadn't a prayer to thwart them. Still, Alderman Aelwin tried. "I disagree," he said. "For all we know, *he* arrived with a mouthful of lies."

He, meaning Brutus, the foreigner, who would style himself Pretania's new High King, even above others who were born here, Gwendolyn's father included.

Doubtless, some feared that with Brutus so entrenched in the West, soon the shift of power would be complete, and

Loegria would have no more use for Cornwall. If this be true, Cornwall's future hung by the slightest of threads—namely, Gwendolyn's marriage. And she, more than most, understood why the aldermen might be concerned... particularly considering the Prophecy—the bane of Gwendolyn's existence.

"Truly," said Alderman Crwys, with narrowed eyes. "Where is this red tide of which he so oft speaks?"

"I, too, am for dissolution," announced Alderman Morgelyn, despite that her father did not call for a vote. But his opposition was a bit of a surprise considering that he seemed to have some affinity for her mother. "*He* lends his warriors to defend our port, but why, when there has not been a breath of discord in so many years?" He did not once meet the Queen's gaze. "I say we've no need of him! And, if you ask me, this is his way of infiltrating our forces to uncover our weaknesses. Indeed, I mistrust the man, and why should we allow a foreigner to seize take our lands, prophecy bedamned!" His gaze slid to the Queen's as he lifted a handsome, golden brow.

A challenge perhaps?

"And yet none of this was at issue until the emissary arrived," interjected the King. "In fact, only this morn, Morgelyn, I heard you say you looked forward to meeting the Prince."

"I, too, heard him say so," said the Mester Alderman. "And, yes, agreed, Majesty. None of this was at issue before the messenger arrived this morn. Must we continue to imperil ourselves for this quarrel? And how preposterous when we've the enemy's own daughter in the King's bed!" Only belatedly, he flicked a glance toward the King and his Queen Consort, lifting an age-speckled hand. "Apologies, Majesties, no offense intended."

The Queen's expression darkened, though she said nothing —not as yet. But Gwendolyn could tell that, like a copper kettle over a flame, her mother's temper was ready to boil.

Looking vexed, her father nodded, though he said nothing, and Gwendolyn understood he must choose his words wisely.

This Konsel was governed, not by the King, but by the statutes of the Brothers' Pact, an ancient code of honor enacted by the sons of Míl—Gwendolyn's ancestors, who'd inherited these lands after defeating the Tuatha Dé Danann.

According to the highest law, no King's right to rule was absolute and despite that a king must bear the blood of the Conservators in his veins, his crown was subject to the will of the Konsel.

Not even a king could remove a duly elected alderman, and, only if one broke faith, or died, could one be replaced. Therefore, the Konsel spoke freely over matters of state, though a king was not without his ways, particularly one so beloved by his people.

Into that bargain, even after all this time, none of these aldermen understood her mother's influence, nor did it appear they anticipated her Prydein temper.

That was a mistake.

"You are all bags of bones with less sense than a salt lick," declared the Queen rather churlishly, but under the present circumstances, Gwendolyn couldn't blame her. As closely guarded as the secret was, her father's illness was no secret to any of these aldermen, and more and more, they tested him without regard.

Her mother continued. "Our Gwyddons have investigated Brutus' steel. There is nothing of its kind, nor can we hope to defend against it. Yet you would advise your king to sever a perfectly biddable alliance? All for what? Because my kinsmen stole a few of your goats and you don't like the woad on their faces?"

Discomforted by the Queen's boldness, some elders shrugged. A few bobbed their heads. "More to the point," she persisted, angrier now as she sought Alderman Morgelyn's gaze. "Will any of you dare call me a liar?"

The word tore like a snarl from her lips, and even the torch flames shivered over her challenge, for the "lie" of which she spoke was the divination witnessed by herself and her maid—and of course, Gwendolyn, although Gwendolyn was only a babe.

No one needed clarification, because everyone knew about the Prophecy, even as everyone knew about the horde of *Gwyddons* her mother called forth throughout the years to examine her only born child, only to ascertain whether, instead of a babe, those *faeries* had left her with a changeling. For years and years, her mother dragged *dewinefolk* from their woodland shelters, promising impunity, should they come forward to verify her child's humanity—Gwendolyn's humanity. And this was the reason she and her mother did not comport: From the morning of Gwendolyn's "visitation" until her seventh Name Day, she had been poked, prodded, and probed.

Seven long years, her mother's servitors tortured her, until, at long last, her father put an end to it all, declaring that, if no proof of the exchange had been discovered as yet, no proof should ever come to light. Yet this was also the end of her association with her mother, and for all the years since, Gwendolyn was left to pine for the love of a mother, all the while the Queen Consort pined for a *true* heir—a son of her loins, as though Gwendolyn were not her child.

And still, in her prayers, the Queen wondered aloud what terrible thing she'd done to anger the fickle gods.

Secretly, Gwendolyn wondered if it might simply be that she had all but cast away the only child she'd ever been allowed, and not that Gwendolyn entirely believed it, but that child, Gwendolyn, was said to be blessed by the gods.

Said only because, at this late hour, there was no proof of

Gwendolyn's "gifts." Her hair was golden, truly, but it wasn't "gold." And if anyone should know, it would be her. By now, she'd had more curls snipped, hacked, cut, trimmed, plucked, and examined than anyone could rightly count.

To be sure, there was *nothing* of the precious metal in Gwendolyn's locks, although Demelza always made certain to remind everyone that her hair would not turn lest it be snicked by her one true love.

"Majesty," entreated Alderman Aelwin, daring at his peril to ignore the Queen. "Might we not... at the least... delay this betrothal? We've only just received this news... If you assent, we'll see our Princess wed in less than six sennights."

Gods.

So soon?

Until now, Gwendolyn hadn't dared count the days.

Alderman Crwys begged, "Please, Majesty..." He peered at Gwendolyn now. "Shouldn't we prefer to take some time to prepare the poor girl's dowry chest?"

Poor girl?

Sucking in a breath, Gwendolyn dared to look at her mother, and found the Queen's color heightened to a color Gwendolyn had never once seen upon her mother's tawny cheeks.

Blood and bones. Was this why they'd summoned her? To play one side against the other? To sway her father against her mother? To entreat Gwendolyn to defy the Queen?

Not bloody likely.

Gwendolyn knew better than to try.

In some ways, her authority surpassed the Queen's, and yet knowing she daren't utter a word against her mother, Gwendolyn pursed her lips. When her expression remained inscrutable, Alderman Aelwin finally gave a pleading glance toward the Queen, eschewing her title as he said, "As I understand, the Princess' dowry chest has not been delivered. Is this true, Mestres?" He hitched his chin at First Alderman Bryok, but the First Alderman averted his gaze, jaw taut, as though he would have no part in this discourse.

Queen Eseld ignored the veiled accusation, and, to her credit, she also ignored the omission of her title. "*My daughter* was *always* meant to wed this Maytide, Konselman. This news changes little."

Actually, it changed a lot so far as Gwendolyn was concerned. Locrinus was hardly Urien. But at seventeen, if she did not wed this Maytide, it could be another long while before another opportunity presented itself—a long, long while, during which her womb could wither and die. Only once in a great while did the new moon align itself with Calan Mai, and for a princess of Pretania, wedding vows must be spoken on this sacred day, with the Llanrhos Druids in attendance, to bid the gods bestow blessings of peace and fertility, not only for the wedding couple, but for the land itself. This was why so many years had passed since her meeting Urien and her upcoming nuptials. They were waiting for the most opportune time to align their houses, and now, for the sake of the realm, her wedding could not be postponed.

Yet the Aldermen knew this...

"Majesty," pleaded Alderman Aelwin.

"Enough!" declared her father. "Enough! Enough!" He reached out to squeeze the Queen's hand. "The Prince arrives on the morrow. What would you have me do, Konselman? Turn him away?"

Gwendolyn blinked, surprised. "Tomorrow?"

She hadn't realized, though of course, it made sense, considering there was so little time remaining before the planned event. She must have at least one opportunity to meet

Prince Locrinus to see how they would comport. Still, she wasn't ready.

"Tomorrow," confirmed her father with a nod.

"Oh," she said, and, truly, she might have said more, but there wasn't a good reason to object, even despite that the alderman spoke true. Her dowry chest had not yet been delivered, much less completed, or even begun, so far as Gwendolyn knew. She had no lady's maid. And worst of all—again, she swiped self-consciously at the blueberry stain on her tunic— she wasn't prepared to face the Prince.

Her heart fluttered wildly as she dared seek her mother's gaze—not to change her mind. Gwendolyn understood they were running out of time. She merely longed for some reassurance.

Sensing her attention, Queen Eseld turned to look at Gwendolyn for the briefest of instants, then quickly averted her gaze, leaving Gwendolyn feeling... that same horrid sense of melancholy she always felt over her mother's rejections, subtle as this was.

Suddenly, the Queen slapped the table and rose from her seat. "Enough!" she said fiercely, and if her mother was passionate about nothing else, she was passionate about this. "Our dragon banners will be united! Now, I intend to go plan for our guests."

She marched from the room without a backward glance, leaving the aldermen holding their tongues. As a daughter of the Northern Tribes, there was that about Queen Eseld that lost its civility whenever she was enraged—a certain gleam in her eye, more than a show of temper. Yet her father remained unperturbed. His face gaunt and pale, he turned to face his only child, giving her a lift of his chin. "You may go, as well," he said. His voice was gentle, yet brooked no argument, and

Gwendolyn's brows collided, not so much because he was dismissing her but because she was worried about his health.

At least now she was free to go inspect the glen. "Yes, sire," she said respectfully.

"And please, please, do as your mother says, Gwendolyn. Make ready."

"Yes, sire," she said again, and rose from the table.

With a hand to her heart, she inclined her head, first to her father and King, and thereafter, afforded the same courtesy to her father's aldermen. Afterward, she left, closing the door behind her, denying herself the urge to linger and listen because come what may, she must resign herself to this fate. Everything her mother said was perfectly true. The dragon banners must be united.

It was her duty to wed Loegria's heir.

And this she had known since the day she was born.

Neither could she allow herself to worry over Prince Locrinus' affinity toward her. If he wished to be king of Pretania, Gwendolyn was part of that plan. Loegria might, indeed, have more sons, but Cornwall had no more daughters.

TWO

An errand boy rushed by with a heap of towels. Spying Gwendolyn, he stumbled to a halt, attempting a hasty bow and nearly spilling his burden.

"Oh!" Gwendolyn exclaimed, rushing forward to help him keep his stack. "Keep your eyes ahead," she admonished once the towels were saved. "No one will fault you for it, not even the King." The boy nodded enthusiastically, then attempted another bow, and Gwendolyn shook her head, smiling with her rebuke. "Straight ahead!" she commanded, pointing down the hall, and away the boy dashed with a mountain of towels bigger than him, his bottom wagging like a pup's tail. The towels were headed for the salt bath, a medicinal *piscina* her father had ordered constructed some years past using blueprints traded by a Phoenician merchant.

After hearing about their healing springs, the merchant asked to see one, and when her father lamented the vanishing pools, the merchant offered his blueprints.

It was really quite inspired, Gwendolyn thought. Constructed so it siphoned sea water into an inner-city pool from the bay below, waders came to ease their joints and for various other ailments. They worked similarly to the hot springs, with two major differences: the hot springs were naturally heated and provided by the grace of gods. The salt bath was made possible by the ingenuity of men, yet there was no way to heat the pool; and therefore, it was not so enjoyable to use during the Winter. But despite this, it was quite the attraction. Visiting merchants came oft to make use of it during warmer months, diverted from nearby ports.

Another servant rushed by with a cart, his sole duty to replace the old, spent torches with fresh ones, newly dipped in pitch. Another came with a broom, and another with a bucket and mop. The spirit of the moment was vastly changed from the sleepy languor Gwendolyn encountered on the way into her father's Konsel. During this short time since her mother's departure, the Queen had already put the entire palace to work.

From the ivy-tangled courtyards to the King's polished-granite audience hall, servants rushed about, making ready for their distinguished guests. But this was when her mother's talents shone best. Whatever "savage" influences Queen Eseld had before her arrival, there were none more sophisticated than she. She was the Mestres of Cornwall, the lady of Trevena, and no one worked harder at being Cornish than their Prydein Queen.

Thankfully, her mother was right about this, as well; there was much to be done—enough to keep her busy and away from Gwendolyn. It had been too long since they'd had guests of such import—not since her first meeting with Urien, five years past, when Gwendolyn was still too young to understand the significance of their union.

She had thought Urien fine, in the same manner one

admired an elder brother, but she'd never once imagined herself on his arm, nor in his bed.

Now Gwendolyn was old enough to understand the import of what was happening here today, and if she didn't like Prince Locrinus, she would be stuck with him, regardless.

Sadly, the chances were far greater that he would not like her, and come what may, tomorrow, she would be meeting her betrothed—her second, at that!

The very thought unsettled her belly so she wasn't hungry. Good thing, because by now, the hall would have been cleared of Alyss' wonderful morning cakes.

And despite this, she continued in that direction, intent upon checking with Yestin, to see if he had need of her this morn. Even now, she suspected her mother's maid was in her bower, waiting with a mountain of dresses, and no doubt this was the reason Demelza had been late this morning. But, if she could, once she was finished with the maid, she intended to steal away, and it was better to check with the steward now than to have him search for her later, and risk involving her mother. Doubtless, they were already planning the welcome feast, everything from the musicians to accompany the meal to the victuals themselves.

Queen Eseld would have her say, of course, but it was the King who must approve expenditures, and in his place, Gwendolyn. No matter that Queen Eseld so oft took his place while he convalesced, the approval of expenditures was a task assigned to the heir, which Gwendolyn was, no matter that her mother despaired of the fact.

Nor did Queen Eseld appreciate having to approve her *dawnsio* expenditures through Gwendolyn, even though Gwendolyn would never dare thwart her.

Without question, her mother would lend her *dawnsio* to

the event, at a cost no one would ever dispute, because the service they provided was invaluable.

Along with the Druids, the *dawnsio*, *Awenydds* and *Gwyddons* all served important roles for the kingdom—as priests, historians, philosophers, and scientists. They continued an ancient tradition, teaching epochs of history through a choreographed dance, which was widely considered to be one of the most esteemed roles a woman could aspire to. To the unskilled eye, it would appear the dancers were posturing to entertain, but every gesture bespoke volumes.

Altogether, there were twenty-one dancers, plus twenty-one understudies—a pair from each of Pretania's tribes, not including the isle of Mona, where the Druids lived—fourteen for Prydein, eight from Westwalas, six for each of Cornwall's boroughs, and two each from the remaining tribes. Each dancer was carefully chosen by the Queen and her *Awenydds*, not merely for her beauty, but for her mental acuity as well. Unlovely people need not apply, and Gwendolyn was rarely even invited to watch. Purely out of necessity, because someday she would be queen, she had been taught to interpret the dance, but her mother clearly didn't want daily reminders that her own daughter didn't measure up to the perfection she'd cultivated in her dancers.

Not once in Gwendolyn's life had her mother ever complimented her face, and this was well and good... if only she hadn't heard a thousand buttery praises fly from the Queen's lips, all for others, including Ely, who at fifteen was now the understudy for Durotriges, whence she and her family hailed. A twinge of envy resurfaced, though Gwendolyn suppressed it, hardly pleased with the sentiment. Her relationship with her mother wasn't Ely's fault any more than Ely could be faulted for her natural beauty. And neither was Gwendolyn's countenance anyone else's doing. Blessing or curse, it was her own burden to bear.

Much to Gwendolyn's surprise, she found Ely lurking outside the great hall, spying on her uncle. Surrounded by sweepers, her father's steward sat hunched over one of the lower tables, scribbling at his ledgers. His loyal hound sat beneath the table, ears perked, eyes peeled, hoping the maids would uncover some disgusting treasure to sweep his way. If he could and his master would allow it, Gwendolyn knew that dog would be out from beneath that table, sniffing at piles of rushes, content enough to gobble greasy straw, but even the dog was afraid of his master's bark. Rightly so; because aside from the King and Queen Consort, and of course, Gwendolyn, Yestin held the highest post in the realm—higher in some ways than the aldermen, because he controlled the Treasury and the men who guarded it. And regardless, he was still Elowyn's uncle, and rather than face him, the silly girl would hide behind the door, chewing at her cheeks.

She was so deep in thought that she didn't hear Gwendolyn approach, and when Gwendolyn laid a hand atop her shoulder, Ely yelped in surprise.

"Gwendolyn!" she exclaimed, then winced, turning to peer through a crack between the hinges to see if her squeal had attracted Yestin's attention.

"Oh, Gwen!" she sobbed. "I am undone! I've been told my uncle means to pair me with the ambassador's son for tomorrow's feast."

"Which ambassador?"

"Trinovantes," she said. "The new one."

Gwendolyn's brow furrowed. "But I thought you welcomed the opportunity to find yourself a good husband?"

"Oh, I do! But, really, Gwendolyn, have you met him? His

face is flat as a morning cake! Indeed," she said, when Gwendolyn's frown deepened. "I'm told he was kicked by a mule."

"Gods," said Gwendolyn, her brows slanting with dismay —not the least bit feigned, though not for Elowyn's sake. Despite that she understood Ely meant nothing by the insult, she was naturally sensitive to the poor man's dilemma. She understood more than most what it felt like to be judged by one's appearance.

"I just know *she* asked for the pairing to turn me off the thought of a husband."

She, being Lady Ruan, although Gwendolyn suspected otherwise. Ely's mother was far too kind. Although it struck her in that moment that perhaps all mothers and daughters were destined to have quarrels—or so it seemed. As kind as Lady Ruan was, Ely clearly took issue with her, more lately than ever. Though at least Ely's mother didn't think her a changeling, and never once employed torture to glean the truth of the matter. Gwendolyn couldn't say the same.

"Perhaps 'tis because she knows you are the kindest of souls, Ely? Someone like the ambassador's son will have need for a speck of compassion."

"Harrumph!" said Ely, though her shoulders slumped. "Mayhap tis true, Gwen, yet this doesn't lift my mood knowing *he'll* come soon to spirit you away."

He, meaning Prince Locrinus whose presence was already felt, despite that he'd yet to arrive. And this must be the true cause of Elowyn's distress, she realized. Sliding an arm about her friend's shoulders, Gwendolyn tried to lift her mood. "*Only* if he likes me," she jested.

"Oh, I *know* he will!" Ely returned. "And nevertheless, if he does not, has he more choice than you?" She peered up at Gwendolyn, her sweet blue eyes swimming with tears, and Gwendolyn frowned. Leave it to Ely to speak plainly. As her own mother had already pointed out once today, the dragon banners must be united—dragons rampant, one to guard the sea, the other to guard the land. Choices such as these were not the prerogative of princes or princesses. Even if Prince Locrinus found her as displeasing as her mother clearly did, he, too, would have little choice. Come Calan Mai, she would be wedding Loegria's eldest son beneath the Sacred Yew, and she would don the torc of his house in a ceremony that hearkened back to the Dawn of Days. This was the indisputable truth.

"What shall I do without you?" said Ely.

Gwendolyn's voice softened. "Never fear, dear friend." She pulled a wisp of hair from Ely's beautiful face. "I'll make another appeal to take you with me when I go."

"My mother will say no," argued Ely, and Gwendolyn knew it was true. Already, she'd asked twice, and Lady Ruan would not part with two children.

So far as Ely's older brother was concerned, he was already bound to come with her. From the day he took his vow to serve as her personal guard, Bryn's fate was sealed. As Gwendolyn's Shadow, wherever she went, so, too, must he go. As was the custom, he even slept in her antechamber, and the only time he wasn't duty-bound to be at her side was when Gwendolyn was safely ensconced within the palace. At the moment, he was probably in the Mester's Pavilion, with his sire, receiving orders for his comportment during the Prince's arrival and Gwendolyn blushed hotly over the realization, because her mother liked to complain that she and Bryn were overfamiliar.

"He's your servant," she would say, yet this was sometimes difficult to recall when the three of them, she, Bryn and Ely, had grown up nearly as siblings.

She gave Ely's shoulder a gentle squeeze. "Loegria isn't far," she consoled, and then she turned Ely about and, with a glance into the hall at Yestin, decided he would be at his ledgers for many hours to come. At the moment, Ely needed a distraction, and Gwendolyn knew how to provide it. "Come," she demanded. "Yestin can wait. I'm off to choose my wardrobe for the visit, and you know how desperately I will need your opinion. Given my druthers, I'd wear a jerkin and keep a spear in my hand."

Ely giggled, allowing herself to be lured away, and the two walked, hand in hand. Alas, though Gwendolyn was jesting, she also spoke true. She was not the most discerning of fashion, but when the Prince arrived, she intended to present herself well enough that he would embrace her as an equal. With all his golden finery, she didn't wish to face him looking like a troll, as so often she felt beneath her mother's scrutiny.

SPYING GWENDOLYN'S COMPANION, DEMELZA LIFTED A BROW. "Shouldn't you be rehearsing?" she asked.

Ely hitched her chin. "I am not needed."

Old as the *faerie* hills, Demelza was her grandmother's maid before she was her mother's. Hence, she was the one who'd taught Queen Eseld all the intricacies of the Cornish court. No doubt, age gave her authority. "Says who?"

To Ely's credit, she stood taller beneath the maid's scrutiny. "So says Mother Superior. She told me to make myself scarce."

Hearing this, Demelza lifted both brows.

So, too, did Gwendolyn because the revelation said so much.

"And what did you do to displease her?"

"Naught," said Ely, with a pink stain on her cheeks. "I merely pointed out that Gwendolyn had terrible taste in attire.

I suggested that, despite all your great effort, Demelza, she might benefit from a discerning eye."

"You said that?" Gwendolyn asked.

And here she believed it was her idea for Ely to attend her.

Very quickly, Ely shook her head, peering back at Demelza, who'd caught the gesture, because one grey brow lifted higher. "Well... not precisely."

Demelza looked at the door, mayhap considering whether she was in any mood to deal with two unmanageable charges, but at long last, relented. "Very well, Elowyn. Go, sit. But do not disturb us. If your opinion is required, we'll ask."

Gwendolyn tried not to smile as Ely grinned victoriously and flounced over to the bed to hide behind a veritable mountain of dresses. No doubt she'd said nothing of the sort to Queen Eseld. If she'd angered the Queen at all, it was only because she wasn't paying attention in class. That else Lady Ruan had whispered into her mother's ear about Ely's reluctance to dance.

No matter the reason, angering Queen Eseld was never a wise thing to do, unless one wished to be saddled with a flatnosed companion at supper. And now that Gwendolyn understood more about what led to that decision, she was quite certain it was her mother, not Lady Ruan, behind the pairing. As it was with her father, whatever Queen Eseld decreed, Lady Ruan would agree to, and if this were the case, there was no one in the palace who could change her mind—not Yestin, certainly not Gwendolyn.

Poor Ely.

Gwendolyn decided she would slip her a dress, knowing it would cheer her.

The Queen might not be too pleased that Gwendolyn had softened her rebuke, but she certainly wouldn't care about the gown, and Gwendolyn should know. By now, she had stained, rented, or ruined so many dresses. Her mother never batted an eyelash. In truth, sometimes Gwendolyn wondered if she ruined them on purpose, only to see if her mother would care.

Unfortunately, to reprimand Gwendolyn, she would have to speak to Gwendolyn, and this wasn't likely to happen, unless perforce.

Mind you, their relationship was cordial, their conversations never heated, but they were rare as *piskies*. And sometimes Gwendolyn felt her mother showered her with so many gifts merely to keep her from seeking an audience to ask for favors.

And nevertheless, judging by the number of gowns she had to try on this morning, her mother was entirely too generous, if not affectionate. Even with Ely's help, it took more than three hours to try on every gown, but thankfully, Ely's tastes were pristine, and Demelza didn't object to her choices, nor did she protest when Gwendolyn offered Elowyn her favorite of the lot. "What time is the Prince due?" asked Gwendolyn anxiously, while Ely sat petting her new dress—a brightly colored *cendal*, dyed in a shade called Nightingale to match Ely's fiery tresses.

She needed to get away, before it grew late, and she sorely regretted not meeting with Yestin because now there wasn't time.

"At first light, so I'm told," said Demelza, pulling at a thread on the dress she was altering.

Naturally, Gwendolyn was shorter than her mother— simply one more way she didn't measure up. Her bosom was smaller, as well, and her hips wider, too. As a daughter, Gwendolyn was merely a pale shade. Truly, for while her hair was yellow, her mother's was dark as night and no matter that her manner of beauty was uncommon amidst the Dumnonii,

Queen Eseld was unspeakably lovely, her eyes warm and rich as loam, lips neither thin nor cruel.

It was little wonder the King had been so willing to set aside a century's worth of discord for the sake of their union.

When the thread did not come away, Demelza bent to set her teeth against the offending strand, snapping it quickly. In the meantime, Gwendolyn stood naked as an oak in Winter, arms crossed to conceal her bosom, the tiny hairs on her arms prickling against a draft.

Winter was gone, Spring had arrived, but April sometimes still harbored a bitter chill. "Have you met him?" Gwendolyn wondered aloud.

"Gods, no. How would I, child? I'm only a maid. Go ask your mother." Demelza rose then, tossing the heavy dress over Gwendolyn's head, tugging the material down.

Instinctively, Gwendolyn searched for the sleeves and sighed, knowing she would ask her mother for naught. "So," she persisted, speaking through the thick material—a heavy, brushed suede, dyed blue, her mother's favorite color. "Do you know if he's anything at all like Urien?"

"Nay, child."

Once Gwendolyn's head emerged through the collar, she hitched her chin.

She wasn't a child any longer. She was seventeen.

"I hear tell he's beautiful," offered Ely. "Perhaps 'tis why Bryn doesn't like him."

Gwendolyn cocked her head in surprise. "Bryn has met him?"

Ely smiled the faintest of smiles. "Oh... I don't know," she sang, and Gwendolyn frowned.

"You mustn't fret, Gwendolyn," said Demelza, her lips somehow moving around the pin in her mouth. She tugged rudely at Gwendolyn's sleeve. "I'm told he's quite handsome, but really, you oughtn't ask such questions. Rather, the question should be: Does he appeal to *you*?"

Gwendolyn felt this way, too. But she didn't like it that everyone seemed to know more about Prince Locrinus than she did, including Ely, though naturally Ely would know more, because she spent so much more time with Queen Eseld.

With a sigh, Gwendolyn allowed her head to fall back, neck sore, and wearied of posing so long, even wearier of dissembling. She glanced at the high window, gauging the time.

"How can I know what I think until I meet him?"

"Verily," agreed Demelza, as though she had validated her point. "And yet, whatever the case, you must get your mind straight, because the result will be the same, whether you find him appealing or nay. You will marry, no matter, and if you are inclined to enjoy your husband, perhaps you will."

"Humph!" said Ely. "That is what my mother says about the *dawnsio* when I say I wish to wed a man instead. This is what it's like, you realize—the *dawnsio*." Ely sighed dramatically. "But my mother says 'tis inevitable I will dance, because Queen Eseld loves my form, and I must embrace my calling."

"She speaks truly," said Demelza. "You have a rare talent, Elowyn." She plucked another pin from the *pinpush* and placed it into her mouth.

And face, Gwendolyn wanted to add. No doubt, it was Ely's face that Queen Eseld loved most, for, in truth, Ely was the epitome of beauty—hair like flames, eyes cerulean, like the sea. As stunning as the Queen was, it was Ely who was blessed with the beauty of their *rás*.

"Humph," said Ely, again. "It is not *my* calling. I'd sooner die a thousand deaths in childbed than dance a single night for fat, greasy dukes!"

"Ely!" exclaimed both Demelza and Gwendolyn, although Gwendolyn said it with a yelp of laughter.

"Well, then, perhaps you will enjoy your flat-nosed companion?" suggested Demelza as she knelt at Gwendolyn's feet.

"See, Gwendolyn! I told you!"

Gwendolyn's thoughts sobered, returning to Prince Locrinus, and perhaps sensing the turn of her thoughts, Demelza said, "This is the way of it. You'll not be the first to wed a man whose face and heart are unknown to you. And yet, no matter, I've known many who found joy in their unions, merely because they chose to, your mother being one. You must decide you will love him, and eventually you shall."

"What of me?" Ely complained. "I shan't be allowed to wed *any* man! Really, Demelza, I don't want to dance!" Elowyn pushed her new dress aside, adding sullenly, "Oh, yes, I know that once I am invested, I can take a lover if I wish, but it does not please me to welcome a man into my bed under a veil of night and never hold my own babe in my arms."

Put so gloomily, Gwendolyn vowed again to speak to her mother. But, at the moment, Demelza had left a door wide open to inquire about Queen Eseld, and Gwendolyn intended to seize the opportunity. "So my mother came to her marriage with a full and willing heart?"

"Of course not," said Demelza matter-of-factly, putting her needle to the hem of Gwendolyn's gown. "What woman does? And yet your mother understood her duty, and she accepted it with grace and faith. In the end, she came to love your father dearly."

Gwendolyn thought about that for a moment, then asked, "So, did you know my mother before she arrived?"

"Nay, child."

Gwendolyn knit her brows. "Then how can you know what she felt?"

"I simply do."

"*Gods.* You are unyielding, as usual," Gwendolyn said hotly. "I am certain my mother commends you for it, Demelza, but I find it boring!"

The maid stood, reaching up to tap a finger against Gwendolyn's cheek, not the least bit perturbed. Very gently, she said, "Have I ever forsaken you, Gwendolyn?"

Gwendolyn shook her head because, nay, she had not. And yet, neither was Demelza sworn to her. She was bound to her mother, and thus would do her mother's bidding in all things.

The maid sighed wearily. "You *must* trust me," she said. But Gwendolyn's shoulders slumped, and the maid immediately reached about to tap her back. "Stand straight," she demanded. "If you slump, the dress will drag."

And that was another thing: While she was shorter than her mother, she was not short for a woman. She had her Prydein grandmother's look, or so she'd been told.

"What if I am taller than he is?" Gwendolyn worried, all the more sullen now, considering everything that could go wrong. "Won't that displease him?"

"You shan't be," announced Ely, peering up from a handful of jewels she was inspecting. "I'm told he's quite tall, and golden—a golden idol for a golden bride! Don't you think this necklace would look divine with that gown?"

Gwendolyn turned to appraise the jewels draped from Ely's fingers—a silvered curtain of sapphires meant to be worn with a matching tiara. But the tiara was not among the pile of borrowed jewels. Evidently, her mother had not seen fit to lend it this time, but the necklace alone was worth more than all the pottage in the city.

"Your mother would be pleased," added Ely, and some part of Gwendolyn longed to run, screaming in frustration, because it was *always* some gem or gown Queen Eseld saw fit to compliment, never Gwendolyn herself. And, really, she lent them so oft, as though her jewels could somehow make up for some defect of Gwendolyn's person. As a consequence, Gwendolyn was learning to despise the accoutrements. "Lovely," she said.

"There," announced Demelza. "We're through."

"At last!" said Gwendolyn, and when Demelza peered up to meet her gaze, Gwendolyn shrugged. "I'd like to go hunting."

Only she didn't actually intend to go hunting. She still meant to inspect that glen. However, though Demelza might know of the King's plight, Ely did not. For obvious reasons, it was vital to the realm that the King maintain an appearance of good health.

"Please, Gwendolyn," begged Demelza. "Go ask your mother. Considering the circumstances, she may not approve."

"Why?" Gwendolyn smiled, lifting both brows. "Because I might harm my lovely face?"

Ely snickered, and Demelza cast both girls a withering glance.

Self-deprecation was the one thing that always upset her mother's maid. "There is naught about your face that is unlovely," she scolded as she retrieved her sewing basket. And then, muttering beneath her breath, she departed.

"So, now you'll go hunting?" said Ely.

"I will, indeed."

"And will you ask your mother?" Ely flicked a glance at the handsome gown Gwendolyn had discarded on the floor, then another at the neatly folded pile of worn leathers on the chair beneath the window. But she knew the answer already.

"Nay," said Gwendolyn.

Ely sighed heavily. "Well, if you mean to defy her, I should not go. She'll tell my mother, and my mother will make me spend the entirety of *your* Prince's visit entertaining Lord Flat Face!"

Gwendolyn laughed despite herself. "I'm sorry," she offered, even as she fetched her hunting attire from the chair. "Where is Bryn?" she asked.

"Oh... I don't know," answered Ely, but it was clear by the way she peered up through her thick lashes, that she knew, and was protecting him, as she always did, whenever she thought Gwendolyn might incur her mother's wrath.

If only she and Ely could trade places, Gwendolyn lamented, for Gwendolyn was not made for gems or silk. Instead, she was more at home in the woods, with a blade in her boot and a bow in her hand. "Never mind," said Gwendolyn as she dressed.

When she was ready, she found her quiver and made for the door. "I'll find him myself," she told Ely. "You stay and play with my mother's jewels."

CHAPTER

THREE

There were only a handful of places Bryn could be: in the stables, pampering his beloved mare; in the Mester's Pavilion with his sire; else in the courtyard, practicing at swordplay. These were the first places Gwendolyn would look. If he wasn't at any of these places, then he would be in the cook's house, charming kitchen maids into parting with a morning cake, or two.

Without question, Ely's brother was a simple soul, unfettered by personal desires—all except for those regarding his belly. He was devoted to his family, unwavering in his sense of duty, and he was also quite good at his occupation—a natural consequence of the long hours spent in training. And he was so good that he held several distinctions, including a few for hand-to-hand combat, archery, swordplay, and not the least of his skills: equestrian handling. Over the years, he'd taught Gwendolyn everything she knew.

And yet, all this said, it was difficult for Gwendolyn to take him too seriously when they'd shared the same wet nurse.

The one thing Bryn was *not*, however, was forthcoming. His

deep, soulful eyes held secrets he was neither willing nor capable of revealing, and more and more, she felt the truth of this as a barrier between them. Like Demelza, Bryn was imperturbable, and no matter what Gwendolyn said or did, he faced her with that same self-assured half-smile that never failed to catch a favor from the kitchen maids. This was only natural because he shared the same countenance with his sister. But unlike Ely, Bryn was far more certain of himself. And this, too, was only natural because Bryn was older. Three years senior to his sister, one year to Gwendolyn. By the time Ely came about, Gwendolyn and Bryn were already close as ticks, and Ely had toddled about behind them like a sweet little pup. It was only later, after Bryn was sworn to Gwendolyn, that his demeanor changed, and she grew closer to Ely.

She found him in the first place she looked—in the courtyard, sparring with his new partner, a pointy-eared *Sidhe* Gwendolyn neither liked nor trusted. No matter that he must be scarcely older than Bryn, and not much more than Gwendolyn, he behaved as though he thought himself better than everyone, despite her station—not that Gwendolyn considered herself superior merely because of a crown. Simply because one's *rás* was the elder *rás*, did not presume one's dominion. Rather, one must earn one's place in this world—everyone, including kings.

And regardless, Málik was quite the swordsman, dancing about on the nimblest feet Gwendolyn had ever seen.

More than anything, she loathed she was so compelled to watch him, and she loathed it all the more that she admired his style. Indeed, sometimes, in the privacy of her bower, she practiced maneuvers like his. And, here and now, determined as she'd been to ignore him, she watched them cross swords from the corner of one eye, holding her breath as he twirled like a dancer, then landed gracefully on his feet, like a cat. Unfortunately for Bryn, seeing Gwendolyn distracted him. To his detriment, he relaxed his sword arm, and that damnable *Sidhe* turned the flat of his blade against the side of Bryn's arm, whacking him hard, his ice-blue eyes glittering fiercely.

Irksome elf!

Even thinking such blasphemy made Gwendolyn feel ashamed, yet no one in her life had ever infuriated her more than Málik Danann, not even her mother.

Danann! Danann! As though he had a right to the name. For all she knew, *his* blood spilled the same as hers. Anyone could claim to be anything at all.

Her cradleside visit notwithstanding, no one had ever actually met a true-blood *fae* in so long, and so much as Gwendolyn loved Demelza, even Demelza's story gave Gwendolyn pause. All her life, she'd sought to meet one, until *him*. But if *faekind* were anything like him, she didn't wish to meet another.

Silver-haired, silver-eyed, he certainly favored the stories of his ilk, including his teeth, which were frighteningly sharp. Whenever he smiled, he looked as vicious as a wolf.

Daring to meet his gaze now, Gwendolyn found a telltale glimmer in his eye, hard as diamonds, and much to her disgust, it sent a quiver down her spine.

In answer, she gritted her teeth because he was both smug *and* arrogant—the difference being that one was all about being annoyingly pleased with oneself; the latter a matter of abundant pride, coupled with a blatant contempt for others. Somehow, Málik managed both, always smirking, never affable, always judging. And if Gwendolyn read his expression right, he had clearly judged her and found her wanting. "I'm off to hunt!" she announced, instead of stopping to ask Bryn to join her. And truly she would have, instead of presuming he would attend her, but it irked her terribly that Málik gave her his usual look of disdain, as though her presence eternally wearied him.

As it was, he was quite fortunate her father no longer put heads on pikes, as her grandfather used to do, because Málik's might be a perfect candidate—not that her father would agree, mind you, because, somehow, the sorry creature had inveigled him, as he seemed to have inveigled everyone, Bryn and Ely included.

Nay, she hadn't missed all the times Ely tried to convince Gwendolyn to go watch her brother spar, when in truth, it was Málik Ely cared to see.

His partner at once dismissed—and she had to confess it filled her with glee—Bryn hurried to catch her. "Gwendolyn... please, please tell me you asked your mother?"

Gwendolyn kept walking, readjusting the strap of her quiver so it wouldn't slip down her arm. "Yes, of course," she lied.

"Good," he said. "Good. The last thing I need today is another rebuke."

She dared not look at him. "Oh? And did you receive one already?"

"Of course."

"What for?"

His voice held a note of pique. "Need you ask?"

"Nay," Gwendolyn said, and kept moving, one foot in front of the other. No doubt it had something to do with her, as always. Bryn had one small weakness. He couldn't seem to deny Gwendolyn when she begged. And yet, Bryn was an intelligent man; she couldn't help if he saw her reason and capitulated.

Lamentably, even once they were inside the stables, Gwendolyn still couldn't look at him. She knew him too well, and he knew her equally so. He would read the truth in her eyes, though her silence did not reassure him. "You didn't ask, did you?"

It wasn't a question and Gwendolyn gave him no answer, insomuch as silence wasn't an answer. But it was.

Grumbling beneath his breath, Bryn reached out to pull open the stall door, cursing as he did so. "Blood and bloody bones, Gwendolyn!" He only ever called her Gwendolyn whenever he was angry. "You'll be the death of me yet!"

"Princess to you," Gwendolyn teased, not so much to remind him of his station as to nettle him—although perhaps in part to remind him, because the last thing she needed at that instant was for Bryn to gainsay her and prevent her from leaving the city. These were the first days of Spring, after a long Winter, and Gwendolyn was eager to visit the glen to see if the blight had returned, and she really wanted for Bryn to come along. If he forced her to go ask her mother, no one would go anywhere today.

And really, though she could leave without him—no one would stop her—he would answer for that as well. Therefore, he might as well come along. It wouldn't go unnoticed if she rode out of the city unescorted.

But it wasn't only the glen she wished to see. She wanted to speak to him privately to ask him what he knew of Prince Locrinus, since no one else seemed able or willing to say aught —except for Ely, if only to reveal he was tall.

Although Bryn might not be so forthcoming with his own cares, he was the one person she knew who understood what was at stake and who would speak to her without prevarication. And yet, he was right, of course. Her mother would be furious, but Prince Locrinus' arrival wasn't anticipated until the morrow and Gwendolyn shouldn't be expected to think only of him, especially where it concerned her father.

Moreover, though she realized the import of the Prince's

visit, she hadn't any clue how long their *guests* intended to remain, or when would be the next time she might get out of the city, and simply be a girl, not a princess, or a would-be queen, and especially not a Promised One.

The Queen Consort would see her immersed in too many preparatory efforts, none of which bore any true value to anyone, including herself. At this point, there was no *magik* cream to change Gwendolyn's countenance, and this was all her mother truly cared about. She would have Gwendolyn bedeviled with beauty regimens—the washing of hair, the combing of hair, the braiding of hair, the powdering of skin, the inking of eyes, the scrubbing of skin, the moisturizing of skin, the painting of skin. It was all too much!

Not to mention the endless reminders about manners and suggestions for how to behave in the presence of her new betrothed—what to say, how to say it, when to say it.

Most significantly, what *not* to say, and how to comport herself as a woman should, keeping a smile painted upon her face, even through a wash of tears.

It was enough to make Gwendolyn nervy as a bat fresh from slumber, despite that she did truly wish to make a good impression.

But if all that were not reason enough, Bryn also needed time for repose. After the Prince arrived, there would be no rest for him at all, and Gwendolyn hadn't any questions about her duties tomorrow. She'd been taught from the day of her birth that her people were her priority, and this wedding would come to pass, if only for them.

She knew little about the Prince, but as far as she was concerned, far more than a perfectly powdered face, knowing something about his likes and dislikes could help her conduct herself so he might find her appealing. No matter what Ely claimed, Bryn must have surely met him at some point. How else would Ely know he was tall, or that Bryn didn't like him? Really, what plausible reason could Bryn have to dislike a man he'd never met?

At any rate, she knew Bryn was keeping secrets of late, and she didn't like it. If he'd met Prince Locrinus, then what good reason could he have for failing to say so?

Already, Gwendolyn's nerves were frayed, and she still had one more evening to wait to see what Prince Locrinus would think of her. It was harrowing, truly, all this doing nothing. Only waiting to be judged. More than anything, it galled Gwendolyn that she should be reduced to caring about such things as her face. But alas, nobody, not once, ever, had said to her, "Practice your swordplay to impress your betrothed," or, "Learn to ride better." "Study harder." But if she was meant to rule well, these were all things that were crucial to her role. Gwendolyn was an adequate swordsman, a very good *aconter*, and an excellent horsewoman. But these were not things her mother cared about, only her face, and at that, a face her mother could not even look at for an instant longer than she must.

Bryn said nothing more, but Gwendolyn heard him grousing as he left to gather the saddles. When he returned with both in hand, she plucked hers off the top without a word, opting to saddle her own mare. She didn't need to be pampered at every turn. In fact, she preferred not to be. Bryn had enough to do on his own. She enjoyed fending for herself.

Anyway, if she were a man, she would have spent her entire life training to lead an army instead of learning to please a man. Wasn't defense still the primary duty of a sovereign? Regardless of what one wore, or how one used the garderobe? Perhaps if Gwendolyn had had a brother, it might not fall within her scope of duties, but she didn't have a brother. *She* was Cornwall's heir, along with the husband she would marry.

And therefore, it was incumbent upon her to learn every aspect of a sovereign's duties.

Mayhap this was why Málik irritated her so bloody much, because she hadn't had a single occasion to practice with Bryn since the day he'd arrived—rotten, misbegotten cur.

Once their horses were ready, Gwendolyn hauled herself into the saddle and exited the stable without waiting, reluctant to subject Bryn to any more rebukes. Perforce, he would pursue her, but she would rather have it said he came unwillingly.

As it was inside the palace, the city conducted itself at the same frenetic pace—merchants peddling wares in the courtyard, suppliers marching in their purchases, people rushing about in anticipation of the Loegrian envoy. Although this was not a usual market day, the market, too, was congested. Gwendolyn had to pass through to reach the narrow bridge that connected Stone Island to the mainland. Most of the merchants were congregated there, just inside the inner gates, hawking wares to anyone who ventured by. "Early spears!" called one merchant.

"Nettle tops!" cried another. "Nettle tops!"

And still another rushed forward to show Gwendolyn a lovely ell of azure cloth that looked like muslin. "Mollequin!" he said with lifted brows. "From the East! Here, let me show you, Highness!"

His black, wiry brows lifted higher as he petted his fine cloth, unwinding a length of the fabric so Gwendolyn could better see it.

"Not today," she said, considering the manner of his dress and the multitude of gold rings on his fingers. She was not too impressed with such things anyway, but if he hadn't worn so many rings, she might have offered him a copper and bade him to sell his cloth again.

Passing the permanent booths reserved for the most sought-after goods, she waved—at the baker and cordwainer in particular—before spurring her mount through the gates, onto the bridge, where there was considerably less foot traffic.

Clearly, it didn't take long for news to travel. By now, everyone within twenty leagues of the city must have heard Prince Locrinus was expected, and every farmer and artisan in the area had come rushing to peddle their wares.

She passed a few small carts, then several men with packs on their backs, and finally a petite woman, strolling with a little girl, talking to her pleasantly, hardly concerned that they might be the last to find a spot in the market. Gwendolyn stopped for a moment to speak with them. "*Myttin da,*" she said, and smiled when the child's brown eyes widened. Her mother was so surprised by the encounter that she stood with mouth agape.

"We've come to sell morels," said the girl brightly, pointing to her mother's meager basket.

"Indeed? I love morels," said Gwendolyn, reaching into the pouch at her belt and producing a silver coin.

"Me too!" The child's curls bobbed with her excitement as she jumped with glee. "Morels are my favoritest!"

Laughing, Gwendolyn said, "I would buy them all from you and save them for myself, but alas, I am off to hunt."

"All by yourself?" asked the child with awe, cocking her neck back like a chicken.

"Indeed, a woman can hunt the same as a man," Gwendolyn said. "Though I do not go alone." She peered back to spy Bryn emerging from the market onto the bridge, and then turned back to address the little girl, thinking that, as dirty as she was, she was more precious than gold.

She tossed the silver coin down for the child to catch, and

when she missed it, and went scurrying after it, the mother finally spoke. "Bless you, Highness! Bless you!"

"Thank you," said Gwendolyn, but when the woman went to hand Gwendolyn her basket, Gwendolyn lifted a hand, and said, "Keep it, friend. Sell it again. Else keep some for yourself and your lovely child. I wish you good luck at the market today!"

"And you!" said the woman.

As Gwendolyn rode away, she could hear the child saying excitedly, "I found it, I found it!" "Keep it safe," said her mother. "That was our Princess! This coin will bring us good luck." A tickle spread from Gwendolyn's heart, like tender little vines in search of the sun. It always made her feel so blessed to speak with her people.

She continued on, enjoying the warmth of the sun, peering down one side of King's Bridge.

Trevena lay perched on an island of precipitous cliffs overlooking an angry sea. Joined to the mainland by a narrow pass, the city was founded by the original conservatives of this land, long gone now, but their *magik* remained—most notably in the Dragon's Lair below the palace. Often by night and by sea, one could spy the dragon's breath inside the cave, a warning to ships to keep their distance, at least until morning, when the churning waters were easier to navigate. This, as she'd learned, was a parting gift from the Ancients, the beacon that lured traders to their bay, guiding them safely within. It was, in fact, this marvel that first brought King Brutus to their lands, with all three of his gargantuan ships, each bearing a thousand warriors at the oars, and Prince Urien at the helm of one.

Gwendolyn wasn't born yet.

The cove directly to the north of the bridge was too narrow for any but smaller vessels to navigate. However, the bay to the south harbored a well-used port. Even now, as she crossed the bridge, she could spy the bustle below—tiny folks from this vantage, and the usual crush of vessels hurrying to unload their hulls, hoping to clear the bay by nightfall.

Of course, even by day, only the most skilled sailors ever dared enter, if not for the jutting rocks, and deceptively strong currents, to steer clear of the staggering number of vessels anchored there, and the remnants of those that sunk.

Ships were far safer anchoring beyond the cove, and gods forbid anyone should be caught in the maw of the Dragon's Bay when the sea god Manannán came to rage.

It was for that reason Trevena had endured so long, protected on all sides by natural defenses. And to this day, because of the gift of their Dragon's Lair, their city thrived as a port—a matter of pride for her father, and for Gwendolyn as well.

Turning her attention from the harbor, Gwendolyn reveled in the lengthening silence. It was a lovely day for the ides of April. The sun shone brightly, warming the countryside a little more with each passing day. At long last, she gave a casual wave to the palace guards as she passed beneath the outer gates and made for the forest at an easy pace.

Only once her mare's hooves bit into softer soil did she feel any true urgency to be away. And then she spurred the sweet beast into a canter, confident that Bryn would follow.

Tilting her head back with glee, she breathed in deeply. The countryside was a welcome departure. Already the grass was greener, and the distant trees were unfurling new leaves, the scent of them more welcome than any perfume from Illyria.

Finally, when she reached the tree line, Bryn dared to sidle up beside her. "There you are," she teased, with a smile in her voice. "I worried you'd abandoned me."

"Never," he swore, and Gwendolyn knew in her heart that

come what may, this would always be the case. Loyal Bryn would follow and serve her till death did them part. And if the need ever arose, he would sacrifice his life for hers. But he would choose to do so, not because it was expected, nor because it was his occupation, but because he loved her, not as a man loved a woman, but as a brother loved a sister. She trusted this and loved him, too.

Indeed, if there was one source of comfort to be found in the adventure to come, it was that she would never have to face her destiny alone. She would always have Bryn. Lamentably, her mood soured as she considered his new sparring partner. "I don't know why you like that *Sidhe* so much," she groused.

"Because he is true to himself," Bryn replied. "Málik is who he is, without compromise or apology."

"Oh, I'd say. Apologies are lost to that ignorant elf."

It was *not* a polite thing to say, and Gwendolyn loathed that she'd felt compelled to say it, and perhaps she was even embarrassed, yet not enough to take it back.

Málik brought out the worst in her.

"Perhaps," said Bryn, and left it at that, until Gwendolyn's irritation got the better of her, and she added, "He is rude!" She cast Bryn a beleaguered glance. "I saw for myself the way he smacked you with his blade, smiling like a fox who swallowed the hen."

Bryn smiled companionably. "I warrant 'tis naught more or less than what I would have done to him. We are friends."

Gwendolyn rolled her eyes. "Truly? And does it not bother you that your father gives him such favor? He came from where, Bryn? Nowhere, truly? Recommended by no one and yet suddenly this man is training our Elite Guard?"

"He has taught me well—more than my father."

Gwendolyn fell silent, not wishing to argue, but not wanting to capitulate.

"At any rate, lest you forget, he was summoned here by your father."

"Humph!" she said, straightening her spine, unwilling to afford Málik Danann any generosity at all. "I doubt this. And regardless, he enjoys showing off."

Bryn's lips thinned. "You know... I find it odd you would hold his *rás* against him—particularly you, Gwendolyn, since you seem so preoccupied with all things *fae*."

She *was* preoccupied with all things fae.

Not anymore.

As children of the gods, the Tuatha'ans were supposed to have ruled eternally. Yet where were they now? Consigned to some dark underworld conceived for their penance, and why? If they were anything like Málik Danann, it must be because they were all arrogant fools.

Annoyed, Gwendolyn returned, "It is not his *rás* I hold against him, Bryn. It is his... attitude. He behaves as though he is born of gods."

Bryn lifted a shoulder. "Aye, well, if the tales are to be believed, so he would be."

Gwendolyn shot him another bedeviled glance, narrowing her eyes. "So *he* claims. Yet anyone could claim to be Danann and appoint himself such." She forced a smile and gave Bryn an exuberant nod, false though it was. "Hello, friend. Have you met me? I am Gwendolyn Danann!"

Bryn shook his head. "I must disagree," he said. "Aside from his name, he speaks little of his kind. You are wrong about him, Gwendolyn. All I know of Málik, aside from his prowess on the court, I only know through the gossip of others."

"Humph," she said again.

For a while, they cantered through the woods in silence. Alas, though Gwendolyn would have liked to have said she enjoyed the sound of Spring—the pitter-patter of creatures, the snapping of twigs beneath their hooves, and the warbling of birds—all she could hear was the sound of fury rushing through her ears.

"Alderman Morgelyn has been even more forthcoming about him than my father. Care to hear what more I know?"

Gwendolyn knitted her brows. "Nay. All *I* need know of him, I see in his eyes."

It was true. According to the *Awenydds*, the truth of a man's heart was like a flame in his eyes, and Málik's flame burned bright with contempt.

"You, of all people, would be impressed," Bryn taunted.

Once again, Gwendolyn rolled her eyes. "Gods forbid that *Sidhe* should win himself another disciple. He has more than enough admiration for himself to last him a hundred thousand lifetimes. And therefore I must sadly decline to allow you to regale me with such heroic tales—if indeed there are any to share."

"There are."

"Good. I don't care."

Bryn sighed, and said nothing more, no doubt loath to argue.

But Gwendolyn didn't like it at all that he seemed so worshipful of Málik—particularly when he was the one who'd maligned him when he'd first arrived, and it was Gwendolyn who'd defended the ungrateful *Sidhe*, not that *he* would ever know it.

"Anyway..." She flicked her reins harder than she'd intended. "I detest the way he looks at me."

"How so?"

Gwendolyn's frown only deepened. "I don't know. I can't explain it."

"I see," said Bryn, far too amiably, and then he changed the subject altogether. "Have you considered what would happen if *your* Prince should arrive early and your mother cannot locate you for his greeting?"

"She'll make do without me," assured Gwendolyn.

A small, ratty badger rushed across the path before them.

"Alas, I doubt my mother would have me as part of the welcoming party, anyway. I suspect that if she could have me wed Prince Locrinus without him ever having to glimpse my face, that is precisely what she would do."

"You mistake her, Gwendolyn."

"Nay, Bryn. And you must know how I adore you, as I do Ely—quite desperately for thinking me so utterly perfect. But we both know the truth. My mother doesn't think me... worthy."

Not for the *dawnsio,* not to carry the weight of the sovereignty, and certainly not to marry the likes of Prince Locrinus, despite that Gwendolyn was the only one who could.

By the by, Gwendolyn also suspected that if her mother could have masterminded some changeling *magik* of her own, she would have switched Gwendolyn and Ely at birth, and perhaps raised Ely as her own. No doubt she rued the day that someone like Gwendolyn ever came from her loins. Not only was Gwendolyn not a boy, but she was cursed, as well.

And despite this, Queen Eseld would never admit how she felt. She would go to her grave before speaking ill of her only daughter, no matter that her disappointment was there in the depths of her lovely Prydein eyes for all to see. Indeed, if the Prophecy held true, then it would seem her mother's heart must not be virtuous enough to see beauty in her child, so she might never dare confess her true feelings, lest everyone else realize this as well.

"I am certain she loves you," Bryn offered. "As we all do," he added quietly.

"No doubt she loves the *thought* of me," Gwendolyn countered.

"You say you wish to hunt?" asked Bryn suddenly, changing the subject once more, and pointing to a mass of grey-brown fur visible between the trees—a strapping, eight-point buck that sat watching from behind a dead bough. Like a stone effigy, the majestic beast stood still, only tipping its great head to keep a wary eye on the woodland's trespassers.

"Too small," Gwendolyn said dismissively, dismounting, and making enough noise to frighten the entire forest. Of course, the buck bolted, and a murmuration of starlings erupted from the treetops, speckled wings aflutter.

Gwendolyn was not here to hunt today. She was here to inspect the glen, nor did she wish to talk about Málik or her mother any longer.

Both topics distressed her, but neither so much as the health of the glen because it was the King who commanded this land, and the land that sustained him. Remnants of an age when the gods still dwelt here, the pool was filled with curative waters that could heal so many ills—if only it could heal a king. And yet, in so many ways, the haleness of the glen was a measure of her father's health, and the reverse was true. It was his sickness that diminished the glen, and the sicker it became, the sicker he became as well. It was a vicious cycle that could lead to his death, and Cornwall's, as well. This was why her marriage to Prince Locrinus was so crucial. The peace their union would foster was critical to Cornwall's survival. Without the alliance, Cornwall wouldn't last long enough to worry about the prophesied Red Tide.

As for Queen Eseld, though she was a conundrum, she was someone Gwendolyn deeply admired. Having come from Prydein as a young woman, she'd not only learned the Cornish language, but the language of the *dawnsio* as well. She'd embraced every role ever given her, always careful never to gainsay her husband, nor to give anyone the impression she acted against his will. In all things, her mother was a dutiful wife, and yes, perhaps mother, as well.

Gwendolyn knew her mother considered her interests above her own. But it was her attention she sought—a loving look here and there, the way she did with her husband.

And yes, of course, Gwendolyn knew that was different. A mother's love for a daughter was not the same as her love for a mate—much as Gwendolyn's love for Ely and Bryn was not the same as the love she someday hoped to have for her husband.

And yet... Gwendolyn often saw the way Lady Ruan regarded her children.

And sometimes she noticed a certain way Bryn looked at her... with a sparkle in his eyes that said he would welcome her embrace. But this wasn't what Gwendolyn sought from him, and she didn't feel the same, though how sorely she craved her mother's arms.

"I am not in the mood to hunt," she said, tilting a glance at Bryn, who was still mounted, watching her curiously.

"Who could have guessed."

Gwendolyn grinned. "Let us swim instead."

Bryn scowled. Neither was he tempted to dismount. He twisted his lips, peering back through the woods as though he considered leaving. "'Tis unwise," he said finally.

"Why?"

"Because your mother will think it unseemly."

"Gods! We've swum together a thousand times."

"Everything is different now."

Gwendolyn twisted her face. "Since when?"

"Since your betrothed is due to arrive at any moment," he reminded, and Gwendolyn's brows collided. She straightened her shoulders, unwilling to be led astray.

"He does not come till the morrow," she argued.

"And still..."

"Well, *I* am going for a swim," she said, turning her back to Bryn, and collecting her mare's reins. "You may remain here."

After today, everything would, indeed, be different, and that was all the more reason she must do what she needed to do. Come tomorrow, Prince Locrinus would be here, and *if* he liked her, they would be bound. After their ceremony, *all* her decisions would be made with him in mind. But right now, Gwendolyn was still Gwendolyn.

Unbound. Unwed. Uncowed.

FOUR

G wendolyn made her way down the familiar path toward Porth Pool, her mood lifting even as she went.

A swim would clear her head, and that could only aid her mother's cause, improving her temperament, and perhaps it would even give her a more healthful glow.

Who could object to such things?

Some people claimed that beauty itself was a gift of the spring, and if that was true, then for the sake of the realm, she could use all the help she could get.

Although, in truth, Gwendolyn didn't know what other people saw when they looked upon her, the most obvious consequence of her "gift" was this: Depending on how they viewed her, people treated her differently. If she feared anything at all, it was the possibility of spending the rest of her life with a man who did not, or could not, love her, because of her face. She prayed that when Prince Locrinus finally looked upon her, he wouldn't see what her mother saw.

Tomorrow she would know for sure.

The thought sent a rush of starlings aflight, this one straight from her heart.

For obvious reasons, she knew Bryn would relent, but she didn't feel too terrible about that, because as reluctant as he was to cross her mother, he also relished a good swim.

He worked too hard, she reasoned, never thinking of himself. If it weren't for Gwendolyn, he might never rest, and therefore, she was doing him a favor. At least that's what she told herself as she skipped along, eager as well to immerse herself in the warm, healing waters.

Porth Pool wasn't as big as Dozmaré, where the Lady dwelt, but this pool was the last of its kind. As near as it was, few ever ventured here until the bloodroot and trilliums bloomed because the Winter woods were inhospitable and Jakk Frost was a tricksy *fae* who guarded these woodlands jealously until long after Spring's first melt. Too many luckless fellows had been discovered hereabouts, bones wrapped in threadbare cloaks, curled up by long-dead fires.

Doubtless, most of these men had been searching for Porth Pool, for its restorative powers, because even during the midst of Winter, its waters remained warm and its ability to heal was strong. Even during midwinter, folks were driven to locate it, but the mists surrounding it could make men lose their way, and some said it was possible to lose their way completely and cross the Veil. Certainly, if the *piskies* had their way, luring men with their foolish fire, no man would ever find the pool. And yet, once upon a time, these pools had been plentiful throughout Cornwall. Now, there were only a handful remaining.

Whereas the rest of the forest was still waking from its long slumber, because of the temperate clime and warm steam, Porth Pool was always lush. Like an oasis, it lay hidden in a glen filled with oak, rowan, and hawthorn trees, all sacred to the gods. About two years ago, all the trees began to form disease—nowhere else in the woods save here. The oaks formed leaf blisters; the rowans ceased to give fruit; and the hawthorns became spotted.

Alas, the *Gwyddons* tried everything in their power to restore them, but 'twas said the land was attuned to the spirit of the age, and the *ysbryd y byd* was suffering.

Much to the dismay of the *Awenydds*, and particularly over these past few years, people coveted things shiny and new, turning their hearts and minds from the Old Ways.

At one point, the *Gwyddons* might have been among those whose minds were turned toward progress, but they were foremost men of spirit, and so now the scientists worked closely with the *Awenydds* to see if together they could make a difference. If, alone, they could not manage, they must call upon the Druids, whose *magik* was ancient, but dangerous.

For now, the best they could do was to mitigate the damage every Spring, and it was important to catch the blight before it took hold for the year.

If not, they risked the chance that the trees would perish, and if aught at all changed in this sacred place, it would alter the environs enough so it might endanger the pool.

A little south of Trevena, near the older tin and copper wheals, there used to be another such spring. Now it was nothing but a *winterbourne*.

Eventually, this, too, could be the fate of theirs, but it was early yet, and if there was any sign of blight, this time, they would call the Druids to tend their glen before it sickened further.

With their long, white beards and frizzled brows, the Llanrhos Druids were simply not men to be trifled with. They, like the Tuatha Dé Danann, were born of ancient blood, and whilst her own father was considered Pretania's first High King, the

Druids were the arbiters of this land, tasked with enforcing the will of the gods.

If her father's goodwill inspired peace amongst the tribes, the Druid's curse inspired fear, with good reason. Any grievances that could not be rectified among themselves could be brought before their door, but the outcome was never certain, for the Druids' laws were not the laws of men, and their resolutions were frightening, and sometimes, the method of their judgment came at the expense of the plaintiff's death.

Gwendolyn once heard of a man who went to plead his case to the Lifer Pol Court, begging them to intervene on behalf of his good name. Of course, being a man, they agreed, and whilst he stood, smiling with satisfaction, they shoved a dagger into his belly, cutting him to his entrails, and made their judgment about his innocence by the way he stumbled and fell, and the way his entrails revealed themselves, as well as the splatter-tell of his blood.

No one should ever summon them without great care.

Feeling a stirring in her heart, a surge of love for her beloved father, Gwendolyn quickened her pace, eager to reach the glen before Bryn, and to see how the trees had fared through the long Winter. Better than Urien, she hoped.

When finally she arrived, she exhaled a long breath, delighted to find that the trees were all hale, mostly, and realizing Bryn would delay his arrival only a moment to afford Gwendolyn a measure of privacy, she quickly disrobed.

No matter, it would be easier to survey the entire glen from the water, with all the trees surrounding her. Trusting the waters to be warm, she dove in and sighed with delight.

Wonderful. Blissful. Soothing.

Gods. This was what she needed today—a dip in the pool to steal all her troubles away. Holding her breath, she dove deeper.

Oh, yes, this!

This was how she imagined a mother's womb should feel —*cozy, warm, and safe.*

Cradling her knees, Gwendolyn spun about, turning and turning, allowing her momentum and the water to carry her as it would.

Acceptance with grace and faith. This was the way of the *Awenydds*—the enlightened ones, those whose hearts were attuned to the Old Ways, and who still believed the warp and weft of all life was biddable through the *Aether.*

When at last Gwendolyn opened her eyes and peered into the crystalline waters, she blinked, fascinated, as tiny points of light swarmed beneath the surface...

Piskies.

It was impossible to see them from above. One could only spy them from beneath the water's surface, and only from certain angles. Their minuscule bodies darted about like water spiders, leaving wakes like silken webs. Their bites were equally vicious, though water spiders were bigger, and skated above the surface, even as *piskies* swam beneath.

Sometimes, during the twilight, they rose above the pool, their wee bodies twinkling like stardust. And yet it was said that if one's heart was not true, *piskies* would assail en masse and sink their fangs into one's flesh, leaving their victim with a fever that would either rent them from their miserable life once and for all, else purge them of the black in their hearts.

Fortunately, they never bothered Gwendolyn, and if only one listened, one could hear them chattering, their tiny voices gurgling like a brook.

Perhaps if the Prince and his father lingered long enough, Gwendolyn might bring him here to share the blessings of this place. She didn't know if they had such springs in Loegria, but a learned soul such as he must surely appreciate its beauty and history.

One of the larger *piskies* rose to the surface, and Gwendolyn followed. Compelled, she reached for it, but it eluded her and vanished into a ray of golden light, the sound of its answering giggles like bursting bubbles.

Emerging into the sunlight that slid between the thickening boughs, Gwendolyn inhaled a hawthorn-scented breath, reveling in the cascade of warm water that tugged gently at her curls.

It was only another moment before Bryn emerged from the woods. Hands upon his hips, he glared down into the pool, shaking his black hair in disapproval. But that didn't stop him from ordering Gwendolyn to turn about, spinning a finger to beg privacy for himself.

Smirking victoriously, Gwendolyn did as he bade her, turning away, wading over to a shallow spot in the pool so she could stand and inspect the low-lying foliage.

Together, she and Ely and Bryn had swum here so many times—as often as they could. No doubt Ely would be heartily sorry she missed the day's fun, but that's what she got for worrying so much about what Queen Eseld thought.

Sometimes, one must take one's fate into one's own hands and follow one's heart.

She heard Bryn's bellow, then felt a hefty splash, and spun about with a wide, happy grin, prepared to splash him once he re-emerged. But her smile died on her lips when she spotted the figures emerging into the glen—one in particular, with arms crossed, the look on his face full of contempt.

Behind Málik came two of her mother's Shadows.

And then, for the ultimate insult... Queen Eseld herself.

EVIDENTLY, KING BRUTUS HAD SENT A MESSENGER AHEAD TO announce their early arrival. Gwendolyn and Bryn missed him by two blinks of an eye. Any instant, the Loegrian party was due to arrive, and despite this, her father had called everyone of consequence into his hall to witness Gwendolyn's censure— the first such reprimand she'd ever received in her life.

Outside, in the corridor, she could hear servants rushing about, shouting for last-minute preparations. But despite Queen Eseld's need to oversee such arrangements, the commotion didn't faze her at all. Her darkened eyes remained fixed upon Gwendolyn, narrowed and wrathful.

"I know not what to say," said the King, and the look on his face was one of bitter disappointment.

Yet Gwendolyn didn't understand why he should be so angry.

Was it the simple fact that she'd gone swimming with Bryn when so much needed to be done? Or was he enraged because her mother was? Or were they both simply furious because she had allowed Bryn to skirt his duties? And with Bryn for allowing her to avoid hers?

Mayhap all these things, but it still made so little sense, considering that the only thing that had changed since yesterday afternoon was the simple fact that her betrothed was en route to the city. She understood that both she and Bryn had other, more important duties to tend to, but the diversion had been harmless, and how many times had she done precisely the same as she'd done today, and each time no one ever said a word.

"You're a woman, grown," said the Queen. "Betrothed!"

Soon.

Not... yet.

She wanted to say it aloud, but the words simply wouldn't emerge through the constriction in Gwendolyn's throat.

Blood and bones.

She had never seen such a look of fury on her father's face.

She wanted to speak in her own defense, but words simply would not come—particularly when she saw her father's face turned so florid, and his trembling hand clutched at his chest, as though in pain. For a terrifying instant, Gwendolyn worried —for the witnesses he'd welcomed into his hall. Would they now discover the illness that was slowly claiming him? All because of her!

The circular window above his throne filtered in the sunlight, bright enough to cast her father's face in shadow to those who were not so near, but she was, and she could see how pallid his skin had turned.

Gods, if he died, here and now, she would blame herself evermore.

Gwendolyn swallowed convulsively, fear clutching at her heart. Behind her, she was acutely aware of both Málik and Bryn, the latter anxious, the former filled with loathing.

Everyone present within the King's hall now waited as King Corineus calmed himself, and with her mother seated at his side, gave Gwendolyn a scolding unlike any she'd had in all her days. "The time for disobedience is done," he said, when he could. "Very soon you'll be consigned to a wife's duties."

"Nay," interjected her mother. She placed a hand upon her husband's arm, perhaps to settle him, despite her own ire. "A queen's duties," she reminded gently.

"Do you know what this means, child?"

"Please, Corineus," begged her mother. "Do not call her that any longer. I warrant 'tis the reason she behaves like one —because we do not expect better. She has lived no less than seventeen winters, and I was the same age when I came to be your bride."

"Truly," he said.

And then, with a heavy sigh, her father pressed two fingers to his forehead, as though he didn't know what more to say or do. Or perhaps he was already taxed by the ordeal.

For the good of the realm, the two must remain in accord, always of a single mind—lately, most often her mother's, Gwendolyn thought bitterly. She would not leave here today without discipline. King Corineus spoke now, only covering his eyes. Like a veil, his hand slid down to cover his face. "So it seems... the time has come for me to take sober measures."

And then, after a moment, he withdrew his hand from his face to reveal eyes that were dark and swirling with disappointment. He flicked a glance at Bryn. "As of today, Bryn Durotriges will no longer serve you," he declared.

Gwen's heart leapt in protest. She found her voice at last. "Nay! Why?"

"Silence!" her father barked. "Your mother speaks true, Gwendolyn. He cannot be trusted to perform his duties like a man. Very much like you, he remains a child, subject to a child's whims. Proof of this is plain to see."

He then turned to Bryn. And it was in that instant that Gwendolyn understood what true peril she'd placed her friend in, because the man who regarded him now was not at all familiar to Gwendolyn. He was not her father, but the King.

He sat straighter, his eyes smoldering like coals. In them, Gwendolyn saw the fury and determination with which he'd once lifted and disposed of the giant Gogmagog, even suffering from broken ribs, tossing his broken body into the sea.

He spoke mainly to Bryn, though his voice reverberated throughout the hall. "Considering how you two were discovered, young Durotriges, if I believed you meant to avail yourself of my daughter, I would have your head, here and now."

"Father!" Gwendolyn protested.

"Silence!" he snapped, without looking at her, and all

sound evaporated from the hall, but not before Bryn's mother cried out in dismay.

Fearful of what was to come, Gwendolyn turned to meet Ely's gaze, and Ely's eyes, too, were round and wide. This hurt most of all—the simple fact that she had by now disappointed everyone, not only her mother and father. Sadly, she was accustomed to her mother's displeasure, but this was the first time in all her life she'd garnered the same from others.

"However, because I know my daughter to be the source of your misconduct, I shall be lenient. From this day forth, you'll no longer serve the Princess."

Clearly relieved, Bryn fell to his knees, bowing his head.

"Yes, Majesty," Bryn said, his voice raw with contrition. "I am deeply regretful for my part in today's misfortune," he said, and Gwendolyn couldn't tell whether it was chagrin or anger that gave his neck so much color, because he wouldn't look at her.

Suddenly dismissing him, her father pivoted toward Gwendolyn. And she knew that whatever he said to her now, whatever it should be, she would best be served by silence.

His eyes, dark as tempered steel, held her gaze so she daren't even look at her mother, but then again, why should she? There would be no sympathy or help to come from that quarter.

"From this day forth," he said, "You'll be served by Málik Danann."

"Father!" Gwendolyn cried, but her father lifted his chin, unmoved by the tears that brimmed in Gwendolyn's eyes.

He offered her the flat of his hand, silencing her once and for all. "So I have said, so will it be! Go now, prepare yourself to greet your betrothed. Do nothing more to shame this house."

"Yes, sire," she said, hot tears burning her eyes.

With the entire hall still planted firmly where they stood,

Gwendolyn roused the nerve to turn and face them, and then made her way between them, toward the doors. No one dared look at her. Save one...

Málik Danann.

His *icebourne* eyes met hers, and Gwendolyn thought she saw him smile.

CHAPTER
FIVE

That swiftly, her joy was lost.

Fury fired Gwendolyn's march down the hall.

Málik?

Málik!

He was cold, taciturn, disdainful, and arrogant, and despite that she didn't know him well, she didn't want to know him at all. Only now, instead of taking her beloved friend with her to Loegria, she would be forced to take a soulless elf.

Gods, she loathed him—loathed him to the core of her being. Even more now that she knew he was the reason her mother had found them in the glen. *He* was the one who'd told her where they'd gone, and then he'd escorted her directly.

Certainly, Gwendolyn knew Queen Eseld would have found them on her own, but it was Málik's scornful face she'd first spied emerging from those woods, with that smug, self-righteous expression she wouldn't soon forget.

By the eyes of Lugh, she wasn't in the mood to forgive, regardless of his promotion—no matter that he would soon be her new Shadow. He could attend to her all he wished, but

Gwendolyn would never, *ever* trust him, nor would she care for him the way she cared for Bryn.

Stupid, heartless elf.

"Go away!" she said as he appeared behind her, even knowing he would refuse.

"Alas, Princess, this would be my greatest joy, but I cannot," he said evenly, and he didn't miss a step, remaining behind her all the way back to her chambers.

Annoying.

Infuriating.

Irksome.

Elf.

Gods, she loathed the appellation and the spirit in which it was given just as much as the *Sidhe* must loathe it as well, because it was never used with any good intention, and still she couldn't think of him as anything else.

It was kinder than the names she'd like to shout at him right now, though she wouldn't give him the satisfaction. Already he was smirking behind his hand. And not even behind his hand, for she wouldn't soon forget the smile he gave her as she quit the hall.

Gwendolyn had once loved the notion of *faekind*, and she felt connected to them through her gifts; so why, for the love of Danu, did he have to be even part-blood?

To Gwendolyn's dismay, if she quickened her pace, so too did he.

If she slowed, so did he, until Gwendolyn was livid and ready to pull out every strand of hair on his too-comely head.

Why was it that the most beautiful creatures were also the deadliest?

And by the by, she loathed the way he called her Princess, as though it were a blasphemy all its own.

Unable to bear his presence, she spun to face him once she

reached her door, prepared to leave him in the antechamber. "You will *not* be welcomed within," she said furiously. "*Ever!*"

It was despicable enough that he must take up residence in her antechamber, sleeping only a few yards from her bed. She glanced at the meager cot that had once belonged to sweet Bryn and noted that her antechamber was already stripped free of Bryn's belongings.

Had this already been decided, even before Málik led Queen Eseld to the glen?

Cold and unaffected, his hands swung to his back, his face devoid of expression, his eyes silvery and bored. *Gods, he was made of stone.*

"Naturally, Princess. Indeed, from here forth, the only male who'll be welcomed within your bower will be your lord husband—*after* your vows are spoken." He smiled thinly, betraying some trace of emotion, but none that was remotely benevolent. "On pain of my life," he added.

Was that a threat?

Worse! Was he implying she would dare entertain men in the privacy of her bower? Not even Bryn had ever attended her within. He'd slept in her antechamber, and she in her bower, always behind closed doors. At most, he had stood upon her threshold, only when the door was open and someone else was in attendance.

"I have windows," she longed to say, but she held her tongue because she would never intentionally disrespect her betrothed. Thus, there was nothing she could say regarding his declaration, because no man had ever entered her chamber, including her father, and none would be welcomed still, most especially not him!

And neither would she crawl out some window, sneaking away like a thief.

She couldn't prove his irksome smile was anything but

courteous, but she felt the cut of his sarcasm down to the marrow of her bones. Somehow he'd reduced her to growling like a dumb beast. "See you do *not* disturb me," she said, and then she opened her door, giving him one last warning glance before entering her chamber and slamming the door.

Hard.

Very hard.

The sound of it shook the rafters.

Gods, she would like to say she'd slammed it in his face, but dutiful as he was, he had already turned his back to the wall, resigning himself to waiting until she re-emerged—a thing that might never have happened so swiftly except for the knock on her door.

Still furious over the turn of events and realizing it wouldn't be Ely—not this soon after her brother's demotion—she marched back to the door and tugged it open, eager to flay Málik with her words. But it wasn't Málik's face that greeted her.

It was Demelza, directing a procession of servants into her chamber to fill a bath. But though Gwendolyn couldn't see Málik, she sensed his presence acutely, and she knew he was privy to every word she uttered. Therefore, she resolved to say nothing, determined to share as little of her life with him as possible.

She might be forced to deal with him as her Shadow, for the time being, so long as she remained under her father's roof, but someday, she would be Queen, and as Queen she would choose her own Shadow, and she would restore Bryn to his rightful position.

If he would have it.

Gwendolyn felt dreadful over her part in his demotion— worse than words could convey. And even though she longed to weep on Ely's shoulder, she knew her dear friend wouldn't be visiting her again this day. Likely their entire family had convened to mourn the loss of their eldest son's status, and despite that none of them would dare speak a cross word to or against Gwendolyn, she also knew they were likely as disappointed in her as were her own parents.

As disappointed as Gwendolyn was with herself.

Indeed, were she them, she might be furious.

Gods, she'd like to believe her father wouldn't carry out his threat to detach Bryn's head from his body, but she couldn't be certain he wouldn't. Illness or nay, her father wasn't a milksop, and he wasn't in the habit of saying things he didn't mean.

How stupid she had been.

How selfish.

How thoughtless.

At the instant, Gwendolyn desperately longed to punish herself with swordplay or something equally physical, but she daren't leave her room, or she'd be forced to suffer *his* company as well. And then it occurred to her: She had also lost her sparring partner and mentor, only to gain a new one—Málik Danann, whose presence even now was as keenly felt as the steam from her tub, scarcely visible, but seeping into every pore of her flesh.

Thankfully, Demelza said nothing whilst there were servants in attendance. Already Gwendolyn was too close to sobbing. But finally when they left, and the bath was full, Demelza spoke. "In the tub," she said. And that was all. No I-told-you-so. No endless lecture about Gwendolyn's solicitation of these unfortunate events. But neither did she offer sympathy.

Sadly, Demelza needn't say or do anything for Gwendolyn to comprehend her own culpability. She was well and truly in the wrong.

She had taken advantage of Bryn's friendship. She had led

him astray. Swallowing hard, she recalled that he'd tried to dissuade her from leaving the palace without consulting her mother, and then again from pursuing a swim.

He was far too kind to gainsay her, all to his own detriment. As his Princess, not his charge, she had a responsibility to look after his wellbeing, even as he should endeavor to shelter her from harm. And yet, she had not. Instead, she'd nearly cost him his beautiful head.

Gwendolyn sighed, a sound not unlike her father's dispirited one.

"Enough self-recrimination," snapped Demelza. "Get in that tub before the water cools. Would you put these servants through another conveyance?"

Nay. She would not.

Gwendolyn didn't argue.

For perhaps the hundredth time this day, after trying on so many gowns, she disrobed, discarding her leathers and hosen, and climbed into the tub.

However, unlike the *piskie* pool, the bathwater was already growing cold after having made the trek in so many buckets all the way from the cook's house.

"I am told the Prince will be in attendance for tonight's supper," said Demelza. "Naturally, you will be paired with him for the evening meal."

Directly to his left, beside her mother, whose place was at her father's right hand. Once their vows were heard by the *Awenydd* priestess, Gwendolyn, too, would be seated at her husband's right hand, though with one significant difference...

Should King Corineus die, it would *not* be her mother to rule in his place, it would be Gwendolyn. Her mother was neither a natural-born citizen of Cornwall, nor could she be recognized as a queen in her own right. She was only Queen Consort, and despite that her father had elevated her so high, the aldermen would never approve of a Prydein princess for succession.

According to the aldermen, Prydein chiefs were as common as magpies and equally thievish. Thus, without her husband, Queen Eseld would have no say.

However, should Prince Locrinus fall in battle and with Gwendolyn's father already gone, she would rule both nations.

In all things, in all ways, she would be her husband's equal, but this was small comfort to her right now whilst she was subject to the will of so many.

And regardless, the one person she would *never* lie down for was Málik Danann. Her thoughts returned to the guard outside her door.

She had swum nude with Bryn a thousand times, and never once had she felt, even for an instant, the way she did right now, only breathing within *his* proximity.

To be sure, a heavy oaken door between them wasn't enough.

She'd prefer an ocean—would that he'd return to Ériu, or wheresoever he was from. Certainly, the thought of swimming with *him* was unthinkable, and Gwendolyn didn't have to ask herself why. She suspected the answer to this question, if she could be honest with herself, hadn't so much to do with her dislike of the man as she would like to confess.

It was something *else*...

And that something *else* was the same something *else* she'd felt as she'd emerged from the hot spring with Málik present.

No matter that he'd politely turned his back—and so far as she knew, *faekind* didn't have eyes in the back of their heads—somewhere deep down, she'd sensed he was just as aware of her as she was of him... and no doubt equally reproving.

Perhaps this was the crux of it all—the simple fact that she must be judged daily, not only by her mother, but by the likes of Málik Danann.

"Did you hear me, child?"

Gwendolyn blinked, peering up at her mother's maid with some confusion.

Nay, she hadn't heard a word she'd said.

Nothing at all but the pounding of her own heart. But it wasn't the thought of meeting Prince Locrinus that had her pulses in a gallop. It was...

Someone *else*.

Inconceivably, that small bit of truth upset Gwendolyn more than anything that had transpired this day, because... of course, she must be thrilled to meet her betrothed.

Málik Danann was only an inconvenience—an obstacle that might soon be removed. Perhaps sooner than anyone realized if she impressed her betrothed?

With that in mind, she finished her ministrations, and removed herself from the tub, then dried herself, and chose the finest of all the gowns she'd tried on today—another blue gown that Ely seemed to favor—and then, when she emerged from her room, with her hair braided and coiled on both sides, wearing the sapphire necklace Ely chose, she emerged with new resolve.

And yet she might have asked herself why it was markedly more important to rid herself of a rude "elf" than it was to impress her new betrothed.

CHAPTER

SIX

King Brutus arrived first, making excuses for his tardy son, although evidently the Loegrian King should take some lessons from his son, and perhaps be a bit more concerned about washing the stench of travel from his person. Wrinkling her nose as her father escorted him onto the dais where introductions were made, Gwendolyn noted that even her mother lifted a finger to the tip of her nose, an unconscious gesture that couldn't dispel the pungent aroma of horse muddled with perhaps a week's worth of sweat.

Thereafter, Gwendolyn sat quietly as her parents made him feel welcomed, all the while worrying over the introduction to come... the *one* that mattered most.

Though perhaps she should take comfort in the Prince's show of courtesy in bathing, she worried he'd heard about the day's unfortunate events, and more than being polite or fastidious, he was only reluctant to meet her? Mayhap even now, he was resisting in his room.

But nay... His father was here, jesting and laughing. If that were the case, he would probably be with his son, trying to win him, and the evening's festivities mightn't continue as planned. Moreover, Gwendolyn knew intuitively that no one in the castle would speak a word of the incident to either, for fear that they might question Gwendolyn's honor.

Only now she was perfectly furious with herself for not considering every possibility. Merely because *she* understood her relationship with Bryn to be that of a sibling's, and Bryn understood this to be the case, and everyone in the palace understood this to be the case, that didn't mean Prince Locrinus would understand as well.

Marriages were sometimes forsworn for less, and she realized, if only belatedly—and stupidly—that this was why her parents were so furious with her.

Viewed through the eyes of a betrothed, a harmless swim, even so innocently done, could be grounds to rebuke their marriage, no matter that amongst Gwendolyn's people, nudity wasn't frowned upon. Quite often the *dawnsio* wore such diaphanous gowns as to be nonexistent, and she was reminded of this as they arrived in the hall, their bodies lithe and every gesture they made suggestive. Ridiculously, she didn't care if Prince Locrinus admired these ladies, but one glance at Málik, seated at a lower table, near Ely, was enough to make Gwendolyn's gut turn violently.

Thankfully, Elowyn's presence comforted her a little, even if Ely still wouldn't look her way...

Was she as furious as everyone else? Only disappointed? Angered by her brother's demotion? Or simply irritated with her present companion?

As forewarned, Ely had been paired with the ambassador's son, but it was worse than she had feared. Flat-nosed though he was, he was also an obnoxious boor who barked like a fox every time he laughed. Three tables away, Gwendolyn could hear him clearly—a hideous sound that carried above the din.

Furrowing her brows, torn between annoyance and regret, both for her sake and for Ely's as well, she nipped at her thumbnail and watched Ely give Málik a doe-eyed glance.

Annoyance gripped at Gwendolyn's belly.

Naturally, there was much she should accept responsibility for. But Ely's dinner companion wasn't one of those things. Ely's not wishing to perform with the *dawnsio* wasn't Gwendolyn's idea; it was Ely's. And no matter that she wished for her dear, sweet friend to live the life she wished to live, Gwendolyn was careful not to lead her astray—at least not in this regard. And truly, if one could be plainspoken, Gwendolyn envied Ely's role with the *dawnsio*. There was much appeal to that life, and in many respects, it was an easier role than that of a wife's—and certainly more so than a princess' or a queen's.

In order to be invested, one must forswear the life of a wife and mother and devote oneself solely to the craft, but most of the troupe lived free from normal constraints.

Also, if Elowyn joined the *dawnsio* as a principal dancer, she would travel. The troupe made its rounds about the tribes, not merely to dance, but to canvass the villages to search for and groom replacements.

But no matter that they were required to live within the women's quarters, and never to wed, they were still free to take lovers as they pleased, so long as they remained discreet.

Even now, as the dancers took their places, she saw that a few of them gave come-hither glances to several of King Brutus' men-at-arms. Dressed in scarlet silk in a shade complementing King Brutus' livery, they swayed and moved to the rhythm of the lute and drums. Everything about them was flawless—their shining hair, painted lips, gleaming nails, the sparkling chains about their waists, chains that swayed and jiggled along with curvy hips and ample breasts.

Under the winking candelabra, the inky shadow of their

mons and the tantalizing tips of their breasts were easily visible through the gossamer gowns.

After all was said and done, the *dawnsio* answered only to their Mother Superior, and for everyone else in the realm, the Queen was a benevolent ruler.

Only for those who knew her best, she had a darker side.

No doubt, Ely was right: the suggestion to pair her with that deadly bore was intended to discourage her from pursuing another path. Indeed, free will was a gift from the gods, but no one ever confessed the truth of the matter—that defying one's parents, or her people, earned a woman little more than a kick in the belly.

Poor Ely.

And yet, for all that anyone could tell, Elowyn seemed to be properly engaged with her greasy companion, neither giddy nor sullen. The message had been received: Come tomorrow, Ely would arrive on time for practice, with slippers in hand. *Mission accomplished, Mother.*

Certainly, there were none in this realm more practiced at subtle machinations. But, of course, Gwendolyn understood why it was so. Were Queen Eseld the sort to gainsay her husband or to wield a sharp whip, the aldermen would complain.

Queen Eseld was too wise to trample toes. Rather, she ruled within the confines of her husband's laws, and there were none here so willing to challenge her, not even Gwendolyn.

Truth be told, her father's conformity did not begin with his illness. It came from a place of trust. Even when he was stronger, he'd never had much issue with allowing his queen to direct his household. And although Gwendolyn found fault with her mother's methods, she knew, as her father knew, all she did, she did for kith and kin—and not the kin she was born to. Gwendolyn wondered idly if her mother ever thought of her parents, or whether she ever longed for her childhood home. So far as Gwendolyn was concerned, she couldn't wait to leave this place, even if she would miss her father dearly. She only prayed to the Goddess that she would find it in her heart to love the man she was promised to wed.

Alas, she could only command her own heart.

What if someone had already warned him she was a hag?

What if he saw the changeling, not the woman?

What if he came to despise her?

What if he simply couldn't love her?

For certain, her mother was not the only one whose ambivalence toward her was notable. Take Málik, for example...

Even now, she seethed over his betrayal of Bryn, and refused to look his way, but she knew precisely where he sat, and she knew this because his spirit burned like a peat-fed torch, calling her gaze like a beacon from across the room.

And this was hardly an exaggeration. She felt his inner light like a firestorm, his flame burning hot and bright, the sound like a roar in Gwendolyn's ears.

He met her gaze, lifted his glass in toast to her, and a lazy smile tugged at his lips, revealing the gleaming tip of one of his fangs. Gwendolyn shivered.

Gods.

With those teeth, he could eat her alive—devour her hope, and Pretania's as well.

Gwendolyn averted her gaze, but as the tapers on the tables burned lower and lower... and lower still, with no sign of Prince Locrinus, she felt more and more uneasy.

In truth, she felt like weeping—in part because poor Bryn wasn't even in attendance. He was very likely banished from the festivities for his part in Gwendolyn's scheme.

Alone. Furious with Gwendolyn. *Hungry as well.*

And yes, she supposed her father was right. Mayhap she needed someone who was stronger—someone who wouldn't cow to her when she spoke, or who cared so much to please her he would be diverted from his duties.

But she mustn't focus on that right now.

She had a duty to perform, and she must do it with a full heart, considering how crucial it was to win the Prince's favor. But one day she would make everything right—one day, when she was queen, when she had more to say about her own fate and the fate of others.

Before she could change anyone else's fortunes, she must first secure her own. So with that in mind, Gwendolyn carefully arranged the table before her, mentally preparing herself for the meeting to come.

CHAPTER
SEVEN

T he tension in the hall grew palpable. Even King Brutus tapped his thick fingers on the lord's table—the rap, tap, tapping heightening Gwendolyn's fears.

One, two, three....

One, two.

One, two, three.

One, two...

She counted dozens—nay, hundreds—all the while trying to deflect all the worried glances. In her heart, she agonized, but she was prudent to be certain none of her suffering was writ on her face. Her expression remained placid, her smile enduring.

Every now and again, when she could take it no longer, Gwendolyn adjusted the order of the small plates before Prince Locrinus' empty chair, repositioning them so he could enjoy whatever delicacies he so desired.

After a while, she studied faces. This one was worried. That one was not. This one was salivating after the dancers and hadn't a thought for anything but the creature in his *braies*.

That one was pinching heads from pilchards, and tossing them beneath the table—why, Gwendolyn couldn't fathom, but tomorrow, Yestin's dog would love him dearly.

She needn't have recognized the faces of the men in her father's guard to note the newcomers who sat so stiffly, and whose hands remained frozen at their middles, as though preparing to unsheathe invisible swords. Instead of livery, they wore finery, and instead of weapons, they wielded poniards, the only blade allowed.

As it was anywhere else, it was impolite to attend a feast girded for war, and that included a sovereign's Shadows. At most, they could keep a dagger hidden in their boot, but visible weapons or armor were forbidden, even for ceremony.

For Cornwall's sake, there were only two within this hall who required the highest level of protection. One was the King himself, the other his heir. But not even for them would exceptions be made. Not tonight. Come what may, they were subject to the Brothers' Pact.

The very most the Elite Guard could hope for was to remain close to their charges, in case of treason, an offense for which the penalty would be death without trial.

According to the sixth law of the Brothers' Pact, no man who supped with a brother or friend should ever do so with a false face. Wine could be spilled, not blood.

Defiance of this law would enrage the gods, and they in turn would curse the land, and the land was higher than any King; its death would be his downfall.

And therefore, since drunkards had no discretion, weapons were simply not allowed. Proximity was the only viable defense, and the highest tables were reserved for the Elite Guards and the Shadows of both royal houses.

Apparently, Málik mustn't consider Gwendolyn's welfare to be of any import because he'd eschewed his rightful place, taking a seat at one of the lower tables, and for this, she bris-tled, again, because it was easier to be angry with him than it was to worry about Prince Locrinus.

However, were this Bryn, he would have fought tooth and claw for his rightful seat, positioning himself as close to Gwen-dolyn as possible.

Alas, he was not Bryn. Only an arrogant pretender, and Gwendolyn was certain he had no more care for her than he did for Pretania.

Why, then, had he taken this charge? More significantly, why would her father assign him to shadow her? Was the illness already ravaging his mind?

Málik might be a worthy opponent for sparring, and he could be entirely capable of fulfilling this duty. Perhaps he was overqualified for the task, considering that he'd been employed to train the entire Elite Guard, but Gwendolyn had never once seen him do obeisance to her father, and neither did he have the bearing for that. She hadn't any sense that he had loyalties to Cornwall, nor to anyone. Rather, his currency was his sword, and he lent it to the highest bidder. Her father's was merely the fattest purse... at the moment.

But fortunately, this was not a Konsel for war, only a cele-bratory feast—not that her intended had deigned to arrive.

"He'll be along soon," offered King Brutus, seeming to read her mind, but even his voice betrayed concern. Gwendolyn reminded herself that it wasn't merely brides who suffered attacks of nerves. She remembered when her uncle Hedrek's elder son married that Iceni girl; he'd combed his hair for a full bell before the ceremony until his own father called him a girl.

Yet what if Prince Locrinus had already glimpsed her and was displeased? What if he'd defied his father and fled the city?

What if, even now, without his father's knowledge, he was halfway returned to Loegria? Everything that could go wrong marched through Gwendolyn's thoughts, demanding attention.

"Smile," her mother said brittlely, then bent to whisper, "A woman must do what she must, Gwendolyn. Come what may, you will face the day with grace."

But no one needed to remind Gwendolyn how momentous this occasion was, nor how much was at stake—at last!

Prince Locrinus arrived, his entrance more dramatic than his sire's. He came, flanked by two red-cloaked guards who were armed to the ears. On sight, they drew gasps from the guests, then swiftly withdrew into the hall. And yet, if his guards' appearance seemed daunting, the Prince's was anything but. He drew another gasp from the guests, all on his own. The rumors had done him no justice, for he was all they'd claimed and more—tall, handsome, imposing... and... yes, indeed... very, very golden.

A golden idol for a golden bride.

Gwendolyn hadn't realized her jaw dropped until her mother cleared her throat. When Gwendolyn looked at her, she tapped the back of a long, painted nail beneath her own chin, even now, unwilling to touch her own daughter.

Gobsmacked, Gwendolyn shut her mouth, then blinked, as though against a bright light. He was... well... he was... the most stunning creature she had ever beheld.

Mayhap not with Bryn's masculine appeal, nor Málik's strange, ethereal beauty, but with a splendor all his own that put a shadow on the sun itself.

"Well, don't stand there," her mother said. "See to your guest."

Yes, of course.

That was the custom.

Since no one but the royal family could ascend unescorted to the dais, he was waiting to be led to his seat. But Gwendolyn suddenly couldn't move. All eyes fell upon her, everyone eager to see how the Prince of Loegria and the Princess of Cornwall would comport.

But this, at last, was the moment of truth, the instant when she might be judged, and her heart pounded like a forger's hammer.

Swallowing with difficulty, Gwendolyn commanded her feet to move, but her legs felt squishy like pudding. And then, like a halfwit, she rose, bumping her knees on the table, and then sliding around the table, her skirt catching on a wooden splinter. She wrenched it free, then stumbled down the first few steps, all arms and legs, without the least bit of grace. Fortunately, if anyone noticed, no one said a word, nor did they laugh.

All chatter ceased as she made her way down the aisle, an emissary for the time, and soon, by the grace of the gods, to be a bride.

His bride.

Dressed in gold, from his head to his boots, the Prince's robes—a creation of intricate embroidery on shining, yellow silk—fit him unerringly. His hair, too, was golden, though not the pale, silvery shade of Málik's hair, nor the fiery gold of hers. Rather, his was more sun-toasted wheat. As though that were not enough gold, she realized as she neared, that his eyes, too, were a curious amber shade.

The visage of him was stunning.

Even his eyelashes glittered beneath the torchlight, and she wondered if he used some type of maquillage. "Highness," Gwendolyn said breathlessly, with a quick, courteous bow and a trembling smile.

Prince Locrinus grinned, and all thought of Gwendolyn's ruinous day vanished, made inconsequential by the blinding light of his beauteous smile.

The most profound relief washed over her, and from that instant forth, Gwendolyn was aware of little else—not their dinner guests, watching so intently, nor her mother, whose rapt attention normally bore spikes into her back.

Indeed, the hall itself was lost to her, as though vanished behind a veil, not unlike the Cloak of Concealment, which guarded the *fae* realms.

Gwendolyn might have found herself red-faced by her gaping, except for the glorious truth that Prince Locrinus seemed equally taken by her.

"Your hair," he said, and reached for a strand, then remembered himself, halting that hand midway between them. "'Tis... extraordinary," he said, and then, with eyes that gleamed as fiercely as his golden attire, he bent to whisper for Gwendolyn's ears alone. "Truly, we shall make a golden match!" Gwendolyn's heart leapt into her throat.

By the eyes of Lugh, was this what it felt like to be struck dumb by love? Remembering herself, she laughed, embarrassed, merely relieved to hear such flattery.

After a moment, Prince Locrinus asked for her hand, and Gwendolyn gave it readily. Lifting it to his lips, he kissed it tenderly, his lips easing into a companionable smile. And then, as though he meant to keep her safe from all harm, he tucked her trembling hand into the crook of his arm, and said, gesturing toward the dais, "Shall we, Princess?"

Disarmed by his courtliness, Gwendolyn nodded. And she couldn't help herself. A wide, genuine grin unfurled as they turned to ascend the dais, thrilled to note her parents' expressions, and King Brutus' as well. Her worries now seemed all for naught, and not even Málik's presence or Bryn's absence could dampen her mood as they took their seats—at least so she believed, until her mother leaned close to whisper in her ear.

"Don't muddle this," she said with a half-frozen smile.

Gwendolyn's cheeks flamed.

Fortunately, Prince Locrinus didn't hear her, and, if her mother was concerned, she worried for naught, because the evening progressed better than anyone could have expected.

The *dawnsio*, without Ely, performed excellently, the choreography never better. The victuals were superb, and even despite having to put together the feast a full day in advance, Yestin's attention to detail was lost to none.

To show off the great many delicacies their city could procure, the high tables were all laden with imported fare—so heavily, in fact, that according to his own admission, not even King Brutus ever indulged so well. Gwendolyn overheard him say so to her father, but neither had she. This was a far grander feast than any they had ever presented to guests before, including for the occasion of her first betrothal, a fact King Brutus must have noted, though he said nothing about it.

On the dais alone, there were more than twenty exotic hens, all placed at intervals along the table for guests to pluck at, most of these imported from Alkebulan, and perfectly roasted.

Instead of pilchards, as was served at the lower tables, some of the small plates were filled with a small, salted fish known as sardines that were imported from Hiberia.

There was also plenty of freshly baked bread, some meant for pulling and dipping in rosemary oil, others hard-crusted, with all the soft interior removed. These were used as trenchers and were placed deliberately for couples to share.

The doughy center of the bread was then used for stuffing of hens, and the stuffing was flavored with fresh oysters fished from their own Cornish beds.

Truly, there was nothing like a good oyster, and there was a marvelous place beyond the Dragon's Bay where the currents aligned in such a way that the pressure salted them delectably.

Sometimes, when fishers hauled in new batches, she and Elowyn and Bryn would fly down to the docks to pilfer a few for themselves.

Only sometimes "a few" turned into "a few too many," and though Gwendolyn never suffered a malaise from oysters, Ely once did, and swore off oysters altogether. However, as a testament to their supreme excellence, her moratorium only lasted until the next harvest, when they once again stood cracking shells straight from the crates they were hauled in.

A sudden surge of nostalgia washed over Gwendolyn as she watched her intended scrutinize an oyster so intensely. That same army of bees took lodgings in her belly, buzzing about with such vigor that it made it difficult to eat.

As she sometimes watched her mother do for her father, Gwendolyn gathered up the small plates as they were being passed, stealing them for Prince Locrinus, and then waiting until he had his fill, before replacing it with another.

"Olives," she said, perhaps too excitedly, as he gave up a plate with a slice of smoked cheese. Only one left, and he set it before Gwendolyn. "From An Ghréig," she explained.

"Ah, yes," he said, licking his finger. "Olives we have. But this cheese is..." He rolled his eyes with an expression of delight. "Extraordinary!"

"Like my hair?" Gwendolyn teased, then felt silly repeating the compliment.

A smile tugged at his lips. "Nothing compares," he said.

Gwendolyn found herself batting her lashes, a ridiculous gesture she had never truly understood until now. "Smoked," she explained, as he lifted a brow.

"Your hair?" he asked, and Gwendolyn laughed softly.

"Nay, Highness. The cheese!"

His tone shifted now, his voice low and serious. "You must bring some home with you when you come."

Home.

He lifted another olive to his lips and Gwendolyn watched him eat it, scraping the dark meat from the pit with his straight, white teeth. She blinked, confused, her heart hammering with such vigor. "My hair?"

"Nay," he said with a chuckle. "The cheese."

"Oh," Gwendolyn said, blushing, embarrassed again. *Of course.* What a silly girl she must seem. "Alas," she said, "no one in Trevena has this recipe. It comes to us by the northern tribes, although I'm quite certain we can have some exported."

"Imported," he corrected, gesturing about the hall with a finger before reaching for her hand and threading his fingers through hers. "Very soon, this will no longer be your home. Any exports we will be fortunate enough to negotiate will be imports for my beautiful queen."

Beautiful?

Disarmed by the compliment, Gwendolyn hadn't the heart to rebuke him, because, well... actually... they were meant to rule *both* kingdoms, not merely Loegria.

Cornwall would *always* be Gwendolyn's home, foremost in her heart.

And yet, he sounded so utterly sincere, and when he flattened her palm against his chest in just such a way, over the beat of his heart, it left her without a voice to protest. The look on his face was so hopeful, so heartfelt, and his lips parted to reveal another blinding, white smile that stole Gwendolyn's breath. All she could do was smile in return.

"So then," he asked. "Of which northern tribe do we speak? The land beyond the north winds? Else Prydein?"

"Neither," said Gwendolyn, eager to regale him with knowledge he might not already have gathered. "From what I am told, they come from the North Seas. Their dragon prows are made to plow through—"

"Ice," he said with a half-smile. "I was only jesting. We have met the Ostmen—barbarians, garbed in whatever pelts they can find, dogs, if needs must."

"Oh," said Gwendolyn, embarrassed again, and to cover her chagrin, she engaged him with a related question. "So, did you meet... these... Ostmen in Loegria?"

"Nay," he said, shaking his head. "Ériu. After my last sojourn, we took a ship home, captained by a helmsman from Hyperborea."

"Hyperborea," she repeated with genuine interest, and he dipped his chin meaningfully. Gwendolyn had never heard of this place, but she didn't wish to be disagreeable.

"At least to me, he seemed no different from any of the barbarian hordes I've met—be they Franks, Suebi, or from the Vandal Kingdom. Every single one has a bent to shout too much, and run about bare-arsed, despite the bitter cold."

Gwendolyn blinked.

Bare-arsed?

Unwittingly, her thoughts returned to Málik, but not because she considered his bare arse, only wondering how much of hers he'd spied.

Sadly, Gwendolyn had never heard of the Vandal Kingdom either, so she said, "Oh. Yes, I see." He was quite knowledge-able, and she suddenly found her meager education quite inadequate. Thereafter, she let him talk and sat back to enjoy the evening, pleased enough that it was going so well. At the instant, everyone conversed contentedly as they filled their bellies with the finest of delicacies. Only Málik, supping at one of the lower tables, seemed bored and disengaged, although at least he didn't appear to be cross.

Rather, his face was again without expression, only now and again flicking glances at the dais to make certain of his undesirable charge—Gwendolyn, naturally.

When she inadvertently caught his gaze, she chafed under his scrutiny, and turned away, though not before wondering if he was alone by choice.

Seated amidst two lords and their ladies, he eschewed conversation as readily as he had his seat at the higher table. Gwendolyn wondered if he knew anyone outside the Elite Guard, and how her father came to employ him. She knew he hadn't been in residence long—certainly not long enough for Gwendolyn to learn much about him. Everything she knew, she knew from Bryn. Though admittedly, she sometimes watched him from the balustrade when he and Bryn sparred; she had learned a lot about him simply through his choices.

He wasn't merciful, neither was he lenient. Rather, he was unyielding, tireless, and shrewd. And yet, despite that he was as arrogant a creature as Gwendolyn had ever encountered, there was something intrinsically magical in his movements.

Indeed, for Málik Danann, even a walk down the hall seemed more like a choreographed dance. In like form, the removal of his sword from its sheath was done with grace, and he wielded that weapon with effortless precision.

Nothing he did was ever... extraneous.

In fact, where Málik was concerned, there was economy in his every movement, and more to the point, he never went out of his way for any reason at all that didn't somehow serve him, which only made his betrayal of Bryn this afternoon even more unpalatable.

What could have been his reason?

He was watching the dancers, but there was nothing in his expression that gave Gwendolyn any sign he was enjoying the show.

Rather, she had the sense that he was otherwise attuned to every movement in the hall—every gesture everyone made, and perhaps all that was said.

The stories she'd heard about the *fae* were innumerable. They could grow silver limbs. They could read thoughts. They could shift shapes.

But how curious the thought, how tedious it would be to hear everyone's conversations all at once. If that were one of Gwendolyn's *fae* gifts, she would certainly go mad.

Once again, averting her gaze from the thorn her father had burrowed in her side, Gwendolyn peered up at the Prince as he, too, surveyed the hall. She hadn't even realized he was talking, and he suddenly knit his brows as he noted the direction of her gaze.

Gwendolyn pretended not to notice. It was that or apologize, and somehow that felt wrong, as though she were confessing to something despicable.

Instead, she dared to ask about the one thing she most wished to know. "Was it fascinating?"

"Quite," he said, and another slow grin unfurled. "Though not in the way you might think. Tell me, Princess... do such things normally entertain you?"

"Immensely," Gwendolyn confessed. "Someday, I hope to visit Cnoc Fírinne for myself, and mayhap when 'tis completed, I should like to see the new Temple in Eastwalas as well."

His brows twitched. "The Æmete Temple?"

Gwendolyn blinked, careful not to frown. "Well, yes, though... that is not what *we* call it. Nor do I believe *they* refer to it in such manner themselves."

They being the Dobunni, a consortium of tribes occupying much of the borderlands. Eastwalas was essentially Dumnonii territory, but it also bordered upon Silures, and Ordovices in Loegria, as well as the Catuvellauni to the east, and Atrebates to the south.

"Æmete is what *they* call *us*," she explained, "Though I do not believe 'tis meant to be kind."

"What does it mean?"

"Æmete?" she asked. "Well—" She lifted her brows. "It means... ant."

He made a scurrying motion with two fingers. "You mean those crawly creatures?"

Gwendolyn nodded.

"Ah, yes, I see," he said. "Alas, if anyone should be called such a thing, it should be them. Shouldn't it?"

Gwendolyn blinked. "Because they are a multitude?"

"Nay, Princess."

The way he said her name—or rather, not precisely her name, only her title—gave Gwendolyn gooseflesh.

"Because they are inconsequential."

The woven spell was suddenly lost.

"They are not even canny enough to join forces as we have."

"Oh," said Gwendolyn.

"Really, had they done so, perhaps Cornwall would not have stood so long."

The furrow in Gwendolyn's brow deepened. So far as she was concerned, no one was inconsequential, not even Málik. But Cornwall had *not* endured so long because Pretania's other tribes were ignorant or insignificant. Although she appreciated the fact that he was treating her as an equal, neither dismissing her opinions nor behaving as though she hadn't the mental acuity to discuss political matters, Cornwall had remained strong because they *were* strong.

Alone, her people had established a well-visited port. They'd learned to mine what the land offered. And they'd learned the disciplines of *metallonourgia*, creating alloys previously unknown. Nay, they did not have such advanced disciplines as did the Trojans, but they certainly had more than the rest of Pretania.

Gods. He mustn't realize what he was saying, and considering his demeanor else wise, Gwendolyn forgave him. Indubitably, his was the perspective of a newcomer to this land. He couldn't possibly understand how much they'd endured, nor how far they had come.

Prince Locrinus leaned close to confide in her. "I'm unsure whether you've heard, but Plowonida recently burned at the hands of the Iceni. It stands unclaimed. As my future queen, I will tell you that, as soon as we can gather an army, my father intends to drive them east to establish a new capital for Loegria. We will call it Troia Nova," he said, grinning broadly. "It is from there you and I will rule."

"Troia Nova," Gwendolyn repeated, though her brows rose of their own accord. She had heard no such thing about Plowonida, but the ramifications of such a campaign would be far-reaching. It was more the custom to abandon a stronghold after a fight, withdrawing to well-defended battlements. According to her father, most often what drove men to battle was not so much the coveting of another's land, but the need to protect what was theirs.

Indeed, Cornwall had thrived so well in part because they did not weaken their defenses by spreading themselves far and wide. However, if Plowonida had been abandoned by the Catuvellauni... if the Loegrians dared to move into Eastwalas... if they truly had the means and numbers to take and keep that city...

What would the Iceni do? Would they attack again after waging and winning a fight with the Catuvellauni? How would they fare against Loegrian weapons?

Troia Nova.

King Brutus had been awarded the land he now occupied by a joint Konsel of Pretania's tribes—a Konsel for which her father was headmester.

Gwendolyn understood the Iceni had a longstanding feud with the Catuvellauni, mostly because the High King of Plowonida had once seduced their beloved queen, but that was a matter of retribution. Not since the Tuatha Dé Danann were defeated so long ago had men seized municipalities that were not theirs to take. Not since the sons of Míl agreed to honor one another's borders. As the Prydein used to do, men might snatch a harvest under cover of night, but they would never, ever bring tillers to plow another man's fields.

And really, not once in living memory had an enemy dared to take a city after a battle was fought, much less lands that were not properly got. What the Loegrians were proposing was opportunistic, and yet Gwendolyn couldn't think it wrong... not precisely.

Simply because something had not been done before did not mean it was not to be done. If the Catuvellauni did not want Plowonida, and the Loegrians did, and if, in fact, it could be sustained, then it might be considered a strong military tack. However, Gwendolyn wondered if her father knew Loegria intended to expand beyond their current borders so deep into Pretania—well beyond the Eastwalas Temple. Gwendolyn longed to ask more about it, but the revelation had completely befuddled her.

"You are quite learned, and it pleases me," said Prince Locrinus, smiling with unreserved approval. "I prayed to have an equal as my partner, as I never intended to rule at all, much less to rule alone."

Gwendolyn's heart warmed to him again, hearing the pain of his brother's loss in his voice. "At heart, I am but a simple man, whose greatest desire it is to discover the mysteries of this world." Reaching for Gwendolyn's hand, he squeezed it gently.

"Now, despite the grief I feel for my brother's plight, I find myself well pleased with our match, and someday, if it pleases you, I will take you on a sojourn to Cnoc Fírinne, and we shall visit the Eastwalas Temple as well."

Gwendolyn's heartbeat quickened. It was the sweetest thing he might have ever said to her. The thought was like a love philter. "That would be a most welcome gift," she said, her heart filling with joy. Thereafter, the evening was a delight. So much so that Gwendolyn put *all* the day's troubles behind her, and all her doubts, as well.

Even Queen Eseld smiled with undisguised approval, and Gwendolyn felt... lovely and brilliant, and... oh, yes... golden... and so full of hope.

All night long, they talked, and talked, and talked.

Only now and again, Prince Locrinus would appraise Gwendolyn with a private smile that seemed so full of promise and possession that it set loose a dole of doves in her breast.

Later, when they said goodnight, leaving their fathers to discuss the final details of their betrothal, Prince Locrinus walked Gwendolyn to her bower door, leaving her with a burgeoning sense of hope... and a tiny seedling of... *love?*

Was this love?

Certainly, it was *something*—something beauteous and satisfying.

Already she admired the man she'd been promised to wed, and now she couldn't wait to share her life with him.

"Until the morrow," he said, before taking his leave, and Gwendolyn sighed contentedly, basking in the evening's joy. Even once he was gone, she lingered outside her chamber door.

But at long last, she turned, with a final, wistful glance down the hall in the direction her sweet prince had gone, only to spy Málik coming around the corner.

The sight of him surprised her as much as it displeased her, even though she should have expected him. Sucking in a breath, she rushed through the antechamber, straight into her room, slamming her door, and thrusting her back against the iron-riveted wood as though she feared he would come bursting through.

Of course, he did not.

He would not.

She heard him enter the antechamber a moment later and settle himself... until nothing but darkness and silence crept beneath her door.

Only then did she make for the bed.

CHAPTER

EIGHT

T he next morning, with Demelza trailing behind her, Queen Eseld called upon Gwendolyn. And then, for once didn't rush away. Wearing a pleasant smile, along with a few ells of scarlet *cendal*, she patted Gwendolyn's cheek, informing her how utterly proud she was.

She also brought with her a very unusual gown that she wished for Gwendolyn to try on—a design that appeared to be an odd mix between a warrior's tunic and a ceremonial robe. It was like nothing Gwendolyn had ever seen her mother wear, and yet it was stunning.

Fashioned of a crimson-dyed buckskin, it bore markings Gwendolyn was only vaguely familiar with—Prydein, she believed.

"My wedding dress," the Queen said.

Having already lifted the gown by its shoulders to better inspect it, Gwendolyn blinked over the modesty of its design. "But—"

"The style of my people," explained the Queen, and Gwendolyn laid it back down, brushing a finger over the exquisite emblazonry.

"'Tis... lovely," she said. And yet, it was the last thing she would ever care to wear—not because it wasn't beautiful. Strange though it appeared, it was also one of the most exquisite designs Gwendolyn had ever had the good fortune to see, much less the opportunity to wear. Alas, though, she was terrified to touch it again, lest she ruin it and earn her mother's wrath.

"It is now yours," said Queen Eseld.

"Mine?"

Her mother nodded. "Aye, Gwendolyn. It may surprise you to learn I never had the courage nor conviction to wear it again after my nuptials, yet I know you will, and it would thrill me to see you do so."

Gwendolyn peered up at her mother with surprise. She had never actually considered that such a thing would take courage or conviction. She had rather believed Queen Eseld only lacked the desire—perhaps even that she was ashamed by her meager beginnings. Not that Gwendolyn ever thought she should be. Her mother was a princess, after all. It was only that her father had always referred to them so... primitively. And her mother never disagreed.

Gwendolyn didn't know what to say.

While she couldn't claim it was the only gift her mother ever gave her, it was certainly the most personal gift she had ever received.

In fact, the dress was precious, and Gwendolyn wondered why her mother had never even shown it to her before, but the question was short-considered.

However, in light of the unexpected gift—generous beyond generous—and after the wonderful evening she'd had with Prince Locrinus, she refused to allow anything to quash her mood today. So much hope was affixed to this union. *So much hope.* And now, for the first time, Gwendolyn had pleased her mother as well.

Things were looking well. Indeed, they were.

She stood there, admiring the dress, pride lifting her spirits higher.

Someday soon, all kingdoms would be as one, a feat that could only be accomplished by the coupling of their dragon banners. But after last night, the "golden one" of prophecy could well be Prince Locrinus. In truth, all that recommended Gwendolyn as Pretania's champion was a tangle of hair that no one had ever proven was aught but unruly.

"Naturally, you must pair it with hosen," suggested her mother, showing the split at the front, then lifting a flap. "Traditionally, a Prydein ceremony is performed upon horseback. To my people, a good horse is the symbol of great leadership, and a chieftain's daughter must come to her marriage with a worthy mount, as her promise that she'll never be a burden to her husband, but an equal in all things."

Was this why Gwendolyn was so good with horses? Had she inherited this trait? One thing was certain, she could ride a horse better than any man. And yet, Gwendolyn knew so little of her mother's people. All she knew was that her mother had come to her father under a suit for peace, and little beyond that —only that Queen Eseld was traded during a civil meeting between tribes, and that her grandmother was also a queen, and her grandfather a Caledonian chieftain.

Even more intrigued now, she peered up, wanting to hear more. "Did you marry my father that way?" she asked.

"Alas, nay," said Queen Eseld, with a sigh. "I did not. I wore this gown, but we took our vows in a consul's tent before a prelate at the festival of Calan Mai."

"Oh," said Gwendolyn.

Her mother sighed again, and it sounded like a lifetime of disappointment must have been released with that breath. "I dreamt it would be different, but this was the way."

How sad, Gwendolyn thought—to be deprived of one's fondest dreams. Her mother should have had the wedding she'd desired, and if Gwendolyn could find some way to make up for her disappointment, she would try. However, she would be content enough to mend this rift between them, a rift she had never sought, nor did she entirely comprehend.

As for her own wedding... naturally, Gwendolyn had her own anticipations—to be wed before her friends and family, to a prince whose heart was as beautiful as his mind.

She would be crushed if any part of this turned out to be false.

And really, though Prince Locrinus' face was covetable, she didn't care about that. She, more than most, understood the injustices of being judged for such things, and she would never do it to anyone else. Even if she did not think him beautiful, she would have endeavored to find beauty in him, regardless.

She was still admiring the dress, but she pondered aloud. "I only wonder, did my father refuse your tradition?"

With such grace of movement, as though it were the gesture of a dance, Queen Eseld pushed a lock of shining black hair behind her shoulder. "To the contrary, dear one. Your father has never refused me aught. From the first, he has welcomed me as befits a queen of this realm. My father would be pleased."

At the turn of their conversation, Gwendolyn's heartbeat quickened. She had to keep herself from blurting a hundred thousand questions, fearful of never having another opportunity. And yet, she knew her mother well enough to know she must proceed with caution.

"Have you not spoken to my grandparents since you wed my father?"

"Nay," said Queen Eseld, with an odd note in her voice. Wistfulness, frustration? "I have not." She exhaled impatiently. "Enough reminiscence for one day!"

She smiled brightly, seemingly unfazed, and perhaps unaware that her refusal to share more would diminish Gwendolyn's spirits. "We have so much to do, and so little time!"

Disappointed despite her mother's enduring good humor this morn, Gwendolyn hitched her chin, wondering if Queen Eseld's detachment from her own mother could be the reason she was so aloof toward Gwendolyn. Mayhap she simply didn't know what it was to be a mother to a young woman? Or even a wee child.

Could it be... not so much that she still believed Gwendolyn to be a hideous changeling, but if she'd never had a genuine relationship with her own mother, she wasn't predisposed to having one with Gwendolyn?

It could be.

It seemed plausible.

Unfortunately, Gwendolyn knew firsthand how Ely's mother behaved with her own two children, and it was nothing like how Queen Eseld ever behaved with Gwendolyn.

In fact, Gwendolyn had never even thought of Ely's mother as Lady Ruan. She was mother to Ely, and mother to Bryn, and truth be told, mother to Gwendolyn as well.

This was why yesterday's ordeal upset Gwendolyn so much. To see Lady Ruan so disappointed in her made everything so much more difficult to bear. Someday, when she dared, she might ask Demelza how her mother had been with her as a babe.

Had she been coddled? Was it always Demelza who'd cared for her?

Gwendolyn wanted so desperately to believe that Queen Eseld had once held her to her bosom, cradling her head, and petting her messy curls. Demelza liked to say she was born with a mass of ringlets so thick she broke every comb she ever tried.

Unwittingly, Gwendolyn lifted a hand to her tresses, running her fingers through the thick tangle of curls. It wasn't fine, nor shiny, but Prince Locrinus had complimented her and the memory of that compliment made her smile a tiny, private smile.

Could it be that it shone for him? Was it possible that he saw not the tangle of curls she struggled to brush each day, but the golden filaments promised by the Prophecy?

The thought alone made Gwendolyn giddy, because so it was said that only her true love's heart could bring out the true beauty in her. And if he saw her tresses as golden, then perhaps he saw beauty in her face?

Her palms dampened simply over the thought of seeing him again, and her breath quickened painfully. She felt a tell-tale flush creep over her body.

Over by the bed, her mother made busy gathering some jewels she'd let Gwendolyn borrow yesterday—primarily the lovely sapphire necklace that matched her tiara.

So often her mother shared from her private coffers, but it occurred to Gwendolyn in that moment, as her mother gathered her precious gems, that her own dowry chest remained empty. So, too, was Ely's, but for a different reason.

How much longer before she must leave? Little more than a month, Gwendolyn realized, counting the weeks on her fingers.

Although her relationship with her mother was bitter-sweet, her bond with her father was strong. She didn't know what she would do if she went away, never to speak to him again. But she felt quite certain they would meet often to parley, except with Loegria as Gwendolyn's newest priority.

Still, she would never stop caring about Cornwall or its people. And gods willing, with her new husband at her side, she would serve the realm well.

"I thought you might wear the gown today," her mother suggested as she prepared to leave. "Really, Gwendolyn, if you must go traipsing about the countryside, as I know you will, I must have you present us to our best advantage."

Startled by the abrupt change in her mother's demeanor, although she might have expected it, Gwendolyn said, "I shall endeavor to do so, Mother."

And yet, escorting Prince Locrinus about a city he would someday rule could hardly be considered "traipsing about." So then, was that what this was all about? Had her mother come only to ensure Gwendolyn presented herself to "our best advantage"?

Gwendolyn's smile faded. Why couldn't it ever simply be about a girl and her mother? "Thank you," she said, resigned. "'Tis beautiful. I adore it."

And she did. *Truly.*

And anyway, it was a compliment of sorts, to be trusted to represent her Prydein kindred. By wearing this dress, not only would she be seen to represent Cornwall, but Prydein, as well. And of course, her mother's people should be represented, even if so oft her mother seemed content to ignore her humbler beginnings.

Gwendolyn sighed then, because it didn't matter *why* Queen Eseld had proffered the dress; what mattered was that Gwendolyn wore it. To that end, she found her best leather hosen and donned them at once. With Demelza's help, she slipped on the ceremonial robe as well, and once she was fully attired, she was surprised to discover how odd the garment felt.

It was firmly fitted, with no extra material about the arms. And now, she regretted all those blueberry cakes! The only free-flowing part of the gown lay below the waist, which was essentially made of four conjoined flaps to give the impression of a full-skirted dress.

And now she realized why it must be paired with her hosen, because any movement at all would expose her limbs. Alas, though she and her mother were approximately the same size overall, her mother was taller and leaner than Gwendolyn; therefore, the buckskin squeezed her upper arms and, if the bosom hadn't been fashioned to accommodate a woman's breasts, it would have flattened her as well, because the girth was too tight.

Additionally, because her mother's breasts were considerably larger than hers, she found the cups entirely too generous.

Testing the bodice, Gwendolyn frowned as the material, stiff with age, collapsed and remained concave. With a gasp, Demelza rushed forward to fill the space between the dress and her flesh with a round of cloth, and Gwendolyn tugged it back out, horrified by the prospect, refusing to make herself look buxom. She tossed it on the floor.

How embarrassing!

Her mother had returned, Gwendolyn realized. Now she stood in the doorway, watching as Demelza flitted about, attempting to dress Gwendolyn to some satisfaction. Her gaze shifted to the cloth Gwendolyn had refused.

"I meant to keep it a surprise. However, for your dowry chest, I also mean to gift you the breastplates and shoulder plates designed to accompany that gown." A wistful smile tugged at her lips. "After all, Gwendolyn, I am aware of how I have failed you. If there's only one thing I wish to remedy before you leave, it is to prepare you fully for your role as Pretania's queen."

Surprised by her mother's admission, Gwendolyn met her doleful gaze. "I—" she began, intending to offer absolution, but her mother pressed a finger to her lips, and said, "Beginning at once, just as soon as our guests have departed, I expect you to train daily with Málik Danann."

Again, Málik?

Gods.

Gwendolyn longed to protest, but her mother's expression forbade it.

Hot tears threatened, but she blinked them away. This was no happy gift! It was the worst thing her mother could have said to her!

"There is so little time, Gwendolyn. Though I can plainly see the Prince is already besotted with you, your future is yet to be written. Your father is right, dear one. You must be prepared."

Besotted?

Gwendolyn's emotions swung again. *Was it so apparent?*

"You must face your role as queen, not merely with the grace of a lady, but with the strength of a warrior, and I must confess I regret I forsook my own education. I allowed my instruction to fall by the wayside, but I would have you do better, Daughter."

How swiftly the mood had changed.

Gwendolyn longed to argue that Bryn's tutelage was good enough for her. She didn't want to study with Málik. But so stunned as she was to spy the sudden welling of tears in her mother's eyes, it rendered her speechless.

Gwendolyn nodded dumbly, and her mother tossed up a hand, turning her back to swipe a finger beneath her eye. "I am away," she chirped. "Demelza will see to it you are properly dressed, and the Prince awaits his lovely princess."

Again.

Lovely?

"Oh, yes!" Queen Eseld returned to the threshold, hand raised, as though just remembering something. But this time, when she met Gwendolyn's gaze, all traces of her tears had gone. "King Brutus and your father have yet to formalize your bride price, but considering the success of last eventide, you may consider it done!"

She tilted her head, smiling with ill-concealed pride. And yet what this pride was for, Gwendolyn couldn't rightly say. "Enjoy your day," the Queen said. "Go wheresoever you please, do as you please, only be in attendance this evening for the Promise Ceremony!"

Tonight, it would be done.

"Yes, Mother," said Gwendolyn.

And then she was gone, vanished with a spin of fine skirts. And with her sudden departure, Gwendolyn felt... again... inexplicably melancholy.

But nay, not precisely.

Rather, bereft. It was... an odd, but terrible void, as though she'd been gifted something of such exceptional value, but only for an instant. Then it was wrenched away.

This was the first time in her memory that her mother had confided in her so directly, and she had a terrible sense it might be the last, particularly considering the short time she had remaining in Trevena.

Gwendolyn swallowed with difficulty, but with her mother departed, she felt more comfortable complaining to Demelza about the state of her dress. "I adore it," she said. "I do! But can naught be done for these sleeves?"

Demelza tugged at the stiff material, sighing. "It should

have been oiled, and then stretched," she said. "If only I'd known she'd meant to do this so soon."

"You did not?"

"I did not," the maid confessed.

"What about these?" Gwendolyn added, cupping her own two breasts, her cheeks burning hot. "I do not relish the thought of walking about with false breasts, but neither will I like it if the material collapses and Prince Locrinus sees me." Her cheeks burned hotter yet.

"Fret not," said Demelza, pulling harder at the cloth. "You are perfectly endowed, my child. Your bosom was made for your body. And no matter, I vow this material will soften and mold itself to your form as though it were made for you."

Gwendolyn lifted a brow, considering her modest breasts. "Small as they are," she lamented.

"Nonsense," the maid argued. "I should not say it, but your mother is overly endowed. 'Tis hardly common to bear such large breasts with such a tiny waist. And there is naught wrong with your form, Gwendolyn. I have heard many a man claim that any more than a handful is a terrible waste, and you have a handful, or perhaps two."

"Not two," said Gwendolyn, and her cheeks burned hotter still.

In fact, she had a little more than a handful, but her hands were fairly small. She dropped them at her sides as Demelza continued fussing with the gown.

"The sleeves will be stretched at the first opportunity," she said, pinching at the material, unfazed by her own frank speech. "In the meantime, I will endeavor to convince your mother to allow the use of the breastplates—today," she added. "I shall go remind her how much your father admired the way she looked when she wore this... at first."

"At first?"

"Well, he did. To begin with. But she came to him a wildling herself, full of her own self-importance."

Gwendolyn pursed her lips. In so many ways, her mother was *still* like that. Not much had changed. And yet she daren't impugn her own mother, so she said, "Is that so?"

"Oh, yes. She carried a poniard to bed for a fortnight, fearing she might be slain."

The maid pulled aside the collar of her gown and revealed a small scar at the small juncture between her neck and shoulder. The look she gave, with both lifted brows, left Gwendolyn aghast. "I made the mistake of waking her too early."

Gwendolyn laughed, though she was horrified. "Did she believe she would be slain by my father?"

"Oh, no, child! Your mother speaks true. Your father worshipped the ground she walked upon, yet this was not something your mother seemed to comprehend until she found her place in your father's court. Eventually, she put her instruction to use with the *dawnsio*, and traded her dagger for a scepter."

Gwendolyn lifted her brows. She would have liked to have known her then. The *old* Queen Eseld was far more intriguing.

Demelza winked then. "She'll give you the breastplates today. As you know, she would deny you naught."

Of course not. Her mother would never say no to something like this. Appearances were everything to her. "Thank you," said Gwendolyn, sorely hoping the breastplate would conceal her bosom. And then she was suddenly excited to see what the vestment would look like altogether—a Prydein princess? How thrilling to represent her mother's people! How magnificent to have a small connection to her grandparents, even despite that she'd never met them. Someday she would, she vowed.

Someday.

CHAPTER
NINE

G wendolyn felt magnificent as she made her way
through her father's halls into the courtyard. It
wasn't only the stunning gown she'd been honored
to wear, but in some part, her mother's attention and approval
this morning as well. At long last, if only for a moment, Queen
Eseld had gazed upon her only daughter with few misgivings,
taking pleasure in her company. It was as close to a true
mother-daughter connection as they'd ever had, and as
fleeting as it was, it set loose a burst of joy from Gwendolyn's
heart that swept into her face and tugged a permanent grin on
her lips. And regardless, something about wearing this dress
really made her feel "beautiful." Today, coupled with the
success of last night's introduction, she could easily imagine
herself capable of fulfilling her destiny, and the anticipation of
it filled her with glee.

Lady Ruan passed by, smiling with unvarnished approval.
Whatever disappointment she'd felt toward Gwendolyn
yesterday, it was no longer perceptible in her countenance.

"Exquisite," she said. "Simply exquisite!" And she clapped her hands fondly, then kissed Gwendolyn quickly on the cheek.

Alderman Crwys bowed as he passed, the light of respect shining in his old eyes. And then Alderman Morgelyn as well, the youngest of her father's aldermen. He gave Gwendolyn a wink, and she blushed.

Even Bryn's father, the Mester of Arms, looked twice as she emerged into the courtyard near the Mester's Pavilion. And if he was still angry with her for Bryn's demotion, he didn't show it. But neither did he smile. The man was not given to many.

Only for show, because, of course, they were at peace, Gwendolyn wore the finely hewn arming sword her father gave her on her fifteenth Name Day. Made of good Loegrian steel, it rested in the bejeweled and furred scabbard that hung about her waist, gems winking brilliantly against the bright morning sun.

But also, because she never left home without it, she'd tucked another small poniard into the sheath at her boot. This one she mostly used to dine with, but it too was finely made, with the emblem of her father's house carved into the hilt—the ancient guardian of Dumnonia, the fiery-winged drake with the thorny head and barbed tongue.

Having come by the Endless Sea, Loegria's capitol flew a standard with the wingless sea serpent and speared tail.

Once joined, it was said they would become invincible.

Today, with the hem of her new garb so much shorter than the gowns she so oft wore, the dragon hilt remained visible over the lip of her boot.

To complete her outfit, she wore her mother's soft scarlet cloak, tied loosely about the throat, and with all her new finery, she felt she looked the part of a warrior queen, more than prepared to take on the entire Red Tide Brutus had so long ago warned about.

Let them come!

She would join the dragon banners into a single pendragon and then let us see whose blood turned the tide red!

Together, she and Prince Locrinus would unite Pretania's clans, and unified, they would stand strong against whatever scourge must come their way—Romans, Trojans, whoever!

This morning Gwendolyn would escort Prince Locrinus about the parklands, only to give him a glimpse of what he would someday rule, with Gwendolyn by his side. She dearly hoped he would be impressed, but not only with the tour. Today, she hoped he would see her, not only as his bride-to-be, but the strong partner he claimed he longed for.

Dressed for the occasion, she marched into the courtyard undaunted, even when the sun glinted off the metal plates binding her bosom, stabbing her in the eyes.

And there he was, precisely as her mother claimed he would be, awaiting her with his retinue, the same two red-cloaked guards that had escorted him into the hall yestereve. All three chatted amiably, including the Prince.

Málik appeared sober beside them. Tall and lithe in comparison, he had the figure of a well-hewn but loose-limbed fellow. Moreover, while the red-cloaked guards were fully armored in fine Loegrian steel, he was garbed modestly in a leather tunic and leggings that, if they didn't protect him so well as the armor, must at least allow for some ease of movement.

Not so unlike her own, his leathers were well-aged, and cut in much the same fashion as her new Prydein robe. And come to think of it, they were similar enough that it begged the question: Were the Prydein acquainted with the Tuatha Dé Danann?

She wondered but didn't wish to think of Málik as *fae*.

He could style himself Danann all he wished, but that didn't mean he *was* Danann.

Whilst Prince Locrinus' guards wore helms, his head remained bare. His silvery tresses were caught at the nape in a pony's tail, with a loose lock veiling his eyes, so that when he lifted his head to assess Gwendolyn, she couldn't even guess what he was thinking—not that she cared to know. Somehow, even without armor, he looked... *formidable*. It was that *piskie-may-care* attitude, she realized—the ease with which he embraced all things, as though the world might find itself ablaze, and Málik Danann would simply march from the flames unscathed.

In true form, not bothering to wait for Gwendolyn to arrive by his side, he swung himself into the saddle. And demons take the man, not once had Gwendolyn ever mounted so swiftly, nor with such grace and ease. Doubtless, in all that armor, neither would Prince Locrinus nor his burly guards, but Gwendolyn should endeavor not to notice.

Inconceivably, Málik made the courtyard feel tiny as he sat, larger than life, upon his modest black horse—a mare, not even a stallion, as was the custom for warriors. Whatever the man lacked in girth, he more than made up for in height and bearing.

Yet it annoyed her to no end that it was *his* eyes she met first, and she told herself it was only because he sat so tall in his saddle, a full head above the rest.

But she knew this was a lie because he hadn't even assumed his saddle when she'd first sought his gaze. Even against her will, her eyes were drawn to him like lodestones.

When finally she dared to seek Prince Locrinus' gaze, his honeyed eyes glinted with what she interpreted to be displeasure, but he hid it well behind his ready smile.

Something like doubt shifted Gwendolyn's mood. Because

of Málik, she would endanger this alliance and anger her prince. What form of *magik* was this that *he* could ensnare her attention so easily, despite that she loathed him?

Henceforth, she vowed to pay Prince Locrinus all due regard and endeavor to ignore Málik Danann, resigning herself to his presence in much the same way a dog must resign himself to fleas. Gracious as always, Prince Locrinus came forward to greet her, holding out his hand.

"My sweet Princess, you are... ravishing," he said, and the gleam of his perfect white smile softened the hard glint in his eyes.

An unexpected shiver sidled down Gwendolyn's spine, and she said quickly, "And you, Highness." Only belatedly realizing how silly she sounded. "I mean to say—"

He pressed a hand against his chest, over his heart. "My humblest of thanks," he said, and bowed, as though the compliment were merely expected, and not some fevered rambling from a giddy maid. "As I have said, we are well-matched. And now I am eager to discover all your sanctuaries and learn everything there is to know about my lovely lady."

Gwendolyn felt a tingling in her scalp, and she inhaled sharply.

Alas, although she would like to say the rush of joy she felt over his compliment was sheer pleasure, it was liberally dosed with relief.

A new, unexpected warmth surged through her as, once again, he tucked her hand into the crook of his arm, then escorted her to her mount.

For the outing, they would be accompanied by Málik and both of Prince Locrinus' Shadows—his two to her one. But then, he was traveling, and often when she traveled, she took two guards or more.

Poor Bryn's absence was duly noted, and perhaps for the

first time since her good friend's demotion, she realized what a disservice she had done to him. But not only to him, to herself as well. She would desperately miss his kinship, and the ready smile he always had for her, no matter the circumstances. She wondered where he was right now—what Ely was doing as well.

Sadly, she realized that both her friends were dutifully avoiding her today, as there was never a time she had not stumbled upon one or the other by now.

Indeed, they had been inseparable as children, and not much had changed since they were dragged wailing from their mothers' wombs. Later, once the Prince departed, she would find both and apologize profusely, and somehow—*somehow*—make amends.

In the meantime, she allowed Prince Locrinus to assist her in mounting, not that Gwendolyn needed his help, but the solicitation seemed to please him.

She was thrilled to discover that, just as Demelza had claimed, her Prydein tunic was already softening, molding itself to her curves. Her hosen, well-worn and supple, afforded ease of movement. She could grow accustomed to this manner of dress, and perhaps when she was queen, she would encourage it for all. But of course, this was only a fleeting whimsy, and she wasn't in any hurry to assume the throne. But it was fun to imagine.

Still, there was something so freeing about the Prydein gown, and she wondered how her mother could resign herself to wearing such confining dresses after donning such a garb—only this made her wonder things she might never discover, such as, what did all the symbols mean?

There were strange half-moons, interwoven with other emblems, fish and serpents, and others besides. Sadly, she could never feel at ease asking such things of her mother, and she wasn't certain Queen Eseld would even welcome her questions.

Certainly she never had before, and despite the short but amicable visit this morn, it was not their usual encounter.

As Gwendolyn waited for Prince Locrinus to find and mount his own horse, she flicked a glance at Málik to see if his leathers bore any such markings. They did not.

His were simple and black, like his horse... like a cold, dark night.

Like his mood.

So at odds with his countenance.

Lamentably, he caught her staring, yet again, and his lips tilted slightly at one corner. Inhaling a breath, irritated with herself for bestowing upon him more attention than he deserved, Gwendolyn offered him her back, hitching her chin.

At long last, Prince Locrinus was ready to ride, and he sidled his horse close to Gwendolyn's, then made to reach for her reins. Gwendolyn stopped his hand before he could retrieve them. "No need, Highness. I am a well-practiced horsewoman."

He froze momentarily, then assented with a nod, and quickly withdrew his hand. "Of course," he said, "I should have guessed. There is *that* about you."

What *that* was, Gwendolyn wondered—particularly as he peered sideways at Málik. And for an instant, she couldn't help but compare the two, Locrinus with his golden beauty, and Málik...

Gods, so lovely as she'd felt this morn, she suddenly felt like a toad in their presence.

Both men were unquestionably beautiful—Prince Locrinus more so than Málik, and it was he that Gwendolyn should endeavor to please.

As soon as they were away, Málik fell behind, and Gwendolyn found herself vexed by that, unwilling to examine the true reason she felt so peeved, regardless of what he did. If he had dared to ride beside her, she would have been vexed by that, as well.

But Málik could remain wheresoever he pleased—hurl himself down a gully if he chose. *He* wasn't her concern, not today.

Clenching then unclenching her fist, she willed away her mounting tension and determined, once and for all, to put Málik Danann out of her mind.

CHAPTER

TEN

Although her father's secret wouldn't be betrayed by the glen, at least not today, the last thing Gwendolyn wished to do was take Prince Locrinus there and have him ask about the pool's significance. She would be honor-bound to tell him everything—about the King's connection to the land, and the trees' recent decline.

But it wasn't just that. On the off chance he'd heard about yesterday's ordeal with Bryn, she didn't believe it would be prudent to take him there and give him a false impression of sweethearts stealing a tryst.

Therefore, even though it was her most favorite place, she decided Porth Pool was better left for another day. Perhaps later, after she and Prince Locrinus were wed?

Meanwhile, though it wasn't quite so beloved as her pool, she took Prince Locrinus to another of her cherished places. And considering their discussion last night, she couldn't wait to share it with him.

It wasn't so majestic as the Eastwalas Temple nor the *lyn yeyn* quoit near Chysauster, where her cousins lived, but it had

115

always impressed her with its perfect circumference. Twenty-six stones altogether, they were said to be effigies of *dewine* maids, whose moonlight dance somehow displeased the Mother Goddess, so she turned them all to stone. Some now lay sprawled upon the moorland in a swoon. Others stood tall, as though their heads and eyes were last turned to the stars. Whichever the case, Gwendolyn hoped they would ignite the Prince's curiosity, and she was titillated by the prospect of discussing *philosophia* with him.

Would he consider their flawless design? Would he think it divine? Would he see any similarities to those places he'd visited in Ériu? She couldn't wait to find out.

Seated betwixt two rocky tors—Bronn Ewhella and Rough Tor, whence many of Cornwall's rivers arose—the circle's utter perfection spoke to the wonder in Gwendolyn, for, no matter how one speculated, no one could truly glean its purpose, nor comprehend the true nature of its design. It was older than Trevena, older even than Gogmagog and his giants, and if these were truly maidens struck down during their midnight dance, it happened long before the Dumnonii were made conservators of this land.

In fact, Gwendolyn suspected they could be *fae*, and some part of her wondered what Málik would think of them, but she certainly didn't intend to ask.

Excited to reveal the stones, she led the small party into the moorlands, and then, once they'd arrived, she led them in a circle, careful not to allow her mare to trample the swooning maids. Her excitement was palpable; all the little hairs on her nape prickling, as they always did in this vicinity.

Prince Locrinus broke formation and moved into the circle. "We have a few of these," he said, hardly impressed.

Gwendolyn furrowed her brow. She was forced to confess:

His reaction was not her first disappointment. No matter; she feigned indifference, asking politely, "In Loegria? Or Troy?"

"Loegria," he said as he circled the stones. All the while, his destrier trod heavily over fallen maidens, snorting at a string of wild ponies nearby.

Gwendolyn's frown only deepened.

Arms crossed, Málik remained at a distance.

So, too, did Prince Locrinus' Shadows, although one of them retrieved his bow and an arrow and sat testing his sights on a pony. But those were sacred, too, and if Gwendolyn thought for an instant that he meant to set an arrow loose, she would fly at him with a vengeance. So long as he did not, she sat smiling, forced though it was.

"You know, I have never been to my father's birth land," the Prince confessed.

"Oh," said Gwendolyn, curious to know why, considering that he'd traveled so extensively. *Was it because his father was no longer welcome in Troy? Or merely because he had no desire to see his father's homeland?* The latter simply didn't fit what she knew of him—the erudite soul she'd looked so forward to meeting.

If only to understand his point, she considered how she would feel if it were her own father who'd been exiled from his birth land, knowing there would be people left behind she would never know—oh, yes, she could see how that would upset him. Presumably, no matter how well their lives had fared since leaving Troy, the subject was bound to be a sore one for the Prince and his father. Therefore, she must forgive his insouciance.

Seated atop his armored stallion, in all its golden armor, the Prince was undeniably beautiful, his hair glistening beneath the midday sun, like a halo.

Considering him, Gwendolyn counted her good fortune

that he seemed equally pleased with her—or at least that's how it seemed.

Admittedly, she didn't know how a "besotted" man should behave.

Abandoning the poor maids where they lay, disappointed in Prince Locrinus' response but undaunted, Gwendolyn led the party away, but when she peered back to see if Málik was following—he'd been so quiet—she found that he'd dismounted, and was on his knees inside the stone circle, one hand splayed upon a fallen stone, his head down as though in prayer.

Without remarking upon it, Gwendolyn watched as he lifted the stone upright, and once it was standing, he brushed his hands on his hosen and returned to his mount.

Prince Locrinus said naught as he followed her gaze, and she was compelled to feign exasperation with her errant guard. She turned and made a sound of frustration, then spun her mare northeast toward the Trevillet. Really, she didn't care what Málik was doing, or why he'd felt so compelled to raise that stone, but right now, she hoped he'd be trampled by ponies before he could rejoin them. Admittedly, this time, she was upset with him by no fault of his own. She didn't like that he'd shown so much more reverence to those Dancing Stones than did her betrothed. But this was Gwendolyn's problem, not anyone else's.

By the time they found the Trevillet, her good mood had returned.

She led the party west along the river to the keeve, a place of natural beauty that gave her so much peace. There, they stopped to enjoy a small treat by the waterfall—sweet meat pies, with a bit of mead—until Málik, the laggard, finally deigned to arrive.

Despite knowing there was one pie left, Gwendolyn stood

without a word, eying Málik with no small measure of annoyance as she retrieved her mare.

The meal had been arranged by her mother, packed in her saddlebags before the horses were ever delivered to the courtyard. Therefore, they were hers to share, or not.

Málik didn't deserve one, as there was naught about his demeanor that gave Gwendolyn the first sign that he felt himself a part of her entourage.

In fact, he was as distant to her as Prince Locrinus' men. Fortunately, if Prince Locrinus noted her mood, he said nothing, and the party returned to the road.

It was past noontide when they came full circle and arrived at a small rift that could only be traversed by foot. Eager to be away from prying eyes, they abandoned the guards atop the lay-by, and because it was only a short jaunt and Gwendolyn knew the way well, she led Prince Locrinus down the gully until they reached the etchings carved into the high stone.

"A blessing from the Ancients," she explained, pointing. Stamped deep into the rock, for all to see, a promise of fertility for Cornwall and her people.

Her father was given precisely the same mark by the Llanrhos Druids when he ascended the throne, and her grandfather had one as well. Little doubt Gwendolyn, too, would be painted when the time came for her to ascend—a small tattoo at the base of her neck. Although she wondered how the Druids would endure it, since they seemed not to appreciate women.

"Fascinating," said the Prince, and once again, Gwendolyn found herself piqued. It wasn't anything she could put a finger on, not precisely.

Rather, it was a feeling she got, a lack of interest that she could only attribute to the Prince's exhaustion—but of course.

He'd traveled two long days to arrive here, and he was bound to have been up too late, then up early besides.

Gauging the hour by the position of the sun, she peered up to find Málik once again in her sights. Like a gadfly, he was always there, irritating to the end.

He was standing atop the lay-by, peering down at them from the cliff top, munching on something he must have taken from his own saddlebag. He held the treat aloft in greeting, with an indecipherable smile tugging at his lips.

Gods.

Whatever sense of irritation she now felt toward Prince Locrinus, she could easily attribute it to her own vexation over the prospect of having that man as her Shadow, morning, noon, and night. How could she bear it? That *he* was not in her antechamber this morning when she'd left was only because her mother and Demelza had sent him away upon their arrival so he could see to his morning victuals.

Alas, no matter what he did, Gwendolyn was bound to be annoyed with him for some time yet—or at least until she had the chance to tell him what she thought of his betrayal of Bryn.

And she would, just as soon as she found him alone, and there weren't any other ears about to catch the blistering she intended to give his pointy ears.

Conforming to his way, Málik said nothing, merely watched.

Once again, Gwendolyn gave him her back, continuing down to the beach, eager to be free of him. Only realizing she must have been a bore these past few hours, sulking over the Prince's response to her Dancing Stones, she brightened her tone.

"There are peregrine nests to be found on these shoals," she said. "If we find one, you may wish to carry one home?" She smiled widely. "As my betrothal gift."

"Falcons?"

"Oh, yes! My father favors them for hunting."

"Indeed," he said, "I should like that." And then he turned to peer over his shoulder, perhaps to assess the steep path whence they'd descended, because he said with a note of admiration, "You are quite able-bodied, *Highness*."

Gwendolyn laughed. "As well I should be, *Highness*. I spent most of my youth climbing these bluffs."

"Alone?" he asked, his voice lifting slightly.

"Oh, nay!" Gwendolyn felt better already without Málik to spy on them. "Always in the company of my Shadow."

"Ah, yes," he said. "Your Shadow."

Gwendolyn couldn't tell by his tone whether that revelation displeased him, or whether it was her own guilty conscience that needled her—guilt for things she'd never until yesterday even questioned. After all, she was the princess of Cornwall, and she'd understood from the day of her birth what was expected of her. Never would she knowingly betray her duties, nor would she have imagined her parents wouldn't trust her implicitly.

Really, it wasn't as though she and Bryn had stood there ogling one another, nor did they swim in close proximity. It was all perfectly harmless, as it would have been with Ely.

And regardless, if anyone ever disrespected Gwendolyn, she wasn't a hapless maid. Thanks to Bryn's instruction, she was quite skilled with her blades, even without Málik's interference. In all things, she was a woman of her own mind, as her father had taught her to be, and yet she was being punished for this now.

She could thank Málik for that.

He was the author of her misery, and though she realized the responsibility of charming her betrothed must fall to her alone, if she failed today, she would blame him, regardless.

Mercifully, though he must have senses keener than most, he couldn't see around corners. The image of him standing atop the lay-by, eating his treat with a half-smile, as though he realized she'd meant to deprive him, and the treat was his recrimination, only filled her with more rancor. Hoping to salvage the day, she led Prince Locrinus down to the cove, and once there on the beach, she dared to entreat his hand, then led him to the Dragon's Lair, a series of passages extending beneath their mountain, accessible only at low tide.

It was quite bold of her, she realized, and deep down, she heard Demelza's note of whispered caution. But Prince Locrinus was now her betrothed—or he would be after tonight.

Still, she hesitated before going inside the cave, placing a hand to the cold stone, and turning to assess the bay, considering whether the tide was coming or going—something she normally knew as a matter of intuition. Today, however, her instincts felt... *wrong*.

"What's this?" he asked, at last with some interest, and Gwendolyn's sense of unease dissipated. Eager to tell him about the place where she used to play as a child, she explained the significance of the caves, and then told him about the Dragon's Lair.

Like many of the rock formations found elsewhere, and the labyrinth carvings in the rock valley, the Dragon's Lair had been here so long as men had memory.

It was only accessible by traversing the caves and emerging through to the other side. From there, it was possible to climb onto a stone alcove—a natural balcony of sorts. And there, nestled in the stone, by night and by sea, one could spy strange lights within the shallow cave—the fiery breath of the dragon, for which their standard was made.

But the alcove didn't simply keep ships from smashing on

their cliffs; it also gave them a great military advantage, because without it, Trevena was completely inaccessible by sea, protected on all sides by natural defenses, approachable only by the narrow land bridge, which during wartime would be heavily guarded. If ever they were attacked, all they had to do was draw down the heavy tarp to conceal the alcove and cast the sea into darkness.

Land and sea would enact their own defenses, leaving the ships to battle angry tides. And then, if anyone dared approach by land, her father's archers would pick them off.

So really, unless one defied the Brothers' Pact and betrayed them inside the gates, the city was impenetrable. And this was the one way Loegria could not compare. Cornish archers were among the best, their bows made from yew wood, blessed by the gods. That wood could last a thousand years without rotting, and the yew's poison was so potent that her father's army often used a tincture made from it on their arrows to poison enemies during battle.

It didn't matter what the efficacy of a man's steel was, nor the skill with which he wielded it, if he couldn't wield it face-to-face. Their archers would ensure no enemy could come near. It wouldn't matter how well-trained an army was or how well-armored—their archers were so accurate in aim that they could find and penetrate the smallest chink in their armor.

But of course, Gwendolyn didn't tell Prince Locrinus any of these things. Like the news of the glen, she daren't share such things just yet—not until they ruled this land together.

"Curious," he said, when she explained about the Dragon's Lair. And then, encouraged by his interest, Gwendolyn continued. "Sometimes," she said, her voice animated, "it sounds like rolling thunder down here, particularly when my father's troops are marching o'er the stone bridge."

Prince Locrinus peered up, examining the cave's interior. It wasn't directly below the land bridge, but the positioning of the cave was just so that a disturbance anywhere along the mountain reverberated throughout the caverns. Even now, there was the faintest rumble, scarcely audible beneath the pummeling of waves—simply men walking along the bridge.

"I would have enjoyed such a place when I was a boy," he said, offhandedly. "If for naught else, to sit and ponder the Fates."

"Oh, yes. I confess, it was sometimes used for this. I did much just the same." For another moment, they stood listening to the roar of the ocean's waves, louder now. Regrettably, the tide was rising already. Even now, water was slipping beneath the soles of Gwendolyn's boots, although she was loath to end the moment, for these were the moments whence love was born. "Quite oft I spent my childhood tears here," she confessed, and smiled, though she spoke the truth. Those particular memories didn't please her, and there were so many days she'd escaped here to weep over her mother's endless trials. Only Bryn ever witnessed her torment, but she was grateful for his counsel and the perspective he gave her.

So he'd claimed: Her mother's pursuits weren't an accurate measure of Gwendolyn's worth, but a testament to the Queen's fears. After all, she'd come to Cornwall to bear the King an heir, and she'd given him, not only a girl child, but a girl child whose humanity was questioned. Alas, that it was questioned most oft by the Queen herself was the worst of it.

"And did you spend those tears alone?" he asked carefully.

Gwendolyn inhaled sharply. "Nay," she said. "Always with an audience, but fortunately, he is sworn to secrecy." She smiled sadly.

"Your Shadow?" he said now, reaching for her hand and drawing her close.

Gwendolyn's heart leapt within her breast as he spun her

about, only to walk her backward, following until she found her back pressed against the cavern's wall.

"I give you my word, Princess, and vow to flay any man who dares make my queen weep."

Gwendolyn blinked, her heart beating faster. A shadow entered the cavern—one that had nothing to do with the bright sun shining beyond the cave's entrance.

"T-thank you," she said, unnerved by the dark look that fell over his comely features. She peered at the cave's entrance, not so much because she was afraid; she was not.

Wouldn't that be silly? The Prince was her betrothed, bound by a promise that could not be broken. And didn't he just say he would flay any man who dared to make her weep?

"Fortunately, I am not so maudlin these days," she said, reassuring him. A smile found its way through the mask of uncertainty, her gaze drawn again in the entrance's direction.

Gods. No matter his promise, his smile made her feel... *nervous.*

Gently, he touched a finger to her cheek, and the tenderness of the gesture sent an odd tremor down her spine. So much as she adored Bryn, she had never once felt such a fluttering in her belly whenever he'd gazed upon her—yet this must be a good thing?

His presence filled the entire cavern, demanding her full attention.

Eyes round and wide, Gwendolyn stared into his eyes so long she felt the tide creeping into the back of her boots. "Prince Locrinus," she began.

"Please, Gwendolyn... call me Loc," he suggested.

When Gwendolyn didn't at once respond, he added, "As you and I are soon to be wed, I would have you address me more... intimately."

Gwendolyn nodded. "Loc," she said, testing the name on her lips.

The weight and feel of it made her lips burn hot, and once again, she turned to peer in the direction whence they'd come... *searching for what?*

They weren't in danger, not really.

The tide never rose too swiftly, and even if it did, those rocks on the other side of the cave were accessible enough to allow them to climb easily to the safety of the alcove.

He smiled lazily, following her gaze. "And yet... I must wonder... doesn't it bother you to keep an elf at your heels all day long?"

Gwendolyn blinked in surprise. "Elf?"

She was startled by his use of a name that most people wouldn't consider polite, no matter that, of late, she sometimes thought it herself. "I—"

She closed her mouth again to better consider her answer.

Really, it didn't bother her that Málik was half-*Sidhe*. She didn't have a problem with anyone's *rás*. She was only nettled by one *Sidhe* in particular—*that Sidhe*, the one she now spied loitering on the beach. "He is harmless," she argued. "Mostly."

"Mostly?"

"Indeed."

"I have never met an elf who knew his place."

Gwendolyn didn't consider her actions—that it might offend her betrothed to correct his behavior. She pressed a finger to her lips to admonish him.

"Shhh... voices carry," she apprised.

In response, Prince Locrinus inched closer, until she could feel the solidness of his chest as he leaned against her breast plate, flattening her breasts. "Don't worry, Princess," he said. "No one can hear us, except perhaps the hound at your heels. My men will know better, to afford us privacy."

CHAPTER
ELEVEN

I n the half-light of the cavern, Gwendolyn found herself pressed evenly against the damp wall, hands flat against cold, unyielding stone, with the roar of the ocean rising like a storm all around them. Prince Locrinus—Loc—placed one hand on either side of her head, right on the stone wall, and peered down at Gwendolyn with an odd glimmer in his eyes.

But then, he neither did nor said anything, and they stood together so long that icy water crept over Gwendolyn's heels.

At long last, he said, "I have delighted in every moment of this day, dearest." And he surprised Gwendolyn by bending to press his soft lips against her own, ever so gently, and the silky smoothness of his mouth gave her an unexpected shiver.

Gods.

She had never been with any man this way.

Gwendolyn swallowed convulsively, knowing that if he took liberties with her now, no one would fault him for it, not even her father, as there was little about their union that was negotiable, unless one meant to sacrifice the welfare of the kingdoms.

And still...

"I beg forgiveness, Princess, but you must realize... there are certain things I will not take for granted."

An easy smile played about his lips, and his eyes grew dark as smoked honey. Suddenly, Gwendolyn felt one hand alight upon her waist and her heart tripped painfully.

"I am told this is no place to linger," reverberated a voice throughout the cavern, the sound of it loud, commanding, and filled with censure.

Prince Loc spun about to face the intruder—Málik.

He was standing at the mouth of the cave, a dark silhouette against the bright afternoon sun, his silvery hair haloed, and his face cast in shadow.

Blood and bones!

Gwendolyn had never been so happy to see him—a truth that nettled her as much as did the fact that he had followed her here without permission.

Tidewater crept up to her ankles, lending truth to Málik's next words. "Not even kings may command oceans."

Instinct spoke, and Gwendolyn felt the sudden, undeniable urge to be away from this place. She slid beneath Prince Loc's arm, moving swiftly toward Málik. Only once she neared enough to see his face outside the glare of the sun, she met his eyes before sidling past and noted the disapproval in his gaze.

How dare he judge her!

How dare he spy on her!

How dare he—

And yet, right now she was also relieved he had disobeyed her orders—a fact that upset her all the more, because while she was indescribably relieved to see him, yesterday's unspoken accusations fell true to the mark. She should have thought better of this.

"Gwendolyn!" Prince Loc barked. Only now that she was away from him, she was furthermore embarrassed by her response. Her throat thick with emotion, she ran toward the rocky path, tripping over loose stones and bruising her knee, rushing up the incline, bewildered and ashamed, wholly uncertain how to face Loc again, or what she might say.

Even as she found her horse, and untethered her mare, even as she mounted and sped away from the Prince's Shadows, she feared he would blame her—or at the least, feel rejected.

That wasn't her intention at all.

Unfortunately, now that she had set upon this course, she couldn't stop.

Giving her mare a heel, wincing over the pain in her knee, she hurried toward the safety of the city gates, only vaguely aware that Prince Loc had rejoined his guards, and Málik was mounted as well, giving chase, even now closing the distance between them.

CHAPTER

TWELVE

G wendolyn returned from her outing alone, with Málik quick on her heels. Her hosen was ruined, torn at the knee, and even now she could feel a small bruise forming. Having abandoned her mare in the courtyard, she rushed into the palace without waiting to secure a groom for her mount. Flushed, with eyes burning, she ran through the corridors, avoiding everyone's gazes, seeking the sanctuary of her bower.

News traveled swiftly. Once in her bower, it wasn't long before Ely came bursting through her door, an unexpected but familiar sight that brought a fresh sting of tears to Gwendolyn's eyes. "What happened?" asked Ely, wide-eyed.

Gwendolyn might have cast herself into her friend's arms and spent her unshed tears, except that she knew intuitively that if Ely had heard, her mother and Demelza wouldn't be far behind. "I don't know," Gwendolyn confessed, shaking her head. "I-I... I don't know. We were in the cavern below the Dragon's Lair—"

"You and Prince Locrinus?"

"Yes," said Gwendolyn, her legs trembling, her hands as well. She sat on the bed, fearing she might swoon, her lips trembling as she spoke. As best she could, she explained what happened. Although truly, there wasn't much to say, and in hindsight, it seemed a very silly thing to do, to run from one's betrothed, for no good reason at all.

Gods, every time she envisioned Málik's face—his dark expression as she'd passed him by, she wanted to spew the meager victuals of the day. Setting a hand to her belly, she attempted to settle her nerves, relieved beyond measure to have Elowyn's counsel.

Quickly, she recounted the events of the entire day—everything, from her disappointment in Loc's response to her Dancing Stones, to the confusing incident beneath the Dragon's Lair. She spoke without taking a breath, afraid that her mother would intrude and the moment would be lost. Thankfully, all her good friend's quarrels seemed forgotten under the veil of her concern.

"He put a hand on your thigh?"

Gwendolyn nodded. "My waist. And then..."

"He said what?"

Gwendolyn tried to recall precisely what Loc had said, her cheeks burning hot. "He said, 'I beg forgiveness, Princess, but you must realize... there are certain things I will not take for granted.'"

Ely's brow furrowed. "What do you think he meant to do?"

Gwendolyn shrugged. "Perhaps nothing," she said.

And then, suddenly, a thought occurred to her, and she peered up, afraid the worst had come to pass. "Do you believe he heard about my swim with Bryn?"

"Anything is possible," said Ely, nipping at her lower lip, and Gwendolyn nodded.

Confused and embarrassed, her eyes brimmed anew, hot

tears spilling through her lashes. "I regret everything, Ely—everything!" Traitorous tears made tracks down her cheeks, and Ely came to her at once, embracing her and saying, "Hush, dear friend. Don't weep."

"I am not weeping," said Gwendolyn, pushing her gently away.

She'd promised herself many moons ago that she'd never shed another tear—not for her mother, not for her circumstances, not for any reason at all. She was a princess of Pretania! She would face many injustices and trials over the years to come, and she must not face them with tears.

"Of course you aren't," said Ely, gently. "You never weep."

"Nay! I do not," agreed Gwendolyn, even as tears salted her lips. She reached up to swipe the telltale moisture away, and said, "No more!"

Ely laughed softly, reaching out to brush still more tears from Gwendolyn's face. "Dry your eyes now," she said. "You are my Princess, and I love you dearly. And by the by, if you really must know, Bryn blames himself, not you. All is well, Gwendolyn."

"It wasn't his fault," argued Gwendolyn, still furious with herself. "He didn't even wish to go to the glen. I never once questioned how things might appear."

They weren't children any longer. To behave as carefree as children were wont to do was inexcusable. They couldn't continue rushing about the countryside, divesting themselves of clothing, pretending to conquer demons, or rushing about chasing *piskies*. It was long past time for Gwendolyn to consider all the consequences of her actions.

She peered up at her good friend and confessed, "I have taken too much for granted. I realize only now how little regard I've had for the consequences of my decisions."

Ely averted her gaze toward the high window, perhaps considering Bryn.

"I am sorry," Gwendolyn offered, with the deepest of sorrow.

"Fret not, Gwendolyn," said Ely, and Gwendolyn took her by the hand and pulled her down to sit beside her on the bed.

"I hope Bryn may someday forgive me," she said.

"Oh, Gwendolyn, I told you. He has," Ely reassured, and then she turned to meet Gwendolyn's gaze, peering straight into her eyes. "My brother is well, if only disheartened. He will grow accustomed to his new duties."

Gwendolyn gave a nod of acknowledgment, and Ely's voice turned up another notch with her curiosity. "Did he truly kiss you?"

"Indeed. Only a peck."

"On the lips?"

Gwendolyn nodded, and Ely said, "How romantic!"

But it didn't *feel* romantic.

Not in the least.

Once again, the thought of Málik Danann brought a rush of heat into Gwendolyn's cheeks. How long had he been standing there? How much had he heard and seen?

With some effort, she cast away the memory of his censure, and considered how she might endeavor to make amends to Prince Loc. Lamentably, there was no good reason for her childish behavior, and now she must endeavor to think of a good explanation in order to mitigate the damage she might have caused to their alliance.

Even now, was he telling his father?

And then, would they complain to hers?

Well, she would know soon enough, because doubtless that's what had waylaid her mother. They were all likely in

Konsel, discussing Gwendolyn's unruly behavior. At any moment, Queen Eseld would come marching into her room with all traces of the morning's joy vanished from her countenance.

"What will you do?" asked Ely.

"Whatever I must."

If she was asked to kiss his feet, for the sake of the realm, she would. Gwendolyn squeezed her friend's hand and said, "I beg you, allow me to make amends, Ely. I cannot do much for Bryn, but I know you really don't wish to dance. Allow me to take you with me to Loegria."

Ely's brows lifted, her eyes brightening, although her objection was incongruous. "We can't! Your mother—my mother!"

Gwendolyn smiled then. "That was *before*. Isn't it you who always endeavors to remind me there is a silver lining in every dark night?"

Elowyn shrugged, and Gwendolyn continued. "Bryn will no longer accompany me, and if you come with me as my maid —something I do not yet have for my own—you might live your life as you please, and perhaps even find a suitor amidst Prince Locrinus' men."

Gwendolyn could see the hope alight in her eyes. "Truly?"

Gwendolyn nodded. "Truly. And no matter how upset they might be, why should your parents forsake you? 'Tis no secret you do not wish to dance, and I am owed a lady's maid of my choosing, which, like my dowry chest, has as yet been denied me. So do not fret," said Gwendolyn. "I will see to it."

Ely smiled then and dared to ask, "How did it feel?"

"What?"

"Your first kiss!"

Gwendolyn sat back, her brow furrowing over the question. Because it should have been... titillating. And yet, all she could think of at the moment was that terrible look in Málik's eyes, and the horrible apprehension she'd felt down deep in her soul.

It was as though... she'd felt... trapped.

"Oh, Gwen! Was it truly so awful?" asked Ely, surprised. How long had they anticipated first kisses—how giddily had they spoken of them?

"No," said Gwendolyn "It... was... fine."

Ely blinked. "Fine?"

"Sweet," Gwendolyn corrected. "Gentle and sweet."

"Do you look forward to more?"

Gwendolyn furrowed her brow, considering her answer...

No.

She did not.

Though why didn't she wish to kiss Prince Loc? He was charming, intelligent, gently spoken, and learned, as well. Nothing about him should give anyone pause, except for that uncomfortable moment in the cave.

He was her betrothed. He was the most beautiful man she had ever met... and despite that, she dared to wonder if Málik's lips would be so cold.

CHAPTER

THIRTEEN

Much to Gwendolyn's surprise, neither her mother nor Demelza came to inquire about the mishap in the Dragon's Lair, and as best as Gwendolyn could determine, Prince Loc must have given her a reprieve. *Did he feel contrite for his part? Was he as embarrassed as she was?*

Whatever the case, she decided that when she next saw him, she would apologize profusely and accept all blame. Too much depended on this union to allow her emotions to rule her, and so, it seemed, she owed apologies to many.

All things in due time.

However, she determined to begin with Ely. And because there was still ample time before the Promise Ceremony, she sought an audience with her mother and father.

Discovering both in convivial moods, she broached the request with abandon, only in a roundabout way. "I do not wish to employ a Shadow," she said.

Seated upon his throne, with a dingy shaft of dust-mote-filled light spilling over his head, her father scowled. "You have no choice, Gwendolyn."

"Please, Father! I despise him. If you cannot condone Bryn's behavior, you mustn't condone his."

Her mother's lovely brows collided. "Málik's?" She sounded surprised.

"Indeed," said Gwendolyn.

Her mother's tone was gentler than Gwendolyn ever remembered. "Has he given you some insult?" *Nay.* He had not. So Gwendolyn measured her answer carefully, knowing that every word mattered. If she accused him unfairly, it could cost him his life.

"Nay," she said, honestly. "I merely dislike him. Nor do I trust him."

Her father sat forward in his chair, studying Gwendolyn's face as though it were his war table. "Odd, you never complained about your Shadow till we took your poppet away."

"Bryn is not my poppet. He's my friend."

Her father lifted one grey, frizzled brow. "With a twist of the hand, he dances as you please. I'd call that a poppet, Gwendolyn. Regardless, the answer is nay. As the future sovereign of Pretania, you must keep an able Shadow."

"Why? The Shadow you've given me is incapable of doing what he's told. Thanks to Bryn, I can defend myself. Instead, I'd prefer a lady's maid."

"You are my heir," he said, as though this explained everything.

"And you are a woman," added her mother. "I would not have it said I allowed my daughter's integrity to be compromised."

Gwendolyn flinched, wondering if someone had told her about the day's outing after all. Her cheeks burned hotter yet, and not entirely with anger. After all, she had no response to that, because what could she say? Remind her mother that a male Shadow, whoever he might be, could as easily taint her honor, even unintentionally?

Yesterday's ordeal at Porth Pool was proof of that.

"At least give me Ely," she entreated, which was her intent all along. Despite that everything she'd said about Málik was true, she had known her father would not give any measure where he was concerned. She was stuck with him... for now.

"Alas, Gwendolyn, we've discussed this," her mother protested. But before she could speak again, Gwendolyn rushed to say, "She could not serve me before because of Bryn. Please, Mother! I wouldst have at least one of my most trusted companions with me in a strange city."

"Oh, Gwendolyn," her mother said, but this time Gwendolyn sensed she might be wavering. "Elowyn is my most promising pupil."

As she rarely did, Gwendolyn met Queen Eseld's gaze directly. "I know, Mother. However, Ely doesn't wish to be your pupil."

Her mother's face twisted over the affront. "Why not?"

"Because she longs for a husband and children. She's not made for the *dawnsio*."

Silence met her declaration, and even as Gwendolyn waited for the verdict, the grey light outside brightened. Although it was impossible to glean what Queen Eseld was thinking, Gwendolyn sensed her capitulation even before she voiced it. No matter what Gwendolyn felt about Queen Eseld as a parent, she knew her mother was neither cruel nor unyielding when a valid argument was presented. At last, she sighed. "And... you propose to find her a suitable husband?"

"I would."

She tilted her head. "And... if we agree to this, you will content yourself with Málik? Your father is convinced he will be your salvation, and I will not have you disappoint him."

Her father said nothing. Nor did he nod, and Gwendolyn sensed he had retreated from this conversation, leaving her mother to do what she would.

"I will," she promised.

"You must receive instruction from him daily!" her father announced, his gaze refocusing, although he was immediately taken by a fit of coughing so dreadful that it turned Gwendolyn's attention from their negotiations.

Alas. The glen was hale, but her father was not.

His fits were getting worse and worse, and more and more, he was secluding himself in his apartments, with only her mother as his eyes and ears... and voice.

Gwendolyn wondered what would happen when she left, and for the first time, she worried she would go and never see him again. *Gods.* The last thing she wished to do was to fight with him now, and then leave, knowing their last days were embattled.

"This is ultimately why we have enlisted him," her father explained, when finally he could. "Gwendolyn... dearest... I wouldst know you leave us with the means and knowledge to defend, not merely yourself, but your kingdom as well."

"Father," she entreated. "Art worse?"

He coughed a bit more, then said, clearly irritated, "I would not have it said I left you ignorant and incapacitated."

Gwendolyn felt a sudden foreboding. "Leave me?"

"Hush, dear one," said her mother now, her voice kinder than Gwendolyn ever remembered. "Your father is well enough. He means only that you are his heir—his only heir. As such, you will someday be called upon to lead."

She sighed with portent, glancing briefly at King Corineus before continuing. "Nothing is certain, Daughter. There will be times you will have only yourself to look to, and he—we—wouldst be certain you have the finest of educations, and this includes your military tuition. I understand this now."

"But—"

"You may take Ely," her mother relented. "I shall gladly part with my best girl if you feel she will serve you better."

"I do," Gwendolyn said, careful not to frown, mostly because the negotiation had been too easy. It didn't even bother her at the moment that her mother had called Ely her best girl. Something was amiss, and she wanted to know what.

A single glance about the hall revealed servants scurrying about, preparing for tonight's ceremony, though it wouldn't precisely be held here. In keeping with tradition, the Promise Ceremony would be performed, not within the great hall, nor beneath the Sacred Yew, where her wedding would be held, but in the courtyard, at twilight, where the villagers could amass before the dais to witness the exchange of torcs.

Later, after the ceremony was done, Gwendolyn would be whisked away, out of the Prince's sight, with no intention of seeing him again, until the day they took their vows.

The Prince, however, would remain with his father and everyone else to celebrate whilst Gwendolyn was escorted to the yew to pray.

The revelry would resume here, in the great hall, with everyone but Gwendolyn in attendance. Even now, the trestle tables were being returned to their dining positions, and soon the entire room would cease to look like an audience hall for the King.

Of course, Gwendolyn was pleased their negotiations had turned out to such great advantage, and that her mother was being so cordial, but the address now left her feeling... unsettled. Although mayhap it was only the stress of the events to come. After all, after this evening, she would no longer be free to love as she pleased, but a bride bound to a Prince she really didn't know. "Thank you," she said finally, discomposed by the thought.

Once more, her father gave in to a vigorous bout of hacking, and then cleared his throat and tilted Gwendolyn a watery glance. The red veins in his eyes were angry and swollen.

"Never fear, my daughter. I am well," he reassured. "I simply find myself... weary. I warrant after the evening's ceremony, and once I retire, I shall sleep well enough and alight from my bed with a spring to my step you haven't seen since you were a wee child."

He gave her a wan smile, and Gwendolyn longed desperately to believe it. After all, the glen was still without blight. And this must truly mean her father was getting better.

Mustn't it?

She wanted to tell him what she'd found, but held her tongue, only because she didn't wish to remind him of yesterday's trouble with Bryn—not now.

Wanting so desperately to embrace him and knowing it wasn't seemly, Gwendolyn knelt at his feet and offered him a heartfelt vow. "I swear it, Father, I will practice daily. I will not leave Trevena without acquiring all the knowledge you deem necessary, and I will..." She couldn't lie and claim she would enjoy sparring with Málik. "I will respect my tutor."

Her mother arched a perfect dark brow. "See that you do," she said firmly, though without ire. "His tutelage comes at a high price, and though we hoped it might be easier for you to have Bryn learn from him and teach you, this is no longer reasonable. You must do as he bids."

Once again, Gwendolyn met her mother's gaze. Queen Eseld was smiling, but sadly. "I will," Gwendolyn said, all the fight having left her. "I swear it."

Queen Eseld gave her a nod and said, "Go now. Prepare

yourself for the ceremony, as I have sent Demelza with a gift for you, and 'tis likely it has been delivered."

Gwendolyn straightened. "A gift?" she asked, surprised. "For me?"

"Indeed," said her mother, her lovely lips lifting only slightly at one side. "'Tis long overdue."

"Yes, Mother."

Eager to see what gift her mother had sent, Gwendolyn rose from her knees, her spirits now lifted so that she barely noticed the bruise on her knee, eased by her mother's agreement. Whatever else her mother had sent, the Queen's capitulation was most welcome.

Exhilarated by the news that she would allow Ely to join her in Loegria, she gave each of her parents a bow and then rushed into the corridor to search for Ely, keen to share the news.

CHAPTER

FOURTEEN

Before Gwendolyn stood an intricately carved coffer, bearing many of the same odd symbols she now wore on her Prydein gown.

Was this, too, her mother's?

Their faces bright with joy for Gwendolyn's sake, both Demelza and Ely stood aside as Gwendolyn approached the coffer with ill-concealed awe.

Like the gown she wore, the coffer didn't appear to be new, but neither did it appear to be any worse for its wear. To the contrary. It was well cared for and smelled of lemon oil. The paint on the etchings was vivid and fresh—perhaps even retouched for this presentation.

It was the finest gift her mother could have given her, with a bit of herself in the bestowal. It was as though she had known how much Gwendolyn longed to know about her mother's kindred. And now, this was a connection to her grandparents she'd never dared yearn for—a glimpse into their life through the gifts she'd been given.

Gwendolyn fell to her knees beside the chest, uncertain

whether she dared to touch the beautiful, finely etched wood. Gingerly now, she put a finger to the figure of a fox, imagining the careful hand that had carved it. The pigment here was bright red, and she wondered if the paint was derived from bedstraw root, because of its shade—more orange than red.

Across the entire lid, there were tiny gems carved into the woodwork and all the fish had sapphires embedded into their eyes. The scales were brushed with gold.

"There were several gowns that wouldn't fit within," explained Demelza. "Along with your betrothal vestige, they are here upon the bed."

Gwendolyn turned to peer at Demelza, finding her patting the bed, and there saw another veritable mountain of dresses. Only this time there were none Gwendolyn recognized. Instead of her mother's usual castaways, they appeared to be new and quite extravagant, judging by the opulent materials—although really, her mother's leavings were far from meager.

Demelza was beaming. "Your mother hoped the wait would be worthwhile. She sent the coffer to Caledonia to be restored by the same artist who painted it for your grandmother and your mother as well."

Had her grandmother had a hand in its restoration? Had it once been filled with her dowry gifts? Gwendolyn inhaled sharply, wishing with all her might that the woman who'd given birth to her mother could be here now to watch her open this chest.

Mayhap all she'd postulated was wrong?

Mayhap her grandmother had loved her daughter—as her own mother loved her, as well? Her heart sang with delight. "'Tis... beautiful," she said. "So beautiful!"

"Only wait till you open it, child. Inside, you'll discover great wonders. Robes from Carthage and Phoenicia, ribbons from Megara, and some fashioned of Imperial silk."

By the eyes of Lugh!

Gwendolyn had yet to process the chest itself, much less what lay within. It was the loveliest thing she had seen in all her life.

"You'll also find chemises fashioned of dimity—no *broella* for you, my dear!"

A soft gasp escaped her. *Broella* was a thick woolen cloth of a dark red shade, worn by the *Gwiddons*. She had never worn that coarse fabric, but she knew many who did, including the aldermen. Blinking in wonder, she marveled that, so well visited as they were, she had never heard of so many of these places, nor of Imperial or dimity, either.

Inconceivably, Demelza continued.

"There's a bit of *baldekin, byssine, cendal, cameline,* and cloth of gold so you can fashion your own gowns in your own style."

She took a breath before adding, "By the by, your wedding attire was commissioned by a seamstress in Troy, in hopes that King Brutus will appreciate the effort. But though your Princeling may not recognize the gesture, perhaps his father will tell him."

Certainly, if King Brutus did not, Gwendolyn would be sure to do so.

So much thought had been put into this dowry gift. More than aught, she longed for Prince Loc to know how much her parents valued this union—how much everyone valued it. Gwendolyn no less than anyone else—and she *must*, for it was vital she do so.

Love where you must.

Love where you must.

Love where you must.

From the night she was brought into this world, her future was writ in stone, with blood. She was the *golden child* of prophecy, the hope and future of Pretania. She was the one who must deliver her kindred to a brighter future, free from disease and discord.

Indeed, her marriage to Prince Loc wasn't only the means to secure Pretania's survival, it was also the key to restoring her father's good health, for only by restoring the *ysbryd y byd* for her people could the land itself be restored.

Alas, if her father wasn't healed, it boded ill for Cornwall, and for Gwendolyn as well, for she was her father's heir. If she failed him and ascended to his throne without curing the country's ills, she would fall prey to the same wasting disease as that which now threatened her father and King.

This was her dowry chest.

This was her fate, now sealed.

This should be her joy and hope as well.

And it was.

Truly.

She was only sorry she had been such a fool this afternoon, flying away from her Prince as though she believed he could do her harm. He would never, for he too held a stake in this marriage, and without Gwendolyn, he would have no right to rule. His blood was not the blood of the conservators; he needed her as much as she needed him.

"How envious I am!" squealed Ely with a clap of her hands. But Gwendolyn could say little intelligent in response. Her stomach was clenched tight.

She glanced about once more, taking in the bed that was overburdened with gifts. During the short time since she'd left her bedchamber this morn, her room had been filled with dresses, jewels, tiaras, ribbons, flowers, and every sort of gift a young lady could imagine—most of which could never have fit inside the modest-sized chest.

"You missed the procession," said Ely, her voice shrill with excitement. "They came when you left, and one by one, carted in one heft after another. After they were gone, I wept with joy to see so many lovely gifts you've been given." Her friend sighed dreamily. "I went to look for you only to tell you, and —" She clapped her hands again, delighted. "Mayhap, some-day, I too will now have my own dowry chest, thanks to you!"

A slow grin unfurled as Gwendolyn took in Ely's joy. After all, *that* was the most wondrous gift of all the gifts her mother had given her today—the chance to take Ely with her when she left and the opportunity to make Ely's dreams come true. That gift was far, far above the rest, although in its entirety, this was a bounty unlike any that Gwendolyn had ever known.

Like last night's feast, no expense had been spared.

"I cannot believe my mother sent me all this," Gwendolyn said, still kneeling by the chest, the bruise on her knee hardly noticeable. Good thing she would have time to heal, so she wouldn't arrive at her marriage bed looking bruised and abused.

Again she fingered the artwork gently, afraid to damage it even with the lightest touch. It was Demelza's voice that broke the woven spell. "And who else would give you so much?"

Who else, indeed?

And regardless, it was such a great gesture that, after all the torment she'd endured in her life, Gwendolyn still couldn't believe it was her mother who'd proffered so much—all for her, and all of it finer than anything Queen Eseld kept for herself.

Gathering her nerve and sucking in a breath, weak and trembling with anticipation, Gwendolyn dared to lift the lid, and there... inside... found...

More Prydein gowns, all made from similar materials as the gown she now wore. Even those fashioned of fine wool bore many of the same symbols that, as yet Gwendolyn had no clue about. She lifted a small pair of earrings, shaped like bees.

"Minoan," said Demelza, and Gwendolyn laid them back down.

She also discovered a silver armband, finely hewn and in the shape of a fish.

Also, an intricately carved forehead crown, covered with rainbow moonstones—three of which were made to drip like tears between her brows.

"It will be some time before you can wear that one," explained Demelza, as Gwendolyn lifted the crown to better inspect it. "This is the tiara you will wear on your bride's day, and a glorious day it will be!"

Gwendolyn's heart tripped painfully. Her bride's day... arriving so soon.

"Your gown will be Trojan, your torc, Dumnonii, your crown, Prydein," Demelza was saying with a smile in her voice. "A symbol of all you embody!"

Gwendolyn swallowed the hefty lump that rose to choke her.

There was so much here... so much... and it was all so... well, incredible. But, by far—even more beautiful than the gift of Ely—the greatest gift of all was her mother's support, which seemed undeniable by these grandiose gifts.

Without question, these were not the sort of bestowals a mother who loathed her daughter would tender. Rather, they were gifts for a beloved child.

The riches could easily be explained away, for any queen would wish her daughter to reflect well upon her house, but not these Prydein offerings. They were far more personal, and Gwendolyn would have supposed they would embarrass her mother more than they pleased her. But nay...

Gwendolyn swallowed with difficulty.

Everything she'd ever come to believe about her mother now seemed... *wrong.*

Moreover, she couldn't help but remember the gleam in the Queen's eyes as she'd bade Gwendolyn to hie away to see her surprise.

Joy? Pride? Love?

And yet Gwendolyn was bemused, because after all she had endured by her mother's hand—all the censure, all the frustrations and doubts, all the neglect and disregard, all the times she'd longed for merely an afternoon with her mother—was this now Gwendolyn's reward only for pleasing a prince?

Was this all it took to appease her mother?

Or could it be she had misjudged Queen Eseld?

Alas, she had only a month to find out. After Gwendolyn was gone, all time for casual visitation would be done, and when she returned here again, to this house she'd been raised in, she would return as the heir, with a husband by her side, and far more on her mind than simply getting to know an errant mother.

At the moment, Gwendolyn's room looked like a king's vault—not that she'd ever actually seen the King's vault. It was kept too well-guarded by men whose oath it was to die for its defense, and who were no more allowed to enter than they could allow anyone else to see what lay within. So far as Gwendolyn knew, not even her mother knew what lay guarded so jealously, and the only man who'd ever defied the King's law was a guard who'd lost his eyes, and his tongue as well. Even her father rarely visited his vault, and the only reason she knew anything of its contents was because she was recently privy to a Konsel meeting, wherein the aldermen had lamented the dwindling of gold in their vaults. Gwendolyn herself would only ever be allowed to enter after she ascended to the throne.

Behind her, Ely laughed exuberantly, and still curious to see what more she could find, Gwendolyn rifled through the trunk, lifting a bit of leather, and discovered...

A silver hairpin with the knob in the shape of a fish. It, too, had eyes made of sapphires.

A lunate-shaped pendant, without gems, though it had small *piscium* etched into the metal.

Last, there was a large but intricate brooch that looked like a wide-mouthed fish with an arrow through its gob.

Interestingly, unlike many of the fineries she'd been given today, none of these gifts in the coffer were new. In fact, like the chest in which they were delivered, they appeared rather ancient, judging by the patina on the metals.

"Your grandmother gifted those to me," said her mother, appearing at her threshold. "And her mother to her, on her bride's day."

Gwendolyn turned with hot tears brimming in her eyes and longed so desperately to rush into her mother's arms. But despite that, Queen Eseld's eyes appeared moist, her arms remained crossed, and Gwendolyn knew embraces would not be welcomed. And yet this was the one thing she had longed for more than anything else in the world—a simple, heartfelt hug from the woman who had given her life.

Alas.

"I do not know how many generations have worn those jewels, but I know they have been in my family's keeping for more than five score years."

"So long!" squealed Ely.

Her mother nodded. "Indeed."

"Thank you," said Gwendolyn, and she choked back another surge of emotion. "Thank you... Mother."

A genuine smile unfurled over Queen Eseld's beauteous face, and she cast her arms down at her sides as she swept into the room, like a maelstrom, passing by Gwendolyn where she knelt and marching straight toward the bed, stirring even the spirits in the room.

The scent of lavender swirled around Gwendolyn, then eddied away. "Come, Daughter," she demanded. "Let us dress you now—no, no, no, not with that," she said, pointing to the lunate pendant that had found its way into Gwendolyn's hand. "I'll not have it said we dressed you so plainly tonight. You are promised to a prince, and you shall face him as befits his queen. However, you may bring that hairpin instead. We will use it to secure a crown of braids."

Gods only knew, there was nothing about anything Gwendolyn had been gifted today that was even remotely plain, but Gwendolyn didn't argue. Swept up in her mother's enthusiasm, she put aside her silly regrets, and rose to join Queen Eseld by the bedside.

Thereafter, as Ely oohed and *aahed* over the shining baubles and all the luscious fabrics, her mother chose the prettiest gown of all—a pearlescent creation that was iridescent in its beauty. The sleeveless overcoat was fashioned of some never-before-seen material that reminded Gwendolyn of the underside of an oyster shell. Apparently, this should be worn over an equally lustrous shell-colored undergown, with wide, diaphanous sleeves, so delicate that it billowed about even without a breeze, only with the hustle and bustle of the occupants in her bower.

If only by sheer will, and by the beauty of the treasures she would wear and the heartfelt efforts of her mother, Demelza and Ely, Gwendolyn would surely arrive at her Promise Ceremony in a fashion to turn heads and hearts.

All together, they gushed over Gwendolyn—Ely scrubbing at her body and face until it stung, then choosing Imperial ribbons for her braids; Demelza brushing her hair until it shone and then plaiting it tightly as Ely handed her the ribbons.

Meanwhile, her mother helped to dress her, moving her

hands this way and that, as though she were a poppet, and finally, taking care not to spill any of the substance on Gwendolyn's new dress, she lined Gwendolyn's eyes with a paint made from ground galena.

When all was done, Queen Eseld brushed more paint on her, this one a shimmering green, like the color of a warm, but shallow sea. This was made from malachite. And placing it over Gwendolyn's eyelids, she sprinkled it across her lashes, and then, for good measure, a little dusting on her upper cheeks and lips, so that Gwendolyn feared her skin had turned green, like that of a selkie's.

Queen Eseld had a steady hand, perfectly skilled for having practiced on the ladies of her *dawnsio*. But for an instant, the powder made Gwendolyn's lashes stick together, and though some grains slipped into her eyes, her mother patted her hand when she made to rub it away.

"You'll smear the kohl," she rebuked, though not unkindly. "Give it a moment. The irritation will subside."

Eager to please, Gwendolyn obeyed, thinking that by the time her mother was through with her, she would look like a gleaming gem. It was hardly her usual attire.

However, Queen Eseld could have dressed her in a meal sack, and Gwendolyn would have beamed with joy, merely to have her mother's regard.

From what she'd been told, the Prydein wore paint, as well, mostly woad. Though it was not of this ilk, nor was it worn in the same way, to adorn. Rather, this was a style of paint her mother had adopted after meeting the wife of a Phoenician merchant—only the black paint about her eyes, perhaps reluctant to be seen as emulating the woad of her people.

The people of Trevena were hardworking, honorable folks, who scarcely had time for such adornment. However, as their princess, on the eve of her betrothal, Gwendolyn would be expected to outshine them all—and so she would... so she did.

When her mother's work was complete, Gwendolyn scarcely recognized herself. She was iridescent and beautiful. Her face was flawlessly painted. Her dress was perfectly fitted, but loose about her hips, so no one could tell they were a little wider than her mother's.

"Perfect!" said her mother, still brandishing the kohl brush in her hand.

"Oh, Gwen!" said Ely, clapping her hands with tears shining in her eyes. "You are like a magnificent jewel!"

"Precious!" said Demelza, and Queen Eseld agreed with an earnest nod and a soft smile that betrayed her pride.

FIFTEEN

Despite that Gwendolyn was formerly betrothed to Prince Urien, she had not been required to exchange torcs with him. Being so young when they'd first met, she'd been spared the prefatory, mostly because free will was a gods-given gift she had been too young to comprehend. Now, because she was seventeen and no one could drag her screaming to the yew, the exchange of promissory torcs served, not merely as an affirmation of her willingness to marry, but as a pledge between Gwendolyn and Prince Loc to remain chaste till their nuptials were honored. Her people bore witness to assist them in keeping these vows.

To break them would be a sin against Cornwall.

As it must be with her nuptials, the Promise Ceremony was held during the Between Times, when the gods might traverse the Veil to bless their union. Their approach was felt like a vibrancy in the air, and even the lowering sun shivered with anticipation.

Something like excitement welled in Gwendolyn's breast, although truth be told, the sensation wasn't entirely pleasant.

A rumble of drums began the ceremony, and the harp joined as Gwendolyn ascended the dais where the *Awenydd* stood waiting beside Prince Loc—today a witness, no more, though on the day of her nuptials, the *Gwiddon* and druid would arrive, as well.

Resplendent as always, Prince Loc's smile encouraged her. And if he nurtured any animosity for her treatment of him this afternoon, it wasn't apparent in his expression. With the torc in his hand, he stood proudly, watching Gwendolyn with that same look he'd given her in the Dragon's Lair...

Yearning? Satisfaction? Possession?

It didn't matter.

She was bound to this now, and if she said nay, it would break her father's heart—her mother's as well.

Acceptance with grace and faith.

Decide you will love him, and eventually you shall.

I will, she vowed. *I will.*

Even so, her legs felt like mushed meal as she made her way toward her betrothed.

The torc of her house was as ancient as the *Sidhe* hills. Symbolic was its passing from her father to her, although he handed it to Gwendolyn without ceremony as she walked by— father to daughter, king to heir. He held it aloft on a small crimson tuft, willingly given, willfully taken.

Her father and mother now wore replicants.

Made of old, braided bronze, the torc came together about the neck with two dragon heads that met snout to snout. And within each of the dragons' eyes lay perfectly polished pearls, four altogether, two in each head. This she would give to Prince Loc, to be held in safekeeping until they met again beneath the yew to become man and wife.

This was her promissory note, and he would give one as well.

She was careful to be certain that the heavy chain came to her untangled, letting it pool into her palm, some part of her thrilled over the adventure to come, even though she was anxious. And yet, it wasn't Gwendolyn's way to face the unknown with any measure of subservience, so she hitched her chin and returned the Prince's smile, holding his gaze until the music stopped. Only then her eyes were drawn to the torc in his hand.

The hue of its metal warmed with the golden hour—fresh from the forge and fashioned of the same alloy for which the recipe was so jealously guarded. And, *gods*, she thought she would swoon. The eyes of his serpents were bright blue sapphires, each of them glinting meanly at her, and she found herself reluctant to take the necklace. Gwendolyn swallowed, staring at the serpents, not daring to meet the Prince's gaze, not yet.

Neither of them could properly wear the torcs until after their nuptials, but the instant Gwendolyn accepted it, she would be honor-bound to carry it about her neck, until they could return them and place them irrevocably about each other's throats—like a noose, she thought morbidly, and then scolded herself for the impulse. Secured on long, heavy chains, they were worn in a fashion that was visible to all, a symbol that their virtues were heretofore spoken for, and no one should put them asunder.

Taking the torc was the right thing to do.

Her father depended upon her.

The people did as well.

And... *Prince Loc?*

What did he want?

Whatever nerves Gwendolyn suffered, there was none apparent in the worry-free countenance she faced across the dais, and this gave her the resolve to move.

Knees trembling, she paused beside the *Awenydd* to wait yet again, all eyes in the courtyard affixed upon her. Gwendolyn willed her feet to stay. Now was not the time to repeat her afternoon flight, no matter that she felt an overwhelming desire to flee.

Silence fell as twilight settled, and no man dared disturb it.

The only sound to reach Gwendolyn's ears was the sound of the Prince's footfalls as he closed the distance between them, and the heavy golden chain shivered in her palm.

The *Awenydd* prayed, and then, before all who were present, the Prince knelt before Gwendolyn, bowing his head to receive the chain with her torc.

Only for a terrible moment, Gwendolyn couldn't move. She daren't look at her father, nor at her mother—nor at the *Awenydd*, for they so oft could read what lay hidden in a heart.

Swallowing convulsively, Gwendolyn peered about, searching for Bryn and reassurance. She found him regarding her with a genuine smile, albeit sadly.

And regardless, he gave her a nod, and Gwendolyn peered down at the torc in her hand, and then to Prince Loc's bowed head, compelling herself to bestow it, until finally she did.

Dutifully, she placed the chain about his head, and then said with a quivering voice, "As you are to me, I am to you, promised and faithful till my end of days."

Prince Loc smiled up at her then, and stood, and Gwendolyn did not need to kneel in order for him to place the heavy chain about her neck. She did so anyway, as a show of respect, and he reached over to settle his burden atop her shoulders. "As you are to me," he repeated, "I am to you, promised and faithful until my end of days."

Gwendolyn swallowed again, her mouth gone dry, and then stood, blinking like a hapless creature, until Prince Loc's smile deepened.

Behind him, grinning with unreserved approval, stood his sire—as her own parents must be as well. But of course, it was done. Come Calan Mai, they would declare themselves man and wife, and receive their blessings from the mester druid on behalf of the gods.

Why then did she feel so horrible?

Oblivious to her turmoil, the people all cheered.

Wine was drunk—a gesture of acceptance for the promises made. A single goblet was brought forth for Prince Loc and Gwendolyn to share, offered first to the bride-to-be.

Gwendolyn took her sip, then gave it up to Prince Loc, and immediately thereafter, she was veiled, and the Promise Ceremony was over—or at least, her part.

Accompanied only by the *Awenydd,* to guide her in prayer, and Málik, to shadow her, Gwendolyn was whisked away to the Sacred Yew to pray. On her knees. In the coolness of gathering shadows. To contemplate the gravity of the promises made.

Forever renewing themselves, and resurrecting, the yews formed massive trunks. This one was ancient, with an enormous hollow in its base.

Guardians of the Underworld, death and the afterlife, their drooping branches would root themselves and form new and twisting trunks wherever they touched the ground.

According to the Gwyddons, yews were immortal, and yet this distinction had so oft fascinated Gwendolyn, considering that nothing ever grew beneath its dense canopy because of the carpet of poisonous spines and the dark shadow it cast over the land.

Beneath the tree, she fell to her knees, placing a palm against the aged wood, the very palm that had held her chain, begging for strength... and forgiveness because her heart was a traitorous fool. "Goddess, please," she began, and stopped, sensing the presence behind her.

Please, what?

Alas, though she knew the answer to this question, she daren't speak it aloud.

The weight of her necklace seemed to tug on her heart—a dreadful heaviness accompanied by a shadow that settled into her bones with the lowering night.

Peering up at the *Awenydd* who'd accompanied her for this occasion, she tried not to consider the Shadow who'd deposed her dearest friend.

"Do you feel different?" asked Ely.

Gwendolyn weighed the question carefully, because truly, although she didn't feel changed, she also didn't feel the same as she did before, though it wasn't merely because of the heavy chain she now wore about her neck.

Somehow, in the bright light of day, it seemed heavier than before.

"Nay," she said, "not truly."

It wasn't a lie, not precisely. She simply didn't know how to explain this restless feeling that had been plaguing her since donning the torc and chain. Even with the Prince's absence, he would remain with her always, morning, noon, and night, only because of the torc.

In truth, she now looked forward to her instruction with Málik, because that was the only time the removal of the chain was allowed.

Last night there had been quite the celebration, or so she'd been told. Everyone, including Demelza, had remained to toast the occasion until well into the small hours.

Ely didn't even arrive at her bower until well after sunup, and she'd barely caught Gwendolyn as Gwendolyn rushed out the door to catch the Loegrian party's departure. This wasn't Ely's way, but she must have been celebrating her own future as well now that she was officially Gwendolyn's maid.

By now, the Prince was long gone.

For at least a full bell now, their silhouettes had vanished from the horizon, and despite that, she and Ely stood, peering down at the littered courtyard. Never once did Prince Loc look back, nor did he seek her on the balustrade.

But of course, why should he? she reasoned. He knew, as everyone knew, that she was not supposed to see him again, nor should he dare to gaze upon her. It was bad luck to do so before her bride's day. But Gwendolyn hadn't cared. She'd needed to see what she would feel as she watched him leave... *nothing.*

But not nothing, precisely.

More like... *relief.*

Why?

Unwittingly, her gaze was drawn toward the Mester's Pavilion, where Málik now practiced with Bryn. At least that much was unchanged.

"I hope one day, I, too, will be wed, Gwendolyn."

"You will," Gwendolyn promised, reaching for Ely's hand and cradling it. "I shall see to it, my dear, sweet friend. I swear it." She gave Ely's hand a good squeeze.

Admiration shone in Elowyn's eyes. "I am so grateful you spoke to your mother on my behalf," she said. "I cannot believe she has released me."

Gwendolyn offered a smile and jested as a matter of habit. "I suppose she must be sure someone will be around to see to *her* interests."

Silence met her declaration. And only after she'd said it did Gwendolyn realize how it must have sounded to Ely, as though she didn't trust her.

"I am loyal to *you*," said Ely after a moment.

"I know," said Gwendolyn, quite certain that Ely would never knowingly betray her confidence, and her mother must know it as well.

"Alas, I supposed in part it could be true," allowed Ely, reconsidering. "Now that Bryn is no longer to accompany you, I can imagine she feels better knowing I will be there instead. But you have always thought your mother to be so ill-natured, and I have never seen her this way, Gwendolyn. Neither does my mother, and my mother's intuition is good. Queen Eseld loves you truly."

Gwendolyn thought about the dowry chest, filled with so many thoughtful gifts—gifts that were not only beautiful, but representative of all the things her mother must hold dear to her heart. All these years she had believed her mother was embarrassed by her Prydein blood, but the opposite must be true. *Clearly.* She had saved everything she'd arrived with, perfectly cared for, and she'd saved it for Gwendolyn. So, was it that she didn't feel brave enough to set herself apart from others? Did she sense Gwendolyn was brave enough to do so? That she would wear her Prydein heirlooms with pride?

Gods. All these years... There was never anything about Queen Eseld that had seemed weak or unworthy. She carried herself like a queen of *all* tribes, although mayhap, deep down, she was still a frightened little Prydein girl, who didn't feel as though she belonged.

Considering that, Gwendolyn stared ahead at the open gates—gates that remained open by day, for it was her father's practice to keep an open door to all people and their grievances. Now that he was ambassador to all, this included people of *all* tribes, although they saw few emissaries from Prydein. And despite this, there was peace. The Prydein were far more respectful these days, although Aldermans Crwys and Aelwin were also right: No matter that everything seemed harmonious at the moment, they would be fools to forget that King Brutus was, in so many respects, an opportunist—someone who had already amassed a powerful army, and who had, for all intents and purposes, lifted himself above even Gwendolyn's father. Gwendolyn hadn't wished to acknowledge this, but she could see it in Brutus' demeanor, and that of his son's as well.

Moreover, Prince Loc's disclosure about Plowonida settled poorly with Gwendolyn, and although she'd yet to tell anyone about it, there was something about Brutus' foray so deep into Pretania that gave her pause.

Now, if King Brutus should smell weakness, would he renege upon his promises? Should Cornwall and Loegria find themselves at war, the rest of the tribes would quickly forswear the alliance, and the land again would bleed.

There was so much Gwendolyn daren't voice—not to Ely, nor to Bryn, not yet. And yet, though the Bearer of Tidings rang bells, crying "All's well!", all didn't *feel* so well.

Something was troubling Gwendolyn, though she couldn't put a finger to it yet.

Something.

All at once, from one of the distant smelting houses, came a shout, catching Gwendolyn's attention. Together, she and Ely rushed forward to the balustrade rails to watch a lone man stumbling toward the palace. Behind him came more men carrying what appeared to be a rolled tarp. "What do you suppose this is about?" asked Ely.

Gwendolyn knit her brows. "I don't know," she said, her hand reaching for the heavy chain about her neck.

Caterwauling now, tripping over his own two feet, the first man rushed into the palace through the doors directly below, and Gwendolyn said, "Let's go find out."

CHAPTER
SIXTEEN

The First Alderman's body had been discovered behind the smelting house.

Gwendolyn stood quietly aside the dais, listening to the account as it was described to her father, and even as she listened, three men unrolled a heavy tarpaulin before the dais, revealing the mauled body of what was supposed to be First Alderman Bryok.

The man was scarcely recognizable. And Gwendolyn should have recognized him. Only two mornings ago he had been alive and well, speaking at her father's Konsel.

She grimaced. Apparently, during last night's ceremony, the First Alderman had taken a blow to the head, substantial enough that he'd never recovered his senses. But then, perhaps because the gates were left wide open to allow celebrants to come and go as they pleased, wolves somehow discovered and mutilated his body.

But wolves? Really?

As to the weapon of his demise, a blood-stained forger's hammer was found not more than an arm's length from the body. The assailant hadn't even concerned himself with the hiding of evidence, which Alderman Aelwin was quick to point out as he held the hammer aloft, bespoke the blacksmith's innocence. Clearly, no man guilty of such a crime would ever leave his own tool, marked with his name, covered in blood, to be discovered so readily.

Anyway, the blacksmith and the First Alderman were not known to be acquainted. Or, at least, they were not connected in any way that seemed notable. Both ran in different circles— Bryok with his colleagues, and the blacksmith with his own kind, two different classes of men who rarely broke bread together, except during a celebration such as the one that was held last night. "The armorer's hut is never locked. Perhaps the assailant only availed himself of what was near," suggested Alderman Aelwin.

It was difficult to say much else about the man's death, considering the state of his body. And, regardless, the physician tried.

Judging by the stiffness of his remains, Mester Ciarán said he believed Bryok encountered his assailant before the Promise Ceremony, or perhaps during, whilst everyone else was otherwise occupied. With a cloth wrapped about his hand, to protect himself from the ill humors that manifested after death, he bent to test the dead man's arm, then the leg, if only to demonstrate his point. "Typically, this rigidity would appear between two and four bells after his death." He released the Alderman's leg, letting it drop with an awkward thud. "Once it appears, a man's body can remain this way for hours, else days. I am afraid there can be no way to note when he died. You would do well to inquire with those who saw him last."

"I spoke with him yesterday morn," said her father's steward.

Alderman Aelwin lifted a wiry brow. "Where?" he asked with interest.

Yestin rubbed hard at his bearded chin. "Here, in the hall, I suppose, whilst I was deciphering my ledgers. He begged permission to employ the kitchen, but I refused."

Alderman Aelwin placed the hand with the hammer behind his back. "And why, I wonder?"

Yestin appeared confused. "Why did I tell him nay? Or why did he wish to employ my kitchen?"

"The latter, of course," said Aelwin, waving his free hand as though to dismiss the question. "Naturally, everyone understands well enough why you wouldst say nay."

"Ah, yes. Well, so he claimed, he wished for Alyss to brew a medicinal."

Mester Ciarán tugged thoughtfully at his beard. "Oh? Was the First Alderman ill? I cannot recall he ever requested anything of me."

"Not that I know," said Yestin. "He seemed hale enough to me."

The physician lifted a finger, as though only just recalling something. "But yes, well, I do recall him asking some moons ago whether I believed hemlock could have a use for mania. However, this was put to me as though he were inquiring for another."

The King glowered. "What other?"

Mester Ciarán shrugged. "I'm afraid he did not say who, Majesty."

Certainly her father would wonder, as Gwendolyn did, what business any man had to inquire about hemlock. It was a deadly poison, and unless it was used precisely by someone who knew every aspect of the plant and its use, it could do more harm than good.

Alyss was trained in simples, but to ask such a thing of her during such an eventful time, whilst the cook's house was otherwise occupied, was unthinkable. Whatever pots she might use for the brew would be laced with poison and thereafter would need to be thoroughly scrubbed. It was a lot of work to be done when no time or hands could be spared. Even Gwendolyn's normal dosing had been temporarily discontinued.

Certainly, she wasn't an alchemist, but she knew enough to know what herbs to mix for what and where. As it was with a tincture of yew, there was little to be accomplished by its application, except death. Gwendolyn knew more than she liked to know about such things, because she'd been ingesting a special concoction of poisons in minute doses since she was only a child, a measure against treason, since poison all too often was a traitor's weapon of choice. In fact, so did the rest of the royal family, including her mother, and this was why their cook's house was sometimes employed to make such brews.

However, whenever this was done, it was done under the strictest of supervision, by men who would die to defend them, and well they could if they ever turned a blind eye to a turn of the hand, because it was also those same guards who would be the tasters.

As it was, now that Gwendolyn was older and drinking the same brew her parents consumed, even the smallest dose to one who did not possess their resilience was lethal. Therefore, she hadn't any clue why Bryok would have any interest in hemlock.

And neither was his wife manic.

"Well?" asked the King, his voice rising with interest. "Is there?"

"An application for mania?" The physician lifted a shoulder. "Betimes," he said. "Betimes. With great care, as you must imagine. For any such medicinals, these plants must be harvested quite late. And yet, come to think of it, if he ingested hemlock, this might account for his inability to respond to..." He gestured roundly at the mutilated body. "This... hideousness."

"Are you saying he could have been alive?"

The physician nodded gravely. "'Tis possible," he said, and everyone's faces twisted grotesquely, as they no doubt imagined such a horror.

"And yet, the lack of blood makes me feel he must have already been dead long hours before the wolves discovered him. Perhaps the dose was intentional?"

It was true. There wasn't much blood, at least not on the tarpaulin, even though his wounds were gaping. The thought of this man lying insensate through such a mauling was horrific.

"Intentional?" Her father lifted both brows. He waved a hand at Alderman Aelwin, at the blood-stained weapon he was still holding. "I don't understand. If the hammer did not kill him, why is it stained with his blood? Indeed, why should anyone bother to beat a man if he's already dead?"

Once again, the physician tugged at his beard. "Majesty, 'tis impossible to say who, or what, killed this man. There is no device known to us, aside from a scrying stone, that can accurately reveal such things, and we have not known a good seer in an age.

"To make matters worse," he continued, seeming to forget himself as he rolled the body over with his boot, inspecting him further.

With his staff, he brushed aside a lock of the First Alderman's bloodied head, then probed the wound with the pointy end of his staff. But it didn't bleed, merely oozed, and Gwendolyn felt bile rise at the back of her throat.

"Yes, yes... just as I suspected, there will be no cruentation

for this poor soul, lest you find what wolves have mauled him."
To prove his point, he handed his staff to Alderman Eirwyn
and bade Eirwyn to provoke the wound. Reluctant though he
was, the Mester Alderman did as he was asked, tapping the
end of the physician's staff against the back of Bryok's head.
Gwendolyn covered her mouth but refrained from turning her
head.

The discussion over cruentation was fascinating. Known as
the ordeal of the bier, Gwendolyn wasn't entirely familiar with
how it worked, but it was a supernatural method of finding
evidence against a suspected murderer. The opinion was that
the body of a victim would bleed in the presence of his
murderer.

"That is enough," said her father, lifting his hand in front
of his face. "Get this man to the chamberlain and give him a
proper rest!"

At once, the same three servants who'd hauled in the
Alderman now leapt forward to roll him back up into the
tarpaulin, before whisking him away.

Regrettably, they could not take the horrid scent, nor the
memory of his oozing wounds. Gwendolyn placed the back of
her hand to her nostrils as she continued to listen.

"What I believe is that he must have died during last
night's Promise Ceremony," concluded Alderman Eirwyn.

"Is there anyone unaccounted for during this time?" asked
her sire.

It was Yestin who answered. "I do not know, Majesty, but I
will inquire at once."

"See you do," demanded her father.

The Mester Alderman returned the staff and cleared his
throat. "Majesty, I am certain *all* of *my* aldermen were
accounted for yestereve," he said. "This must have happened
after Bryok's shift."

"All were accounted for?" asked the King, with a note of reproach to his voice.

"Except Bryok," allowed the Mester Alderman, red-faced.

"Was he supposed to have been on duty?" asked her father, with narrowed eyes.

"No, Majesty," said Eirwyn. "He was not. Although he may have intended to join the celebration for a while, it was his time to change his schedule and he was supposed to have taken a shift at first light. Thus, he was apprised not to imbibe."

"I see," said the King. "And was he inclined to drink?"

"Alas, Majesty, I do not know him well enough to say," interjected Alderman Aelwin.

"And his wife?"

"I am told she left him, Majesty," offered Alderman Eirwyn.

"Left him?"

"Aye, Majesty." The Alderman nodded soberly. "She took her children, so I am told, to visit family in Chysauster." He gave the King a meaningful look. "Indefinitely."

"And who told you this?"

The Mester Alderman shrugged, then peered about the room and said, "I believe it was Alderman Aelwin."

"Aelwin?"

"Not I, Majesty." Aelwin shook his head vehemently. "I did not know him well enough, I fear."

For a moment, the Mester Alderman glowered, then he shrugged, and said, "Ah, well, I suppose it could have been anyone. He's been quite despondent since she left." He cleared his throat. "To be the wife of an alderman is not suitable for all."

"In such a case, might we presume the hemlock was for his own consumption?" asked Mester Ciarán.

"Perhaps," said Alderman Eirwyn with another shrug.

"I ask," said the physician. "Because... were it not for the blow to his head, and the hammer, I might rule this a natural death, insomuch as it must be when a man falls prey to his own vices, and thereafter the perils of nature."

Gwendolyn furrowed her brow. Did the poor fool truly mean to poison himself? Or was it someone else he meant the poison for?

There were easier ways to die than to suffer the effects of hemlock. He would have choked to death in the end, although not before foaming at his mouth and spewing his meal.

Gwendolyn found she had questions, and she longed to voice them aloud, but suddenly catching her father's eye, he inclined his head toward the door, and ordered her out from the hall.

Sensing his mood, Gwendolyn obeyed at once. She found Ely outside, still waiting for her, twirling her thumbs. Gwendolyn took her aside and told her everything she'd heard.

"Foul play?" said Ely, and Gwendolyn shrugged, though she shared the sentiment.

At the instant, there were more questions than answers, and now that she was privy to so many facts, she found she didn't wish to leave the investigation to others.

Wretched as it might seem, the First Alderman's death was a welcome distraction—from what, she dared not confess.

Not even to herself.

CHAPTER
SEVENTEEN

O ver the ensuing days, it was all anyone talked about—the dead alderman, not Gwendolyn's Promise Ceremony, nor anything at all pertaining to her nuptials.

Save for the burden about her neck, evidence of her pledge, it was as though the Promise Ceremony never even happened.

What was more, Prince Loc's absence now lent the entire occasion a sense of foolish fire—like those *piskie* lights in the forest that led men astray, here one instant, not the next.

Gwendolyn wasn't sure how this made her feel.

In some ways, relieved, perhaps? Certainly not over Bryok's death, though she supposed she was pleased enough that the poor man's untimely death now had everyone's rapt attention, including hers, because she didn't wish to confess how she felt about her upcoming nuptials, nor Prince Locrinus himself... because... well... she didn't know how she felt.

Except for the encounter in the cave, and his disinterest on the day of their outing, there was truly nothing wrong with him—at least nothing Gwendolyn could point a finger at.

He was charming, handsome, learned—all the things one hoped for in a mate. And he seemed to admire her erudite nature, which was so utterly important to Gwendolyn, because she didn't wish to be relegated to being someone's prize, as her mother appeared contented to be.

Alas, but it was true, as much as Gwendolyn was loath to say it. As kindly as her father might be, he'd never actually encouraged her mother's uniqueness, nor did he cherish her Prydein blood beyond the alliance it brought to their kingdom —or at least this is how it appeared to Gwendolyn. Rather, he praised the Queen most when she looked and behaved like all the other high-born wives of his court, and perhaps because her mother had so long ago embraced her role as Queen Consort, Gwendolyn scarcely knew anything at all about her Prydein lineage.

Duty first, always. This is what her mother so oft said. And this was the crux of the dilemma: her mother was right. Duty *must* come first. It didn't matter what Gwendolyn wished for herself, nor was she raised to seek anything but fairness from a mate. Cornwall was her foremost responsibility.

Love where you must, she'd been told.

Love where you must. And this she would do.

Duty first.

Always.

Only, now that she'd met Prince Loc, and she'd had a moment or two to consider all that transpired, she found his nature to be... *odd.*

More to the point, if she could be truthful, she didn't particularly enjoy him. All his golden finery and his blinding white smiles couldn't hide a vain demeanor.

And nay, as angry as she was over Bryn's demotion, it wasn't so much the thought of leaving Bryn that upset her; it was more this: She knew what her mother had become since leaving her Prydein home, and it settled poorly in her belly, like a gut full of soured oats.

Worries spun round her head, old and new.

Moreover, she adored this gown her mother gave her, and now, having examined all the finery in her dowry chest—the emblazonry on the cloth, the fine needlework—she had determined the Prydein were anything but wildlings. Insomuch as their artistry was equal to, if not finer than those of Cornwall's artisans, it was now impossible to think of them as crude, woad-painted people, running about like savages in the northern woods.

Also, considering the way her mother had cared for those few treasures she'd brought along with her, it was clear to Gwendolyn how much she valued them. That she had taken such care to present them so finely and considering how long it took her to part with them, it was evident to Gwendolyn that no matter how fervently Queen Eseld had adopted her new life, she secretly cherished, and perhaps even longed for her own people and customs.

It was sad, really, the way her mother had felt compelled to shed her former life. And perhaps more than ever, Gwendolyn understood something vital about her mother's heart.

She longed more than ever to go see Prydein for herself, but some part of her felt such uncertainty over her own betrothed, because there had been nothing in Prince Loc's demeanor that had led her to believe he would appreciate her people, or any other, particularly her mother's. "Barbarians," he'd called the Ostmen. "Garbed in whatever pelts they can find—dogs, if needs must." Was this how he viewed her mother's people as well?

And then, he'd said of the people of Eastwalas, "If anyone should be called such a thing, it should be them because they are inconsequential."

Gwendolyn didn't want to feel embarrassed, or defensive about her land or her people, but considering Prince Loc's own words, she didn't believe he was predisposed to giving others their just due, which only left her feeling strangely bereft.

She was also quite torn—already fiercely protective on the one hand, and reluctantly embarrassed on the other, as her mother must have felt after coming from Prydein. Should Gwendolyn also forsake her people, only to be subsumed by Prince Loc's Trojan ways?

Gods.

That would be horrific.

Gwendolyn found she didn't wish to leave her friends, nor her oysters, nor her beloved glen, nor her mother, in truth— not now, when it seemed she finally had some opportunity to know her better.

As for Prince Loc...

Her mother might be content enough to conform to life with her husband, eschewing her own people and customs, but there was one crucial difference between them: Queen Eseld adored her husband and respected him no less. Love would make all sacrifices worthwhile, but Gwendolyn worried she could never love Prince Loc.

She feared that glimpse of him she'd spied in the cave.

Not because she would be hapless to surrender to his passions once they were wed. She was not. She'd been taught to defend herself, and wedded or not, Gwendolyn would demand all due respect as a princess of Pretania. But this too she feared, because she knew herself all too well: If her husband dared mistreat her, she would castrate him, and damned be their heirs—damned be Cornwall as well, because their discord would be its downfall.

How could she reconcile this?

Mayhap it would be possible to see him again? If only to

determine whether she would feel the same way after spending another afternoon with him. People had bad and good days, and Gwendolyn had plenty of bad days herself. Perhaps yesterday was a bad day for Prince Loc. And certainly, the man she'd spent time with that day on the moors wasn't the same man she'd spent time with during the welcome feast.

Or was it?

At any rate, merely because she didn't crave Loc's kiss, nor did she seem inclined to fantasize about kissing him, that didn't mean she never dreamt about kissing anyone, just not him.

There was only ever one person Gwendolyn had ever fantasized about kissing, and this was not something she ever meant to confess—*dear gods.*

Unhappily, the object of her conflicting emotions was yet another burden she must endure and simply couldn't bear. Thusly, she was still distracted when she arrived for her first session with Málik Danann.

"You are late," he said.

"Am I?" Gwendolyn asked, feigning dispassion, although she felt anything but. And neither was it a question. She knew she was late and didn't care.

What was he going to do? Give her a lashing? And if he did, good. Because then, in truth, her father would reinstate the custom of placing heads on pikes, namely his.

Really, she might be forced to tolerate this creature by her father's mandate, but this didn't give him leave to treat her like a misbehaving child. Nor was her schedule subject to his whims.

Rather he answered to *her*, and despite this, she had seen hide nor hair of him these past two days. She hadn't intended to inquire over *his* whereabouts, even despite that he hadn't slept even once in her antechamber. And why was no one asking him where *he* was during Bryok's murder? Gwendolyn last saw Málik during the *Awenydd's* prayer, and not again for two days thereafter. He might easily have slipped away after Gwendolyn was abed, and she wondered, meanly, if he was the one who'd mauled poor Bryok to death.

Certainly he could do so with those teeth.

"I should argue that *you* are the one who is late," she countered. "Where have you been?"

Unsheathing a small dirk from the back of his belt, unconcerned over her inquiry, Málik picked at a bit of dirt beneath his fingernails. "Did you miss me, Princess?"

"The way one misses a rash!"

He laughed in response but re-sheathed his blade. "If you must know, I escorted the *Awenydd* home."

Gwendolyn arched a brow. Well, it was thoughtful of him, for the *Awenydd* was ancient, and despite that there were few brigands about these parts, she was ill-equipped to defend herself against any. However, no one ever bothered to tell Gwendolyn, so she said, unsheathing her practice sword, "And you are now her keeper, too?"

"Keeper?" asked Málik with a lifted brow. "This is how you see me?"

And then suddenly, his lips tilted at one corner as his gaze settled on Gwendolyn's practice sword. "Art still playing with toys, I see."

Narrowing her eyes, Gwendolyn brandished the sword she'd been using to spar with since she was young, only now regretting her choice, because she saw the telltale twinkle in his ice-blue eyes. She'd chosen this sword because she'd recalled the way he'd swatted the flat of his blade against Bryn's arm and didn't relish the thought of more bruises. She'd hoped he would use a practice sword as well. He did not, alas. With one hand, he unsheathed the bastard sword from the scabbard at his back, and brandished it between them, displaying the sharp, gleaming edge. Thereafter, he made a point of turning the blade to reveal the dull edge, and said, "Don't worry, Princess. I will endeavor to remind myself that you'd rather play with your nursemaid."

Nursemaid? Gwendolyn constrained herself from snarling at him. Still, her lip curled menacingly. How in the name of the Mother Goddess, had this man risen to such rank with his biting tongue? Did her father not realize how disrespectful he was?

Somehow, he infuriated Gwendolyn beyond reason. It was all she could do not to fly at him and tug out every strand of his lovely silver mane, even loathing that she considered anything about him to be lovely.

Her face burning hot, she could scarcely look at him, but she forced herself to do so—too late. He advanced upon her swiftly, and then, just as he had with Bryn, he popped the flat of his blade against her arm. *Hard.*

"Oomph!" she cried, and nearly dropped the practice sword as her hand flew to her abused arm. If her sword had been any heavier, she might have twisted her wrist.

Without remorse, he tilted his head, smirking, even as he drew back his sword arm, poised to strike again. His smile broke into a wide grin. This time, open-mouthed, bearing those shining white teeth—teeth that were not entirely even, yet inexplicably perfect. "Unlike your poppet," he suggested, using her father's word for Bryn, "I will *never* coddle you."

Blood and bones. Why must she bear this? Why would her father burden her with this man? "Poppet?" she countered, tilting him a narrow-eyed glance, only this time, imagining herself flaying him head to foot. "And by poppet, do you mean one who is dutiful and loyal? Because *he* is." Loyalty in a Shadow was paramount.

Doubtless her parents kept secrets from one another, even as they kept separate quarters, but neither would dare keep secrets from their Shadows, even were it possible. Nothing escaped their Shadows, not even the most private ministrations, a certainty that unsettled Gwendolyn immensely—that *he* should be privy to her most vulnerable moments was unthinkable.

"Nay, Princess. By poppet, I mean Bryn," he said, grinning still, and Gwendolyn couldn't bear it, or him. There was that about his expression that promised, as it would be with swordplay, she would never best him with words—not today, perhaps never.

And still she vowed to try. "On your toes!" she demanded.

Alas, if it was the *Sidhe*'s intent to unsettle her so her performance would suffer, his aim was well and duly satisfied. Not having practiced in more than a fortnight, and with Bryn, who was far, far more lenient, she presented herself poorly, missing every opportunity to best the damnable elf.

Gwendolyn loathed so much that he could reduce her to such hatefulness—that she would revile him for the very thing she most admired, his *fae* blood. Gwendolyn was never hateful, except apparently with *him*—this tall blur of hands and feet.

Next to Málik, she found herself ungainly, ungraceful, and entirely unpleasant. To be sure, she could feel her own fury rise like a poison into the back of her throat. And, just for an instant, only an instant, she wished it had been him they'd discovered behind the smelting house.

Though suddenly, having envisioned him lying lifeless and mauled before her father's throne, she felt inexplicably ill.

The sickness manifested itself physically, with a rush of bile that erupted from her lips without grace or forewarning. One minute, she advanced upon her tormentor, sword in hand, and the next she dropped it to cover her mouth, only after spewing the morning's victuals over Málik's tunic. A little stunned perhaps, he sidestepped the rejected meal, somehow avoiding the worst of it, but then he, too, cast away his sword, rushing forward to catch Gwendolyn before she could disgrace herself further by planting her face in the dirt.

Dizzied and sick to her belly, the world spun as Málik swept her into his arms, then settled her down on the ground. Much to Gwendolyn's dismay, she found her head resting on one of his thighs, and one long, muscled arm cradled beneath her to support her back.

Worse, a small crowd of onlookers had formed, everyone waiting for Gwendolyn to rise.

Málik was staring as well, but the concern in his eyes did not match the flippant tone of his voice. "If you did not wish to practice, Princess, you might better have served us both simply by saying so." His lips remained curved ever so slightly. "I have not feigned illness like this since I was a boy, untried."

Gods. It wasn't feigned! But though Gwendolyn hadn't any explanation for the sudden malady, she resented the over-whelming desire to exonerate herself from his accusation.

She would not, however. Her gaze narrowed on the spot of retch on his tunic, drawing his attention there as well, filling her with chagrin. "I am fine," she said, lifting her head and rising from his lap. "Not that you asked."

"What did you eat this morn?"

"Not much."

"Why?"

"I—"

Gwendolyn didn't know. Perhaps she was unsettled, nerve-wracked by the simple truth that she must face *him* this morn. To be certain, it had nothing to do with having sneaked into Mester Ciarán's laboratory to ask him a few questions. The man had tasked himself with performing a posthumous examination, to see if he could determine the true cause of the First Alderman's death, but it was an impossible feat, with Bryok's flesh already so smelly and rotten. Bloodless and grey, as though he were drained of all blood, his extremities were already turning black, particularly the fingers and toes. Even so, Gwendolyn had a robust constitution, and aside from the awful smell, she wasn't the least bit fazed.

In fact, the physician had had a bowl full of prunes in his laboratory, and because she loved them so much, she'd sat, eating them whilst Mester Ciarán explored his cadaver.

"So eager as you must have been to join me this morning, you mustn't go without breaking your fast."

"As if you care?" Gwendolyn said.

"Oh, I do," he argued. "Immensely."

But there was nothing at all sober about Málik's expression, and Gwendolyn doubted he spoke true. She rose, brushing herself off, and, satisfied that she was unharmed, the crowd dispersed as well.

Málik, too, rose from his haunches as Gwendolyn moved to retrieve her practice sword. "If you'll pardon me," she said. "I am done for the day." And, only because it gave her some measure of confidence to assume her position of authority, she added, "As for you... you should plan to visit the pool, else you'll find that mine is not the only spew you'll wear today."

Sadly, it was the worst thing Gwendolyn could find to say, and it fell far from the mark, which annoyed her all the more.

She couldn't escape quickly enough. Not daring to look back, she ran toward the palace, passing Ely as she came out into the courtyard. "Gwen!" she said. "I heard—"

"Nothing happened," Gwendolyn snapped.

"But—"

"I am fine!" Gwendolyn said again, and then she quickened

her pace, unwilling to explain, not even to one of her dearest friends.

"Gwen!" shouted Ely again.

But Gwendolyn still didn't stop, and she was relieved to hear someone calling Elowyn's name—her mother, she believed, although Gwendolyn didn't wait to find out.

CHAPTER
EIGHTEEN

S he could hear the cur moving about her antechamber.
Did he finally intend to move in? More's the pity, because it wasn't merely his right to do so, it was also his duty, and the thought sent needles through her gut.

Only remembering the mocking look upon his face when he'd glimpsed her practice sword, Gwendolyn wondered: What in the name of the Mother Goddess was she thinking?

Perhaps she'd simply not trusted herself to keep from running Málik through?

Certainly he brought out the worst in her, and she was mortified by the impassioned response she so oft had to a creature she oughtn't even notice.

Except she did.

Gods.

From the first.

Whatever thrill she'd felt over meeting Málik that first day, it wasn't shared. She sighed, remembering the cold Winter afternoon he'd ridden into Trevena.

His arrival had so much intrigued her. After all, how long

she'd yearned to meet a true-blood *fae*—someone who could corroborate the stories of her crib-side visitation.

He'd arrived wearing only thin black leathers and a simple cloak, his manner of dress so odd, considering how cold it was outside. From the ramparts, Gwendolyn had watched him canter through those gates, horse and rider moving as one, the two black as night against the Winter so white, with his bastard sword strapped to his back, and his silvery hair billowing behind him. From Gwendolyn's vantage, it had been nearly impossible to distinguish snow from hair, as it swirled about him, until he'd neared, and then, the very first time he'd peered up to meet Gwendolyn's gaze, his eyes were like an *icebourne* sea, chilling her to the bone.

Even now, they had the same effect, no matter his mood, and yet at first, not even his sharp, pointy teeth had disenchanted Gwendolyn.

Indeed, it wasn't until he'd revealed his true self that she'd decided he wasn't worthy of her admiration—not when he so oft felt inclined toward smugness, and most of it was directed at her. Only why? What had she ever done to him?

Like a lodestone, her gaze was drawn to the lone door separating them. In the antechamber, she heard more noises and wondered what he was doing.

During these past few days, whilst he was gone, she had found it far easier to pretend she was pleased with her betrothal, but here and now, with *his* abominable presence, it was impossible to feel aught but misery, and he was surely the cause. His presence was like a dark shadow hovering over her life—if only he would go.

Instead, she would sleep here, in this bed, and he would be... out there... doing whatever *elfkind* did by night.

Creeping about?

Too close for comfort.

Verily, something about performing personal intimacies with Málik Danann so near, struck her as... not wrong, precisely, but discomforting.

Even now, fully dressed and doing naught more than sitting on her bed, she was entirely discomposed by his nearness.

More cacophony.

By the eyes of Lugh, what was he doing?

Doubtless, making himself at home, and the prospect made Gwendolyn gloomy. Her belly grumbled in protest, and she decided it truly must be nerves, all because of *him*.

Already, after one altercation, she hadn't the fortitude to endure another, and that she would suffer this contentious association every day from here forth, until she arrived in Loegria and was free to replace him without answering to her father, was enough to make her ill.

If for no other reason but for that, her marriage was a blessing, because soon she would be mistress over her own life. And in the meantime, if only to keep the peace, her one concession to her father was *Málik Danann*.

He who bore the designation of the Tuatha'an, and who dared to torment and tease her, despite that he hadn't the right.

He who had betrayed the only friend he'd ever made in this city.

All too easily, he'd forsaken Bryn as he had Gwendolyn.

And really, though he was supposed to be the best swordsman in the realm, and Gwendolyn's father was the first to attest to his reputation, Gwendolyn had discreetly inquired and found no one—not one soul—who knew anything about the so-called *fae* in their midst.

So then how was it possible that this man, so utterly mysterious and so full of contempt for the King's own heir, could find himself as the head of her father's army, training men to defend not merely her beloved city, but her family as well.

Curious, that. And suspicious as well.

If only for a moment, Gwendolyn's thoughts returned to the First Alderman. It had been years now since anyone was slain within the city limits. Naturally, there were deaths aplenty, and sometimes people came to her father's hall to complain over petty crimes—the theft of a goat, or the ruination of a man's daughter, or the swindling of a few pieces of copper. There was so little crime to speak of, thanks to her father and his alliances. But somehow, Málik had been a guest in their city for scarcely over two moons, and here they were, investigating the death of a respected alderman—a man who, by the by, must have surely taken his turn in training with Málik Danann, as had Bryn, and most of her father's guards. After all, wasn't that Málik's initial charge? To bring the King's men to heel after too many years of being idle? Particularly now, when all their plans were reaching a crowning moment?

Gwendolyn's mind reeled with questions—such as, why was Bryok skulking about that smelting house during her Promise Ceremony? The location where his body was found was nowhere near the courtyard, nor the Treasury, nor was it close to his home. So what was he doing there in such a remote part of the city, when her father had declared the evening to be a public holiday?

There were several blacksmiths in Trevena, all of them quite well esteemed, but that shop boasted the only forger who knew how to work with Loegrian steel, and he was also the only blacksmith who ever received Loegrian ingots. Not a clue, precisely, but curious just the same.

The cooper was next door as well, with the furrier and tanner two doors down, although most of the merchants were on the opposite side of the city, closer to the barracks and the market and city pool.

What Gwendolyn really wished to know was why that bloody hammer was left in perfect view of anyone who could find it? Why had Bryok been seeking the tincture of hemlock? For himself? Was he, as Alderman Eirwyn claimed, so despondent over the abandonment of his family that he had intended to end his life? If so, why go about it so publicly, even so far as requesting the use of the cook's house for some unknown party suffering with mania?

Howbeit if, by some odd turn of events, Bryok really was inquiring for someone else, and was poisoned, intentionally, or else wise, that hemlock should have done the worst on its own. There was no need for violence, unless the hammer was meant to let blood, to attract wolves no one even suspected were in the area.

In truth, wolves had been absent from these parts for quite some time, and though they could still be encountered in the northern woodlands, why would anyone bother with such malefaction, when any weapon would have sufficed on its own? The hammer, or the poison, not both.

Really, the wolves could be a simple matter of ill timing, but it felt to Gwendolyn as though too much effort had been exerted into hiding the true cause of this man's death.

But then a thought occurred to her as she sat, considering the Alderman's widow. Ia was a woman Gwendolyn had long admired. Younger than her husband, she was perhaps a few years older than Gwendolyn, but already she'd born the Alderman four healthy children in the space of a little over four years. It simply didn't ring true that she'd left him, and neither could they have loathed one another so vehemently and still made so many babes.

Any good apothecary could easily have taken care of that.

Although it wasn't sanctioned, Gwendolyn knew many women who'd sought a dose of *silphium* for this purpose.

Even their ancestors had abandoned unwanted babes to the cold and the will of the *fae*. Sadly, unwanted children were not to be suffered.

Nay, deep in Gwendolyn's heart, she did not believe the Alderman intent upon his own demise. And now, someone would have to tell his poor wife that he was gone.

Perhaps it should be Gwendolyn?

And regardless, someone must now discover the true reason for this malefaction, and Gwendolyn didn't believe anyone was taking it very seriously, except Mester Ciarán, who was concentrating so hard on his cadaver that he couldn't take time to eat his prunes.

Much to Gwendolyn's chagrin, she'd stolen the last handful for herself, and not for a moment did he bother to notice. She'd sat eating one after another right in front of him, and he'd never said a word, not even to caution her about digestive repercussions.

Indeed, he'd been entirely preoccupied with examining every spot on the man's flesh—perhaps looking for evidence of hemlock poisoning. His conclusion: There was, indeed, some potential sign of the poison, but it was impossible to say without asking Bryok about his symptoms—a pounding heart perhaps, or a burning in the belly, increased salivation, paralysis of the muscles, and sometimes convulsions. Unfortunately, despite the unpleasant scent of the plant itself, there was none discernible in the cadaver.

"Inconclusive," he'd said.

Suddenly, without warning, Elowyn came bursting through her door, but she did not pounce upon the bed as usual. Instead, she stood in the middle of Gwendolyn's room, without bothering to close the door.

Outside, Gwendolyn sensed, rather than saw or heard, Málik, and she motioned furiously at the door, glowering at Ely for leaving it open.

Elowyn didn't even notice. She placed her arms akimbo, then announced, "I was strongly admonished by your mother!"

Gwendolyn's brows lifted. "I don't understand..."

"'Tis the truth, Gwendolyn. Your mother hailed me as I made to follow you within. She advised me that a friend is not what you need, and said that you had a duty to perform, that it was high time you prepared for it." Gwendolyn would have responded, but Ely was quick to continue. "Thereafter, she reminded me how wrongly Bryn served you, and then she cautioned me to learn all I can from Demelza ere we part for Loegria. Else, she said, I'll be ill-prepared to serve you, and if she suffers worry o'er it, it will be all my fault!"

Gwendolyn's belly roiled again, her bellyache returning. She frowned. "You *are* my friend, Elowyn, no matter what my mother claims. You are more kin to me than she is."

Gods. It appeared Queen Eseld was purposely divesting Gwendolyn of her closest friends. Forsooth! She no longer had Bryn, and now it seemed her mother would deprive her of Ely as well—not as a servant, perhaps, but as a companion.

All warmth toward her mother vanished in a heartbeat, considering that Queen Eseld had seemed perfectly contented to saddle her with Málik—a puffed-up, spike-toothed gobdaw!

Again her gaze was drawn toward the antechamber, and she wondered if her mother had somehow conspired with the *Awenydds* to bring him to the palace for some purpose Gwendolyn couldn't fathom. Once more, she gestured toward the door and when Ely didn't move quickly enough to close it, Gwendolyn bounced off the bed to shut it herself.

"I would like to lock him in a garderobe," she said.

"Gwendolyn!"

"Please! Already, you sound like Demelza."

How miserable she was. How truly miserable when she should only feel joy and hope. Scolding or no scolding, Ely smiled as the conversation turned to Málik. "Oh, Gwendolyn! You ought to be over the moon to have *him* assigned to you. Why are you not?"

"Oh, I am," assured Gwendolyn. "Over the moon!"

Poor, sweet Ely was enamored with the cold-hearted elf, and Gwendolyn suspected Málik was the reason her friend no longer wished to dance. Ever since he'd arrived, she had been moony and filled with sighs. And yet if that were true, her adoration for Málik was ill-fated. No matter how highly anyone thought of that bloody elf, there was no chance he would ever agree to such a thing. She sensed in her heart that he, like Prince Loc must consider himself better than her, and considering his haughty demeanor, she wondered, not for the first time, why he would attend her, when he clearly didn't like her, and he had no connection to her kindred, nor any loyalties to her father, nor even to Trevena.

To be sure, he was an opportunist, selling his sword to the highest bidder, and that he had remained in Trevena so long as he had, to train her father's men, was the subject of much speculation. Gwendolyn only wondered what was so special about Málik Danann that her parents should place him in charge of the kingdom's only heir.

After all, what duty had he to keep her safe? If indeed he was *faekind*—but he was not—he probably believed it the King's obligation to serve him, not the other way around.

"*Gods,*" Gwendolyn said softly, "I loathe that man."

Poor Ely could swoon all she liked over the rotten elf, and he would never return her affection. Already he had proven that even a princess of Pretania was worth little.

At the moment, she wished with all her heart that she could leave this city and fly away.

She fell back on her bed, glaring at the door, then peered at Ely, eyes narrowed, scheming. "We're going to Chysauster," she decided on the spur of the moment.

Elowyn screwed up her face, confused. "Chysauster?"

Gwendolyn hitched her chin. "At once!"

"But Gwen! I cannot. I told you—"

Gwendolyn arched a brow. "Am I not your lady now?"

"Aye, but—"

She tilted her head, entreating her friend. "Would you leave me to travel without my maid?"

"But Gwendolyn? 'Tis grown late!"

Gwendolyn grinned. "All the more reason to leave at once."

Ely shook her head. "But Gwen..."

"Must you leave me alone with *him*?" She gave a nod and glance toward the closed door, and Ely's eyes widened, and then she said, "Oh, nay!"

"Then please, go prepare," Gwendolyn demanded. "We depart at once."

And then, determined to have her way, Gwendolyn went to seek an audience with her father. Someone must inform Bryok's poor widow of his untimely death. Gwendolyn was as good a person as any. Besides, she had cousins in Chysauster, and she really must insist upon inviting them in person to her wedding. It was the proper thing to do.

CHAPTER
NINETEEN

J ust in case her father might object to the true reason
Gwendolyn wished to travel to Chysauster, she didn't
bring up Bryok's widow at all. As a concerned father, he
would have told her to avoid Bryok's affairs, and leave the
investigations to Yestin.

Fortunately, he didn't question her motive, and before she
left, he handed her a missive to deliver to her uncle, which
Gwendolyn accepted with a thank-you and a smile.

Thereafter, reconsidering the position she'd placed Ely in,
Gwendolyn left her sweet friend behind, realizing only belatedly that before Ely could leave the city, she would feel
compelled to tell Lady Ruan, and if she should do this, Queen
Eseld might discover Gwendolyn's intentions and thwart her.
Nay. Ely could remain—particularly since her dear, sweet
friend had never been away from home a day in her life.

Immediately after quitting the hall, Gwendolyn searched
for and found Elowyn, knowing her well enough to know she
would deliberate too long before telling her mother,
fortunately.

Instead, Gwendolyn gave her a list of chores to complete whilst she was gone, and when Gwendolyn gave her the list, Ely held the hastily written note in her hand, and asked, both brows slanted in dismay, "You intend to go without me?"

"I must," said Gwendolyn. "But do not fret, and please do not speak a word of this to my mother, nor yours."

Ely placed the list into her pocket without sparing it a glance, although Gwendolyn knew she would pore over it once Gwendolyn was gone. Despite that the *dawnsio* was an oral tradition, Gwendolyn made good and certain both Bryn and Ely learned to decipher their letters and numbers—an education well received, because everyone knew that without it, there was no way to hold a profession like Yestin's.

"Yes, Highness," she said, using Gwendolyn's title for the first time in recent memory. Doubtless, she was angry, though Elowyn's displeasure could not be avoided, not today.

Alas, she knew her friend well enough to know she would get over it, and no matter whether she did or did not, this was for everyone's benefit.

Then came Málik.

Of course, she must reveal her intentions, but because *he* served *her*, Gwendolyn didn't request for him to accompany her. Rather she demanded it. She gave him half a bell to prepare for their journey, and meant to be in the saddle, with or without him.

Fortunately, though it took her longer to do what she needed to do, he was waiting for her by the stables, accompanied by two more guards of his choosing—men presumably trained by him, perhaps loyal to him as well. But to his credit, at least he didn't go tattle to her mother, as he did last time. Although perhaps Gwendolyn should have wondered why he was suddenly so compliant, she daren't stop to consider it.

She didn't enjoy being so deceitful with her mother, but if

her father didn't disapprove of the sojourn, she didn't wish to linger to give Queen Eseld an opportunity to deny her. Gwendolyn had never been more confused by her mother's motives. Sometimes it appeared she might be warming to Gwendolyn; then other times, it seemed she was never more contentious. And regardless, Málik was Gwendolyn's Shadow now, assigned to her by her father and king. Gwendolyn had every right to employ him howsoever she pleased. Whether Málik liked it or nay, he was hers to command, not the other way around.

So if he wondered why, after stressing the importance of leaving so promptly, she arrived so late to meet him, she wasn't inclined to report that she'd paid another visit to the blacksmith. She didn't know why it was important, only that it seemed pertinent to do so—now, before the man's story could change. However, having found nothing amiss with the blacksmith's story, she quickly checked the alley where Bryok's body was discovered. And then made a swift detour to inspect Bryok's home, finding and seizing an entire bowl full of those delicious prunes to carry with her in her saddlebag. No one was going to eat them anyway, and they were so good. Indeed, she wondered how they had escaped Yestin's notice for the feast. Hereabouts, plums were never ripe until August, and therefore, prunes were never available until later in the year. They must have come to Trevena by one of the southern merchants, and she must remember to tell Yestin about them and have him ferret out the source.

Three hours later, she was in her saddle, eating another prune, taking great pleasure in every small nibble, when Málik crushed her joy, merely by speaking. "Straight ahead, there's a good spot to make camp," he said.

"We've scarcely left the city," Gwendolyn answered impatiently.

Two bells gone, and still too close to her mother.

"It would be a good place to watch the road," he argued.

There was nothing to watch. "The road" was nothing more than a poorly marked trail that barely anyone used anymore. Gwendolyn had traveled this route more times than she could count. No doubt he was speaking of the promontory where she and Bryn used to spy on cavalcades when they were more apt to travel to and from Land's End.

"It would have been wiser to wait to travel in the morning," he suggested—an entirely useless observation that would do them no good right now. The fact was that they didn't wait, and here they were. Nor did Gwendolyn appreciate his tone.

"Art afraid of the dark, *fae*?"

His lips lifted at one corner. "What do you think?" He bared a sharp, pointy tooth, licking it suggestively. What did Gwendolyn think indeed? What did she really think?

She thought him a wretch and a contemptuous beast. But since he didn't bother acknowledging the question behind her barb, she refrained from answering, and thereafter said nothing more. All the while, he sat chewing on a short whip of reed.

Gwendolyn wondered if he was hungry, and for an instant, considered sharing her prunes, but decided he didn't deserve any. She pointed to the reed between his lips and asked with no small measure of disdain, "So, is this how you sharpen your teeth?"

Her question only seemed to amuse him, and he responded with a chuckle, the sound dark and rich. But then he said, "Indeed." And again, grinned, once again baring his teeth, and chomping loudly. "Better to defend you, *Princess*."

Again with that tone.

Gwendolyn shuddered. Considering he could rip out a man's throat with those teeth, it wasn't a jest. There was something about him—something primeval—that Gwendolyn persistently ignored, even despite sensing she shouldn't.

"I am not your princess," she reminded him.

"Ah, but you are... for the time being."

Gwendolyn lifted a brow. "For the time being?"

Málik shrugged. "Till the gods determine else wise."

"Gods!" Gwendolyn scoffed. "More like, till you've found a better appointment, and a bigger purse?" She slid him a withering glance. "I should make it easy for you. You are not needed here, Málik Danann!"

"Am I not?"

His tone was glib, though Gwendolyn had a sudden sense that, for once, her words had cut him. He averted his gaze, continuing to chew his reed.

Why should she care whether he was wounded?

Málik was neither kin nor kith, and Gwendolyn still hadn't been able to determine what had brought him to Trevena—and less so, why he should attach himself to someone who loathed him as much as he loathed her. To put it precisely, Gwendolyn didn't trust him. But lacking the patience to spar with him, she, too, averted her gaze.

"We'll continue," she said. "There'll be another 'good place' soon."

"As you wish," he said, without looking at her, and Gwendolyn endeavored to ignore him, keeping her eyes on the road.

These days, there were so few brigands along these parts. They were scarce as wolves. But, if there were any to be encountered, they would be found along this stretch of road, where merchants sometimes gathered to peddle their wares, though not in a long time.

No matter, Gwendolyn wasn't overly concerned. As annoying as Málik was, she knew he could cut a man to bits as skillfully with his blade as he could with his words.

Or his teeth.

Resigning herself to a full night's discomfort, she sighed.

Regrettably, because of her haste to leave the city, she hadn't planned well enough for this journey, and despite knowing Málik would have, it galled her to have to depend on him perforce, yet this was what she got for keeping a head full of intrigue. But at least she had her prunes, and if she must, she could endure the entire journey with little more, especially knowing her uncle would greet them with plenty.

They traveled in silence, and only for an instant, she dared to look at Málik in profile. He had a generous mouth and an aquiline nose. He carried his head high, and the golden light gave his silvery mane a warm hue that it didn't normally possess. His skin was pale, though not too pale, his lashes inky black, and it almost appeared as though he wore kohl about his eyes—eyes that were slitted now as he assessed their surroundings. But no matter that he didn't look at Gwendolyn again, she felt his scrutiny regardless—enough so that she belatedly realized she was staring and was chagrined. At once she averted her gaze, and to her utter dismay, she heard him chuckle.

Blood and bones. It was going to be a long, insufferable night!

TWENTY

Naturally, because it was the shortest route, they chose the Small Road along the high, sloping moors. At intervals, this road veered east to avoid the worst of the crags, intercepted here and there by patches of woodland. Yet no matter how far east one ventured, the sound of the ocean was a constant roar, and the sea remained a fixture upon the horizon, every now and again revealing a brightly sailed ship.

Positioned between the southern wheals and nestled along a hillside overlooking both land and sea, her uncle's village lay beyond the Bay of Dunes, close to where the River Hayle rushed into the sea. These days, few people ventured so far south, and Duke Cunedda made certain not to give anyone a reason to do so by regularly exporting his copper and tin.

Until about three years ago, when the yields grew mean, twice every month, even during Winter, her father's troops had ventured south, then north again, and these were the opportunities Gwendolyn seized to visit her cousins, sometimes accompanied by her father, sometimes not. However, over these past few years, because her father's envoys were fewer and farther between, her uncle developed a series of *fogous* beneath his village—underground passages wherein he stored most of his yields until her father could send proper escorts for the journey north. Gwendolyn hadn't been there since he'd begun construction of those and judging by the vanishing wheel ruts along the coastal road, it had been a long, long while since any of his yields were conveyed. Soon the path would be carpeted by rock sea-spurrey, sheep's bit, and sea campion, the red, white, and blue of them brilliant against a carpet of green.

Gwendolyn hoped this didn't mean the southern wheals were exhausted, and she made note to ask her uncle about them, although, no doubt this was the reason for the missive in her satchel—an inquiry over the state of the Crown Wheals. It was no wonder her father hadn't balked over her request to travel. With the aldermen so distressed over the Treasury, she'd given him the perfect means to inquire over the southern wheals without raising alarms.

The journey would take maybe two days, but they made good time, and neither of the accompanying guards complained at all about spending the entire evening in a saddle.

With the cooler temperature, neither were their horses better left standing about, and the pace they kept was easy.

Up ahead, a small rabbit crossed the road, and Málik's head swiveled before Gwendolyn even realized it was there. His sharp eyes followed the creature long after it vanished from her sight into the safety of a thicket, his eyes shining like a predator's.

Intensely curious, Gwendolyn longed to ask if *fae* eyes were keener than most, but since she didn't wish to believe he was anything more than a crude beast, she bit her tongue.

Gods. Who could have imagined her childhood dream of meeting a true-blood *fae* would go so terribly awry? All those nights she'd lain in bed, imagining another visitation from these elusive creatures, dreaming of all the questions she should ask—*pah!*

She was beginning not to believe in *faekind* at all.

No doubt Málik looked different from other men—his eyes a little brighter, his teeth a little sharper—but for all his oddities, it didn't mean he was *fae.*

Trying to ignore him as best she could, Gwendolyn reached back into her saddlebag to grab a few more prunes, wondering if she'd given too much weight to her father's trust in Málik Danann. Indeed, tonight she was shadowed by two men she didn't know by name, and yet another, whose loyalties she questioned.

Willful and bold, she heard Demelza say, "Ye've more pride than caution. Someday it'll lead you astray."

Was today that day?

CHAPTER
TWENTY-ONE

The night grew long and cold—colder than a miner's knob. Still Gwendolyn persevered, even as she teetered in the saddle, her mood turning sour as sorrel.

Meanwhile, Málik rode taller even as she slid lower, until at long last, she collapsed atop the horse's withers, with the pommel stabbing her in the belly, though sadly, it wounded her pride far more than it did her belly, and not even that prompted her to cry halt.

Make no mistake, Gwendolyn understood she was being unreasonable, and still she persisted, until after a while, Málik sidled up beside her and plucked her from her mount, like a berry from a bush, placing her before him on his mare, far too close for comfort.

"Rest," he demanded.

Rest?

Rest!

"I need no coddling," Gwendolyn complained, as he dragged her back to rest against his leathered chest. "Considering that my father put me in a saddle when I was only two, I am in little danger of falling from this mount. Nor do I care to tussle with you. Please, unhand me!"

Releasing her at once, Málik said evenly, "Forgive me, Princess. I'd not have it said you came to harm on my watch."

"Fret not," she reassured. "I am now awake."

Wide, wide awake, every inch of her body attuned to the creature at her back, his proximity filling her with nearly as much irritation as it did chagrin, and nearly as much titillation as it did warmth—more, she was horrified to confess.

What was worse, this close to him, she could actually smell him, and she discovered that his essence was curiously appealing—like rain... and wood.

By now, the moon had risen to its highest point, and the air was bitterly cold—far too cold to be traveling without provisions, although at least it wasn't raining as it did so often this time of the year. Gwendolyn took comfort in that.

Admittedly, something about Málik Danann severed every measure of good reason from her mind and heart. Deep down, Gwendolyn suspected that even this sojourn to Chysauster had more to do with him than it did with Bryok, or even her cousins. If only he'd not come into their lives, she would be snug in her bed, dreaming of Prince Loc...

But mayhap not.

Feeling guilty for pushing them so hard, she peered back at the two guards who had accompanied them, noting their squinty eyes and bent backs.

Unfortunately, this time of the year it was warm enough by day, but night still harbored a vicious chill. If she'd taken more time to prepare, she might have brought a proper tent for the journey, knowing they'd spend at least one night beneath the stars.

Instead, she'd been in such a rush to leave that she hadn't

even secured gifts for her cousins—three sisters from three different mothers.

Her uncle Cunedda had no sons, despite that he'd married four different wives.

Sadly, his new wife, Lowenna, could carry no child to term —mercifully for her, because despite that they were girls, her cousins were all born with such enormous heads their births had resulted in the deaths of their mothers. Luckily, by now all three had grown to match their heads, even if their hearts were still far too large.

Gwendolyn couldn't wait to see them.

Last year, she'd brought them a curious red dye called *kokkos*, made from crushed insects from *An Ghréig*. They'd sewed themselves three dresses that year and went about looking like triplets. This time her head was too filled with... *other things.* She would arrive empty-handed, except for the missive from her father.

An ocean-scented breeze swept by, raising gooseflesh, and Gwendolyn shivered. Inconceivably, the man at her back wore only thin black leathers, with hosen, and a modest cloak— precisely as he'd arrived during midwinter. And still his body was as warm as a low-burning brazier. So warm, in truth, that despite that it vexed her to do so, she slid back in the saddle so her back was pressed firmly against his soft leathers.

Just like that, she rode with her teeth clamped to keep from chattering, and her lips pursed, only wondering why her tongue would not stir, when there was no way they could travel the distance without resting their horses or taking respite. Indeed, the surest way to get Málik to put her down would be to assent to his request to make camp. And yet she did not.

Once more, she peered back at the guards, and this time

relented. "We should stop," she said, and added, "For their sakes." How prideful she was.

"For their sakes?" he asked, with an unmistakable note of amusement.

Gwendolyn nodded. "Indeed."

"It couldn't be *you* are weary?"

"Of course, I am!" she confessed. "Aren't you?"

"Nay," he said blithely, and Gwendolyn bristled, wishing she'd stopped when he'd first suggested it. Now he would perforce make her beg. "Naturally," she said.

And there it was, again, that low, throaty chuckle he smothered before it could find his beautiful lips—lips that appeared so lush and soft and generous, until he opened his mouth, and filled it with sharp words to match his sharp teeth.

"You'll fare better on the morrow if you rest now," he advised.

They would *all* fare better, but Gwendolyn longed to see *him* grovel. "I do not need a keeper," she assured.

"And yet you have one. But though I am not your *first,* I'll not be undermined," he said, and Gwendolyn gritted her teeth, uncertain which of these veiled insults most displeased her.

She did *not* undermine Bryn. Nor was Bryn her lover—first, second or otherwise, as implied by the tone of his voice. "If you are referring to Bryn," she said, "he was never my keeper, nor my lover."

"A least we are agreed you undermined him," he argued. And *dear gods,* she had. Although she wished more than anything to protest, she couldn't. And regardless, Gwendolyn needn't answer to Málik, nor to anyone else.

By Cornish law, on the night she gave Loc her torc, she became a woman unto herself, beholden only to her word, which she willingly gave to Prince Loc. "Tell me," she demanded. "When all is said and done, do you answer to me, or do you answer to my father?"

There was a lingering note of mirth in his voice that grated on her nerves. "Unless my ears deceive me, Princess, this appears to be a trick question?"

"It is not," Gwendolyn said primly. "It is quite simple, really, and I'd like to know where your loyalties stand."

"At the moment, I am sworn to you," he said.

"And yet I never saw you swear any such oath."

Silence.

"If I ask you now, will you bend the knee?"

"I find it interesting, Princess. First your concern for the guards, now you wish to see me on my knees? Art certain this isn't your way of begging a halt for the night?"

"I beg nothing."

Gwendolyn loathed the way he made her respond—as though a harpy lived inside her skin, someone she didn't recognize. And still he made no effort to answer, nor did he stop, and Gwendolyn was prepared to leap from his mount, ready to be away from him.

Trotting along beside them, her mare was clearly fatigued. Proffering another glance over her shoulder at the guards, she found them riding with shoulders slumped, and despite that, Gwendolyn persisted, "You seem to be ignoring my question, *fae.*"

"Which question, precisely?"

"Will you bend the knee?"

"There is only one reason I have ever found to bend the knee... and 'tis really quite pleasurable. Would you like me to demonstrate?"

Gwendolyn's cheeks heated, though she didn't entirely understand his meaning. Enough to say there was a note to his voice that suggested if she made a complaint to her father, he might lose his head. "Well?" she persisted, overlooking his suggestion.

"I bend the knee to no man," he said finally, and Gwendolyn lifted a brow.

"As you can hardly have failed to note, I am not a man."

"Neither any woman," he added.

"Not even to my father, the King?"

For a long, long while, he didn't respond, and then when he did, all puckishness fled from his tone, and he said soberly, "My loyalty is to Pretania, though I care deeply about the King's welfare."

"And mine?"

"And yours."

Some of Gwendolyn's anger deflated—only a little. But there was a certain verity to his words... a truth as elusive and ancient as the *faerie* glens. If indeed he were true-blood *fae*, he would have been not only one of the original conservators of this land, but perhaps its maker as well. After all, it was the *fae* —whether one called them *Sidhe*, *fae*, or elf—who were Cornwall's true forebears. She wished she had the nerve to ask him directly, but alas, she did not. Instead, she fought a tug of war within herself, thinking him yes, thinking him no.

Being children of the gods, all these lands—from Ériu to Land's End, to the farthest reaches of the Caledonian confederacy—were once created for those even-tempered creatures whose armament of choice was *magik*, not swords.

They had already vanished from Pretania long before Gwendolyn was born. All the stories she'd ever heard came from the *Awenydds*, and these were tales told by the *dawnsio*.

The Tuatha Dé Danann were said to have descended upon Ériu from a place called *Tír na nÓg—the Land of the Ever Young* —borne by ships that were carried upon a sea of blood clouds, ushering in a darkness that lasted three days and nights. From four sacred cities, they carried with them four great talismans, all graven with spells. The first was the Sword of Light, which was forged in Finias, and belonged to Núada Airgetlám, the Tuatha'an king, who'd named it Claímh Solais.

It was a fiery sword of glowing light that was said to render the bearer invincible when it was wielded, and could deflect weaves of power, depending on the requirement of its wielder, with the sole exception of balefire, which eventually killed Núada.

The second talisman was the Lúin of Celtchar, fashioned in Gorias, and known to some as Lugh's spear. This was a long, flaming lance that must be kept with its head in a vat of blood to prevent it from igniting and consuming its wielder. Made from darkened bronze, and tapered into a sharp point, it was fastened to a rowan haft by thirty rivets of gold.

Then there was Dagda's Cauldron from Murias.

This talisman was said to be kept to this very day in Ériu, and it was a blessing to its house, for none with a pure heart was ever sent away with an aching belly.

Last, there was Lia Fáil, hailing from Falias. This was the crying stone upon which the true kings of Ériu were crowned, and the stone no longer cried Danann.

Of the four talismans, three were said to remain in Ériu. One, the sword, was lost, never to be seen again. And yet, with talismans like those, it was no wonder Ériu had thrived so long beneath the Tuatha'an rule. In fact, it was said that, during this time, even mortals lived longer—a thousand years and more. Under the hand of the *fae*, the land prospered, nourished by sacred pools like the one that graced their glen. But as the tale would have it told, the Tuatha'an arrogance grew to such great proportions that the gods sent the sons of Míl to teach them a lesson in humility.

Before that Ending Battle was fought, it was agreed the

victors would choose the spoils, and when the time came to choose dominions, the sons of Míl chose the half of Ériu that lay aboveground, forcing the Tuatha Dé Danann into the Underworld.

Manannán himself escorted them there via the *Sidhe* mounds, after which he raised an enchanted mist to conceal them from mortal eyes.

This was why the Tuatha Dé Danann were sometimes known as *fae* or *Sidhe—fae* for the *Faeth Fiadha* that concealed them, *Sidhe* for the mountains that swallowed them whole.

Never intended to be polite, "elf" was the appellation given to them by the sons of Míl, who'd named them "white beings."

The man riding at her back could easily pass for such a "white being," with his silver hair and *icebourne* eyes. And yet his armament of choice was not *magik*, but a sword.

Unwittingly, she reached up to pull a curl of her own hair between her fingertips, considering the *fae* who'd descended upon her crib.

There had been two, an elder and a younger, called Esme. Her mother and Demelza had stood watching from the threshold as the two chittered over Gwendolyn's crib. Demelza once told her both were extraordinary—skin translucent like stardust, with eyes that burned with the light of two suns. Upon smiling, both revealed sharp, savage teeth—and this, too, reminded her of Málik. If he opened his mouth and looked at her in a certain way, his entire look was transformed... *Savage. Wild. Untamed.*

For a moment, Gwendolyn embraced the silence, scarcely aware that she'd relaxed against his chest, until she felt his chin settle atop her pate. The feel of it softened the armor around her heart. No matter his attitude, he had willingly come to serve her father, and no matter if he did so with such egotism that it disgusted her to her core, there was no crime in that.

Furthermore, as annoying as he could be, he had without protest accepted a position as her Shadow, even despite that this was not the promise made to lure him to Trevena. This was not so prestigious an occupation as one might suppose. It was far more rewarding to be a Mester at Arms, or a mentor to the Elite Guard, but if one must serve as a Shadow, it was more prestigious to serve as a guard to the king himself. In serving Gwendolyn, he suffered all the bother and aggravation—long hours, often thankless, with few rewards to speak of—and truly none of the glory. It was for that reason Gwendolyn had treated Bryn so much like a brother, and she'd tried so desperately to make sure he took time for himself.

This was also why she'd coaxed him to the glen that day and now... Gwendolyn was ashamed to say that at the instant, she wasn't missing him at all.

Poor Bryn.

Nor could she explain it, but she'd hardly thought about Prince Locrinus since his departure a few days ago, even with the heavy torc and chain about her neck. And really, it was so much heavier than hers, fashioned so that no one wearing it could forget it was there.

Indeed, with half the day gone in the saddle, and Trevena long in their wake, the Promise Ceremony seemed years away.

Up ahead, distinguishable as a gnarled silhouette against a waning moon, there was a small tree atop a mound. This seemed like a good place to rest for the evening.

"Shall we stop there?" asked Málik, as though he'd read her mind.

"Aye," Gwendolyn relented. "Let's do."

In silence, they left the road, ascending the hill, until they reached the tree. There they settled the horses, and Gwendolyn took her cloak, then found a dry spot, though not before remembering the rest of the stolen prunes she'd placed in her satchel.

There were plenty enough remaining. Keeping some for herself, she dropped a handful into each of the guards' satchels, and another in Málik's—a peace offering.

TWENTY-TWO

A meadow ant crawled about Gwendolyn's nose; still she didn't stir, watching it lazily from the corner of one eye, thinking about Prince Locrinus and the insult wielded against the people of Eastwalas. Above, sun spears stabbed through the boughs of an ancient wych elm. One glance up revealed the flowers had already dropped, and the leaves were still unfurling. As weary as Gwendolyn had been last night, she'd had trouble falling asleep, not simply because of Málik. But, in truth, there was something about the Alderman's death that continued to vex her... something that spoke to her woman's intuition.

Something...

It was like a riddle of sorts, except the clues were all there, she sensed; there were only missing questions—questions she didn't yet know to ask.

To begin with, she was troubled by the lack of blood in the alleyway where the body was discovered. Like that tarp Bryok was carried upon, it was strangely unsoiled. A man mutilated in such a fashion should have surely bled, so where was the blood?

Neither would he have gone silently into his Good Night, all the while being bludgeoned to death by a forger's hammer. In truth, this had been Gwendolyn's impetus for visiting his home. And instead of bloodstains, she'd only found prunes. His house was tidy and well cared for, a testament to his wife's loving care.

Certainly, it was not the home of a man who'd been alone too long, nor the house of a woman who loathed her spouse.

The bed, however, was made, a seemingly inconsequential detail that also troubled her, perhaps because Gwendolyn didn't know many men who troubled themselves to make a bed, and less to clean a house, particularly on such an unrelenting schedule as his.

By the eyes of Lugh, Gwendolyn had never even once made a bed for herself. Nor had Bryn. How many times had Demelza complained over the messes he'd left?

Countless times, Gwendolyn had found her straightening his cot.

As Gwendolyn saw it, with Ia gone, the state of Bryok's house should have suffered—or at least, his bower. But it was as though someone had gone through his entire home and left it speckless... *why?*

Truly, none of these things alone would tickle the hairs on her nape. But all together, they left her flummoxed. Only the fact that she was the one poring over such questions should be the biggest mystery of all. *Except it wasn't.*

Gwendolyn knew good and well why she'd allowed herself to become so preoccupied by Bryok's death—she knew but didn't wish to say.

Moreover, there was no chance someone wouldn't have

noticed a pack of wolves skulking about the crowded streets after her Promise Ceremony. This she knew for certain.

Considering that, her gaze sought Málik, seated atop a boulder in the distance, legs crossed, palms up as though in supplication... *or prayer?*

The towering length of that sword at his back was sorely at odds with the form he presented. And though it should have been the worst place to sheathe a weapon, and no man she'd ever met could do so and still unsheathe it during battle, she had seen him do so countless times with Bryn, taking that sword in hand, and wielding it so effortlessly as though it were made of tin. And yet, it was not, she knew.

Gwendolyn sat, stretching, turning to find both guards attending their mounts.

Clearly, everyone had come more prepared than she had, with blankets for their mounts, and blankets for themselves.

In fact, the guard wearing Hedrek's livery had an interesting mantle for his horse—a coat of colors, fashioned from sundry pelts, as though he'd cobbled it himself. Ingenious, she thought as she rose, brushing herself off. When she turned again, it was to find Málik gone.

CHAPTER
TWENTY-THREE

L eaving the guards to make ready, Gwendolyn ventured over the rise and found her new Shadow kneeling beside a small stream—a rivulet so small that Gwendolyn didn't even realize what it was until she arrived by his side. "A *winterbourne*?" she asked.

He shrugged. "Not yet," he said, though with an unmistakable note of concern. All the while, his hand remained splayed over the trickle of water, as though he were inspecting its essence by touch. At last he said, "The land is struggling."

Gwendolyn took it as an accusation, but not so much directed at her as it was at her father.

"What are you doing?"

As though her question nudged him from a stupor, he turned his hand to scoop up a bit of the water into his palm, then splashed it into his face, before combing his long, wet fingers through his silver mane, darkening his hair.

Gwendolyn shivered, rubbing her arms for warmth. Doubtless the water was frigid, and until the sun re-appeared in full, the air was still cool.

By midday, perhaps, it would be warm enough to swim, and yet who could swim in such a meager stream? The river was so tiny, it was impossible to say whence it had come.

The land wasn't particularly flat here, but neither were there mountains in the immediate vicinity. She supposed it was possible for it to have bubbled up from some long-vanished spring. "Is it hot?" she asked.

"Warm," he said, and Gwendolyn sighed over the terse response.

Gods. She didn't wish to fight any longer. If she must be forced to coexist with Málik Danann, she must really learn to manage him. But they couldn't make peace until she knew what quarrel he had with her. "Why did you tell my mother where we were?"

"We?" His shoulders tensed, but he lifted another handful of water to his face, and this time didn't bother to wipe it away, leaving the droplets to glisten like diamonds on his flesh.

"You know... the pool."

"Why else? Because it suited my purpose," he confessed, and Gwendolyn lifted a brow.

"What purpose might that be?"

In answer, he cast Gwendolyn a backward glance and his lips split into a not very pleasant smile. Indeed, with the morning light glittering throughout his silver mane, and shining over his iridescent skin, he was like... a feral creature, particularly with that gleam in his eyes—savage and danger-ous, and sinfully handsome.

Gwendolyn shivered again, but this time because a tiny niggling thought reentered her head—hideous, but compelling, just the same.

There were no longer wolves in these parts.

Quite easily, she could imagine Málik shredding a man with that mouthful of teeth. All that was missing from his person were a pair of claws, and yet... did she not hear tell *faekind* could shift forms? Could he have been the one who killed Bryok?

"I only wonder... did you perchance know the First Alderman?"

"The dead one?" Put so succinctly, and without a trace of remorse.

"Indeed," said Gwendolyn, frowning, peering back toward the wych elm, where the guards stood waiting. "The dead one."

"Nay," he said.

"So, then, you never met him, even once?"

Málik stood, meeting her gaze directly. "Nay. I cannot say I ever did."

"I hear tell his wife left him, but I guess you wouldn't know such a thing since you've never met him. She's in Chysauster," Gwendolyn revealed.

One brow arched, and his eyes seemed to shine a little brighter with the revelation. "Truly?" he asked.

"Indeed," said Gwendolyn, hitching her chin. "In fact, I intend to speak with her."

"In Chysauster?"

Gwendolyn nodded, and Málik continued to stare at her a long while, before widening his smile. "You must realize, Gwendolyn... I know what you are doing."

Gwendolyn blinked at his familiarity.

"You do?"

"Indeed, I do."

Gwendolyn swallowed, wishing he would enlighten her, because really, she didn't know. And most especially, she didn't understand why she seemed so inclined to bedevil a man who seemed, by most measures, so dangerous a creature. Did she mean to corner him?

So what now? If he was Bryok's murderer—for whatever reason—she was now at his mercy, and far, far from home.

He pushed back a lock of hair that fell into his face. "Only keep this in mind as you play at your game, Princess... curiosity is like a *drogue*. Even in small doses it can be deadly."

He walked away then, leaving Gwendolyn to stare after him.

Was that a threat? Because if it was, it would behoove her to climb atop her horse and fly away home, and yet, Gwendolyn did no such thing. Instead, she followed quick at his heels.

"What does that mean?"

"You know what it means," he said, without turning. "Only be sure of this: Your father put me to a task, and I'll not rest on my laurels, Gwendolyn; neither will you. Whilst we are in Chysauster, I expect you will attend me daily to practice."

Gwendolyn halted, crossing her arms against the chill. Clearly he didn't like her, but why? She had never actually done anything to him, not really.

Certainly not until he'd shown her such disrespect!

He was the one who had given her insult, and then betrayed Bryn. *He* was the one who should apologize, and yet, far be it from him to consider it.

Long hours later, Gwendolyn was still brooding over their conversation by the stream.

Gods. He was the most insufferable creature she had ever encountered.

And now, not only was he not riding beside or behind her, he had taken the lead, so she was forced now and then to spur her mount in order to catch him or not lose sight of him over the hilly terrain. When finally Gwendolyn had enough, she sidled up beside him and said through clenched teeth, "I am not playing at games, you must realize." She really needed him to understand that the mission she'd embarked upon was delicate and important.

"Are you not?"

He couldn't possibly understand. He didn't know how things worked amidst her people. Clearly he hadn't any notion how important the First Alderman's position was to her father's court. Something about his death was terribly wrong, something aside from the obvious, and Gwendolyn intended to find out what that was. She opened her mouth to respond, to explain, but something else occurred to her—that smell. It was horrible in the hall, but worse in Mester Ciarán's laboratory. It was not the odor of a man newly deceased.

Beside her, Málik cast her a dubious glance, perhaps wondering why she fell silent, and Gwendolyn loathed the fact that she admired the shape of his lips, even when they were set so firmly against her. "If you must know, the true reason I am going to Chysauster is to invite my cousins to my wedding," she lied, but she didn't know if she'd said it to remind herself she was having a wedding, or if it was because she needed to apprise Málik of this.

Gods. All she really knew was that she had less right to notice the sinew in his thigh than she did to investigate the Alderman's death.

He answered with silence.

"You do recall I am to be wed, yes?"

Nothing again, merely the sound of one guard hacking up a pit and spewing it out. She heard it land in the grass and cast the man a backward glance, noting he had a full handful of prunes, and even as Gwendolyn watched, he chewed another mouthful, moving it from cheek to cheek as he stripped the pit of its meat.

They were less than half a bell from Chysauster now, and Gwendolyn was desperate to engage Málik whilst she still had his full attention. After they arrived in Chysauster, she would be forced to keep him at arm's length, as much as possible.

For the sake of her own sanity, if not her reputation, neither could she allow him to call her Gwendolyn anymore, even despite that she found she liked it.

"But perhaps you didn't realize," she said haughtily. "After all, you probably weren't invited to the Promise Ceremony, nor the wedding."

"I was not," he confessed, without concern, and Gwendolyn fell behind to admire the cut of his shoulders... the way his leathers and hosen fit so snugly.

By the eyes of Lugh, what was wrong with her? Málik wasn't the man she was promised to wed, and neither did he care one whit for her.

"Of course not," she said meanly. "You are not one of us. So why should my father trust you so implicitly with the most important asset he possesses?"

That got his attention, and he flicked Gwendolyn a backward glance, and the only sign she had that her words might have cut him was the way he also snapped his reins.

"You value yourself highly, Princess."

"I—"

But she didn't, not truly.

She didn't enough, so Demelza claimed.

Gwendolyn found herself with a lack for words, much less a proper defense. Indeed, she was the King's most valuable asset, his heir, but this was not what she'd meant. *Not at all.* Rather, she was speaking of Málik's affiliation with the palace guards, the Elite Guard her father had trusted him so quickly to train. And really, Málik could be training them to serve the enemy—*him*, for all they knew. In fact—she glanced back at the men riding in their wake—proof might be plainer than the nose on her face. Neither of these guards had seemed remotely inclined to see to Gwendolyn's welfare. They answered to Málik, and scarcely ever even looked at her, despite that Gwendolyn was their princess.

Neither had even thanked her for the prunes she'd gifted them, and the one had already eaten a handful. "I must wonder how you came to be in my father's service?"

"More questions?"

"But you give me no answers."

"I was summoned," he said.

"By whom?"

He turned to look at her now and smiled. "You truly enjoy playing the sleuth-hound, I see."

"I—"

"You can fool many, Princess, but you cannot fool me. You think I do not know why you were delayed before leaving the city, but I know."

"You can't, possibly."

"I know more than you think," he said.

"Then perhaps you will help explain the discrepancies I found?"

"I would if I cared to."

"But I care! Something is wrong, and I mean to find out what it is."

He lifted his brows. "Wrong with you? Your marriage, or something else?"

Gwendolyn was confused now. Did he, or did he not, know about her investigations? She grit her teeth. "I mean to say that something is amiss with the Alderman's death."

"So, you confess you are not traveling to Chysauster to invite your cousins to your wedding?"

"Nay! But—yes! Of course I am. I am, and you will see me

do so. And yet I also have a... certain... intuition, and I must speak to the Alderman's wife."

"And this was not something you were inclined to share with your father, the King, to whom you owe your fealty?"

Gwendolyn lifted a shoulder, resigned to the truth of it. "If I had, he would not have allowed me to come."

"Because he wouldn't wish to see you meddle, perhaps?"

Gwendolyn's cheeks burned hot.

Frustrated now, she popped the reins, deciding she'd had enough. "You are the most infuriating creature! I'm grateful our time together will be short," she said, veering her mount toward a thicket of trees, inclined to find herself a moment's respite.

Chysauster was over the next rise, and she needed to repair herself as best she could. If nothing else, she must steel her nerves—to put Málik in his place once and for all.

No matter how familiar he was becoming, he was not her betrothed. She could simply not allow him to speak to her the way he did. She was the Princess; he was her Shadow.

TWENTY-FOUR

Gwendolyn expected her uncle would ride out to greet them and escort them the rest of the way into the village. She also realized that, even as he greeted them so warmly, there were archers concealed in the nearby trees, ready to strike if he gave word.

He would not, however.

With a genuine smile, Gwendolyn offered the missive from his brother, and Duke Cunedda accepted it, sliding it into his belt without breaking the seal, offering her a nod and smile. Whatever that letter contained, it was for his eyes alone, and like the Treasury itself, Gwendolyn would never think to pry. For all she knew, her father was merely adding his own invitation to her wedding.

"Your cousins will be pleased to see you've returned," he said.

"I am, too," said Gwendolyn, wondering what her uncle thought of the *Sidhe* in her company. So much as he had yet to confess it, his *rás* was clear in his features—the hair, eyes, ears, teeth, and lucent flesh. And this was if one ignored his indefatigable arrogance. Though thankfully, if she worried how Málik would comport himself in her uncle's presence, she worried for naught. He fell back before the Duke joined them, assuming a subservient position, ahead of the other guards, as was his right. Duke Cunedda's men assumed the rear, because despite that this was her uncle's land, and his borough to govern, he served her father. As she was heir of Cornwall, he served Gwendolyn as well; therefore, her guards outranked his. But unlike her uncles Arthyen and Hedrek, Duke Cunedda had no pretensions or ambitions. He was content enough to be his brother's keeper. On the ride into the village, they spoke at length, mostly about Gwendolyn's wedding plans. She told him about the Promise Ceremony, eschewing the tale of Bryok's death. The two events were hardly connected anyway, and she didn't wish him to suspect the reason she'd come. Let him believe it was simply to invite them to the nuptials, because the less he knew about her true purpose, the less he would say to her father.

"I hope you'll join us," she offered.

Her uncle grinned wide, a smile that split his face. "I wouldn't miss it," he said. "So, tell me about your prince?"

Gods. It was only then Gwendolyn realized she'd forgotten to mention Prince Locrinus at all. Odd for a woman newly promised. "Well... he's... quite... princely," she offered.

"And you don't like him?" guessed Cunedda.

"I do," Gwendolyn lied, and her uncle lifted a brow.

"You forget how well I know you," he suggested, and Gwendolyn considered what to say in her defense, when suddenly, there was a thud behind them.

Startled, she spun about. One of her guards, the one wearing Hedrek's livery, had toppled from his horse. He fell face-first on the ground, smashing his nose, so it bled.

But this was the least of his concerns. He was foaming at

the mouth, his body convulsing violently, and he was making terrible choking sounds.

At the tips of his fingers lay several of the prunes Gwendolyn had given him.

His reaction swift, Málik dismounted, flying to the man's side and thrusting his fingers down the man's throat, coming away with nothing.

The other guard sat stupidly on his mount, mouth agape, while Cunedda's men did the same. After a moment, her uncle dismounted, moving to the guard's side, and while Málik tried to help him, her uncle pried open the man's fist to reveal...

A half-eaten prune.

Stunned though she was, Gwendolyn dismounted, too, hurrying to Málik's side to discover the guard's tunic soaked from so much dribble. His pupils were large and round, his skin turning blue... and she knew... even before she had finished processing the scene before her... she knew.

She shared a knowing look with Málik, eyes wide.

Poison.

"Lift him!" demanded her uncle, and Málik obeyed at once, scooping the twitching man into his arms, even knowing it was too late.

"We'll take him to the healer," apprised Cunedda.

Alas, Gwendolyn placed a hand on Málik's arm to stay him where he knelt. She met his *icebourne* gaze. "There's no cure," she whispered, wanting him to understand.

There was no remedy for this poison, and even if there were, he would asphyxiate before they brought him before a healer. At this point, the poison would work swiftly, and his final moments would be unimaginable. Gwendolyn shook her head, hot tears brimming in her eyes.

Trusting her, Málik nodded. He unsheathed his dagger, then plunged it straight into the man's heart.

THE BODY OF HEDREK'S VASSAL LAY ATOP CUNEDDA'S SUPPING TABLE. Deprived of life, his skin was already turning grey. "Poison," said the healer, confirming Gwendolyn's fears. But really, she'd known. The convulsions, the increased salivation noted by the soaking of his tunic, and the inky-blue stains beneath his fingernails, so soon after his demise—these were signs. She once watched a taster end this way, and it was the worst thing Gwendolyn had ever witnessed. If Málik had not put his blade into the man's breast, they would have watched him suffocate before their eyes, his eyes round and bulging, blood-rimmed, mouth open and gasping for air.

His death was all her fault. She blamed herself. She was the one who'd put the prunes into his saddlebag. And, if she had not done so, he'd not be lying here stone cold.

Gods. She had never even bothered to ask his name— Owen, so she learned only today. Her head had been so full of Málik and court intrigue that she had never ever considered.

"I don't understand," said her aunt. "If you ate some, why are you not affected?"

Her husband heaved a sigh, his big shoulders deflating. "You mustn't ask, Lowenna."

Sharing this knowledge could make her father vulnerable. Her uncle knew this, as well. That his wife was not aware of it made Gwendolyn believe he did not share the practice of dosing, or if he did, he did not share it with his wife or his children.

Arms crossed, Málik stood on the other side of the table, studying the now lifeless form of the guard. He flicked a glance at Gwendolyn when she spoke.

"I..." She shook her head, uncertain what to say. "Mustn't..."

"You mustn't have eaten much," suggested Málik, and she nodded.

"How do you know the poison was in the prunes?" asked Lowenna.

"I... I... don't know."

Here and now, Gwendolyn met Málik's gaze, and they shared another knowing look, and she knew... he knew.

"We'll put him on a pyre," suggested Cunedda.

"Thank you," said Gwendolyn, and she turned to quit the room, if only to go make certain the leftover prunes remained untouched. She went first to the other guard's mount, only because she felt certain Málik knew better than to eat his. Luckily, all the prunes were still there, precisely where Gwendolyn had put them, although the guard was nowhere to be found, quite likely pouring ale down his gullet over the loss of a fellow.

Málik followed Gwendolyn out, watching as she unsheathed the blade from her boot and stabbed it into the meat of the prunes she held, cutting it to the pit. Handing part of it to Málik, she put her own nose to the part she held, frowning as she smelled it.

There was the faintest mousy scent. Still, it was there.

Dropping the prune, Gwendolyn did what she'd not done in years—acquiesced to a full fit of fury, crushing the meat beneath her heel, furious with herself for missing this clue.

When finally she was in command of herself, she eyed the half Málik held, and confessed, "I took them from Bryok's home."

Málik nodded as tears stung her eyes.

"It wasn't your fault," he allowed, and his tone held none of its former reproach. However, it simply wasn't true. The one thing she had known was that poison was suspected in Bryok's murder. Why, then, had she taken his fruit?

Alas, Gwendolyn needed an ally—and more. She needed Málik's help to uncover this conspiracy. But she needed more than poison prunes before she could go running to her father with accusations. For all she knew, these prunes could have been a parting gift from a wife to an errant husband—a rude farewell. And yet, deep down in her heart, she knew that wasn't true.

Clarity came swiftly to her in that instant.

Someone left the prunes in Bryok's house to intentionally kill the Alderman. What was more, it didn't happen when everyone said it did. He couldn't have smelled so terrible in the space of a single day. He'd died long before his morning shift, and long before the end of his last. Someone failed to report it. Someone then moved his body from the place of his death and tidied his home, then took his body to a place where they could do him some violence to deflect suspicion. Except, when they cleaned the Alderman's house, they forgot to take the prunes.

Now, Gwendolyn must determine whether the Alderman's wife had a hand in this, or if she was innocent of the crime.

TWENTY-FIVE

I a took the news of her husband's death poorly, sobbing in her hands whilst her mother ushered the older children out of the house and held the youngest on her hip.

Once they were out of the room, Gwendolyn explained, as gently as she was able, about the discovery of her husband's body in the alley behind the smelting house.

She didn't tell her about the hammer, nor the state of his body after the "wolves" had their way with him. Some details were unnecessary, she decided, and it didn't take long for Gwendolyn to realize that Ia had had nothing to do with her husband's death.

Indeed, whoever filled those prunes knew she and her children would be gone, and that only Bryok would have access to them.

Moreover, whoever poisoned them must have known enough to know how to handle the cuttings. The fumes alone could kill as readily as the ingestion. But if one did not know how to harvest or prepare the potion, as the physician implied, it could cause blisters to form, or discolorations that lasted days, even weeks; perhaps this was what Mester Ciarán had been searching for during the examination in his laboratory?

Only now Gwendolyn wished she had inspected the most obvious suspects for evidence on their hands. Especially considering that Mester Ciarán also had a bowl of those same prunes in his laboratory. Was it Mester Ciarán who injected the prunes?

If so, and he allowed Gwendolyn to eat them, he would face the executioner. But something told her he did not. And there was also that strange encounter between Mester Ciarán and the Mester Alderman in her father's hall the day they'd brought in Bryok's body.

Gwendolyn knew it took about six bells after death, or thereabouts, before a body's humors ceased to flow. She knew this because she was a hunter. Once the blood congealed, cadavers didn't bleed, except through the ordeal of the bier. Considering that, it was rather odd Mester Ciarán should hand his staff to Alderman Eirwyn to poke at the body. Why should he do so, unless he, too, suspected the Mester Alderman of Bryok's murder? Furthermore, if Mester Ciarán suspected Eirwyn, and Eirwyn knew it, mayhap those prunes in his laboratory were meant to silence Mester Ciarán once and for all?

As soon as Gwendolyn returned, she must seek the physician. Perhaps he would corroborate her suspicions, or mayhap he'd discovered something more.

She was only glad now that she'd taken his prunes. And then suddenly, she remembered something. The day she'd eaten Mester Ciarán's prunes... this was the day she'd retched over Málik. By far, that was the most she'd eaten at once, and not so many since.

She peered up at Málik, who stood beside her, reminding herself to tell him about this later. In the meantime, Gwendolyn laid a hand over Ia's, and said, "Do you know of anyone who might have wished your husband ill?"

Ia shook her head.

"Did you find he was angry when you left?"

"Why should he be?"

Gwendolyn lifted her shoulders. "Because you *left* him?"

"Nay! I did not!" cried Ia. "I did not leave him. He told me to go!" The woman sounded utterly incensed, as though she must be telling the truth. "He said he would follow," she said. "He said he would speak with the Mester Alderman. He said he would leave his position." She blew her nose then, and added, "He promised me a better life."

With Ia's youngest on her hip, her mother patted her daughter on the shoulder, and said, "There, there."

Unfortunately, Gwendolyn had no words to console the poor woman, and neither did she dare elaborate further when Ia was already so distraught.

Offering thanks for her time, Gwendolyn and Málik left her to be consoled by her mother, and Gwendolyn took the opportunity on the way home to tell Málik about her suspicions. With her cheeks burning hot, she reminded him about the spew on his tunic, and explained that she'd eaten prunes from Mester Ciarán's bowl.

"Interesting," he said.

"Don't you think so?"

"Indeed."

IA'S FATHER'S FARM WAS ONLY A STONE'S THROW FROM HER UNCLE'S village.

They'd been gone so short a time that Gwendolyn was surprised to return and discover a pyre already aflame, with

Owen's body atop it. As casually as though he were a rack of lamb, they'd tossed him onto the bier, and then stood watching as he burned. He was surrounded by strangers who would shed no tears for him and Gwendolyn forced herself to stand and watch as well, a final gesture of respect.

Beside her, Málik kept her company.

After a while, he said, "Gwendolyn." And, far from loathing the way it sounded, Gwendolyn was moved by the way her name sounded upon his lips... breathless, like a whisper.

"Yes?"

"Those prunes must have been costly, don't you think?"

Gwendolyn nodded. *Indeed.* Particularly at this time of the year when they must be imported. In fact, they were so costly that she saw none on the table at Prince Loc's welcome feast, despite that she knew her father meant to impress.

"Moreover," he said, perhaps wondering aloud, "only ask yourself... why would someone bother using a hammer if the method of death was poison?"

Gwendolyn blinked.

Of course she had wondered. Many times. It was part of the reason she had embarked upon this investigation, but when Málik posed the question, the answer seemed as clear as the nose on her face.

They'd used the hammer to deflect suspicion—for the same reason they'd moved the body... and for the same reason they'd cleaned Bryok's house.

Whoever killed Bryok wasn't a stranger.

It was someone who'd known him well enough to offer an extravagant gift of imported prunes. Someone who known him well enough to worry his death would reflect upon him poorly.

Find *that* man, Málik suggested, and therein discover his motive.

CHAPTER

TWENTY-SIX

I f only to see if the woman's story would change, Gwendolyn returned to the farm a few days later. Ia had been weeping since Gwendolyn gave her the awful news. So, it seemed she must have truly believed Bryok would join her in Chysauster.

Curious about Bryok's relationship with the Mester Alderman, Gwendolyn inquired further, wondering if Alderman Eirwyn ever called upon their home, or whether he and Bryok might be acquainted more intimately than their positions should allow.

He did not, she said, although sometimes Alderman Aelwin attended her husband at home. "Aelwin?" Gwendolyn asked with surprise, remembering that not once, but twice he'd denied any fellowship with Bryok. And yet, it could be that while it was not precisely unlawful to befriend another alderman, alliances between her father's councilmen were not encouraged.

Moreover, the aldermen were commonly at odds, currying favor at all times. And if Gwendolyn recalled correctly, both

Bryok and Aelwin were foremost in the line of succession for the position of Mester Alderman after Eirwyn retired or died. However, as First Alderman, Bryok had the advantage. Jealousy made for strange fellows.

Indeed, if Alderman Aelwin was jealous of Bryok, perhaps he'd meant to remove his rival, and the prunes were Aelwin's, meant for Bryok.

To that end, Alderman Aelwin had also seemed overly intrigued about the reason Bryok wished to employ the cook's house. Perhaps he was the one who'd sent Bryok to inquire, if only to deflect suspicion from himself.

Gwendolyn had so many questions to put forth upon her return, but though there was little to be accomplished from so far away, she was in little hurry to face the journey home, nor the changes to come—changes to her life, that would be enforced the moment she returned.

The only reason she'd escaped—and make no mistake, it was an escape—was because of her own expediency and her mother's ignorance in Gwendolyn's day-to-day activities. However, Queen Eseld would not allow Gwendolyn another reprieve. Therefore, against her better judgment, she lingered in Chysauster, poring over the clues in her mind, telling herself that what was done was done. The First Alderman was already dead. There was nothing she could do to change that. And neither had she any evidence, except her own suspicions and a handful of poisoned prunes she intended to show her father, though alone they proved little.

Moreover, if Gwendolyn's suspicions were true, there was no one left but Aelwin to inherit Eirwyn's position, and there-fore no one else should be in immediate danger, except for perhaps Eirwyn, although Aelwin would be a fool to murder two aldermen in so short a time.

Nay, he wouldn't dare, she decided.

At any rate, she was quite certain she'd taken all the remaining prunes, much to Owen's lament, and hers as well. And this wasn't the only reason she wished to stay in Chysauster, with Málik, even despite that she wasn't willing to confess it aloud.

Instead, she endeavored to convince herself it was because this would be the last opportunity she would ever have to enjoy the company of her cousins as a girl unwed.

Aside from Bryn and Ely, her cousins were the closest to siblings Gwendolyn had ever had, and now that she was here, she intended to make the most of it.

Mornings she spent with Málik, sparring in her uncle's courtyard. Afternoons she spent with her cousins, reminiscing over times past.

But *gods*, whosoever believed men were bawdier than women had never met her cousins, and Gwendolyn wondered if perhaps they'd spent too much time with their father in the hinterlands. Scarcely older than Cunedda's daughters, poor Lowenna listened raptly to her stepdaughters' tales, perhaps hoping to learn more about the young women she must raise.

More than once, she lifted a brow. And Gwendolyn wondered where Cunedda had met the sweet woman— certainly not around these parts, considering her accent.

"Whence do you hail?" Gwendolyn inquired.

Smiling, Lowenna bowed her head before speaking, far more deferential than her cousins were ever inclined to be. "Thank you, Highness," she said politely. "Dobunni, born and raised."

The borderlands.

Gwendolyn hitched her chin. Depending on which part of that dominion one hailed from, loyalties could be suspect—at least regarding Cornwall. And yet, wasn't it the Dobunni tribe that had granted those lands for the Temple of the Dead? They imagined themselves to be peacekeepers, and ironically, it was also through Dobunni lands Prince Locrinus must secure passage for his army to take Plowonida.

"Have you seen the new temple?" Gwendolyn asked.

"Nay, mestres," said Lowenna. "The first stone was raised after my departure. I've not returned since. Now both my father and mother have... gone. Perhaps someday I will go."

"I as well," said Gwendolyn. Although she'd never been called mestres before, she wasn't about to remind the lady of her correct title. As it was, the look on the poor lady's face was so uncertain that Gwendolyn had the sudden yen to embrace her. All at once, she recalled the word Prince Loc used to describe her people—Æmete.

Really, she couldn't imagine Lowenna ever using such a name for anyone, and she considered perhaps she was told wrong. No doubt, it was a dangerous misunderstanding, and wars were fought for lesser insults.

When Gwendolyn was queen, she vowed to make certain there were ambassadors for *all* tribes, not merely the most respected or feared—that their voices had the chance to be heard.

No doubt her father had gone to great lengths to bring them closer together, but there was still much work to be done.

"Have you any brothers and sisters?" Gwendolyn asked.

"One—an elder brother," said Lowenna. "I was the only girl. My village suffered a pox when I was young. My youngest brother died, with my mother and father, and Mawgan, my elder brother, found himself chieftain too young. He was the one who offered me to Cunedda, and for that I shall be eternally grateful."

Her eyes softened when she spoke her husband's name.

"I see," said Gwendolyn, understanding more than she wished to. Likely it was the pox that had kept her from conceiving. Sadly, Gwendolyn knew it could ravage the womb.

How sad.

Lowenna was sweet, scarcely deserving of a life without children. Like Elowyn, she deserved to hold a babe of her own, and Gwendolyn hoped the gods might see fit to favor them someday. But clearly, the lady was quite contented, if perhaps ill-versed in the social graces.

Perhaps wishing to make everyone feel welcomed, she unknowingly paired Gwendolyn with Málik at the lord's table. From the first night, they shared a trencher and cup, and if anyone wondered why Gwendolyn would dare enjoy such intimacies with a man not her betrothed, no one spoke the question aloud.

If nothing more, Gwendolyn found she enjoyed the freedom afforded her as a woman grown, without her mother about to rebuke her choices, or Demelza to advise her.

Also, so much as she loathed to confess it, it was also a relief not to have Ely about, scrutinizing her association with Málik... nor to catch her giving him such warm glances.

Indeed, with the hostilities behind them, she found she enjoyed his company, and despite that it was unheard of— one's Shadow supping with his charge—Gwendolyn also discovered she didn't care.

Upon her return to Trevena, she would be expected to comport herself as a Promised One, but here and now, in the hinterlands, so far from her father's court, and so far from the eyes of all who'd witnessed the exchange of torcs, she was content enough to live as her cousins lived, free from convention and demands, free from all who might judge a simple friendship.

And neither did her uncle seem to care, though she knew that, unlike his naïve young wife, Cunedda knew better. No doubt he had turned a blind eye, perhaps considering that Gwendolyn would someday be his queen.

Every now and again, he gave her a knowing glance, either winking or smiling, and making her blush, most notably whenever she laughed at something Málik said.

And this she loved most about her uncle's house: There was laughter aplenty. A far cry from her father's hall, his was modest and warm. The lord's table was long, offering seats to all, including the neighbors, whenever they came to call.

Any time a farmer came with a grievance, Cunedda listened mindfully, then invited the man to sup and drink whilst they ruminated over solutions.

Certainly, there was much about Cunedda that reminded her of her father, but though Cunedda was scarcely younger than her sire, his face did not show the same hard years, and his laugh lines were deeper than the lines in his brow.

In like form, his servants jested with their lord and lady, and her cousins told jokes as ribald as any man's. Wine flowed. Small plates passed hands—not olives from An Ghréig, nor sardines from Hiberia, but simple pilchards, fished from nearby shoals, served with *hevva* cake and mead.

Borlewen was bolder than Jenefer and Briallen, and extraordinarily talented. One evening, she played the harp by the hearth, making up stories that put a blush in her father's well-hewn cheeks. Yet another evening, she took a dagger from her belt—the one she'd been using to sup with—and splayed her hand on the supping table, stabbing quickly in succession between her fingers to illustrate her prowess with the blade. Everyone watched with halted breath.

The dagger itself was quite unusual. Poniards were normally meant to be used for slicing. Usually slender, with a triangular blade, this one was longer and double-edged, similar to a sword, and far more suitable for stabbing. More than the trick itself, impressive as it was, Gwendolyn was interested in the blade.

"Want to try?" her cousin asked with a wily grin, and Gwendolyn shook her head, crossing her arms.

"Indeed, I do not!"

"And you?" she inquired of Málik. "Art certain to be braver than a silly girl?"

Gwendolyn laughed at the barb, knowing her cousin meant no harm. To the contrary, there was a certain look in her eye that left Gwendolyn quite certain that Borlewen considered herself far superior to all men, Málik and her father included.

"Am I?" asked Málik with a half-smile. And then, after sharing a brief look with Borlewen, he shrugged and offered a hand.

Borlewen grinned victoriously.

Calmly, Málik spread his fingers, and once again, without waiting to bolster her courage, or taking time to assess the position of his hand, Borlewen stabbed quickly in succession, accurately missing flesh and bone and embedding the sharp blade deep into wood at the end, so it hummed for a moment as the grip shivered.

Gwendolyn lifted a brow, only now noticing the multitude of pock holes in the table, and she wondered how many fingers Borlewen had taken before perfecting her trick. Fortuitously, she still had all of her own.

"'Tis quite the talent," offered Málik as he withdrew his hand and slid it back into his lap. And if he'd held his breath for a good end, it was not the least bit apparent.

Then again, Gwendolyn thought, without truly believing it, if he was *fae...* perhaps he could regrow his fingers and toes, like Núada of the Silver Hand, who was said to have lost his arm, then his crown, and regained it all after growing back the arm in silver.

"May I see the blade?" Gwendolyn asked.

"Certainly," said Borlewen, proffering the dagger, hilt first. She grinned. "'Tis long enough to slide betwixt ribs, and prick a heart," she said, with one lifted brow. "My father had it made for me."

The marking on the hilt was the ancient guardian of Dumnonia—the King's standard, of course—and there was a small black pearl in the dragon's eye. These were rare, and one legend claimed that black pearls were formed in a dragon's head, and that one had to slay the dragon to claim his pearls. However, this was clearly not true, for there were no dragons anymore, if ever they had existed. And still, it was quite an extravagant gift. Even amidst their own Cornish oysters, a simple white pearl was rare as a ghost orchid.

Cunedda entered the room, laughing boisterously as he overheard his daughter speak about the dagger. "And still she never took my hint. Notice the tongue?"

Gwendolyn looked again and found the barbed tongue missing—how clever!

"If he thought that alone would hush me, he must think again!"

Gwendolyn laughed, her brows lifting, and everyone joined her, Borlewen's laughter ringing louder than all. Handing back the blade, Gwendolyn felt wistful for a family like this—a father that would laugh with her, far more than anything else. Gwendolyn had more than enough gifts of silver and gold. And they were all the same blood, but... Gwendolyn longed for such ease.

Alas, this was bound to never change. She was raised differently, and though some would say better, Gwendolyn didn't think so. She had more, this much was true, but more was not better—take her cousins, for example. They lived as they pleased, plainspoken and free. And even Ia, with all her grief, had clearly experienced a love that was sweet and true, for no woman wept so bitterly over the loss of a man if she could despise him, nor wish him dead.

That night, nestled in bed with Jenefer, Gwendolyn and her cousins talked about the evening, laughing about the way her uncle seemed to believe no one could see him when he slid his hand beneath the table into the crook of his wife's thighs.

"He doesn't care," said Briallen.

"Oh, he does," argued Jenefer. "Rather, he believes himself too cunning—like Kitto, every time he nugs you behind the ale casks, Borlewen."

Borlewen laughed. She drew up the woolen blanket to her lips to hide a smile, but her blue eyes twinkled fiercely.

"You must like it," offered Briallen.

"Indeed, she does," said Jenefer. To which she added. "Alas, you'd best take care, baby sister, lest you end with a child in your belly and no torc to declare you."

"Blood and bones!" exclaimed Borlewen. "Better this than waiting so long my womb withers and dies, like Lowenna! At least this way I will have a child of my own to raise and plow my fields."

"More's the pity. They'll be the only fields of yours to ever be plowed again," countered Jenefer.

"Nay," argued Borlewen. "One child will merely recommend me. I know how to please a man well enough that I'll have six more in line behind him."

"Six!" squealed Briallen, and Jennifer added, "*Gods*, you're a wanton."

Borlewen shrieked with outrage and flew out of her bed with a pillow in hand to pummel Jenefer. For a moment, the sisters grappled in jest, with Jenefer screaming and Borlewen trying in vain to shove her pillow against her sister's face.

"Stop! Stop!" screamed Jenefer, laughing. "Stop!" Until all three were shrieking with laughter, and Gwendolyn even, despite that she took a knee in the thigh over Borlewen's feigned fury. Later, when they were settled again and the laughter subsided, Briallen dared to ask, "By the by, Gwen, I must ask... have you never seen Málik's cock?"

Appalled by the rude question, and from the meekest of the sisters, Gwendolyn slapped a hand over her mouth to stifle her horrified laughter, and the sisters all recommenced to giggling.

"I have not," said Gwendolyn, though she was smiling— perhaps as much by the prospect as the question itself.

Gods. The last time she'd spent any time with her cousins, they weren't nearly so man-crazed. But that was a long time ago, and now they were women grown—plainly far more experienced than Gwendolyn. Or at least the way they spoke made her think they were.

"Why not?" asked Jenefer, baldly.

Borlewen was the first to remind them. "Because she is promised, silly twat. And yet, one needn't bed a man to see his bald-pated druid."

"Borlewen!" exclaimed both Jenefer and Briallen together. And again, all three girls fell into fits of laughter, and Gwendolyn, too. But thereafter, even when the room quieted, she couldn't stop thinking of Málik's "bald-pated druid."

Bawdy as they were, her cousins had merely spoken Gwendolyn's thoughts aloud.

Oh, to be so free of thought.

It was a long, long while before anyone spoke again—so long that Gwendolyn thought mayhap her cousins had fallen asleep. Suddenly, Briallen turned, and said, "Really, why do we need men? You should raise an army, Gwen. Take Pretania for us!"

"And then what?" suggested Borlewen, snidely, yawning loudly. "Live like Druids, giving each other green gowns, and waggling the occasional man to get ourselves a babe?"

The Llanrhos Druids were said to love amidst their own kind, and women were not well received. If a woman ever arrived on their doorstep, no matter her grievance, she would be turned away, for theirs was an ancient order that did not welcome creatures with menses—not even for sacrifices. Only a man could seek their counsel.

"I would like that better," said Briallen wistfully.

"Of course, you would," said Borlewen sleepily. Then everyone fell silent, leaving Gwendolyn awake, and longing... not merely for the easy banter of these three sisters, but for something else... something she daren't name.

Forcing herself to think of Prince Loc instead, she tried to imagine their coupling, and... failed. Her brain simply did not wish to entertain such thoughts.

And neither did she.

Thankfully, she'd had enough strong ale to drift to sleep, even as her cousins began to snore.

THE FOLLOWING MORNING, GWENDOLYN FOUND MÁLIK IN THE courtyard, stretching to prepare for their usual morning routine. With the blush of the early morning light painting his form, his silvery color was awash with a dusky rose, and for a long while, Gwendolyn stood back, as she had in those early days after he'd first arrived in Trevena, only daring to admire him—his graceful movements, his long, sinuous limbs... the outline of his well-muscled form... the confidence with which he negotiated each exercise.

However, at the moment, he seemed, for the first time ever, oblivious to her presence, and Gwendolyn found herself with a trickster on her shoulder.

Oh, how she'd love to best him, *only once*.

Having come prepared to practice, she was ready. Careful not to make a sound, she unsheathed her sword, then flew at him, falling upon him just the way he'd taught her to do, minding her feet, so she stepped out precisely at the right moment with the sword positioned, ready to strike. Without warning, Málik spun to face her, withdrawing his sword from its scabbard more swiftly than he should have been able, considering their proximity.

He struck Gwendolyn's blade so forcefully it might have cut the weapon in twain were it not good Loegrian steel. The force and sound the impact made sent a tremor down her spine, and a pang through her hand.

"Well done!" he said. But then, without hesitation, Gwendolyn spun about and parried, hoping to catch him unawares.

Once again, he found her blade, striking harder than he did the first time. "Bedamned!" Gwendolyn cried, her fingers screaming over the abuse.

"Never spin."

"You did!"

"I am me," he said. "You are you."

"Bryn said—"

"I know what your poppet says, Princess, but you'll gain little advantage with a spin. It will not give you more force, nor any more leverage, and will present your back to your opponent. Always remember, your single directive is to avoid being skewered. To do this, you must keep your eyes on your opponent's blade."

Like a strange, sensual dance, he seized Gwendolyn by the hand, spinning her about, showing her what he meant, and, suddenly, she found her back nestled against his leathered chest, and he shoved the tip of his sword against her back. The sharp blade did not penetrate her tunic, but it came dangerously close. She swallowed convulsively, trusting him, even though every instinct told her not to.

Gods.

With Bryn, she had never once allowed herself to be so vulnerable, and here they were, leagues away from the safety of her father's court, with a man whose loyalties she'd once questioned, allowing him to prick her with his deadly blade.

"Notice where the point is," he whispered, and she heard the pop of the fabric of her leather tunic as the blade penetrated to kiss her sensitive flesh. "If you ever find yourself in this vulnerable position, do not aim for the heart. 'Tis difficult to hit anything of consequence when you stab a man in the back."

"Here," he said, pressing the tip a little harder, so it gave her flesh a sting. "Here, to the right, not the left, you will pierce the reins. The pain will be excruciating, and your opponent will drop like a stone."

Gods.

Gwendolyn found herself frozen, and breathless, torn between longing to extricate herself from his embrace... and wishing to submit...

She had not felt this way in Prince Loc's arms.

Never did she imagine herself so ready to kiss a man, so acutely aware of every nerve in her body, every inhale and exhale of breath... her own as well as his.

From across the courtyard came a sudden clang of metal, and Gwendolyn peered over to discover her uncle's farrier working on her mare's shoe—a favor she didn't ask for but was grateful for. However, realizing they had eyes upon them now, her body flushed hot, and, after an excruciating moment, Málik withdrew, and Gwendolyn felt the sharp, cold blade ease away from her skin, somehow leaving her strangely bereft as his hand abandoned hers in midair. She turned to eye his sword, dazed and confused, but too curious not to ask. "Why does your sword have so short a grip?"

Málik leveled it before her, positioning one hand against the sword guard, the other on the pear-shaped pommel, demonstrating the proper way to hold it.

"Should I be using this design?"

He shrugged. "Depends."

"On what?"

Far more swiftly than Gwendolyn could follow, he performed a crooked strike, meanwhile unsheathing the parrying dagger at his waist, and said, "Whether you wish to fight one-handed or two."

Gwendolyn inspected her own arming sword, tilting it one way, then the other, attempting the same maneuver he'd only just displayed, but to no avail. She could easily wield a second blade with her own sword, such as the one she kept at her boot, but not whilst employing such an awkward maneuver. And yet she could see why this could be necessary. The most important thing in battle, so Bryn once said, was to remain flexible.

"It's not possible," he said. "For two reasons. First, most people need two expert hands to employ such a gambit, but your sword has design limitations as well."

Gwendolyn attempted the maneuver again and found she lacked the mobility to hold the sword without finding herself in danger of losing it entirely.

"I understand why you were given that sword. Most

women don't have the strength or cause to wield a two-handed weapon. But you are good enough, Gwendolyn."

Gwendolyn couldn't help it. She grinned. These were the times she felt most alive—when she was sparring with a partner, wielding her sword. It gave her a sense of control over her life that she wouldn't trade for all the lace in Damascus.

"Someday I will teach you the other master strikes."

"Master strikes?"

"The Strike of Wrath, the Cross Strike, the Parting Strike and the Squinting Strike—some of the finer techniques of a longsword."

"I would like that," Gwendolyn said, though, at the moment, she was far more curious about his sword. "May I try yours?" she asked.

"Of course." He traded swords with her, testing the length of hers by measuring it to his heel. It was too short.

Gwendolyn did the same, finding his blade far too long. She had to bend her elbow to avoid scraping the tip across the ground. Clearly, his arms were much longer, and this sword was fashioned particularly for him. Even hers was not so well honed, for she had grown much since her fifteenth year.

"You could have one made," he suggested. "Of course, yours would be shorter, but this would suit you, and it would allow you more freedom to parry as you please. I have already surmised this is your strength."

"Parrying?"

"Indeed," he said, nodding. "Try the sword. Go on. Make use of the grip as needed for leverage. Aim diagonally by raising the pommel and pull back as you thrust forward with the hilt, but don't forget to step and add your hip into the cut as you would any other strike."

Smiling, Gwendolyn positioned her hand, one fist near the

guard, the other on the pommel, then tried his crooked strike again.

This time, it felt better. Indeed, she sensed the longer grip would allow her to place more strength into a swing when she needed it most, thereby avoiding the impulse to spin.

In fact, if she used both hands and kept the swing closer to her body, she could parry quicker, and if she needed to, she could use it one-handed as well.

Feeling emboldened and thinking perhaps that while she had the advantage of his sword, she would test Málik again, she stomped her foot to bait him.

Without delay, he positioned her sword in his hand, closing the distance, stepping into her, and cutting the air before her, even as he stabbed the parrying dagger toward her side, right at the level of her heart, as he came to whisper into her ear.

He grinned. "Most knives will not reach the heart from this angle, Princess, but mine will." His breath was warm, and sweet, like mint grass, and his mouth was far too close.

Gwendolyn's breath hitched as he withdrew and said, "Take heart, I never once saw your poppet parry with such skill."

Warmth spread through Gwendolyn's breast, into her face, and though she lifted a brow over the compliment, it thrilled her, nonetheless. "Truly?" she asked.

"Truly," he said, and winked.

And then, once more, within another blink of an eye, he had Gwendolyn on her bum, red-faced and embarrassed to have been bested only by his simple praise.

His lesson for the morning complete, Málik grinned unrepentantly, like a wolf, his sharp canines revealed, and then resheathed both his blades, and offered Gwendolyn a hand, lifting her up from the dust. Only now she wondered if he'd anticipated her all along. "Did you know I was watching you?"

"Of course," he said, with a smile as crooked as his strike.

"How so?"

He touched the tip of his nose, and his nostrils flared as he confessed, "I know your scent, *Princess*."

TWENTY-SEVEN

O ver dinner that evening, the spirit between them was changed, something slight, though of consequence.

Gwendolyn noted Málik smiled more readily, and he teased her mercilessly, taking their shared cup every time she drank, and turning the glass ever so purposefully, lifting it so his lips fell upon the very spot her lips had only just touched.

It sent a shiver to her womb each time.

Did he realize?

Was it a game?

And yet, no matter. Instead of rousing her pique, it somehow stirred Gwendolyn's blood—a fact that was nearly as disconcerting as was the truth that she thoroughly enjoyed it.

Over these past few days, he had ceased with the chiding remarks. Reserved though he remained most of the time, he was more forthcoming when she dared put forward a question about something she longed to know.

"How came you to be in my father's employ?"

"I was sent," he said.

"By whom?"

"My father."

"Your father? I thought you said you were summoned?"

"Both, if you must know." He gave her a sad, cryptic smile, and Gwendolyn found she hadn't more nerve to pry.

Perhaps on some level, she feared that knowing the truth about him would change her life in ways she wasn't prepared to allow. Only for now, his newfound good humor was a welcome distraction. So were his outlandish tales.

For one, he claimed the *lyn yeyn* quoit near Land's End was a portal stone, like the one that stood southeast of Fowey Moor. He claimed it was used to travel betwixt realms.

"Gods, nay!" argued her uncle, burping very loudly after gulping down an entire tankard of ale. "That is a nurse-maid's tale, meant to frighten wee children. The truth is far less fantastic. Rather, 'tis meant to place bodies atop as leavings for the carrion—a gesture...of—" He burped again— "Gratitude to our gods... for the lending of life." He slammed down his tankard, then lifted it again to show his maid, requesting more. "All to dust," he said. "To dust we go again!"

To this argument, Málik merely shrugged and said, "Ah, well, what do I know?" Though he sent Gwendolyn a conspiratorial glance, and the tiniest trace of a smile.

Naturally, Gwendolyn was eager to learn more. All the questions she'd ever longed to ask of his kind now resurfaced and vied for play on her tongue. And yet, for all she knew, he was teasing her for sport—not *fae* at all, and not remotely sober.

Gwendolyn's gaze shifted between her uncle and Málik, comparing them side by side. Was she the only one who saw him differently? Did they not note his pointed ears and sharp teeth and think *fae*? Or his pale complexion and silvery hair, or *icebourne* eyes?

As far as Gwendolyn could tell, her uncle didn't appear to be treating him any differently than he would any other man, nor did he take Málik's tales as truth.

Shifting his gaze from her uncle, Málik caught Gwendolyn staring again, and she averted her gaze, embarrassed now, wondering if she'd only imagined some *fae* relation, though shame on him for telling such tales.

Danann, they called him, it could be in jest.

What if none of it was ever meant to be taken as truth?

Indeed, what if the stories were only meant to be cautionary, as her uncle claimed, and her crib-side visitation only the fevered ramblings of a drunken maid?

Certainly, Gwendolyn had never known Demelza nor her mother to imbibe, but that didn't mean they hadn't.

Gwendolyn had never considered herself to be different, except by virtue of her royal blood, and there was nothing, truly nothing, about her condition that gave any truth to the Goldenchild Prophecy, except for the tales told by her mother and maid.

Her appearance was simply not proof. One person's notion of beauty was not another's. Some people treated her one way, others treated her another, and the person she spied in the mirror was neither beautiful nor hideous. She was only Gwendolyn—with breasts too small, hips too wide, mouth a little too full, and eyes neither green nor blue. Instead, they were the dullest shade of grey—the color of a storm by twilight.

Feeling maudlin this evening, Gwendolyn peered down into her cup, drained of mead, and considered pouring herself another. But nay, the beverage was too strong.

She glanced once more at Málik and, this time, found him watching her instead, his pale blue eyes all too knowing.

Where once she'd spied condemnation, she now saw something else... something warm and sweet... something dangerous and deep.

But this could not be entertained. She was already bound to Prince Loc. That would not change. Ever since the day she was born, her future was writ in blood by Málik's own kind—or those he claimed were his kin, by the appellation he chose.

Straightening her shoulders, Gwendolyn offered him a tremulous smile, then rose, excusing herself, and made for her bed, feeling flushed and drained as her cup. *Too much mead. Too much frolic. Too much laughter. Too much... everything.*

None of this would serve her on the morrow when she must, at long last, leave and return to her true life. And despite this, before climbing into bed, she dared to remove the heavy chain from about her neck and set it gingerly on a bedside table.

If only for tonight, she would like to be free of the reminder.

Tomorrow would be soon enough to yield to duty. Tonight, she only wished to be Gwen... cousin to Borlewen, Jenefer, and Briallen. Friend to Málik.

BUT THE FOLLOWING MORNING, SHE DIDN'T REACH FOR THE TORC.

One more day, she decided—one more day.

The time was at hand to prepare for her nuptials and remaining here, no matter how pleasant the diversion, would do her little good. She was already bound, promised by her own word and free will.

And yet... at least... at the very least... she could keep the memory of this time close to her heart. So, for now, she left the torc where it lay on the table, unwilling to don it again so soon.

No one questioned her about her bare neck when she arrived to break her fast, and when Borlewen found the necklace upon rising, and tried it on, coming out of the room to reveal it about her throat, Gwendolyn smiled, and said, "It looks beautiful on you."

Borlewen struck a pose. "Verily?"

Gwendolyn nodded. "Indeed." And when her cousin made to remove it from her neck, Gwendolyn lifted a hand to compel her, and said, "Nay, please. Wear it awhile. I shall have worn it more than enough by my dying days."

"Oh!" said Borlewen, twirling happily. "I am a princess! Promised to a great and mighty prince!" Gwendolyn laughed softly.

Indeed, it was a lovely torc—shinier than the torc of her house. Yet the sapphire eyes of its serpents glittered with vengeance, and Gwendolyn found the look of it disturbing. At least for the time being, she was content enough to let Borlewen pretend.

Later that night, after supping, whilst they were seated outside by a bonfire—a nightly occurrence in these parts—Gwendolyn found herself alone with Málik.

Once again, he did not comment on her bare throat, though his pale blue eyes found the torc about Borlewen's neck and filled with questions—questions that Gwendolyn hadn't any answers for, so she let it pass without explanation. Yet truly, her heart had grown heavier than that bloody torc, and she could simply not tolerate the weight of both. In due time, she would wear it again, and she would meet Prince Locrinus beneath the Sacred Yew, because that is what she was born to do. But that didn't mean she must enjoy it, nor should she feel guilt-ridden for taking a few more days to enjoy this liberty, free from reminders like that glowering torc.

Let Borlewen wear it awhile. Her cousin certainly seemed

to like it well enough, petting it like a precious lover, all the while her Kitto drooled over her shoulder.

Meanwhile, Gwendolyn sat cross-legged on the grass beside Málik, covering her hosen with the flaps of her tunic, whilst two of her cousins sat flirting with visiting neighbors, Jenefer with the father, Borlewen with the son.

Prickles of grass poked through Gwendolyn's hosen, but she didn't care. She was far too contented at the instant.

"This should be fun to watch," she said tartly, eyeing Borlewen with her Kitto. "If both should succeed here tonight, one will find herself a mother and sister, the other a sister and daughter by law."

Málik chuckled low, a sound that never failed to stir Gwendolyn's blood. At the instant, she was feeling a little melancholy, knowing they must soon leave... for everyone's sakes. And, in part because she still needed to determine how and why Bryok was murdered. Alas, the longer she remained here, supping with Málik, sparring with Málik, laughing with Málik, the more she wanted to stay... the more she dreaded her wedding to Prince Loc. Coming closer every day.

Already the moon above was a waning crescent, smiling down on them in this place where, mostly, no lady wore gems or silk.

No doubt her mother was up in arms over her continued absence. And doubtless she was furious that Gwendolyn wasn't around to take instruction to prepare for the nuptials to come.

But more and more, Gwendolyn dreaded her wedding night, and all the while she fretted. Everyone except Málik seemed oblivious to her travails.

Gods, she was a mess.

Across the courtyard, Borlewen cozied with the farmer's son, the two of them hiding in the darkest corner, behind a wall of ale casks, completely unconcerned that anyone might spy them—her father, if she wasn't too careful. And yet would he care? Gwendolyn thought mayhap not, because he himself was out in the dark field, perhaps fondling his wife. In the meantime, her cousins seemed free enough to love as they would, though she knew her uncle, as any father would, must have limits to his indulgence.

Even as they watched, the farmer's son took a generous helping of her cousin's ample bosom in his hand, squeezing as his lips found Borlewen's mouth. Only, to see this stirred Gwendolyn in ways she daren't confess, but whom would she tell?

Málik?

The night was peaceful. The stars above winking, and with the moon spilling down over his silvery hair, the effect of it was like a halo. He was too beauteous for words, almost surreal. "What of you?" she dared to ask. "Do you ever intend to wed, Málik?"

"Who? Me?" he asked with a chuckle, as he chewed on a long blade of grass. "Nay, Princess, I was not made for that." He winked at her then, but Gwendolyn knit her brows.

"How do you mean?"

He gave her the barest hint of a smile that sent her pulses skittering, even as it left her with more questions than answers. Gwendolyn heard tell that in some faraway lands, the queen's Shadows were emasculated, and made into eunuchs. Perhaps Málik didn't have the parts, and this would explain so much, although it would be such a waste, because his body seemed made for touching. By the light of a silvery moon, his wondrous skin shimmered like a pearl, and Gwendolyn found her mouth ever so parched, as it always was in his presence, only thinking, thanks to her dearest Borlewen, of his "bald-pated druid."

A pox on you, Borlewen!

Málik's ever-present smile turned lazy now.

"I know what you're thinking," he said. "And nay, I'm no less a man than that silly fool over there, tripping over his tongue to impress your cousin."

Not for the first time, Gwendolyn wondered if he could read her thoughts. He seemed to have the uncanny ability to always glean what she was thinking.

"In fact, I wonder if you will wish to wear your beautiful torc again, with Kitto's drool all over it." It was Gwendolyn's turn to laugh, but at the instant, she didn't care about that torc, not at all. "I never see you tripping over anything to impress anyone," she said, to which he replied, "Don't you, Princess?"

Disarmed by the question, Gwendolyn averted her gaze, somehow embarrassed.

Gods.

"Gwendolyn," he whispered, watching her intently.

His gaze lingered on her lips as he once again removed the reed from his mouth and lapped his own lips, ever so slowly. "Have you never... wondered..."

Her heart beat madly.

"... what's inside your father's Treasury?"

Gwendolyn sat back, her eyes going wide.

His question was a surprising diversion from their conversation. And though she was perhaps relieved, she hadn't expected it. "Well, of course," she said. "Naturally. And yet, the secrets it holds are for my father's eyes alone. I shall know in due time."

"And you believe the aldermen feel the same?"

Gwendolyn thought about that a moment, and said, "What do you mean?"

"Well, do you believe they are content enough to leave this

knowledge to your father alone? Have you never considered whether they have, for a moment, taken a gander within?"

"I—well, no," Gwendolyn said, shaking her head. The entire notion was preposterous. "Only once in my life has anyone ever defied the King's Law, and that man paid for his offense with his life. Why, by the eyes of Lugh, would anyone dare?"

"Unless they didn't believe they would be caught," he suggested, giving her a single, meaningful nod, and Gwendolyn thought about that another moment, watching as Málik tossed away his blade of grass and plucked himself another.

What if someone defied the King's Law?

What if he was caught?

What if Bryok was the man who'd caught him?

The question posed all new possibilities.

The Treasury guards were always on duty, else waiting to assume a shift. Only once every new moon were they allowed a day of rest, and then they resumed a shift of opposite hours. But each shift was assumed in pairs, two guards for every watch.

When Gwendolyn returned, she really must inquire who was Bryok's shift mate.

Was it Aelwin?

She eyed the blade of grass that had returned to its place between Málik's teeth. "That must be delicious," she teased.

"A mere distraction," he allowed, and Gwendolyn asked, "What for?"

"For what I'd really like to be tasting instead..."

CHAPTER
TWENTY-EIGHT

T oday must be the last day, Gwendolyn decided.

The very, very last.

The last, last, last.

And yet, much to her dismay, the questions Málik posed the night before were rifling through her head, revealing more and more questions, and they all desperately vied for attention, seeking answers. Mayhap it was a simple matter of two aldermen scheming for the same position, else it could be something more sinister... possibilities she really didn't wish to entertain, because she was enjoying this time away—far, far more than she should.

Intending to break the news to her uncle before the noon-tide, she and Málik stood sparring in the courtyard, sweating off last night's mead.

The muscles in Gwendolyn's arms burned atrociously. Never had they practiced so ruthlessly. She punished herself for her wayward thoughts, continuing to spar, even when her belly roiled in protest over the heat of the warming sun.

In fact, for the first time, beads of sweat formed upon

258

Málik's brow, and his movements were dawdling and unsteady, at least for him. For anyone else, they would still be quick.

Even now, Gwendolyn despaired of besting him, although he was definitely slower to parry than he should have been, and then, she noticed he went to defend without stepping, and because his feet were ill-positioned, he had to lean to defend himself.

Gwendolyn struck when she had the chance.

"Well done!" he announced, lifting an arm to wipe the sweat from his brow. His cheeks were rosy and his lips flushed bright red.

Her cousins were still in the house, lingering at their father's table after breaking their fast. Borlewen, she knew, hadn't found her bed until the small hours, and as yet, her uncle and Lowenna hadn't emerged from their bower. Gwendolyn was quite certain they were trying again for that son he hadn't yet been blessed with. If nothing else, she must leave this place, because she was surrounded by the scent of sex. It was distracting her in ways she had no business being distracted. "You let me win, didn't you?"

Málik grinned.

"Why?" she demanded.

Málik peered at Gwendolyn sideways and said innocently, "Are you accusing me of playing favorites, Princess?"

His use of the word Princess always sounded so suggestive.

She smiled back at him. "Well, you are, aren't you?"

"Nay," he said. "I would not. What good would that ever do you in battle? A 'favor' now would be to do you no favors at all."

Knowing Málik as she did, Gwendolyn knew better than to re-sheathe her blade just yet. He was a master at seizing opportunities to put her down. "So, you are saying I beat you justly?"

Málik shrugged. "Perhaps so," he said. "You are quite good, Gwendolyn, and I will be certain to tell your sire that your good little poppet served you well."

Rolling her eyes over his favored barb against Bryn, Gwendolyn inhaled deeply, imbued with pride, at least for the moment. More oft than not, Málik's compliments came with advances that sent her to her knees, but today she dared to rejoice.

Indeed, she was filled with ferocity, and she'd kept her head during Málik's endless advances—never so simple as that might seem.

"For the hundredth time," she said, "Bryn is *not* my poppet!"

Málik shrugged. "So you claim."

Gwendolyn lifted a brow. "And yet you never seem to hear it, my friend."

"Friend?"

"Friend," she said, and meant it ardently.

Gwendolyn was heartily pleased now that he would join her in Loegria, relieved, in fact. He was more worldly than Bryn, and unlike Bryn, he didn't coddle her, nor did he treat her with so much deference, even despite that he should.

As an instructor, he was merciless, and she had already improved so much, more thanks to him than to Bryn, though he always gave Bryn the credit.

"I hear everything," he said. "But ears will sometimes lie."

And then he froze, tilting his head, listening, with a hand to his pointy ear.

Gwendolyn thought he must be teasing her again, listening for her lies. But then, she heard the sound, as well—a soft, but distant rumble that grew louder as it neared.

It was only another moment before she spied the cloud of dust billowing toward them over the moorlands.

Hooves.

Horses.

Many.

The sound of their approach grew from a rumble to a roar, and Gwendolyn felt a quiver rush down her spine. She swallowed convulsively, for despite that she'd trained for this, she'd never once expected to have to use her skills. So long they'd been at peace. Never even once had she actually heard war horns. She heard them now, quite unmistakably—a shrill wail that pierced her ears and sent another quiver down her spine.

Fear?

For a moment, Gwendolyn stood, feet planted on the spot, her boots unwilling to move, realizing how ill-prepared she was for battle.

"Raiders!" shouted one of her uncle's sentry men from a nearby tower.

"Attack!" bellowed another. "Attack!"

Men scurried about.

Gods. As placid as their visit had been, it was easy to forget that this hill fort was a stronghold for all the nearby wheals. So it seemed she would experience a raid firsthand.

Sword in hand, hair mussed from sleep, Duke Cunedda came bursting from the door of his home. He lifted the arm that only hours before had raised tankards with glee.

Her cousins all emerged behind him, all three bearing weapons of their own choosing. Borlewen, still wearing Gwendolyn's torc, arrived wielding a massive hammer. Briallen came with an axe, wearing a leather jerkin over her *chainse*. Jenefer came wielding a two-handed long sword. All three girls surrounded their father, but he shoved them toward Gwendolyn instead.

Her uncle's men were quick to join, but this was unlike Trevena, where there were layers upon layers of defenses—two gates, and here there was none.

Aside from the *fogous* below the village, there were few protections here—no walls, only one mean tower whence archers could take aim.

And yet, for all the modesty of this place, her uncle's men were well trained. Even as Gwendolyn watched, his men took positions on the rooftops—one on the garner, one on the blacksmith's hut, another two on the barn.

A few guards rushed to his side. The rest all found places wherever they could—two behind the wall of ale casks that only last night had harbored want-to-be lovers.

Another horn wailed, calling liegemen from nearby farms.

Málik took Gwendolyn by her arm, dragging her roughly behind him. "Stay close," he commanded.

Across the village came shouts, women ushering children into the nearby garner. A few scrambled down a well. And then, once the children were safe, the rest of the women rushed to arm themselves to join the fray. Gwendolyn felt a rush as she assumed the fighting position, only this time it wouldn't be for practice.

This time, she knew blood would spill.

This time she would not use the flat of her blade.

This time she would strike to kill.

Only when the column of roiling dust neared enough so she could see who had raised it, did she exhale in relief and reach for the back of Málik's tunic, trying to pull him back.

"Nay!" she said. "Rest easy. 'Tis our own men, fear not."

His pale eyes darkening to steel, Málik turned to meet her gaze and said, "Nay, Gwendolyn. These are not your father's men. On your toes, Princess! Prepare to fight."

Even as he said it, the riders tossed down their dragon

pennants and bore down on the village, trampling her father's pennants, and leaving them ragged and tumbling in their dust.

Gods.

This was happening in truth, a battle waged. But nay! Cornwall was at peace, allied with Loegria. Who would dare?

The first crack of metal rang, and the horrid sound made Gwendolyn's teeth ache.

Even as they trampled the first line of defense, cutting down her uncle's men, still Gwendolyn doubted her eyes.

Scarlet sprayed the air and splattered the ground.

In horror, Gwendolyn watched as the lead rider's sword cut down a weaker iron blade that met his midair, and then the man who'd dared to wield it—a bare-chested man who'd never even had time to dress from his drunken slumber.

Bile rose at the back of Gwendolyn's throat, but she readied herself to swing, even as riders dismounted and her uncle joined the fray with a roar.

"To me!" he shouted. "To me!"

Ahead of her, with a mighty bellow, Málik joined as well, and, with her heart in her throat, Gwendolyn swung for the first time in all her life to maim or to kill.

Metal sang against metal, a terrible anthem of death.

Crying out as she felt her blade slice into flesh, she saw more crimson spray. And despite that, she thought... this must be a dream... a terrible, terrible dream.

TWENTY-NINE

I n the courtyard, where last night's casks of wine were opened and drunk, and Borlewen flirted with Kitto, the battle waged so near to her uncle's table, and the hearth where his wife only yesterday morning stood baking bread.

The flashing of swords against the bright morning sun stabbed her eyes, even as the crack of metal rang in her ears. Dust rose with the scrambling of feet.

No time for tears, no time to be afraid. A true leader would not run; neither would she. All her life she had prepared for this moment, and she would not fail her uncle and his family.

You can do it, she told herself. *You can do it.*

Don't scream! Don't run!

Her uncle's battle cry was unmistakable. It sent tendrils of fear snaking about Gwendolyn's heart, squeezing so hard she thought she might cease to breathe.

Fighting beside her, Borlewen raised and slammed down her great hammer. It cracked a man's skull like an egg. More blood sprayed. His knees buckled as he rolled atop Gwendolyn's boot, and with a furious bellow, Málik rushed forward to kick the man away, once more jerking Gwendolyn behind him, and cutting down another man who sprang at Borlewen.

Keep your eyes on the sword.

Don't spin.

The courtyard was red with blood.

Cunedda wielded his sword with a mighty bellow, commanding his wife to fight. "Fight!" he encouraged her. "Fight, damn you, fight!"

Beside him, Lowenna did the best she could, struggling to lift her sword. Alas, her arms were not practiced for war, and neither had she the strength to wield it.

She lifted it, at last, in defense of her husband, but missed her mark. The man turned to face her, but she didn't raise her sword again in time, and the man's blade found her breast, running her through. She buckled to the ground, clutching at her breast once he removed his blade.

Blood.

Screams.

Dust bit Gwendolyn's eyes.

Blood spattered her face.

Aim diagonally!

Move your sword with your body!

Raise the pommel!

"Lowenna!" her uncle cried. "Lowenna!"

More blood.

More screams.

The smell of smoke thickened about them.

With horror, Gwendolyn realized the garner was on fire. From that moment on, she heard nothing more than her uncle's vengeful roar as he cut down one man after another, trying between parries to drag his wife's twisted form aside.

Gwendolyn saw Lowenna didn't stir, and it tore a sob from her throat, even as she hoisted her own weapon to thwart another man who rushed Málik. She missed, and if she thought her muscles burned before, with only their morning's practice, they were weak now with pain. *Your arm is weak, but your body is strong!*

Don't close your eyes!

Raise the pommel!

Move your sword with your body!

If only she could find a way through the tangle of flesh to open the door to that garner. But they were surrounded—she was surrounded. Only Málik was her shield.

Another man rushed at them, and as big as he was, it took both Gwendolyn and Málik fighting together to bring him down, although Málik didn't seem grateful.

He cast Gwendolyn a withering glance, commanding her once more to fall back, and then returned his attention to the battle, defending against another man who rushed them.

These were not her father's men. They were mercenaries, wearing no man's livery. Neither were they poor. Their swords were among the finest to be had, their armor shiny and new, the look in their eyes, not hunger, but greed.

How many had descended upon them by now?

Twenty, more?

Revulsion warred with relief as Gwendolyn ducked a swing to take the blade from her boot. She sprang up to cut her blade across the man's throat, so cleanly and furiously it nearly severed his head. Blood spurted from his wound, spraying her face and tunic—her mother's gown. More's the pity, she'd left the breast plate at home, never imagining this could be their fate. *And where was the other guard who arrived with them?*

He was not here. Come to think of it, she hadn't seen him for days.

By now, the rich, red-dyed buckskin of her tunic was painted full red. Covered in sweat and oily with blood, her hands could scarcely wield the sword. Every moment it threatened to fly from her hands, but Gwendolyn clutched it desperately, grateful for the grade of her steel, even as she watched Jenefer's sword snap and spin away.

Gods.

This was like nothing she had ever experienced, a taste of war she'd only ever heard tell of through bards' tales. Neither did these men intend to leave survivors, a fact that became apparent and sent a surge of outrage through Gwendolyn.

What treachery was this?

Who would dare?

Lifting Lowenna, dragging her to safety—as safe as a dead woman could be—Cunedda was suddenly blindsided by a heavy broadsword. It cut through his bare shoulder, leaving one arm limp. Still, somehow, he cut down his assailant, even as he bellowed with pain, and, leaving his wife, he rushed into the melee to defend his daughters.

Gwendolyn's heart wrenched at the sight of them all battling together. Borlewen cut down one man, piercing him once through the gut and another good slice to the throat with a dagger she produced from her belt. Thereafter, she turned her back to her elder sister, and she and Jenefer fought together, shoulder to shoulder.

Gods!

What is happening?

Gwendolyn cried out as the sharp edge of an axe whizzed by, nicking her thigh, and barely missed severing her wrist. Málik rushed at the man who hurled it, taking him down with a single swinging blow. Yet another man went after Borlewen, and a sickening fear rushed through Gwendolyn's heart with a sudden, inconceivable revelation.

The torc.

Her eyes scanned the embattled courtyard, and she noted how many more had their eyes on her cousin's throat.

Whoever these men were, they came for Gwendolyn. *She* had led them here, and her uncle had surmised this as well. He cut down one more man who rushed at Borlewen, and sidled over to Gwendolyn and said, "The *fogous*. Now! Go!"

"Nay," she refused. "I'll not leave you to fight alone!"

Cunedda's eyes bulged with rage as he turned to Málik and demanded, "Do your duty, Shadow! Take her! Go!"

Málik nodded, and Gwendolyn shrieked with protest, "Nay, Uncle! I'll not leave you!" she screamed furiously. "I'll not go!"

The smoke thickened so it was impossible to see anything beyond the courtyard, and the screams in the garner suddenly ceased.

"Under my bed," hissed Cunedda. "You'll find a door there—go!"

Gwendolyn shrieked with outrage, even as Málik seized her by the arm, dragging her backward into the house. To no avail, she fought his unrelenting grip, even as she watched Jenefer crumple to a hammer, her lovely face twisting with surprise and pain.

Gwendolyn bellowed in outrage, and this was the last coherent thought she had.

"Gwendolyn!" Málik shouted, shaking her hard. "Gwendolyn!"

Briallen was the next to fall. Gwendolyn watched it happen with eyes wide and filled with fright. Her father intercepted a downswing, cutting the man's belly with his sword, then turned to Gwendolyn to say, once more, "Go! Damn you! Go!"

"Borlewen!" Gwendolyn sobbed, if only to warn her. "Borlewen!"

Gods.

Did none of these men recognize their princess?

"To me!" she cried, beating her breast with a fist, only hoping to divert their attention from these innocents. She dug in her heels, fighting Málik's grip. "To me!" she shouted. "To me! I am—"

"Gwendolyn!" hissed Málik, slapping a hand over her mouth so hard it stung.

Only this time, when she tried to fight him, he lifted her up and tossed her over his shoulder, heading into the house.

The last thing Gwendolyn saw was Borlewen unsheathing the little blade at her waist. With his foot, Málik slammed the door behind him, somehow seizing a massive bench and spinning it about as though it were only a child's toy, settling it in front of the door.

He moved swiftly, with sure feet, toward her uncle's bower, and once inside, he swung another heavy coffer to bar that door. The sound of it landed with a boom.

"I cannot leave them to fight without me," Gwendolyn begged him, pummeling his back as he threw her down on the bed, but still he grasped her by the arm, his grip unyielding, holding her away from the door.

"Stop!" he pleaded. "Stop!"

When Gwendolyn fought him still, he reasoned with her, "Would you have them die in vain?"

"I would have them not die at all!" she returned madly.

"Gwendolyn!" he said, shaking her again. "They *will* die! Everyone will die! The question is, will Pretania's future perish as well?"

Pretania's future?

A strangled sob escaped Gwendolyn's tightening throat, but finally comprehending, she allowed him to pull her away from the barricaded door, and then watched haplessly as he shoved her uncle's heavy bed aside with a boot, revealing a hidden entrance to the underground passages—the *fogous* he guarded so well.

This was just like her uncle to keep the entrance so close. No one would dare enter his bower, and who would think to look beneath the Duke's bed?

It took Málik only a second to pry open the heavy trapdoor that should have taken two men to hoist, revealing a dark tunnel beneath that appeared to descend into the Underworld.

For a long, grief-stricken moment, Gwendolyn stood, staring without moving, peering back once more at the door, before Málik urged her down.

With frightening clarity, she heard her uncle's shouts, as the door to his house split and gave way to axes. More smashing and clanging. Swords crossing. Something large clattered to the floor. More crashes, and suddenly, a tongue of smoke licked beneath the door.

"Go!" demanded Málik.

Swallowing a lump of grief, Gwendolyn descended, slipping on a length of the rope ladder in her rush to climb down. She felt loosening rubble rain down over the pate of her head as Málik moved to follow her down, and somewhere above, she heard distant shouts, then the rude splintering of her uncle's bower door. Panicked for Cunedda's life, she tried once more to climb up, but her arms burned and Málik pushed her head down with the toe of his boot, and said, "Go, go, go!" With a thunderous crash, he pulled down the door, immersing them in darkness. "Go!" he said again.

Swallowing her grief, Gwendolyn did as she was told, hurrying now, never daring to scream, even when Málik's boot caught her fingers. Muffled voices and coughing came from above as she reached the end of the ladder and felt blindly about for solid ground.

There was none. Gods. There was none!

Gwendolyn had never actually descended into these *fogous* before, nor did she know whether there was any way out. What if these tunnels weren't yet complete?

Anticipating her moment of panic, Málik shoved her one last time, and Gwendolyn tumbled backward into darkness, her sword clattering down beneath her. She fell atop it, landing with a heavy thud on her tailbone, gulping back a sharp cry of pain.

Only an instant later, Málik fell atop her, but he scrambled quickly to his feet, and Gwendolyn could hear him rushing about, but could no longer see him.

"Move!" he said urgently.

Where!

"Move!"

Up above, there was a furious scraping at the trapdoor as though someone might be searching for a handle, and Gwendolyn could see the faintest crack of light through slits in the wood. Having little sense of direction, she turned swiftly to crawl away, uncertain whether she could stand, but her head encountered a stone wall, and she cried out in pain over the force of the blow.

Everything happened so quickly. A loud crack sounded above, and she saw the axe blade penetrate wood. Málik seized her by the leg and tossed her aside, sending her tumbling like a doll against the wall. Then suddenly, without warning, the entire shaft collapsed within itself.

THIRTY

Fear squeezed at Gwendolyn's heart as complete darkness enveloped her.

Was she dead?

Alive?

It was so dark!

After a moment, she coughed and sputtered, spewing more dirt than air. Her fingers still ached from the crush of Málik's boot, and her stomach protested violently.

Even after the dust cleared, it seemed an eternity that she sat, trying to catch her breath in the damp, musty air. She knew Málik survived the collapse, only because she heard him breathing... *or was this the echo of her own breath?*

Gods.

What if she was alone, with no way out?

What if the collapsing shaft buried Málik beneath it?

What if—she heard digging.

Sudden, furious digging.

Coughing.

Bellows.

Screams.

Then, all at once, the digging ceased abruptly, and the heavy silence lengthened, until Gwendolyn heard the hiss of Málik's blade as he re-sheathed his sword.

Holding back her fear, she slapped a hand against her trembling lips, if only to keep from sobbing. After a long moment, when the muffled voices did not return, a tiny blue flame flickered to life... in the palm of Málik's hand, wobbling uncertainly, perhaps vying for the same air Gwendolyn needed to breathe.

But now she could see what happened.

Somehow, Málik had cut down the wooden braces supporting the shaft, leaving the earthwork to collapse. Whoever was above trying to open the door must have been sucked into the shaft and smothered with dirt.

The flame he held now danced in his palm, forming itself into the shape of a small moon, spitting bright blue flames like arms that embraced the orb, twisting and swirling, emitting embers like a damp flame. His eyes met hers, and in the dancing reflection in his pupils, Gwendolyn saw the truth.

A mountain of rubble lay where she'd once crawled. The rope ladder was gone. *Buried.* As dust settled more and more, the little light grew brighter and stronger, lighting more and more of the environs. Apparently, when Málik tossed her away—like a rag—she'd landed against the far wall, but her foot lay close enough to the rubble that it was covered by a small mound of dirt. Blinking, confused, Gwendolyn sat, testing the movement in her limbs. Nothing seemed broken, so she shook her leg and drew up her knees.

In the meantime, Málik grabbed the hilt of her fallen sword, drew it out of a larger mound of dirt, and handed it to her. Only then, as he faced her, every tumultuous emotion that warred within Gwendolyn was reflected in his pallid face, a mirror against her own pain.

She didn't cry, nor did she speak.

There was nothing to say.

So, it appeared they were trapped. In a small cavern. With myriad tunnels creeping further into darkness.

"What now?" she asked, and shivered as she asked, "Will there be *spriggans* in those tunnels?" Ill-tempered creatures, like *piskies*, but grotesque, with wizened features and gnarled little bodies, although they could swell to gigantic proportions if threatened. They were also the ones responsible for leaving changelings in the place of babes.

With a hint of his usual mordancy, Málik arched a brow, then cast Gwendolyn a sideways glance. "*Spriggans* do not exist," he said, tossing the flame in his hand in her direction. Wide-eyed, she watched as it flew—flew!—then paused, like a deer suddenly wary of a hunter. She gasped softly as it crept closer, then poised itself over her, sprinkling light like fairy dust over the pate of her head. Open-mouthed, Gwendolyn watched the swirling orb of blue.

"What... is... that?"

She met Málik's gaze.

"You call them *piskie* lights. Tis *faerie* fire."

Gwendolyn blinked.

Incomprehensible.

He came to sit beside her, nudging it slightly away, then down, so that it burned directly before Gwendolyn's eyes, bright as stars.

Gwendolyn lifted a hand to its vicinity and found it cold to the touch. "*Faerie* fire," she said, with wonder, realizing what that meant.

His eyes *were* keener than most and his strength was

greater than any man's she had ever met—because he *was fae*... well and truly *fae*.

Seizing her by the leg, but gently, he brushed off a clump of soil on her hosen to better inspect her weeping wound. He said, "*Spriggans* are but a figment of your mortal imagination." He pulled off her boot and set it aside. "Shadows play tricks," he explained. "Men too long in the mines carry fantastic tales."

He gave her a pointed glance, peering up at the orb of flame that seemed to obey him like a small pet. "Not that there are not worse things to be found in the dark."

He returned his attention to her wound. Perhaps because it was closer than his, he plucked up the blade from her boot, and cut her hosen from the hem halfway up her leg. Ripping it, he turned the material inside out to brush at the wound on her leg, removing all dirt from the vicinity. It was still bleeding, though not much. "Fortunately, it appears to be superficial," he said, sounding relieved. He returned Gwendolyn's dagger. "Art hale otherwise?"

Gwendolyn nodded quickly, even though she wasn't precisely sure. In fact, she could be dead. That would certainly explain what she was witnessing here.

Her gaze returned to the glowing blue sphere, as he handed her back her boot and wrapped her leg with the strip of cloth he'd made from her hosen.

Gods. Her entire body hurt, and even if she'd not sustained some greater wound, her heart ached too much to admit. He tied the cloth, then gave her a nod. Then, with some effort, and a little help, she slid her foot back into the boot.

As for Málik, his face was no longer quite so glowsome. His skin was grey with filth... as hers must be. His hair, once so silken and shiny, was dull and covered with dust.

Somehow, probably during the descent, he'd sustained a small scrape on his cheek that was... bleeding... *red blood*... like hers. Worry lines furrowed the edges of his beautiful mouth, and it was all Gwendolyn could do not to cast herself into his arms and sob.

She did not need to go back and see the carnage above to know what was left. The screams of the children in the garner would haunt her until her dying day. There had simply been too many to defend against.

Her uncle. Gods. Her throat constricted. He'd sent them off only to battle those men by himself. There was no way he could have defended against so many.

Poor Lowenna.

Her throat tightened again. Sweet, sweet Lowenna. She was gone before the battle ever began, dead and twisted, trampled underfoot.

Briallen and Jenefer.

Were they both dead now?

And what of Borlewen? What became of her with no one left to defend her?

So many questions hovered at the tip of Gwendolyn's tongue, but she hadn't the courage to ask a single one.

THE *FOGOUS* RAMBLED EVER ONWARD, TWISTING THIS WAY AND THAT, leading to nothing, always nothing. Every tunnel too narrow, barely wide enough for a single person to crawl through, much less two, although sometimes they heightened to allow one to walk with a bent back.

The walls were built of stone, all except for the shaft area beneath the trapdoor. Braced only with wood, Málik had somehow brought it all tumbling down.

He insisted upon leading the way, sometimes leaving Gwendolyn with the strange orb of light whilst he scouted the path ahead. Curiously, he hadn't any need to touch the flame, ever. It followed like a pup, seeming to read his mind, moving ahead into the farthest reaches of the tunnel to light their way, and sometimes lagging, or else to one side, but never between them.

Twice Málik returned to say the tunnel ahead had ended, and they needed to turn back. Three times they encountered dead ends together.

Once, he was gone so long, leaving Gwendolyn with the curious blue orb long enough that she worked up the nerve to reach out and pet it. It didn't move away, allowing her to wrap her hand about the spherule, but it wouldn't budge, as though he'd purposely commanded it to stay—no doubt so Gwendolyn wouldn't stray.

Well, it worked. She hadn't any desire to discover if *spriggans* truly existed. Indeed, if *piskies* were real, and *fae* were real, why not *spriggans as well?*

Staring at the orb, Gwendolyn found herself intensely curious about how it worked. Lifting two fingers to tap it gently, she started when it showered her with tiny blue embers that took on a life of their own, wheeling about in circles until they joined the rest of the embers encircling the flame, like a tiny orbit of stars chasing a moon.

When Málik returned, though she wished to ask him about the light, she couldn't find words to speak, not yet. For the first time in her life, curiosity fell prey to her mood. Grief settled into her breast, crushing her heart like a stone.

Hours later, Gwendolyn was exhausted, filthy, freezing, and she needed to find a place to relieve herself. The problem was that she didn't actually wish for Málik to leave her again, and every time he did, she held her breath till he returned.

Gods help her, there might not be *spriggans* in these tunnels, and *spriggans* might only be a figment of some miner's imagination, but she swore she heard breathing that wasn't her own, nor Málik's. Although perhaps this, too, was her imagination.

She'd also heard some wheals were infested with *knockers*, but these were helpful creatures, given to song, who aided the miners. And regardless, she'd had more than enough of the supernatural for the moment, and whether they existed, good or bad, she didn't want to know.

A rat rushed by, stopping to assess them, its eyes reflecting the blue of the *faerie* fire. Abruptly, it scurried away, and with its departure, Gwendolyn longed to weep. She wanted to follow but knew that wherever it had gone, she couldn't go.

Now and again, they encountered brown bats hanging from beams along the tunnels—braces meant to sustain the passages. Wrapped in winged embraces, their black eyes shone against the flickering light, seeming to watch them curiously, though ultimately uninterested in their plight. Disturbed by the *faerie* light, one suddenly awoke, shrieking, and flew away.

In the silence that followed, Gwendolyn wondered who the raiders were. It was impossible to say whether the attack on her uncle's village could be connected to her investigations, but she couldn't help but feel everything was her fault. Could it be that someone—Alderman Aelwin, perhaps?—learned of her intention to speak with Bryok's widow?

Was he so willing to murder the King's only heir to hide his crimes?

For what reason did he wish Bryok dead? Was it only rivalry, or something more? Something like what Málik proposed? To hide the truth of what they had done, perhaps alone, or together—greedy for what lay inside that Treasury?

Here and now, there was no one to ask, and if she dared voice these questions aloud, Málik seemed to be in no mood to converse. As the hours crept by, his mouth drew tight, and his face grew pinched.

Was it her imagination, or was the air getting harder and harder to breathe?

Gods. At one point, even Málik's spherule of blue flame dimmed, and Gwendolyn held her breath, hoping desperately that it wasn't depending upon the same air.

Later, as the hours lengthened, she became certain the air was growing thinner. And though Málik's lungs seemed no worse for the wear, she could tell he was worried—*for her?*

Later there would be time enough for questions, she decided.

However, when they met yet another dead end, she cried out in dismay and finally cast her back against the wall, sliding to her bottom, miserable and fighting back tears. To keep from crying out again, she placed the pad of her thumb into her mouth and bit till she tasted her own blood. Without a word, Málik sat down beside her and drew her into his arms, putting out the *faerie* fire with only a gust of his breath.

"Málik," she protested.

"Shhh," he said, twisting a finger through her curls. "Do you trust me, Princess?"

Gwendolyn nodded, but words wouldn't come. Tears, like dust, clogged her throat.

"'Tis late," he whispered. "Let us rest." And he held Gwendolyn as she wept—for her uncle and his family, for her responsibility in all their deaths, for Owen, for her father, for the mess she'd made of everything, for Bryn, for the situation in which they now found themselves, and for every cross word she ever spent on Málik.

It was all too much, and she couldn't bear it.

CHAPTER

THIRTY-ONE

T he blue flame was already burning brightly when Gwendolyn awoke. Sadly, there was no warmth for the flame to impart.

"Feel better?" Málik asked.

"I do," she confessed, although, as familiar as she lay in his arms, she didn't stir. Here again, he was warm, and it was cold here beneath the dark, damp earth.

Her heart hurt, her leg hurt, and her brain recoiled against thought.

He caressed her arm with two fingers, tickling her softly, and Gwendolyn could feel small prickles of power and warmth even through the sleeve of her gown, like tiny little bolts of lightning. "Your gown is rent," he said, when he discovered a tear.

Hearing this brought another sting to Gwendolyn's eyes. What did a simple tear matter when she was covered in the blood of loved ones and enemies? And yet, this was her mother's dress, the only gown she'd ever cherished. If she had to learn to use needle and thread, she would mend it if it was the last thing she ever did. But it was sweet he would notice and care. Her emotions were in tumult, and she had to swallow hard around her words.

"I wonder if 'tis night or day," she said.

"I don't know. But you've slept a good long while."

"And you?"

As near as they were, she felt him shake his head. "Did you recognize any of those men?"

"Nay," she said, turning her face up to peer into Málik's pale blue eyes. She averted her gaze and stared at the earthen wall, swallowing hard. At some point, the stone had disappeared, and here there was only dimpled clay. A beetle crawled out of a small hole and shook its wings at her. From somewhere along the shaft behind them came the squeaking of another bat.

"Do you think anyone survived?"

"No," he said honestly, and the whispered word blew hot against Gwendolyn's ear.

Once again, her throat constricted. But she understood that weeping wouldn't help anyone right now, most especially not them. What was done was done, and the only thing that might have made a difference would have been if she'd remained in Trevena, as Málik had once suggested she should. Barring that, there was no more she could have done.

Gwendolyn was to blame.

For everything.

Three guards she'd brought with her to Chysauster. Only one would return—the one she hadn't even thought she'd cared for... the only one she now felt safe with.

"I fear there's no way out," she said.

"Shhh... there is naught to fear."

"How can you know?"

"I simply do."

"How?" Gwendolyn persisted, as she slid out of his arms.

The sapphire glow of his *faerie* light illuminated his face, giving it a cool hue. Its fire danced in his eyes, enhancing the blue, making it appear as though they burned, as well.

"Watch," he said, and Gwendolyn did, only not the flame as he'd bade. She tried but couldn't avert her gaze from Málik's luminescent face.

Suddenly, there was another blue light, bouncing about, and he caught it and tossed it like a ball, toward the far end of the tunnel, where it swelled, its glowing blue tendrils standing on end, like strands of hair blowing in the wind.

"A breeze?" she whispered, aghast.

He nodded, and when he smiled, he gave her another glimpse of the sharp, pointy teeth behind his lips. Gwendolyn had the sudden, unimaginable thought that *he* could be the *spriggan* children feared, a nightmare by night that vanished by day.

"Let me look at your leg again," he demanded.

Gwendolyn sat, shifting positions to give him access to her leg. Carefully he unwrapped the strip of leather—a poor means to soak up blood, but thankfully it was no longer bleeding. The wound had already crusted.

"It could have been worse," he said. "We'll need to clean it as soon as we can. We'll find a stream as soon as we're out."

Gwendolyn smiled, exhausted. "What?" she teased. "Can't you produce water, too?"

"*All* things are born of the *Aether*. I merely... cajole them."

On some strange level, that made sense. "So it's true?"

"What's true?"

"You're *fae*."

She knew he was but needed to hear him say so with his own two lips.

"*Fae* is your people's word," he said. "Not mine. I am Danann."

From the beginning, he had styled himself Danann, and Gwendolyn had but chosen not to believe it. Rather, she had felt justified in calling him *Sidhe*, or even elf when she was so furious with him, but never once had she truly stopped to consider the consequences of this truth. His *rás* was the oldest *rás* in all the lands. Had her father known of this affiliation?

What about her mother?

If so, it cast his presence in Trevena under a whole new light.

Repeatedly he had said he was summoned or sent—no doubt by her parents—and something told Gwendolyn it might have been her mother.

"I cannot wait to tell Ely what I've learned."

Málik lifted his gaze, peering through his lashes, his eyes suddenly hard. "You shall tell no one," he said, and then he finished wrapping her wound and once more tested the edges of his bandage. Without understanding why, she nodded obediently.

"They were after Borlewen," she said.

"The question is why?"

"Because she was wearing my torc."

He lifted a brow. "Indeed, but what I want to know is why they were seeking you."

"Why do you believe?"

"I hesitate to say."

"Why?"

"Because the answer is one you'll not wish to hear."

Curious, Gwendolyn persisted. "Do you believe they discovered my mission to speak with Ia?"

"Perhaps." He stood now and drew Gwendolyn up. "Can you walk?" he asked, and Gwendolyn nodded, letting him help her to her feet. "Stay close," he said, moving ahead, and Gwendolyn followed, wondering how she could do anything but. There was nowhere else to go, and even if death itself lay ahead, she'd never turn back.

THIRTY-TWO

Through the faintest crack in the ceiling, it was possible to spy a brightening sky—another trapdoor that might have gone unnoticed save for the *faerie* fire.

The second orb followed it up, leaving the tunnel below flirting with darkness. It stopped just over Málik's head as a thin, feathery breeze blew at the orb from above, scattering tendrils of white and blue light. "Ladder," he said, and even as he reached for it, Gwendolyn felt the kiss of a cool breeze. The rope was tucked to one side, hanging on a wooden dowel that was half gnawed—rats, perhaps—and Gwendolyn feared for a moment that the rope itself would be compromised. She held her breath as he released it, but one firm tug revealed it was secure and ready to climb.

This time, Málik ascended first, if only to be certain no one was waiting above, and Gwendolyn watched him with halted breath, praying that none of those raiders knew about her uncle's *fogous* and where they led. But they mustn't, because if they'd known, they would have already found themselves beset upon in these tunnels, rather than waiting for them to emerge.

They must have believed that shaft only a cellar and fully destroyed. And yet, only now, after wandering those tunnels, did Gwendolyn realize they'd encountered no ingots nor ore. The main cavern beneath her uncle's bower had been empty, despite that no shipments had been made to Trevena in so long.

Were his wheals so depleted that he'd had nothing to send? Or was her uncle secretly trading with someone else? More questions for which Gwendolyn hadn't any answers.

Once again, as Málik climbed, dirt rained down over the pate of her head, and her heart hammered savagely, anticipating another collapse. But the shaft remained sturdy, and Málik made quick work of the ascension. Reaching the top, he bumped his fist, and popped opened the trapdoor to find the night clear, and stars twinkling above. Only to be certain, he withdrew the sword from his scabbard and leapt from the shaft more nimbly than Gwendolyn could have managed. By now, every muscle in her body was sore, if not from battle exertion, then from crawling and stooping through furlongs and furlongs of dark, twisting tunnels.

The wound on her leg ached—not so much for the cut, but for the bruised flesh beneath. Her bottom hurt as well, completely overshadowing the tiny bruise she'd previously had on her knee.

Following its maker, the *faerie* fire—both orbs—vanished once they emerged into the night, dissipating like a puff of vapor, and Gwendolyn didn't linger. The tunnel behind her fell into darkness as she reached for the ladder, body aching and muscles burning, as she followed the silvery moonlight to freedom.

To her surprise, she emerged into a quoit that reminded

her of the Giant's House near Fowey. Yet, unlike that quoit, this one appeared to be more of a tomb.

The sky was brightening, but the capstone above kept the moon's full light from the trapdoor, so that, even by day, it must be difficult to spy from below.

As children, she and Bryn used to run about that Giant's House, wielding wooden swords and taking turns at defending it. Demelza used to say they were built by a tribe of giants who'd hurled these stones together in a game of Quoits. This one sat in the middle of nowhere, with no sign of anyone having used the premises for any reason at all, not for years.

In fact, the stones were all covered with undisturbed lichen, which led Gwendolyn to believe no one had been here since the tunnel's creation.

So then, were those *fogous* meant to store her uncle's yields or were they only a means for escape? In the end, he'd sent Gwendolyn into the tunnels with Málik, only to die with his family in defense of her. Sorrow tugged at her heart and she fought back another painful sting of tears as she inhaled deeply of the fresh night air.

After so long crawling through damp dirt, she had grit between her teeth and her nostrils were encrusted with tears and filth. Much to her dismay, the quoit lay nestled in a small fen, along a ravine, and they had to wade through more wet muck and climb a steep hill to see anything beyond the reeds. Again, Málik led the way, sword in hand, until he reached the summit, and then he re-sheathed his sword and waited for Gwendolyn to join him.

Before them, the land lay cloaked beneath a mantle of *kobold* blue. The sea was only a shimmer in the distance, and the moon but a thin, mocking smirk in the sky.

"Where did your *faerie* fire go?" she wondered aloud.

"Gone," he said, placing his arms akimbo. "It served its

purpose."

"Really?" said Gwendolyn, tugging at an eyelash to remove a bit of dirt. Every part of her ached, but it was only now that she really dared to notice. "I always heard they were more apt to lead men astray?" Indeed, the *piskie* lights were well known for leading men so far into the woods that they never again found the light of day. It was a wisp with a will of its own, and they were no doubt responsible for leading men to their deaths in the woods surrounding Porth Pool.

With every fiber of her being, she resisted the urge to sit now, knowing that if she did, she might never again rise.

Málik winked at her. "I suppose it depends on who it means to lead."

"Ah," said Gwendolyn, dumbly. Her brain hurt as well, as it tried in vain to make sense of everything that had transpired— not merely the attack on her uncle's village, but Málik's disclosures as well... the truth of who he was...

Fae.

She blinked, and the things he'd told her scattered like dust in the wind. Moreover, when she tried to ply him with more questions, she found she hadn't any to ask.

"It's too far to walk to Trevena from here. We'll have to go back for horses," he said, and Gwendolyn nodded, noting with a pang in her heart that he didn't suggest it should be to check for survivors. Clearly, he really didn't believe there would be any.

He looked at her then, and Gwendolyn saw not the arrogant creature she'd first met, but the friend she'd come to know. His heart was there in his pale blue eyes and this, too, squeezed at hers. *Gods.* She admired the firm features of his noble face, the confident set of his shoulders that bespoke such power and ageless strength.

There was so much Gwendolyn longed to say—*I'm sorry,*

for one—but the words wouldn't come.

To her shame, she had dis-served him... merely because.

She'd once told herself she admired his *fae* folk, and yet despite that she knew for herself what it felt like to be forsaken for what other people perceived, she had treated this man with the same contempt.

"I can go quicker without you," he suggested.

"I'll not remain here."

To that, he nodded, his lips lifting at one corner, as though he'd already expected her to answer that way, and he said, without argument, "Stay close."

THE VILLAGE WASN'T FAR. THEY ARRIVED AT THE EDGE OF TWILIGHT, with the sun only just waking. A soft blush lit the horizon, painting her uncle's village a dusky shade of rose. Smoke rose from the landscape, like a smoldering brume arising from a warm, *piskie* pool.

Whoever those men were, they were gone now, but they'd left nothing intact. The garner was consumed, and Gwendolyn hadn't the stomach, or the heart, to look inside. If there were any survivors at all—perhaps the children down the well—no one remained here.

Her uncle's home was burnt to the bedrock. Within the rubble, they spied several charred bones, though it was impossible to say to whom they belonged. The fire was spent already, but the embers still burned hot, making it impossible to sift through the remains. Though at least there was no need for a pyre; these bodies were already consumed.

Gruesome as it was, they spied the top of a man's head, with one long arm twisted before it. Evidently, one of those raiders had been trapped in the shaft, with his torso buried and his head exposed to the fire—at least she hoped with all her heart that it was a raider, and not her Uncle Cunedda, meaning to follow them down.

The stable, too, was destroyed. There were no horses to take. However, Gwendolyn discovered her bridle and satchel hanging on a small wooden horse, most likely set aside when the farrier was fixing her mare's shoes. Inside the satchel, much to her horror and relief, she found the prunes she intended to show her father.

Her belly protested loudly, having gone so long without sustenance, but more than the ache in her gut, the one in her heart could not be denied. Still, she held back more tears as she considered her part in this travesty. What would she tell her father?

She had lied about the reason she'd come to Chysauster, and now so many good people were dead. Someone would have to return to give them a proper funeral.

Satisfied that nothing could be recovered, they made their way south to Ia's farm in funereal silence. Only once arrived, they found it, too, abandoned.

Most likely, Ia's father had spied the village smoke, or heard the war horns, and rushed his family to shelter. There were many caves along the shoreline, and perhaps this was where they'd gone. They would return to discover they had no liege lord, and no one left to defend them—at least until her father could award these lands to another of his vassals.

Lamentably, they would also return to find they were minus two horses, though at least their animals seemed well enough in the interim. A few goats roamed about a small enclosure, a fat hog wallowed about a mud hole, and a lone hen scratched around a small but sturdy coop. Gwendolyn didn't like to think herself so savage, but it was all she could do not to take that hen and swallow it whole.

Fortunately, she discovered a few eggs inside the coop and took those inside to boil. There, she found a small kettle and a dying fire in the hearth. She rekindled the flame, set the eggs into the pot, precisely as she'd watched Lowenna do, then returned to the stable to choose the two strongest horses for the journey home, fully intending to repay Ia's father the instant she could.

In fact, she would trade him two for one, and if her father objected, she would stand her ground. The old Gwendolyn mightn't have known how to boil an egg, or how precious a single hen was, but she was changed—all things were changed. Her actions had consequences, she realized only belatedly, even the most inconsequential decisions.

A swim in the pool with Bryn could easily have cost a dear friend his life, and Cornwall its alliance with Loegria. Her uncle and his family had paid in blood for her journey to Chysauster.

Perhaps at one time she and Bryn had marched along those shoals, searching for peregrines, but she was not seven any longer. She was seven-and-ten, a woman betrothed, with an ailing father and duties she must withhold.

"Let me see to your leg," Málik demanded.

"It's fine," Gwendolyn said, as she saddled the second of two mares.

He arched a brow. "Your leg, Gwendolyn."

Gwendolyn, too, lifted a brow, wondering when precisely she'd ceased to be "Princess" in his eyes. But this was not entirely unwelcome. With him, she'd much rather be Gwendolyn.

"You're right. 'Tis healing," he said, only after making her sit on a bench and unraveling the bandage to peek beneath.

"As you said, 'tis only a flesh wound," she allowed, with a hint of a smile. "I shall live."

"Indeed you will," he reassured. "Indeed you will."

And regardless, he cleaned the wound for her, then made her a strong-smelling poultice of mashed juniper leaves, smearing this smelly concoction on her wound, before rewrapping the bandage. Thereafter, he disappeared for a while, and meanwhile, because everything they'd arrived with was gone, Gwendolyn searched the house for supplies to travel with.

She found two cloaks, one in a heap by a sewing basket, another in a coffer, neither in good repair. Thin, and made of wool, she wondered how they could keep anyone warm. But no matter, it was better than nothing, and this, too, she intended to repay twofold. She would gift them two of hers, else steal a few from her mother.

Gwendolyn pushed both cloaks down into the saddlebags, one for each, then slid her arming sword into the saddle's fur-lined scabbard. In these parts, even a poor farmer must be prepared to defend his farmstead.

At long last, Gwendolyn stole an old blanket from another trunk in the master's chamber and rolled it up, then tied it to the back of her mare, intending to share this with Málik.

The master's bed had one more coverlet to spare, but she couldn't leave the family with nothing. It wasn't as though they had the benefit of a good port with merchants to trade with. These blankets were handwoven, and likely they'd taken Ia's mother long months to weave.

Gwendolyn figured they would have taken the better of their blankets with them, but it wasn't as though they had plenty. The house itself was quite mean.

It was only a short while before Málik returned, and Gwendolyn supposed he was ready to leave, but without a word, he dragged her into the master's chamber, then shoved her down beside the bed.

CHAPTER
THIRTY-THREE

"Stay," he whispered.

Outside, Gwendolyn heard voices.

"Saddled," said a man, his voice not at all familiar. "They can't be far."

Raiders?

Those same men returned?

Or could it be Ia and her family?

But nay.

It was not.

As though he'd read her mind, Málik shook his head, then lifted a finger to his lips, begging Gwendolyn to remain silent. And then, quietly, carefully, he unsheathed the sword at his back and disappeared into the common room.

Gwendolyn's heart hammered fiercely.

"Check the house," bellowed another man, this one coming closer. Then booted steps, coming quickly, loudly fiercely, like the beating of her heart.

Gods.

She'd left her sword on the horse she'd meant to ride.

Instinctively, her hand moved down along her thigh, past the bandages, to her boot, reaching for the small blade she kept there. It wasn't big, but it was sharp enough to put out an eye, and she would do it.

For a terrifying instant, Gwendolyn considered what she would do if they found Málik and harmed him. It spurred her into motion. She didn't think, only acted.

She couldn't remain here, hiding like a coward, whilst they hurt him! Moving swiftly to the bower door, she found a burly man entering the cottage, his hand still on the knob. Málik stood hidden on the other side of the door, his entire body cast in shadow behind it. Gwendolyn didn't even have the time to worry about the glower he sent her.

She faced the scene with wide, frightened eyes, recognizing this man as the raider who had attacked her uncle's home. Only for an instant, his head tilted, as though surprised to see her, but his surprise was his undoing.

Málik moved swiftly around the door, seizing him by his long, scraggly hair, and then dragged him into the room. In what appeared to be a swift, macabre dance, he slit the man's throat, then pushed him aside, dragging him by the hair until he, too, vanished behind the door.

From her vantage, Gwendolyn could see that there was one more man outside. Now, he stood in plain view of the door, and he turned, drawn by the noises in the cottage.

Gwendolyn froze at the sight of him marching in her direction, his face splitting wide with a malevolent grin. She couldn't speak or move.

Once more, Málik placed a hand to his lips and though Gwendolyn could only see him in her periphery, she daren't turn her head in his direction. Not wanting to give him away, she tried hard not to look away from the approaching warrior, no matter that every bone in her body screamed for her to flee. The knife in her hand trembled.

Or perhaps it was only her hand?

He came closer.

Closer.

Closer.

Closer.

"I don't know how you escaped," he snarled when he was close enough to see inside the darkened hovel. "But I won't give you another chance."

His dark eyes glinted with ill-intent.

Somehow, Gwendolyn met his gaze squarely, showing him the blade in her hand, so it glinted against the morning sun. But this only made him bark with laughter, and still he paused... just inside the door, where his gaze found and settled on the boots of his fallen companion.

The smile abandoned his lips.

Málik moved with haste, deftly pressing his sword against the man's throat. Only this time, the man was quick as well. He shoved backward, butting his thick head against Málik's face.

Gwendolyn heard him cry out, and both men tumbled to the floor. For an instant, she stood frozen as they battled, swords too unwieldy to use in such proximity.

The raider put a knee on Málik's sword hand, pressing his full weight against it, and Málik bucked beneath him, trying to displace him. Perhaps he could have, but the instant the man gave Gwendolyn his back, she rushed forward in defense of Málik, thrusting her small blade precisely where Málik had taught her, straight into the man's reins.

Just like he said, the man dropped like a stone, and Gwendolyn stood back, staring dumbly at the body as Málik pushed him away, then sprang to his feet, and dusted himself off.

His gaze narrowed on Gwendolyn. "I told you to stay," he said.

Gwendolyn hitched her chin. "I couldn't."

"Why?"

Why, indeed?

She shrugged, unable to confess the powerful surge of emotion she'd felt over the possibility of losing him. "You should say thank you," she returned with a tremulous smile. "This time, *I* saved *you*."

"Indeed, Princess," he said. But the smile he returned didn't match his tone or his words. "But don't be too pleased with yourself; we *fae* have eight lives."

In answer, Gwendolyn furrowed her brow. "I thought this was cats?"

"Alas, cats curry more favor with the gods. They have nine," he said, winking. "One more than *we*. But let us go before his friends come searching."

Gwendolyn needn't be told twice. Re-sheathing the blade at her boot, she preceded him out the door.

CHAPTER
THIRTY-FOUR

G wendolyn had never worried overmuch about being outside the palace gates, but the landscape had never appeared more sinister, with the road ahead and behind swarming with shadows. The near moon-less night was a ready cloak for betrayal.

Their chosen horses were sturdy blue roans, accustomed to hard work, if not so much travel. The journey was slow, because they were forced to stop often to water and rest them, but fortunately, they encountered no one along the Small Road, and night descended into near blackness. The pain at Gwendolyn's thigh was a nagging reminder that there was treachery at hand, and the galloping gait of their horses a constant reminder of their urgency.

She daren't consider what she might discover when she arrived home and feared the worst—a coup. After all, if someone dared attack the King's daughter in the home of her uncle, a powerful duke, they might not have intended to answer for it later. No matter that she'd said nothing of this to

Málik, for fear of making it true, she worried they would arrive to find the gates locked and her father's head on a pike.

Whatever should happen, Gwendolyn trusted Málik to protect her, a prodigious change in feeling since their departure from Trevena. This man she had once so loathed had become the one man she didn't wish to live without. And yet, having wielded a sword unto death, and watching her beloveds cut to pieces before her eyes, she understood how vital it was that she never rely on anyone but herself. Málik taught her that.

He gave no mercy and expected none in return. And neither would Gwendolyn, once she discovered who was behind this murderous affair. Vengeance took root in her belly and she could feel its rootstock strengthen and grow.

Now, at last, she understood why her father had reprimanded her over Bryn. She must *never, ever* allow herself to be a pampered princess, and she realized, despite all her bluster, that she had been precisely that.

Worry roiled through her belly, though not for herself. Her father was a well-respected man. Their allies had benefited under his rule. The last time war had come to their gates was during her grandfather's reign, when all the tribes were still at war and there was no High King to rule them all. Only now, she feared her people had grown discontented, and her thoughts returned to the glen.

The land was the life of the people; the king was the strength of the land. Little by little, that glen had deteriorated. And what would happen once it was gone?

Gwendolyn could feel it, she thought... a shift and darkening of the future, storm clouds forming ahead, like the blood clouds that ushered in darkness for Ériu.

By the time they reached the vicinity of the promontory, the horses were well-winded, sides heaving, and Gwendolyn dismounted as soon as she dared, leading them quickly off the road, toward shelter, a refuge she knew so well she could find the way even in the dark.

Málik followed without a word. Perhaps knowing intuitively why she made the rest of the way on foot, he, too, dismounted, and swept forward to seize the lead from her hands, guiding both horses away. "I'll tend to them," he said. "You, go."

Trusting him to do what he should, Gwendolyn obeyed, only first retrieving the blanket from her horse's backside, and then, whilst Málik sought a secure place to hide the horses for the evening, somewhere off the road, where no one could see them, she ascended the cliff alone, anticipating a cold, discomforting night, even with the blanket in her hand, because they couldn't risk a fire. At the moment, she would have given a hundred coppers to have that horse pelt she'd so admired on the missing guard's horse. It would have been far warmer than this.

Her muscles aching, and her calf burning, she made the climb, and grimaced when it began to sprinkle—a cold, spring rain that seeped into everything it touched and settled deep in the bones. Grateful for her good, sturdy boots, Gwendolyn ascended with care, knowing firsthand how slippery these cliffs could be.

The promontory itself was deceiving. At first glance, it would appear there should be no easy way up, but there was a path on the ocean-side, where the trail wasn't quite so steep. However, the shelter was merely a shelf against the cliff side, exposed landward more than seaward and visible for leagues —both good and bad, because they could spy on anyone who traveled by, but if they were spotted, they would be trapped here, with no way down, except one... those rocks below. But the fall would be deadly, and if the rocks didn't kill them, a vengeful ocean surely would.

Weary to her bones, Gwendolyn defied the pain in her legs, and the need to stop to weep. Finally, reaching the promontory, she ferreted out a good place to make a pallet, far enough from the edge of the cliff, against a small nook that should protect them from the wind and rain.

To make the pallet, she pushed aside all debris, knowing it would be impossible to find enough bracken here to pad a good bed. Shivering already, she crawled beneath the thin woolen blanket and huddled as far as she could into the nook. Sadly, this was how she must sleep, with her back against the wall, as rain pattered her boots.

Thankfully, Málik wasn't long, and neither did he question the need to share a pallet, though he doubtless needed his sleep and the blanket far less than Gwendolyn. Yet knowing they must rise together with the sun, neither did he hesitate to join her, especially once he heard the chattering of her teeth.

Gods.

Even her lost cloak would have been better than this, but that, too, was gone, likely burnt in the fire in the room she shared with her cousins—Málik's as well, though his place of slumber was not in the house. Like everything else she possessed, or nearly, that cloak had been her mother's. Thankfully, she still had her beautiful Prydein gown, soiled as it was from so much dirt, smoke, blood, and sweat. Pulling the blanket to her chin, Gwendolyn acknowledged the disparity between her true life... and this...

All her given days, if she'd thirsted or hungered, she could ring a bell for sustenance. If she was dirty, she rang for a bath. If she needed a blanket, she sent Demelza to procure one. If she needed clothing—well, she never needed clothing. Her mother saw to it she wanted for naught. Only now, as she shivered beneath a threadbare blanket, feeling the chill wind creep into her tattered, wet clothes, she understood what it felt like to need things she couldn't have.

As for that continued lesson... Her belly grumbled loudly. There was nothing in their saddlebags, and neither did she get to eat her eggs. Quite likely, they were still sitting in that hearth pot, over a long-spent fire... as cold as she was.

Her mood sour as the smell of this blanket, she started as Málik pinched the coverlet between two fingers and tossed it off her legs. Without asking permission to do so, he lifted her hosen to inspect her wound. Finally, satisfied with what he found, he tugged the hosen back down and settled himself beneath her blanket, drawing Gwendolyn close, before producing a bit of salted meat from the purse at his waist.

"'Tis healing," he said. "I was worried the shivering could be a sign of fever."

"Where did you get the meat?" Gwendolyn asked, grateful but guilt-ridden that he had taken it upon himself to shield her from the rain.

"The cupboard at Ia's, before those idiots arrived."

Gwendolyn nodded, her lips trembling miserably, though if she dared give into her grief right now, she would find herself a puddle on the ground. And therefore, she refused to cry, even when Málik drew her close to keep her in the warmth of his arms. Not once did she recall such a warm embrace, not from her father, nor from her mother.

Never from Demelza.

Nor Ely.

Certainly not Bryn.

Only once, ever, did she remember Lady Ruan lifting her up into her arms, when Gwendolyn fell and skinned her knees. Lady Ruan then carried her straight to the healer, and dumped her on a cold table, and left to fetch her mother—who never came.

This...

This was different.

Like the way he'd held her down in the *fogous*.

Some part of Gwendolyn longed to stay here and never leave. *Forget the world at large. Forget her duties. Forget Prince Locrinus and her promise. Forget her vows and crown. Forget the treachery... and the dead.*

Only to be held... like this.

Always.

Forever.

Two hearts, beating as one.

"Did you eat?" she dared to ask, after a while, only hoping the miserable cold hadn't stolen her voice.

"Not yet," he said, and by the way he spoke, Gwendolyn knew he didn't intend to. He was saving whatever food there was for her, and though she wished to reprove him, they were only a half a day's ride from home. If she must herself, she could go without, and empty the larders when she returned. And no matter what anyone said, she would sit Málik down at the lord's table, and would command him to be fed—anything his heart so desired.

He deserved that, and more.

Eventually, her teeth stopped chattering.

Málik's heat was enough to keep her toasty. Up above, the moon was scarcely a sliver in the sky. Judging by its shape, only a few more days till she must take her vows.

For Gwendolyn's people, a new moon represented a time for rebirth. Whatever was wrong before that moon was reborn, it could be undone by the new cycle. And yet, here and now, she feared there were mistakes to come.

Unwittingly, her hand moved to her bare throat, where the

torc no longer rested, and, for this, there would be a consequence to pay.

Tomorrow.

Tonight, she didn't wish to think about that.

She snuggled closer to Málik, sighing.

Tonight, she was safe.

Alas, everything she'd ever believed of this man was true. He was arrogant and cold—not to mention overbearing—when he hadn't any right to be. He spoke to her as though he thought himself a prince above all, and Gwendolyn only a poor servant. And yet...

She shivered anew, this time not because of the cold... but with a sudden, intense awareness of the man beside her. After a while, the rain stopped, though Gwendolyn still didn't stir. She could pretend to be overjoyed by the prospect of wedding Prince Loc.

But she was not.

A sob tore from her throat.

A tear slipped past her lashes.

Instinctively, Málik drew her closer.

"Hush," he whispered. "All may seem lost, but the daylight will bring you clarity."

Gwendolyn nodded gratefully.

He shifted suddenly, turning to face her. "You aren't alone," he said, reaching up to brush a hand across her brow and then back to tangle his long fingers through her hair. "You were never alone, Princess, and I will not leave you."

More tears slid past Gwendolyn's lashes, and, not for the first time over these past few days, she dared to lay her damp cheek against Málik's chest to weep, so grateful for his soothing words, trusting in her heart that he spoke true.

She wasn't alone.

Gwendolyn had never been alone, not even when it felt as

though she was. She had her mother. She had her father. And now she had Málik.

"Tomorrow will be brighter," he promised, and Gwendolyn's throat tightened as she shook her head, more tears dampening his leathers. "Not for my cousins," she said. "Not for Cunedda."

"I know," he said. "I know." And his voice was deep and hoarse as his hand petted her hair. "You are not the spoiled princess I once believed."

Gwendolyn strangled on a bit of laughter. "Neither are you the hideous creature I once conceived." And yet, and yet...

Giving lie to her words, she saw the moon glint on the sharpest of his teeth as he smiled, and the smile was as intimate and minacious as... a kiss.

The moment was rife with tension, filled with anticipation, tender, but bittersweet.

Longing and sadness.

Málik tapped a finger beneath Gwendolyn's chin, lifting her face to his gaze, although she couldn't actually see him so well as he likely saw her. "You needn't do it," he said.

Gwendolyn blinked. "Do what?"

"I should not say it, but I will... come with me, Gwendolyn," he pleaded. "Forswear the crown and come to a place where no adversity may seek you."

Gwendolyn laughed softly. "And where would that place be, Málik? If there is one thing I have learned, it is that there is adversity everywhere, always."

"Not where I am from," he said, and then, after a long, excruciating moment, when Gwendolyn did not push him away, he dared to press his lips over her own.

They were not warm, but hot, too hot to deny.

It drew Gwendolyn like a moth to flame, but where his mouth was soft and pliant, his teeth were not.

Somewhere in the fog of her brain, she understood these teeth represented danger, and yet not the sort she'd once supposed. Even knowing she should not, she dared to cling to him, pulling him nearer, greedy for the taste of his mouth.

Gods.

Aside from Prince Loc, she had never tasted a man like this before this, even despite that she had imagined herself kissing Málik just this way, full-mouthed, with lips pressed hungrily together, bodies melting into one another, as she sipped greedily from the nectar of his mouth.

His teeth, so sharp, dared to catch her lip, and he pricked it ever so gently, then lapped her thereafter. And on his tongue, Gwendolyn could taste the copper tang of her own blood.

She sensed his restraint in the grip of his hands about her upper arms, and hadn't even realized he held her so firmly, until she felt him shudder... and... if she uttered a word... a single word... only *"yes"*... he would dive deeper into her mouth, to plunder its depths.

Tentatively, Gwendolyn offered him the tip of her tongue, and he suckled greedily, then offered his own, the trading of these forbidden caresses titillating but... prohibited.

Greedy for more, she dared to deepen the kiss, and some small noise escaped him that sounded suspiciously like a growl. Her body responded at once, as she longed for his hands to roam her body, but daren't ask.

This was how her body was supposed to hunger, like lovers coupling in the woods on a summer solstice, with the sweet scent of pollen heavy in the air.

Dearest gods...

Deep in Gwendolyn's heart, when she imagined herself carrying a babe, her belly swollen with child, it was Málik's she envisioned.

She didn't know when this had changed, or if ever it did.

Perhaps she'd wanted Málik all along, only knowing in her heart this love was forbidden.

"Gwendolyn," he rasped.

Gwendolyn's heart hammered against her ribs, like a prisoner begging to be set free. She desperately wished to give herself to him, but... she was... promised.

It was Málik who tore himself away, staring expectantly through the shadows. "Gwendolyn," he begged.

"I have a duty to Cornwall," she said brokenly.

"You don't love him," he argued.

"I *will*," she vowed. "For Cornwall, I *will* love where I must."

"I understand," he said, and the look on his face was thoughtful.

Gwendolyn felt the need to explain. "I cannot deny what I feel for you, Málik, but I was born to serve my people, and I cannot fail them now. I am my father's heir—his only heir—and I am duty-bound and promised by my word."

"I understand," he breathed. "I do." And then he pulled her close again. "Sleep, Princess. The day has been long. Tomorrow will arrive too soon."

CHAPTER

THIRTY-FIVE

G wendolyn opened her eyes, momentarily relieved
to still be drawing breath, but then her belly roiled
to find Málik gone, though she suspected he must
have descended to ready the horses, and she calmed herself,
knowing he wouldn't have gone far.

He said he would not leave her, and she trusted him to do
what he said.

Puffy white clouds sailed by on a watery firmament. Occa-
sionally peering between them, a golden sun was busy at work,
burning off the last traces of last night's rain.

On the cliff side overhead, a grey and white peregrine
falcon sat perched, discernible only for the stark white of its
underbelly, because its wings were dark as the granite upon
which it sat. It peered down at Gwendolyn with a curious tilt
of its head, showing her the yellow of its beak and blinking
down at her with piercing gold and black eyes.

If this had been a crow, she might have wept for fear of
what was yet to come, for even as starlings were harbingers of

spring, crows were harbingers of death. But crows and starlings aside, the falcon also had a message to bring, for this was
the familiar of kings.

More than anything, Gwendolyn dreaded facing her father
—not so much because she believed she had misbehaved, but
because she would arrive today with grimmer news than any
he had ever received since her paternal grandmother perished
of yellow fever in a borough far away. With a party of ten, her
father had gone to attend her funeral, and now, someone must
return to see that her uncle and his family received a proper
end, as well.

Someone would have to sift through those ashes and find
their bones.

Someone would have to speak rites.

Someone would have to mourn them the way loved ones
ought to be mourned, not left so their charred bones could be
bleached by the sun, and dogs could fight over the remains.

Heart sore, Gwendolyn arose, seizing the grizzled blanket
to follow Málik down. She exhaled a long breath when she
spied him beside her mare, patting the soft, brown cheek.

For an instant, she watched, fascinated by the way he
cajoled the beast, smoothing a hand across its brow, the
gesture as tender and sweet as the one he'd offered her last
night.

He peered up. Their gazes met and held. His normally pale
eyes darkened to the shade of steel, and he averted his gaze.
Thereafter, Málik was perfectly civil, but there was a new,
underlying tension between them. Imagined or not, it held
even polite words at bay.

The journey home was quick. Their arrival at the gates
uncontested. The city was still and placid, all things as Gwendolyn left them.

Only she was changed.

Evermore.

Saddle weary though she was, she sent Málik ahead to announce their arrival, needing a few minutes to gather her thoughts before facing her father, and meanwhile, she led both horses into the stable, blinking in surprise as she spied the horse with the multicolored pelt.

Had the guard escaped after the battle at Chysauster? Peering about to see if she could spy him, she wished now that Málik had remained so she could send him to check the barracks.

Particularly considering their trek through the tunnels, he certainly could have had plenty of time to arrive before them, but if he'd made it back, unharmed, with news of the attack on her uncle's village, why then wasn't her father mounting a search party to look for Gwendolyn?

The stable was still full of the army's horses, the peace of the morning heavy in their morning routine. Neither had the sentries at the gates behaved any differently toward her than they would have if she'd returned from an afternoon jaunt. Their waves had been casual, even as her heart tripped madly. Curious, she thought, as she started away, but then, remembering the prunes in her satchel, she went back to retrieve them, fearing some groomsman might find them, and not wishing to see anyone else suffer on her account.

There were only a few remaining, not more than five. She stuffed them into the purse at her belt, and at once sought the King's Hall, marching in wearing her tattered clothes only to discover her father in session with an audience—a farmer with his son, begging for the King to call upon the Llanrhos Druids. He claimed there were signs of locusts, and only the Druids could charm the birds into banishing their plague. Hearing this, Gwendolyn worried anew over the glen. Those locusts portended worse matters yet, and if the glen was plagued as well, it boded ill for her father... but even more for Cornwall.

Not wishing to interrupt, Gwendolyn skirted the perimeter of the tribunal, coming to one side of her father's dais, not meaning to call his attention, not yet.

She wanted to speak to him privately, without an audience. At the moment, several aldermen were present, including Aldermans Aelwin and Eirwyn, and Mester Ciarán. Only there was something about the look in Alderman Aelwin's eyes when he spied Gwendolyn—one of maybe surprise—that gave her a sudden epiphany. Suddenly, she changed her mind about speaking to her father alone and stepped into the tribunal.

"Gwendolyn!" exclaimed her father, no doubt shocked by the state of her dress. She was still dirty, bruised, her hair all in tangles, and her mother's gown and hosen were rent.

"Forgive me, Father," she blurted, turning to address the physician, removing a dried plum from her pocket. "Mester Ciarán," she said, hitching her chin. "I must apologize for stealing your prunes."

"Prunes?" he said, looking confused. He tilted his head like the peregrine. "What prunes, Highness?"

Gwendolyn handed the prune in her hand to Mester Ciarán, then took a few more out of her pocket, revealing them in her palm, smiling as she turned to offer one each to the aldermen present. Aelwin took one, if reluctantly so, and so did Alderman Eirwyn, again, disinclined.

"Ah! Well! You are most welcome to these," said Ciarán, handing back the dried plum. "I must confess they give my belly a fright."

Gwendolyn smiled, because she understood what he meant, but thankfully they didn't affect her this way, not usually. Nor had she eaten enough after the initial ailment to repeat the offense she'd perpetrated upon Málik. Thankfully, her dosing was strong enough nowadays that the poison itself hadn't affected her adversely—or at least not the way it had affected poor Owen. She was certain now that the bellyache she'd suffered after eating so many that first day was because of the poison.

Emboldened by the aldermen's confusion, Gwendolyn placed one sweet fruit into her mouth, allowing her eyes to roll back in her head with absolute delight. All the while, she watched the physician's expression for some sign that he understood what she was ingesting.

The man seemed oblivious, only perhaps confused about why the King's daughter had interrupted their tribunal to rave about prunes—and especially looking as though she'd fought and lost a battle with soot-snorting dragons. "Delectable!" she said, swallowing.

"Gwendolyn?" her father said, sounding perturbed. "What goes here?"

However, Gwendolyn still needed proof. As yet, she didn't have any. She understood what was intended and how, but the guilty party could be anyone, and until she determined who it was who'd poisoned these prunes, there was no chance to decipher the bigger mystery—*why*? Why, precisely was Bryok murdered. Certainly, Ia's account had painted Aelwin in a very poor light. "Might you tell me where you procured these?" she asked Mester Ciarán, trying not to look at Aelwin, for the moment, daring to ignore her father.

The physician looked about the hall, perhaps a little uncomfortably, pulling at his beard, until his gaze settled on Alderman Aelwin. "Why, I believe I acquired them from Alderman Aelwin, though I did not have the heart to say I did not favor them, neither dried nor else wise. Alas, though I have prescribed them many times, because they are nature's remedy, I am fortunate to have a strong constitution and I do not relish spending time in garderobes."

"Oh, but they are so delicious!" Gwendolyn lamented. "I must have more," she said, like a child seeking sweets. She turned to Alderman Aelwin. "Have you tried them, Alderman?"

"Ah, yes," he said, clearing his throat. "I have, I have," he said, fidgeting, and Gwendolyn smiled thinly. She turned for a moment to look at her father, and then back at the alderman. "Should I congratulate you yet?"

"For what, Highness?"

"I would presume, with Bryok's death, you must have been promoted to the position of First Alderman. Yes?"

His face colored red. "Indeed, Highness, though this has not been made public as yet. I cannot claim the honor till after your nuptials. It has been agreed that nothing should distract from your... happy occasion," he said, peering up at the figure now emerging into the hall.

"Go ahead," she pressed, gesturing toward the prune, well aware that Málik had joined them.

"Oh, no!" the Alderman refused. "Please, Highness! I've eaten too many already!"

"Have you?"

"Indeed."

"And where did you procure them, I wonder?"

"One of the southern merchants, I believe."

"Which one."

"Oh, I don't know," he said. "I don't remember. Perhaps the latest shipment from Alkebulan?"

"Gwendolyn," her father said, a frown in his tone.

"Father, I must insist the Alderman try one," Gwendolyn persisted, without daring to look at her father. He would order her out of his hall, without listening to her story, and she would never disobey a direct command.

Málik paused beside her, arms crossed, and said, nodding at Aldermen Aelwin, "I believe your Princess commanded you to eat... so eat."

The Alderman suddenly looked, for all the world, like a man who had eaten far too many prunes. The blood drained from his face, and he appeared as though he might retch.

"Gods," said Alderman Eirwyn. "'Tis only a prune, man! Eat it already! If it means so much to the Princess, simply do it!" He himself lifted the fruit to his mouth and Gwendolyn slapped it from his hand before it could touch his waiting tongue. At that very instant, Alderman Aelwin must have realized she knew. He bolted. Málik moved swiftly to apprehend him.

Only then did Gwendolyn dare turn to her face her father, her King. Straightening her shoulders, feeling older than her years, she said, "Father, I have cause to believe this man has conspired in the death of your brother and his family."

She nodded soberly as her father's brows collided, and Gwendolyn added, "*My* attempted murder as well."

"Aelwin?" her father said, sounding bemused.

"Lies, and more lies!" the Alderman shrieked as her father's Elite Guard came forward to take him from Málik and arrest him. Even as he was dragged away, he continued to proclaim his innocence. But Gwendolyn was certain now. All evidence pointed to Alderman Aelwin. Now it was up to her father's guards to wrest the truth from him—the entire truth.

Having heard the commotion, Queen Eseld swept into the hall. But though Gwendolyn braced herself to meet her mother's wrath, it never came. Queen Eseld took one look at Gwendolyn and cried out, rushing forward to embrace her.

"Gwendolyn," she said, "Oh, Gwendolyn!" But though

Gwendolyn returned the embrace, reveling in the feel of her mother's arms, she couldn't allow herself to show any weakness—not here, not now, not yet. There was terrible news to be imparted, and more answers to be sought. Enough tears had been spent already. "Cunedda is dead," Gwendolyn said. "Cut down by assassins. His daughters, and wife, as well."

"Everyone... gone?" the King asked weakly.

"Yes, sire," said Gwendolyn, grief clutching at her throat, clawing at her words. "Were it not for Málik, I, too, would be dead. He has served me well."

A sober air embraced the hall. Queen Eseld ascended the dais, moving swiftly to the throne, beside her husband, setting a hand atop his ruby sleeve, and, not for the first time, but for the first time of consequence, Gwendolyn noted her father's sunken cheeks and bent back.

His hand trembled as he lifted it to his mouth, clutching his face, as though to stifle a sob, but no sound came through his broken lips.

"Cunedda," he said finally, wretchedly, for Cunedda, the youngest of his brothers, had been his indisputable favorite.

Moved beyond words, Gwendolyn knelt before her father's throne, bowing her head, as much to hide the haze of tears as to show him her utmost respect.

It was a long, long, painful moment before she found her voice again, but when she did, she was quick to thank him for Málik's service, and she revealed everything he had done... nearly everything. She told him about the battle at Chysauster. The misadventure in the *fogous*. The story Ia told about her husband and Alderman Aelwin. The prunes she'd discovered in Bryok's home. The dead guard. Only despite that she knew he could see the evidence of it—her bandages—she did not speak of the wound at her thigh, nor the care with which Málik had tended her. Nor could she seem to form words to speak aloud everything Málik had revealed—the spherule, his birthright, the confessions he'd made. None of it seemed able to rise to her tongue. It was as though some spell were cast upon her to keep these words from ever being spoken aloud. Curious, but this was a question for Málik... later.

But suddenly remembering the pelted horse, she asked her father to search Ailwin's home, and also for the guardsman.

"Do it," said the King, pointing to one of his favorite Shadows.

It wasn't long until the man returned, and as Gwendolyn suspected, there, in Aelwin's chamber, they discovered irrefutable proof of his treachery, Gwendolyn's missing torc.

Only this was not the proof she'd expected. Rather, she thought they might find some trace of the poison, or evidence of his plot against the Treasury. But not this. Arrogant as he was, the torc lay revealed upon his table, left in plain sight whilst he'd hurried away to comply with a summons from the King. Much to her grief, there was no sign of Borlewen, only the necklace. No sign of the guard, either. Her father's Shadow revealed the ill-begotten prize in the palm of both hands, nestled within a blood-soaked cloth, and Gwendolyn's heart seized painfully—not merely over what this meant for her cousin, but for the return of her torc. A tumult of emotions warred within her, both dread and relief at once, only one more so than the other.

Without a word, she retrieved her torc, and then, with her heart as heavy as the torc, she fastened it to her chain, with barely a glance toward Málik, who averted his gaze.

No one caught the exchange, and Gwendolyn straightened, resolved, for she'd spoken the truth last night. Her fate was not her own. By her own words during the Promise Ceremony, she had sealed her own destiny. Last night's kiss, wrong as it was, must remain in her memory, warming her heart when she was old and grey.

No one must ever learn of her secret, and she must hold it dear—for Málik's sake and her own. *Fae* or not, her father would take his head.

Upon his throne, King Corineus sat, his Queen Consort by his side, his expression grim, his cheeks more hollow than his eyes. "Leave us!" he barked to all remaining witnesses, but he motioned for his Shadows to remain. And then he said to Gwendolyn, only with a tip of his head toward Málik, "Come." With great effort, and the help of his Shadows, the King slid from his throne, and Gwendolyn feared he had grown so much worse since she'd left.

Had she failed him so?

As she'd failed Cunedda and her cousins?

The very first thing, as soon as she could, she must seek the *Gwyddons,* and she was glad the farmer and his son had already requested the Druids as well, because this would save her the trouble of asking.

Gods.

A lump of emotion stuck in Gwendolyn's throat, and she longed so desperately to seek solace in Málik's arms, but she followed dutifully where her father led.

To Gwendolyn's surprise, he took them to the cliff side vault, the Royal Treasury.

Unlike so many other magnificent edifices in their city, which had been designed by the greatest of builders, this cave was merely a cave, like a sepulcher, ancient as the granite from which it was hewn. As a little girl, Gwendolyn had always marveled that so rich a treasure must be kept in such a humble place, with only a heavy stone to place before it.

The guards assigned to the shift moved to one side to shove

the stone until there was a man-sized gap between the rocks. Her father reached for the torch beside the entrance and thrust it in before him to light their way into the vault.

When Gwendolyn hesitated, he turned to beckon her within. And Málik, too, much to Gwendolyn's surprise.

THIRTY-SIX

The torch in her father's hand gasped for air in the darkness, the sound of its struggle like a dying man's breath. Peering back at the crack of daylight at their backs, she tried not to allow her recent ordeal to keep her from following deeper.

Every muscle in her body begged her to flee, but she took comfort in her father's presence in front of her, and her Shadow's defense at her back.

Once they reached the darkest heart of the cave, her father thrust his torchlight over an altar made of stone, and the breath left Gwendolyn's lungs as she saw what treasure it held.

Not precious ingots as she'd once believed, nor gold.

It was an ancient sword, resting atop a crude table of stone.

With a tremor in his hand, her father handed Gwendolyn the torch, moving closer to the altar to reach for the sword. Sliding it out of its granite bed, he lifted it up, taking the hilt with both his hands and straightening it so the tip faced the ceiling.

With his wasting body, he could scarcely hold it upright,

but once he steadied it, he whispered some indiscernible word, and the sword glowed until it became a white glaive of light.

He sighed then, as his gaze slipped past Gwendolyn's to meet Málik's pale eyes—brighter now, against the reflection of the sword. Her father gave Málik a sober nod, and the two shared a look, before he spoke, his voice weaker now for the effort.

"You spoke true, Málik de Danann. I can no longer trust this sword to my keeping. This sacred talisman must be kept safe till my heir has need of it."

Gwendolyn blinked, confused. Why should he give the sword to Málik if she was his rightful heir? "Father?" she protested.

In Málik's hand, the flame extinguished, and the silver returned to its resting state, a dull, aged metal. But Gwendolyn suddenly understood what this was...

Claímh Solais, the *Sword of Light*, the sword with which Núada conquered Ériu. The greatest of the four talismans once belonging to the Tuatha Dé Danann. Like the crying stone, Lia Fáil, it would not burn for any but the rightful heir. And just as surely as she knew this, she suddenly understood why Málik had come.

He'd come for that sword.

The treasure in her father's vault.

All those questions he'd asked about the Royal Treasury, and the aldermen... he'd only wished to know if they knew what lay hidden within the vault. And yet he had surely known. She could see the truth in his eyes, and in the way he now avoided her gaze.

"Forswear your father's crown," he had said. But if she had done so, would her right to bear this sword also be forsaken?

Without a word, he took the sword her father offered, the prize he'd coveted all along, and then turned from her ailing father, giving Gwendolyn only the briefest of glances and a single nod as he passed her by, the look on his face perhaps one of regret, though not so much regret that he would refuse the damnable sword. He walked past Gwendolyn without a word, and then he was gone.

Gone.

Simply gone.

Not to the antechamber she had so hatefully longed to deny him, nor to the barracks where he'd spent so much of his time after his arrival. Neither to the courtyard, where he'd trained her father's men.

Gone.

And just as surely as Gwendolyn now understood his intent, she knew he'd lied. He'd told her he'd never leave her, and now he would.

Something like vines with thorns twined about her heart, like the arms of that blue orb of flame in the *fogous*, twisting, twisting, turning.

GWENDOLYN'S MOOD WAS FOUL. UPON RETURNING TO HER CHAMBER, battle weary, her clothes threadbare, and her wounds aching, she wanted to rush about screaming through the antechamber, kicking at beds, doors, and coffers.

She did not, however. She was a woman grown, or so she'd claimed so many times, and now she must behave like one, facing *all* her trials with her head high and shoulders straight.

Naturally, Málik had brought nothing into these chambers, so he took nothing, except the sword on his back, and the one her father gave him.

That's all he'd ever wanted, she thought bitterly.

That bloody sword.

"You aren't alone," he'd said, but it wasn't true.

She *was* alone—far more alone than she'd ever felt in all her life.

Much subdued from her former self, Ely arrived soon after Gwendolyn found her chambers. Sullen and perhaps still angry, she went about her duties, tidying Gwendolyn's room, ordering a bath for her new mistress, and laying out a clean, new dress for Gwendolyn to wear.

Demelza didn't come at all, and neither did she so much as pass to wave.

Apologies seemed in order, though Gwendolyn didn't know *what* to apologize for. For giving her heart to a tricksy *fae*? At least now it wouldn't be Ely shuffling about these halls, with downcast lips and eyes. Gwendolyn would take her place.

Some things returned to normal—at least normal *before* Málik de Danann. Reassured that he had learned his lessons, her father reinstated Bryn as her Shadow.

Mercifully, her mother also assured Gwendolyn that she meant to keep her word and allow Ely to travel with her to Loegria. Lady Ruan would be compensated for the absence of both her beloved children. Now that Málik was gone, and after everything that Gwendolyn had endured, Queen Eseld wouldn't think of allowing her to travel without both.

Ely and Bryn were changed as well—Ely by whatever trust Gwendolyn had failed to live up to, and Bryn by his punishment for allowing his heart to rule his head. Alas, though, Gwendolyn had truly believed she was doing him a favor, just as she'd believed she was doing her father a favor by unveiling the treachery in his court.

After everything, she still couldn't regret having exposed the traitors, but she regretted the way she went about it. Only because of her, Cunedda was dead. Her cousins were dead. Lowenna was dead. At least one of their loyal guards was dead.

And the other? Like Málik, he, too, had vanished. Though at least Ia and her family were safe. Her father's men traveled south to see to Cunedda's affairs, but not even to bury his brother could the King suffer a moment in the saddle. His condition worsened more every day.

By the evening before Prince Loc's return, the King was lying abed, with only Gwendolyn and her mother allowed to attend him, aside from the two Shadows he trusted most.

Gwendolyn was beside herself with grief, because how could she leave? How could anyone expect her to wed Prince Loc now, and leave her dear, sweet father to waste away and die with no one to defend him?

Gwendolyn was the one who'd spent her entire life training to take his place. She was the one who would rule in his absence, yet she would give up everything with only the assurance that her father would survive. And here, once again, she found herself outside the palace gates, accompanied by Bryn, asking him to escort her to the glen.

"I will not say no, Highness," he said tersely, his chin lifting defiantly. "Yet I will not say, yes. You must command me."

Some part of Gwendolyn burned over his words, though she understood why he insisted. This time, if he must be castigated simply for doing his duty, it would not be because he was equally culpable. As his sovereign, Gwendolyn must demand his participation.

"It's not what you think, Bryn," she said. "I only wish to see the glen. My father," she said, and then she hushed abruptly, because Bryn was not among those who needed to know her father's condition. "I merely wish to see the glen."

He nodded. "As always, I am yours to command," he said stiffly, and Gwendolyn found herself torn between sending him back to the palace, and leaving him here, to watch her go.

"Very well, then. I command you to accompany me," she

said through clenched teeth. And then she felt like weeping—for all she'd lost.

Her youth.

Her innocence.

Her friends.

Her throat constricted.

Her father all too soon.

And Málik...

Gwendolyn could scarcely bear it, knowing her pain was in her eyes for everyone to see, especially Bryn. Though he was clearly furious with her, he knew her better than anyone, and she knew... he would know.

Without further ado, she led the way into the woods, thinking about that *piskie* light Málik had produced. Yet even now, her tongue would not form the words to share what she'd learned. He had done this to her! As surely as she knew he'd lied, she also knew he'd cast a spell on her to keep the things she'd learned from ever being spoken aloud.

Once again, fury seized her, and she spurred her mare to ride ahead of Bryn because she couldn't bear for him to see her cry.

She dismounted, tied her mare to her favorite oak—a stranger to her, because now her faithful horse was lost. And, even before Gwendolyn emerged into the glen, she saw the wasted trees, and fell to her knees, a knot forming in her throat.

The leaves... they were blighted.

The fruit flowers were wilted.

Worse yet, so much worse... the pool itself had grown stagnant, murky, and green, with black algae growing in pockets. Dark lichen crept up the shore to the base of the trees, scaling the oaks and hawthorns. The oak leaves bore ugly blisters, and the hawthorn leaves were stained with black, the yellowing foliage scarcely clinging to their withered boughs. A bed of ravaged leaves lay puddled at her feet.

Whatever part of Gwendolyn that entertained any notion of staying in Trevena, and refusing her groom... this, too, withered... and died, like the ravaged leaves that floated downward from a once-green canopy, into a bubbling, corrupted pool.

How could she leave her father alone?

Yet how could she not?

As surely as she knelt here, her fingers catching the cold, damp, corrupt soil, marrying Prince Locrinus was the only way to save the land, and ultimately bring it peace.

"Father," she said, brokenly. "Oh, my dear, sweet Papa!" She had not called him Papa since she was young, small enough to bounce on his knee.

Bryn stood behind her now, and whatever steel he'd set in his spine seemed to soften at the sight of her, kneeling with her hands splayed over the dark lichen, fingers clawing the perverted earth.

"The land is struggling," Málik had said.

And then he'd abandoned her to this fate.

Bryn came to one knee beside her, placing a steady hand atop her shoulder, and he said, "I am sorry, Gwen." But he couldn't possibly understand it, even though he understood, as all understood, the king's ties to this land.

"I know," she said brokenly. "I am... sorry, too—for everything, Bryn. Truly, I am. I shall never again place you at odds with your duties. I give you my word."

He squeezed her shoulder, and said, "You are not alone, my dearest friend." And then, when Gwendolyn choked on a sob, he said once more, "You were never alone."

But that wasn't true.

She.

Was.

Entirely.

Alone.

With the burden of saving her father and the land, weighing upon her as heavy as stone.

Resolved now, Gwendolyn struck Málik from her thoughts, if not her heart, and stood, dropping the clump of stinking soil from her hand.

No more tears.

No more uncertainty.

She understood what she must do.

THIRTY-SEVEN

"Please, Gwendolyn. Smile," her mother rebuked, as they stood observing the preparations in the courtyard below, awaiting their cue. In only a few moments Gwendolyn and her party would be expected to descend the ramparts, and together, she and Prince Locrinus would ride to the Sacred Yew together, trailed by all of Cornwall, so it seemed.

The Loegrian party had only just arrived. King Brutus had dispatched his messenger to advise Gwendolyn to be ready to depart the city immediately following the ceremony—in his words, "To give the couple privacy and time alone."

But, perhaps more significantly, Prince Locrinus had heard of Gwendolyn's ordeal in Chysauster, and, to avoid further treachery, he had arranged for the two of them to travel by some unexpected route... alone... with a small entourage to serve them, so they could travel more swiftly. She was grateful for this care, but whilst the entire kingdom remained in Trevena to make merry, and celebrate their nuptials, the Kings' heirs would slip away, to consummate their vows in the privacy of a tent in the middle of nowhere, with only Gwendolyn's lady's maid to witness her blooded sheets.

This was not the way she had imagined her wedding night would be. But it was far too late for regrets. And even were it not, there was no other choice to be made. She was her father's *only* heir, and as the Prophecy demanded, the dragon banners must be united.

The afternoon sun burned hot, making Gwendolyn sweat in all her layers of finery—something she evidently wasn't supposed to do, and one glance at her mother made her feel even more unbecoming, as she imagined kohl melting about her eyes, beneath her veil.

According to custom, Gwendolyn could not yet see her betrothed, not till the instant she was unveiled, like a sculpture meant to be admired, or a gem to be worn.

It was a silly custom, she thought, mortifying, no matter that it was intended as flattery. As pretty as he was, Prince Locrinus wasn't wearing a veil. And yet, Gwendolyn was grateful for hers, because it would hide her tears as she marched to her fate.

Gods.

There was nothing wrong with Prince Locrinus, she told herself. So what if he wasn't interested in her Dancing Stones, or that she didn't like the way he'd made her feel in the cave.

For an instant, Gwendolyn had liked him, and she could, and *must*, endeavor to do so again. Simply because she had unreasonably allowed a cold-hearted fae into her life, into her heart, was not the Prince's fault. As betrotheds were concerned, hers was quite certain to be envied, and if the scene below was any sign, he already was.

In anticipation of the Prince's arrival, all the young ladies of her father's court were attired in white or gold, else both, and all the men with robes to match. The setting sun shone on their metal accoutrements, blinding Gwendolyn where she stood on the ramparts.

It was clear to all who had eyes to see that Prince Locrinus had won himself the hearts and minds of her people, and no matter that he was not yet their rightful King, they were no doubt pleased he would someday be, and this he had managed with only a single visit, and a winsome smile on his too-comely face.

Indeed, *he* was the golden child, the sort for whom life came so easily—not that Gwendolyn had cause to complain, considering her station.

Whatever anyone thought of her countenance, no one would dare mistreat her, although it vexed her to no end that he could so easily win everyone over, and she, as a woman, had to work so bloody hard to gain the same respect.

And regardless, she was ashamed of the resentment she felt in her heart for one so beauteous as he.

After all, who shouldn't favor beauty?

Were Gwendolyn not already beguiled, she mightn't have found anything to complain about, and yet... she was... and did.

By the eyes of Lugh, the only thing she had ever coveted—beauty—was the one thing she now reviled, for what was beauty alone without a heart and soul to match?

Look at him, she thought. *Only look at him!*

Even his golden robes were finer than hers. Why must *he* always arrive with such pomp and ceremony?

Gwendolyn's bridal gown was simple, but quality. Its design reminded her of an elder woman she once met from An Ghréig, with straight, flowing lines that hid her woman's curves and a golden belt cinched high beneath her breasts to accentuate her bosom—Trojan, or so Demelza claimed.

Her crown this eve was the intricately carved forehead

crown her mother gave her, the one embedded with the rainbow moonstones—Prydein.

Simple as it was, by her finery alone, she would represent three great tribes. And yet, even from this distance, Prince Locrinus was so blindingly golden and so beautiful that it put Gwendolyn to shame.

"Gwendolyn, please! Don't look so glum," her mother persisted, and then, turning once more to watch the Prince, she said, "This is the difference between a woman and a child, my dear. A woman faces adversity and makes the best of her situation. I will apprise you what my mother once said to me: If you look for joy, you'll surely find it. If you look for grief, you will find that, as well. But, if you accept your fate with grace and faith, you may yet discover your greatest joy." Essentially, it was the same counsel Demelza had given her.

Her mother smiled then, and said, "At any rate, I have never seen a man so fine. You are fortunate, indeed!" Then *you* wed him, Gwendolyn thought glumly.

And truly, it galled her that she had vied her entire life to receive an instant of the regard her mother so willingly gave to her betrothed. Even now, Queen Eseld found it far more appealing to gaze at *him* than she did to consider her only daughter.

Only Málik had ever truly seen her.

Only Málik had ever treated her as an equal, expecting her to live up to her promises.

Unwittingly, Gwendolyn lifted her fingers to her lips, remembering the feel of his mouth, the sharpness of his teeth, the taste of his tongue.

I am undone, she thought.

Undone.

Unquestionably, if she refused to consummate this marriage, her mother would gladly offer to catch her by the ankles—and merely to think of it, something like bile rose at the back of her throat over the thought. Battling the urge to weep—a thing Gwendolyn rarely did but was doing quite oft now—she caught her hands and held them before her, if only to hide their trembling. But it wasn't merely nerves that made her belly ache. It was something else entirely.

Time was growing short.

Already the sun was beginning its descent.

Awaiting their cue as well, Ely and Demelza joined them on the ramparts, but neither spoke. Both stood aside, stone-faced, and in the presence of Queen Eseld, both were mindful to keep opinions to themselves. And yet, Gwendolyn knew intuitively that Ely was grieving as well, her heart heavy knowing that she, too, would be expected to depart the city within the next few bells, dragged away from the only life she had ever known... these halls wherein they'd played together, the fields where they'd run, the shoals they'd climbed, the oysters they'd loved.

Gods willing, perhaps Ely might eventually forgive Gwendolyn for her duplicity, even despite that Gwendolyn couldn't regret having allowed herself the time with Málik.

Even now, she couldn't regret a single moment.

If he asked again, would she go?

Knowing her father's plight, how could she not wed Prince Locrinus?

Not for the first time, Gwendolyn cursed the infernal Prophecy.

But no matter, even if she refused to marry, she might never see Málik again. He'd run away with her heart and the sword. Even now, standing next to her mother, Gwendolyn longed to cast herself into her mother's arms and beg not to go. But no one was more adamant than Queen Eseld that Gwendolyn must fulfill her destiny.

"Our banners will be united!" her mother had said fiercely, and if she was passionate about nothing else, she was passionate about this.

Below the ramparts, Prince Locrinus was making his way toward the gathering place whence the procession would depart, appearing contented to soak in the praise. Apparently, his younger brothers were attending, as well as his mother.

By now, the entire countryside had gathered, and the city gates were left wide to admit all who cared to follow the procession.

There was a crush clear through the courtyard, all the way past the Mester's Pavilion, past the barracks, across Stone Bridge, and clear out the gates, onto the King's Road.

Down below, to one side, Gwendolyn could see that same little girl with her mother, the one she'd spoken to on the bridge on the way to the market. They were both holding brightly colored flowers, waiting for their chance to give these as an offering.

Conspicuously absent from the celebration were three of Gwendolyn's favorite cousins... and their dutiful father and his wife. A knot formed in her throat as she remembered their final moments—Lowenna's twisted body being dragged by her grieving husband.

It was a sight Gwendolyn would never forget.

Her own father stood below, flanked by his Shadows, and for now, he was steady on his feet, looking resplendent, and quite golden by right, for his livery, like their dragon standard, was gold and white. But this was a curious thing Gwendolyn only now realized: the choice of Prince Locrinus' colors, the absence of crimson, even in his cloak, despite that he was flanked by his red-cloaked guards. Curious as well was the fact that he never once peered up to seek his bride, though Gwendolyn could have missed his glance, as she was peering out over the palace gates, over the parklands, searching the horizon... for someone else.

Someone who was long gone from this place, and perhaps even this isle.

Someone who had likely already cast her out of his mind and his heart.

She would never forget that final, hardened glance.

And still, some small part of her prayed he would come trotting through those gates, as he had during that *wintertide* evening, that he would ride into the courtyard and pause before the ramparts, begging Gwendolyn to leap into his arms —but this was impossible.

Down below, the *Awenydds* were gathered now as well.

The entire city seemed to hold their breaths.

Prince Locrinus assumed his mount, and beside him waited Gwendolyn's mare. The entire procession to the Yew would take no more time than it would to descend to the harbor. Gwendolyn could see the great tree from her perch, stately and majestic, like a twisted, old sovereign guarding its land. That's where the Elder Druid awaited now.

"Art ready?" asked her mother.

No.

She was not.

Gwendolyn nodded, and with all her heart, longed to reach for her mother's hand. Alas, Queen Eseld was not the hand-holding sort. She gestured for Gwendolyn to precede her, and Gwendolyn dutifully obeyed. Her mother and maids fell into step behind her, and Gwendolyn made her way toward the stairs.

CHAPTER
THIRTY-EIGHT

F ew knew how long they lived—Druids or yews—but this ancient tree had stood in Trevena's shadow so long as Gwendolyn had memory.

Newly arrived from Llanrhos to officiate her ceremony and later to take measure of the glen for her father, the elder druid appeared to be the yew's very twin, with crags in his wizened old face, gnarled old limbs, and skin pocked with age.

Some yews were ancient as the *faerie* hills, present when the world was made, elder witnesses to the passing of ages, never so silent as one might believe, for they were also known to be bringers of dreams, and the Druids oft took their visions from the vapors they produced.

All things were made known during these waking dreams, and even now, the elder druid stood inside the hollow, eyes closed as he summoned the *ysbryd y byd*, the *spirit of the age*.

As warm as the day was, anyone else standing below the tree's branches risked more than hallucinations, and the holding of breaths was less a response to the occasion as it was to the yew itself. When finally the druid spoke, there was a collective gasp of relief. He looked at Gwendolyn, seeing her straight through the veil, even despite that his old grey eyes were milky with age.

"Today, we call upon the elements to bring unto this union the harmony they share. From Air, we beg curiosity and peace. From Fire, we beg courage and passion. From Water, we beg stillness and strength. And, from Earth, we beg humility and gratitude. Join hands!" he commanded, his voice like thunder, and Gwendolyn offered hers though it quaked.

At once, Prince Locrinus accepted it, placing it gingerly over the back of his own, as the Druid sang, "Now is the time between times, when all light is swallowed by darkness...

"This be the hour for our dead to return to our realm, while *piskies* dance through the sacred glens, shifters may change forms and the *ben-Sidhe* howls against the wind.

"It is also a time whence all possibilities and promises are born. Are you prepared to fulfill your destiny together?"

The question seemed posed solely to Gwendolyn, and though she knew it wasn't so, she must be the first to reply. "I am," she said, her chin quivering behind her veil. She daren't even look sideways at her betrothed, and she willed away tears that threatened to spill.

"Indeed," said Prince Locrinus, with such confidence that Gwendolyn wished she could borrow from him.

The druid's voice carried over the field, amplified from his hollow in the tree, as though he spoke through a herald's trumpet.

"With hands joined, and by your own free will, bound by the laws of man in accord with the Brothers' Pact, and betokened by the torc of your noble houses, we call upon you now to claim one another! Your marriage will be your gift to the realms, binding each together!"

Knowing this was her cue, and with the yew's fumes

already making her feel heady, even with the added protection of her veil, Gwendolyn retrieved her hand to remove the heavy torc from her chain, her fingers fumbling with the latch, and then moved forward to place the torc itself about Prince Locrinus' neck, discarding the chain. Someone rushed forward to scoop it up from the ground at her feet, and with trembling fingers, Gwendolyn arranged the torc so his dragons' heads were staring at the apple of his throat.

The hue of the torc's metal cooled beneath the shade of the ancient yew, and the eyes of his serpents winked a dull grey—a chameleon, perhaps like its wearer.

Prince Locrinus smiled at her then, with so much warmth and so genuinely, that Gwendolyn's heart filled with hope. Indeed, this was the man she should love.

Resolved, she stepped back again, and Prince Locrinus quickly removed Gwendolyn's torc from his chain, and then he, too, stepped forward to place it about her throat, discarding the chain and placing it quickly about her throat.

Made for a woman, hers wasn't nearly so heavy as his, and it settled easily, with the dragon snouts so close together they appeared to be kissing. Gwendolyn couldn't see them, but she could definitely feel them.

Compelled to, she adjusted her torc. And then, as he had done for her, she gave Prince Locrinus a tremulous smile, and vowed to be the wife he deserved.

Between them, the druid nodded approvingly, and said, "You are now joined in matrimony as Prince and Princess of Pretania! Go forth this day to your dwelling place, together, never to be put asunder! May you live long and prosper!"

And then it was done. Gwendolyn lifted her veil, revealing her face, and Prince Locrinus smiled, straightening to his full height, seizing her by the hand, forgoing the customary kiss of peace, and turning her about to raise their joined hands so everyone could see.

A great huzzah rose amidst the gathered crowd, rippling over the field in waves. At once, the celebration removed itself from the vicinity of the tree—all save for the druid, who remained, eyes closed again, his lungs filling with fumes, and both his hands splayed upon the yew as he prayed. Gwendolyn marveled that as decrepit as he appeared to be, his tolerance for the yew poison was so great. Much like hemlock, the toxin was strong, the vapors equally so.

And regardless, the druid would remain this way throughout the twilight, and on the morrow, he would attend her father to tell him what visions he saw, including those he would call upon for the sake of the glen. Gwendolyn only hoped the blight would be curable, though tonight, she daren't dwell on such things, not when she must keep a smile on her face.

King Brutus was the first to rush forward to congratulate the newly wedded couple. He kissed Gwendolyn on the left cheek and said, "What joy you will bring to our house!"

Prince Locrinus' mother was quick to do the same. She gave Gwendolyn one soft cheek to nuzzle, then the other, and then embraced her fully. "Daughter," she said. "I will treat you as though you were my own." Her voice was kindly, and Gwendolyn's breath hitched over a lump of sudden joy.

Locrinus' brothers followed—Kamber and Albanactus, each more winsome than the other. "Alas," teased Albanactus. "If only I were the one born first!" He lifted Gwendolyn's hand and kissed it swiftly. Then Kamber did the same. "Princess," said Kamber, and then added, "We shall forever remain your humble servants."

Gwendolyn's father was slower to reach her, but whatever strength he'd lacked these past few days, he now mustered for this embrace, squeezing Gwendolyn so tightly as he whispered in her ear. "You are beauteous, Daughter. I am proud." And then he turned to Prince Locrinus and crooked a finger at him, and said, "Get me a grandson, young man!"

Embarrassed, Gwendolyn smiled, once again mentally preparing herself for the night to come. Queen Eseld came to embrace her next and for the first time in all Gwendolyn's life, the embrace was genuine and long, so very long, and so terribly bittersweet. It brought a new sting to Gwendolyn's eyes. "Mother," she rasped, as Queen Eseld held her close.

"My dearest, sweet child," said Queen Eseld. "I am so pleased for you. Today you have brought great joy and healing to our people and our lands. I only wish with all my heart that your grandmother and grandfather were here to witness this day!"

Gwendolyn nodded, her voice too thick to speak as her mother extricated herself from the embrace, and then patted Gwendolyn gently on the cheek.

And that was that.

Prince Locrinus stood by her side, solicitous and kind, making Gwendolyn rue the moment she'd dared give her heart to a heartless creature—who, by the by, couldn't even remain in attendance long enough to see she was wed, less to celebrate her moment.

One last time, she allowed herself a sudden and over-whelming surge of fury over Málik's abrupt departure, but she vowed this anger must be a cleansing. After today—this moment—she would think of him no more, and she would be a wife and princess.

Prince Locrinus took her by the arm, drawing Gwendolyn away from the bantering crowd. Drawing her aside, he lifted his hand to a wayward curl and brushed it away from Gwendolyn's face, his eyes shining with...

Love? Joy? Desire?

"Beautiful," he declared. "I cannot wait to have you to myself. But first!"

He turned to wave a hand into the air, and the throng parted to reveal Gwendolyn's bridal gift... a grey-white mare with a golden mane and tail, to replace the one she'd lost.

Its lithe body was armored with golden scales, including a *croupiere, crinet* and *peytrol*, with a *shaffron* that bore a golden horn. "From Gaul," he said. "Imported for you. This breed is highly prized, loyal to a single master."

He smiled companionably. "As I will be loyal only to you. Until the day we are called to serve, my lady, we will travel together, east to west, north to south, if only so our people may gaze upon their beauteous queen. This is my gift to you, not only the horse."

He bowed then, humbling himself before her, and Gwendolyn's heart did a small, tentative leap of joy. Not only because of his kind words, or his sweet gift, or his promises, but more than anything, Gwendolyn wanted to travel, and clearly he'd heard her and understood this, and he cared enough to give her such a wondrous gift.

Without warning, he swept Gwendolyn into his arms and carried her to the golden saddle, then settled her atop. Thereafter he grinned broadly, like a wee boy, and waved for his own horse to be brought forth. "Shall we begin our journey together, Princess?"

"Oh, yes!" Gwendolyn exclaimed, excitement bubbling up within her as a murmur grew throughout the crowd. All at once, she felt heartily ashamed for all the terrible things she'd thought of him. *Love where you must,* she heard Demelza say.

Love where you must.

Love where you must.

And now she understood why he'd wished to take her

away so soon after the ceremony, and the knowledge swelled in her breast until her heart must surely be twice its normal size. This was his Bride's Gift to her, she realized, and it was splendid. Whatever reservations she'd given asylum to, she set free, ready to fly with her prince by her side. Hope sprang from some unforeseen well. Gwendolyn peered down at him, commanding her heart to change, and her mother's words whispered into her ear...

If you look for joy, you'll surely find it. If you look for grief, you will find that, as well. But, if you accept your fate with grace and faith, you may yet discover your greatest joy.

Gwendolyn reveled over the feel of the horse's flesh between her thighs, and she sat tall and proud in her new saddle as the Prince found his own horse and mounted beside her. Indeed, he was fine, every muscle in his body straining against his golden garb, his legs encased in glittering hosen, his arms and chest with painted gold leather, emblazoned with a version of his own dragon, also in gold. But nay, she looked closer, and saw it was *both* their standards combined. *His dragon. Her colors. Their house.*

A new standard for a new age.

Another huzzah swept through the crowd, and this time, though Gwendolyn noted her husband bent to take her reins, he constrained himself, and smiled instead, straightening in his saddle to give her a flourish of his hand. "Where you go," he said, "I follow."

And with those words, a tiny seedling of love unfurled within Gwendolyn's breast, tiny but strong. One last time, she peered back to seek her mother's gaze and found Queen Eseld smiling happily. Her father and mother were bantering easily with their new relations, and she knew in that instant... she had chosen well.

Eager now to meet the entourage they would travel with,

and keen for a new adventure, Gwendolyn gave her mount a nudge with her knee, but then, something caught her eye... a lone figure in the distance, on the bluff over the sea, a dark silhouette against a lowering sun, and the sight gave her heart a little twist.

She knew who it was but turned away.

Love where you must, Demelza had said. Well, the one thing Gwendolyn loved most in this world, more than anything else, was her father, this land, and her people.

Resolved at last, she turned her back to the glittering sea.

CHAPTER

THIRTY-NINE

T he last rays of sunlight glanced off the armor on her gilded mount—a gift from her prince, as majestic as she... The Dragon Princess, for whom his heart burned, and for whom the land yearned. But if there was a choice to be made between them, he was destined to lose.

The burden on his back was twofold, his own heavy sword and the sword of his people. But neither lay heavier nor cut more deeply than the burden he now carried in his heart.

She is not your destiny, he told himself.

But you already knew that, didn't you?

What made you believe you alone could turn the hand of fate? Thanks be to a youngling princess for keeping her head better than you.

This was all he cared to see. Now that it was done, he could leave.

Shifting the weight of one sword from his back to his shoulder, he turned from the celebration, heading northeast along the Small Road, his back to the city, his eyes to the sea.

Alhough he was not a seer, it didn't take one to understand

Gwendolyn's journey was only beginning, and her trials, as well.

"Gorthugher da," said Esme, materializing by his side. With long, graceful fingers, she shoved back her blood-red cowl and grinned, revealing sharp, savage teeth to mirror his own.

As stunning as she was, as cunning as she was, Málik now found her beauty a much paler shade, like shimmering pearls against a vivid flame.

"I have the sword," he told her crossly, displeased with her presence, yet knowing this was what she'd come to find out. If he gave her what she sought, perhaps she would leave.

"Yes, I see," she said excitedly, and her ensuing laughter was sharp, like a cackle. "Does it burn for you the way she does?"

"It does not," Málik said, but lower, "Neither does she."

"You mustn't allow yourself to be chased by the shadows in your mind, young *drus*. Remember, we were born for this."

For what?

To watch an innocent fall prey to her mortal enemy?

Feeling betrayed, Málik refused to speak again.

Once before, he was sent to intervene against the Fates and he failed. The Trojans were not to be trusted. And Gwendolyn was not the first they would use.

Too long without the practice of using her feet, Esme glided along beside him. "There is a charm to the forbidden that renders it unspeakably desirable," she suggested. As though this would be the reason he did not choose her, the woman his own sire would see him wed.

"Málik," she said, more soberly, a note of pain in her voice. "Your enemy does not come cloaked with pointed ears. It comes to you as the one thing you most desire."

Not you, he wanted to say, but he continued to ignore her, placing one foot firmly in front of the other, stubbornly using his limbs because if he stopped now, if he gave himself over to the *Aether*, he had a fear that he would fade from this realm, become only a specter, and then a memory, too soon to be forgotten.

"She is not Helen," Esme suggested, and old wounds bled afresh.

No, she wasn't. Gwendolyn was nothing like that lady. She was sweet and innocent and far too uncertain of herself to understand the sway she held, whereas Helen had been a siren, playing kingdom against kingdom, friend against friend.

Even so, Gwendolyn, too, would lure a wooden horse into her father's gates, and Esme was the one who, both times, had orchestrated his collusion.

"Go away," he said. "Tell my father I am on my way."

Her voice held a pleading note. "You will disappoint him if you tarry."

"It is not me he wishes to see, but this sword, and it comes when I come," he said. "Now, leave me."

"As you wish," she relented with a sigh, and her fading was not gentle, more like a tear from this realm, a bandage ripped from a wound.

Alas, everything she'd said was true. His only comfort was this: Gwendolyn was where she should be. The dragon banners were united, and someday... his golden princess would be Pretania's queen.

FORTY

T hey traveled so long into the night that Gwendolyn wondered whether they would ever stop to rest, much less to consummate their vows.

Only considering her recent misadventure, and the fact that there were no pack horses along for the journey, she worried they would spend the evening under the stars—not something she would normally bemoan, save that it was her wedding night, and she knew Ely would not fare well sleeping so meanly. Nor did she like the simple fact that they were women, traveling alone with a troupe full of men—not that she was worried, except for modesty. She had her husband to protect her, and Ely had Bryn. Yet Ely would sleep poorly, despite that she was already half-asleep in her saddle, with her brother poking her now again to keep her from sliding off her horse. By now, Gwendolyn's own bottom was sore, and despite that she'd been born to a saddle, or nearly, anticipation was killing her as much as the newly fitted saddle on her new horse. She'd forgotten how much a simple thing, like acquainting herself with the rhythm of her mount, could make such a difference in her riding pleasure. Right now, more than Gwendolyn could say, she desperately missed her old mare. She hoped that sweet horse fared better than her cousins, though she daren't even think of such things right now, not now.

Presently, when they spied torches alight in the distance, spreading a dull yellow glow over the horizon, all Gwendolyn's worries eased, because she knew then that Locrinus had taken every care to make this night a memorable one.

And now so much made sense. If he knew they would pass this way, and he'd intended to leave directly after the ceremony, of course he would make certain there were tents erected for their pleasure, and every comfort was extended to Gwendolyn and her guests.

She was also pleased that both Bryn and Ely had accompanied her. In the end, her mother blessed her, considering Gwendolyn before her *dawnsio*. And no matter that Ely was nervous, she too seemed excited to begin a new life, and for a chance to find and marry a man of her own choosing, someone who could love and keep her as Ely deserved to be kept.

As for Bryn, he was back where he belonged, in the position he'd trained for all his life. Gwendolyn knew he would do well amongst her husband's warriors, and as her Shadow, he would have every opportunity to rise in rank. Perhaps someday he might earn his own troop. And in the meantime, although there was still some underlying tension between them, he was back to his old self.

At the moment, Gwendolyn rode beside Ely, and though Prince Locrinus rode ahead of his troops, leading his men, she saw him peer back now and again, as though he feared she might change her mind and flee. It was really quite endearing, and despite how nervous Gwendolyn was about the coupling, she was now eager to have it done.

"Gods!" Ely gasped when she saw the illumined campsite.

The sight of it was utterly enchanting, with torches lit in a circle, and a village of golden tents already assembled, looking like radiant little moons, winking up at the black night. "It's so... charming!" said Ely.

Indeed, it was. But once again, those buzzing bees returned, stinging Gwendolyn's belly until Gwendolyn thought she might retch.

Now was the time.

She watched with her heart in her throat as Prince Locrinus turned and fell back, rode down the line to retrieve her, riding high and proud in his saddle, smiling a smile intended only for her. "Wife," he said, when he reached her, and Gwendolyn gave him a silent nod, unsettled by the foreign word... *husband.*

Gods. Even now, it was loath to rise to her tongue. Thankfully, Locrinus didn't notice, and he motioned for Gwendolyn to join him and leave Ely with Bryn.

Demelza said to expect nerves. She said it was only natural. But this felt... *dreadful.*

Soon, all too soon, she would be expected to disrobe before him, and he would see all of her, not as a stranger, but a lover.

His hands would find her breasts and hips, his tongue would tease her mouth, and come what may, she would give him the one thing that was only hers to give.

All eyes were on Gwendolyn as she rode at Prince Locrinus' side to the head of the line, her limbs suddenly feeling like jiggly pudding, so much that she feared she would slide from her saddle and disgrace herself, all legs and arms and tears.

Perhaps sensing her disquiet, Prince Locrinus bent to take her reins, and for once, Gwendolyn allowed it. The camp was eerily silent as they wended their way through the village of tents—mostly men present, completing various duties, and in one corner of the camp, there was a fire burning with a large cauldron over it, and a cook standing beside it, ladling what must be porridge into bowls, in anticipation of the party's arrival.

Most of the men traveling with them made straight for this corner, their voices heard at last as they produced flasks for the evening's enjoyment.

Of course they should wish to celebrate with their prince, but something made Gwendolyn glance back over her shoulder to see if she could spot Ely.

Ely was lost now amidst scattering troops, and Prince Locrinus turned away from the cook's corner, leading Gwendolyn straight to the largest of the tents.

Naturally, it would be.

Inside, Gwendolyn found it well provisioned, with an enormous bed in the center, and her dowry chest already delivered for her convenience. Remembering the gossamer *chainse* she'd discovered within, she blushed hotly over the thought of wearing it, because it left nothing to the imagination. Doubtless, the rest of her belongings had been sent ahead.

"Make yourself comfortable," he said, with a new eagerness to his voice that sent another swarm of vicious bees through her belly.

Gwendolyn nearly swooned.

Gods.

How could she bear it?

Forcing Málik out of her mind, she started for her dowry chest, to locate that special gown her mother had given her, only hoping Prince Locrinus—her husband—would give her time alone, to prepare for the coupling.

"Sit," he said, and the single word was a command.

Gwendolyn froze midway across the tent, turning to face her husband with her back toward the canopied bed.

The golden lamplight shone upon him as fiercely as it did the sapphire eyes of his dragons. Like a golden statue, he shone. His hair, long and fine, was loose, flirting with the breeze at his back. And suddenly, Gwendolyn was cold, and far too aware that she was so far from home. She rubbed her arms for warmth as he grinned at her, and the grin transformed his face, both lusty and greedy at once. But though she recognized lust, something about it gave her pause.

Without a word, he reached into his pocket, advancing upon her, his look so dark that she instinctively stepped backward, and kept stepping backwards, until the back of her knees encountered the bed—and still he advanced, his eyes burning with a strange, unnerving light, a fire not unlike the fire in his dragon's eyes.

Once he reached her, he shoved her back none too politely onto the bed, and Gwendolyn landed on her rump, throwing her hands behind her to support her fall.

"Loc?" she said.

Still without speaking, Prince Loc settled himself so Gwendolyn's knees lay nestled between his hard thighs. And gods—she swallowed convulsively. Something about his demeanor was different tonight, though he didn't touch her, nor did he move to disrobe. Instead, he revealed what he'd taken from his pocket—a shining blade, sharp and gleaming against the lamplight. Smiling now, he reached out and rudely pulled Gwendolyn closer and before she knew what he intended, he had already sliced the first lock of hair.

It fluttered to the bed.

But it was only hair.

Not golden.

Not gold.

Only hair.

The sight of it suddenly enraged him.

Rudely, growling like a beast, he seized Gwendolyn by the hair to cut even more, tugging at her curls, until she cried out in protest.

Snick.

Snick.

Snick.

Hair.

Not gold.

Not golden.

Only hair.

There was a growing pile now, and Gwendolyn blinked herself out of her stupor, finally comprehending.

He didn't care about her.

He only cared about her hair.

He wasn't her true love.

Snick.

Snick.

Snick.

More hair.

Not gold.

Not golden.

Only hair.

"Gods!" he exclaimed. "I am such a fool!"

He went another round with her hair, furiously cutting, tugging, pulling and snipping, hacking and snipping, until another furious roar rose from the depth of his bowels, erupting from his throat.

At long last, Prince Locrinus stood back, glaring at Gwendolyn as though she were a hideous beast, and shouted, "Liar!"

His lips twisted cruelly, as he said, "I'd not bed you if you were the last woman in all these lands. I'd bugger a filthy druid before I'd ever touch you!"

And then, with a snarl, he hurled his blade into the bed,

embedding it there in the center, where he and Gwendolyn were meant to lie. Without another word, he left, and Gwendolyn blinked down at the mess on the bed.

Only hair.

Not golden.

Not gold.

In the lantern's light, it was dull, with only a shade of red.

Their love was not true. Their courtship only a ruse.

Prince Locrinus was *not* the man she'd supposed.

But the blade...

Drawn to it, Gwendolyn blinked again, her hand trembling as she retrieved the dagger to inspect it, and her heart squeezed more painfully than she ever knew possible when finally she held it in her hand.

The blade... it was double-edged, similar to a sword, meant to be used for stabbing, long enough to slip between a rib and stab a heart. The marking on the hilt was painfully familiar— the ancient guardian of Dumnonia, without the barbed tongue... and... there was a tiny black pearl in the dragon's eye.

Bile rose in Gwendolyn's throat, the taste bitter, like betrayal, and something like fury simmered through her blood, filling her with a dragon's rage.

Those tender twines and thorns, newly spun about her heart, now slid painfully through her veins, sending roots so deep they sank into bone and marrow. Because the blade... it was Borlewen's.

AFTERWORD

I first came across Gwendolyn's story in my research for another book and was gobsmacked by what I learned. Hers is the first account I ever read, historically speaking, of a strong woman, who kicked a cheating husband to the curb. But then, she raised an army to defeat him, taking his throne and crown to rule as Briton's first Queen Regnant—talk about the wrath of a woman scorned.

However, while this book gives props to her, and I make every attempt to stick to the historical record, there's no doubt I took a hard left turn into Fantasyland, incorporating many of the great legends of the British Isles, including the advent and eventual defeat of the Tuatha Dé Danann. Alas, there's so much more I could (and want!) to say, but not wishing to spoil the fun, I'd rather you take this journey along with me. If you enjoyed book one, you don't want to miss book two.

Preorder The Queen's Huntsman

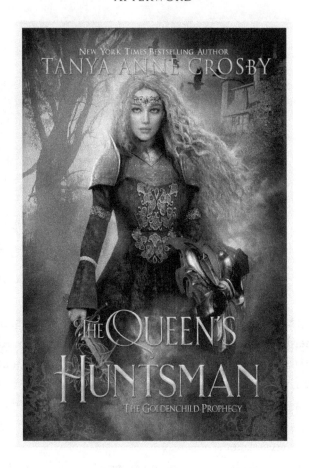

A HEARTFELT THANK YOU!

Thank you sincerely for reading The Cornish Princess. If you enjoyed this book, please consider posting a review. Reviews don't just help the author, they help other readers discover our books and, no matter how long or short, I sincerely appreciate every single one.

Would you like to know when my next book is available? Sign up for my newsletter:

Also, please follow me on BookBub to be notified of deals and new releases.

Let's hang out! I have a Facebook group:

Thank you again for reading and for your support.

ALSO BY TANYA ANNE CROSBY

THE GOLDENCHILD PROPHECY

The Cornish Princess

The Queen's Huntsman

The Forgotten Prince

ONE KNIGHT FOREVER SERIES

One Knight's Stand

DAUGHTERS OF AVALON

The King's Favorite

The Holly & the Ivy

A Winter's Rose

Fire Song

Lord of Shadows

THE PRINCE & THE IMPOSTOR

Seduced by a Prince

A Crown for a Lady

The Art of Kissing Beneath the Mistletoe

THE HIGHLAND BRIDES

The MacKinnon's Bride

Lyon's Gift

On Bended Knee

Lion Heart

Highland Song

MacKinnon's Hope

GUARDIANS OF THE STONE

Once Upon a Highland Legend

Highland Fire

Highland Steel

Highland Storm

Maiden of the Mist

THE MEDIEVAL HEROES

Once Upon a Kiss

Angel of Fire

Viking's Prize

REDEEMABLE ROGUES

Happily Ever After

Perfect In My Sight

McKenzie's Bride

Kissed by a Rogue

Thirty Ways to Leave a Duke

A Perfectly Scandalous Proposal

ANTHOLOGIES & NOVELLAS

Lady's Man

Married at Midnight

The Winter Stone

ABOUT THE AUTHOR

Tanya Anne Crosby is the New York Times and USA Today bestselling author of thirty novels. She has been featured in magazines, such as People, Romantic Times and Publisher's Weekly, and her books have been translated into eight languages. Her first novel was published in 1992 by Avon Books, where Tanya was hailed as "one of Avon's fastest rising stars." Her fourth book was chosen to launch the company's Avon Romantic Treasure imprint.

Known for stories charged with emotion and humor and filled with flawed characters Tanya is an award-winning author, journalist, and editor, and her novels have garnered reader praise and glowing critical reviews. She and her writer husband split their time between Charleston, SC, where she was raised, and northern Michigan, where the couple make their home.

For more information
Website
Email

Newsletter

9 781648 391170